BEAR
WITH
ME NOW

BEAR WITH ME NOW

Katie Shepard

BERKLEY ROMANCE

NEW YORK

BERKLEY ROMANCE
Published by Berkley
An imprint of Penguin Random House LLC
penguinrandomhouse.com

Library of Congress Cataloging-in-Publication Data

Names: Shepard, Katie, author.
Title: Bear with me now / Katie Shepard.
Description: First edition. | New York : Berkley Romance, 2023.
Identifiers: LCCN 2022045377 (print) | LCCN 2022045378 (ebook) |
ISBN 9780593549292 (trade paperback) | ISBN 9780593549308 (ebook)
Subjects: LCGFT: Romance fiction. | Novels.
Classification: LCC PS3619.H45425 B43 2023 (print) |
LCC PS3619.H45425 (ebook) | DDC 813/.6—dc23/eng/20220921
LC record available at https://lccn.loc.gov/2022045377
LC ebook record available at https://lccn.loc.gov/2022045378

First Edition: April 2023

Printed in the United States of America
1st Printing

Book design by Alissa Theodor

FOR MY CHRIS:
THE BEST CHRIS, CHRIS OF CHRISES.

AUTHOR'S NOTE

This work strives to realistically depict issues of mental health and disability and includes depictions of ableism, including ableist language. This book also depicts substance abuse, prior death of a parent as a result of drunk driving, misogyny, an animal attack, explicit and graphic sexual content, and vulgar language.

BEAR
WITH
ME NOW

"SLOANE, IS THIS A RESORT?" TEAGAN ASKED HIS sister as soon as his confusion grew strong enough to overcome the inertia of his medication.

He didn't know where he was. But he knew that giant tents—if the word *tent* could adequately describe a canvas-and-wood structure larger than his condo back home—were found only in resorts. A luxury resort at that, because there were thick, soft carpets around the king-sized bed, a full living room set in rattan and batik-print cotton, and enough cheerfully twee Edison bulbs strung among the rafters to illuminate most of Williamsburg. It looked like a space specifically arranged to trend under the *glamping* hashtag or grace the front page of the *Wall Street Journal* travel section. "Are we . . . on vacation?"

Gracie Square Hospital had doped him up for discharge this morning, so he'd been high as a kite when he boarded the plane to Montana. And his sister had shut down his initial inquiries about their destination. But now that he was slowly swimming toward full consciousness, Teagan had a *lot* of questions about what he was doing here.

"No, this is a wellness retreat," Sloane corrected him, as uncharacteristically attentive as she'd been during the entirety of their journey from New York. "Wilderness therapy. It's run by a doctor." She emphatically flapped her hands in the sleeves of the oversized sweater she wore over her thin frame.

Sloane and Teagan didn't look very much alike. Sloane, slender and brunette, looked just like their mother, her father contributing just as much to her features as he had to her upbringing. It was startling, sometimes, how much Sloane looked like Teagan's earliest memories of their mother, even though *worried* was not an expression that had typically graced her face.

"But why am I at a wellness retreat? I'm not actually sick. I was cleared to go back to work," he protested. Under a cocktail of medications that kept all sharp-edged thoughts at bay, Teagan was having trouble following the reason that Sloane had dragged him to a wellness retreat in Big Sky when all he'd been instructed to do was enroll in outpatient therapy. He had not, in fact, had a heart attack. Physically, he was fine.

Sloane's eyes—blue to his hazel—welled up with concern.

"Oh my God, Tiggie," she said. "Your brain is like a bowl full of betta fish right now, isn't it? You can't go back to *work* like this. But don't worry. I've got it. I told your secretary you'd be gone for at least a month."

That too was hard to follow. Teagan didn't have a secretary or any kind of PA—he couldn't justify it, despite the swamping press of calls and invitations and correspondence that had threatened to drown him even before this current misadventure. The family charitable foundation he'd run for the two years since his mother's death was bleeding cash. He barely even paid himself a salary.

"You talked to Rose, maybe? The investment officer?" he

clarified, heart beating faster. Who else knew by now? He wouldn't have willingly gotten anyone at his office—let alone his sister—involved in this painfully embarrassing situation. He'd thought he was dying. A heart attack would have been easier to explain than this. His *not* dying would be easier to handle if fewer people knew he was only struggling to cope with his very ordinary professional obligations.

"Whatever! Rose, yes. She told me you'd need a responsible person to be released to, then probably some outpatient treatment too. I said I'd take care of it. This is me taking care of it."

It took Teagan a minute to process that. It wasn't as though he'd left Rose much in the way of instructions during his ambulance ride to the hospital, but only someone who didn't know Sloane well would consider her a *responsible person*.

"This will be, like, so good for you," she told him, wrapping her hands into the slightly grubby cotton sweater he wore over his very grubby oxford. "This is a place where you can get healthy. You need to be somewhere you can relax, deal with your stress, maybe get some space to feel whatever you need to feel about Mom. Not the hospital, not your stupid little condo building that doesn't even have a fitness room."

Teagan ran a hand through his hair and looked around the tent where Sloane was proposing he stay. Great purple mountains towered over golden hills. The camp was on the edge of a sparkling blue lake ringed with gray pebbles and green fir trees. There were a dozen luxurious canvas tents with their sides rolled up to admit the sweet July breeze. Each tent had a wooden patio adorned with strings of fairy lights and tasteful groupings of cream-colored pillar candles.

The big fluffy beds within the tents, set with half a dozen pillows and a faux sheepskin throw, promised hours of seductive rest. But Teagan didn't need any of this—he had prescriptions and a safety plan, and as soon as this last round of benzodiazepines wore off, he had a week of missed work to catch up on.

"I can't take that much time off," he protested.

"Rose said you could," Sloane insisted.

He really couldn't. His mother had left the foundation's finances in a shambles, and two years of drudgery spent cleaning up the books had only clarified its current dire straits. And even if it had been hubris to think he was qualified to fix that with no professional experience besides trading municipal bonds, he couldn't let everything drop now. He'd be no better than his mother.

"Sloane, this all looks very nice, but—"

His sister shoved him lightly. "Did you see there's horseback-riding?" Sloane asked, eyes wheedling.

Teagan groaned and put his hand on his forehead. *Horses.* He needed ten million dollars in new endowment commitments and a direct flight back to LaGuardia, not *horses.*

"The last horse I was on was a pony in Central Park. I was eight."

"Forget the horses, then. There's plenty of other stuff to do. We need this," Sloane argued.

Teagan began frowning over *we* as Sloane pushed the admissions paperwork into his hands. Setting aside the question of why there were *two* admissions packets, he humored her by opening the folders and flipping through the glossy brochures.

There were pages of information on the nutritionists, physical trainers, and astrologers he might expect to encounter. There was sunrise yoga, sunset yoga, crystal-guided mindfulness, and—on full moon nights—full moon yoga. There were painting classes, jewelry-crafting workshops, canoeing, archery, and gourmet plant-based dinners served under the stars. Did this place even have therapy? Finally, Teagan reached the professional biography of Dr. Goedert, the program director's husband.

He was a clinical psychologist, which seemed like overkill. Teagan's own doctor would handle his medications, and he didn't think his other therapeutic needs were large. But when Teagan reached Dr. Goedert's professional specializations, he stopped. Dr. Goedert specialized in the treatment of addiction.

"Oh," Teagan said, feeling very confused again. "This is rehab?" Dislocation was becoming a familiar sensation. He'd gone to the emergency room for what he'd been certain was a heart attack. Somehow he'd ended up in the psychiatric hospital. Somehow he was in rural Montana with a questionnaire about his nonexistent drug use and a second questionnaire about his equally nonexistent skin care routine. He couldn't make the progression of events make any sense.

"It's not really rehab," his sister said, a little too quickly. "It's personal wellness, tailored for the needs of people with chemical dependency issues."

"Sloane, what I have is brain chemistry issues. And I'm already treating those."

"Well, even if that's true, maybe we still need to talk about substance abuse with a professional." Her face wrinkled in consternation as she wrung her hands. "Given everything with Mom?"

"But that problem is not the problem that I have," Teagan slowly explained to her. He rarely drank. He didn't do drugs—save and except for whatever he'd been prescribed during the past week. "I don't need to go to rehab, and I can't take a vacation."

Sloane snatched the admissions packets away from him.

"You're not listening to me," she complained. "They have yoga and mindfulness training, and all the food is organic and anti-inflammatory. Don't you think that would help you?"

"It probably won't hurt me, but I think twenty milligrams of daily Lexapro have it covered already."

Sloane grimaced. "We could spend some time together," she said, trying a different tactic. "I barely see you anymore."

"Of course we can spend some time together," Teagan said. "Anywhere. Regardless. School doesn't start back up for another month or two, does it? I can stay at the house in Irvington with you until you go back to Claremont."

"You'll just spend every day at the office if we do that. We could go hiking here. Don't you like hiking?" Sloane suggested instead, sensing that he was wavering.

Teagan squinted at her, more thoughts penetrating the gray fog shrouding his mind. Sloane didn't like the outdoors. Their mother had tried to ship an eight-year-old Sloane off to Teagan's childhood sleepaway camp in Vermont in the first year that he didn't come home from college for the summer. Sloane had bribed a staff member for use of her cell phone, called Teagan to inform him that it was *hot*, there were *bugs*, and she wanted to go *home*, then waited at the camp entrance with her suitcases until Teagan drove up in the middle of the night from Boston to collect her.

"Sloane, are we here because *you* need to go to rehab?" he asked, slowly working through it.

She licked her lips, considering.

"Sloane."

"I mean, everyone in our family had issues," she said. "We probably needed more therapy. All the therapy, for all of us. Remember when you got so mad that mom left me home alone while she went to Art Basel that you called CPS on her? Like, you should have probably talked to someone about that too."

"You were ten! And that still doesn't explain why you want to go to rehab." Teagan paused, stomach dropping as he began to imagine everything she could have gotten into out of sight in California. "What have you been taking, exactly?"

Sloane scrunched up her foxlike features. "Just pills. A little coke. But you know, given everything with our family, I thought maybe we could both stay at a place like this and work on ourselves . . ." Her voice delicately trailed off as she looked up at him in open appeal.

Teagan rubbed a week's worth of stubble on his cheeks, then ground his palms into his eyes. He should have paid more attention to how Sloane was handling their mother's death. He'd been too absorbed by all the estate work, by the foundation. None of it was more important than his sister. Jesus. He should have been on top of this too.

"Okay. Okay. How much does this place cost?" he asked. He hadn't worried about that so much until now, but he hadn't planned for a month of luxury accommodations for two people.

"What do you mean, how much does it cost?" Sloane asked, alarm visible in her eyes.

"I *mean*, how much does it cost? Or does this place take insurance?" Teagan was abruptly glad that he'd resisted his directors' suggestion that he cut employee health benefits.

"Why does that matter?"

"It matters because I need to figure out if I can afford it," he said.

"You have a literal trust fund. This is literally the reason why people put together trust funds for their kids—so they can go to rehab after all the shitty parenting."

"I don't have one anymore, actually. I poured it into the foundation when mom died."

"Jesus Christ. Why would you do that?" Sloane asked, appalled.

"I thought it would make me feel better," he said, turning and heading for the main building. He couldn't justify inheriting money from his mother when the foundation had been two months from missing payroll under her mismanagement. It had been a moment of triumphant moral clarity— but moral clarity was not a good and consistent source of serotonin, as it turned out.

"Doesn't look like it worked," Sloane called as she followed him. "And now you have to worry about paying for stuff."

Teagan put what he hoped was a soothing expression on his face and paused. It must have been hard for Sloane to articulate that she needed help. He turned to put his hands on her narrow shoulders. She'd always been small for her age, and it was still hard for him to consider her full grown now that she was taller than most women. "Don't worry about it. Dad left me some money too. I'll take care of this." His dizzy attempt to project reassurance must have worked, because she finally nodded.

He let them into the camp's main building. Everything was decorated in shades of white and cream, in travertine stone and pale wood, like a spa. He supposed it was a spa.

"If this place is too expensive, I'll find a place we can afford. Rehab's important."

"But I wanted to go to *this one*," Sloane said. "They customize your diet to your personal immune profile." She waved the nutrition brochure, which depicted a soft-focus bowl of raspberries, pistachios, and what appeared to be . . . butter? Had to be margarine—the place was vegan. Teagan kept his skepticism of the therapeutic benefits of raspberries and vegan butter to himself. The best rehab program was one that Sloane would actually stay at; their mother had dabbled in sobriety, but never for long, or long enough. Better to get this right the first time.

Teagan halted on the plush sisal rug covering the pineboard floor of the reception area. Rachel, the program director who'd greeted them upon their arrival, was typing on a computer in a glass-sided office, but she stood up to intercept them as they approached the main desk. She was in her fifties, with one of those immobile, ageless faces achieved via high-quality medical intervention.

Rachel brought over two little copper cups of ice water as she greeted them. There were bits of unidentifiable red leaf floating in each cup. Possibly some kind of cabbage. Sloane smiled, the expression honest and delighted for the first time since she'd signed him out of the hospital. Some small knot in Teagan's chest loosened; he didn't feel like he'd delivered for anyone recently, and if Sloane's sobriety demanded leaf water and hot yoga, he'd liquidate investments to get them for her.

"Did you have any trouble filling out the admission paperwork?" Rachel tactfully asked, no doubt eager to get paid.

"I can do that while my sister gets settled," Teagan said,

resolved to staying with Sloane until the charms of the outdoors failed her.

Sloane gave a muted squeal of approval, tugging on his
arm with both hands.

Rachel favored them with a polished smile. "This afternoon we have a class on rock garden design using crystal
healing methodologies. Does that sound like fun?"

"Yeah, of course," Sloane agreed, as eagerly as though
she'd been waiting her entire life to design rock gardens,
with rock crystals especially.

Teagan set his shoulders back and blinked at the ceiling
for a moment, willing his mind to fully wake up, even though
thoughts oozed out like the last ounce of toothpaste in a roll.
He needed to call his bank. Call Rose and maybe the program officer of the foundation. The front desk of his building,
maybe a couple of the people on the planning committees
whose meetings he'd miss . . .

His gaze landed on the pile of luggage at the front desk.
He had no idea what Sloane had even packed for him, and
he otherwise had only the clothes he'd worn into the hospital. His skin itched to change out of clothing he'd sweated
through a week ago.

"Can I bring our bags to our tents first?" he asked Rachel.

"Oh no," she said. She opened the door and craned her
neck outside, shouting at an unseen person around the back
patio. "Don't worry about carrying a thing here. Darcy does
all of that."

two

IT WAS ALMOST MIDAFTERNOON BEFORE DARCY
got the chance to duck into Rachel's office to use the telephone. With the arrival of Teagan and Sloane Van Zijl the
day before, the ranch was at capacity, and that meant Darcy
could barely make it from one chore to another without being intercepted and asked to explain, fetch, or fix something.

She cradled a package of lightbulbs under one arm as she
punched up her voicemail. Two messages from zombie debt
collectors looking for her father, one from her dentist telling
her she was four months overdue for a cleaning, and one from
the shitweasel she'd been calling every day for the past week.

"Hey, babe," said the cheerful voice of her ex-roommate,
scratchy and distant on the recording. "It's Travis. I'm almost done over here in Washington. I should be able to
bring the car back by next Friday. I'll give you a call when
I'm in town. Just hang tight till then, okay? 'Kay! Later."

Darcy's hand clamped down on the phone receiver so
hard she thought she might crack the plastic. The car? *The*
car? The lack of a possessive pronoun made her so angry her
vision nearly whited out for a moment. That was *her* car—
the car she'd spent almost all of her savings to purchase from
Travis, and which was supposed to have been parked at the

wellness retreat next to Rachel's pickup truck as soon as the finance company returned the title.

Resisting the strong urge to throw something, Darcy called Travis back.

"Travis," she gritted out when she went straight to his voicemail. "Like I told you yesterday, you need to drop off *my* car. Right now. Not next week. Turn around and drive back to Montana this instant. Or I'll—" She broke off, swearing under her breath. She wouldn't call the cops on him, and he knew it. "Or I'll have you killed." Yeah, that felt satisfying to say. "Assassinated! I will have you *assassinated*, by a bunch of big, scary guys. I know guys from the Navy. Like Navy SEALs, but worse. Black ops, wet work, off the books guys. Who owe me favors. Who owe me their *lives*. I am sending them after your lying, stealing ass if you do not have my car here by *this* Friday. Call me back and confirm that you do not long for the sweet embrace of the grave, otherwise they're coming for you." Darcy slammed the receiver down.

She didn't actually know any goon squad, but one would have been really handy. She pinched the bridge of her nose between the fingers of her free hand as she massaged the tension there. It had been a mistake to fall for Travis's aw-shucks, single-dad schtick—that was on her, fine, she should have known better—but trapped out here in Big Sky without transportation or cell phone reception, she couldn't even hunt the creep down.

For just one moment, she let her knees sag.

Et tu, Travis?

She'd covered for him on more than one shift at the warming hut, because he had a kid to visit back in Tacoma, and she'd felt bad about his long commute. But doing nice things for other people was no guarantee they wouldn't cheerfully screw her over if the opportunity arose. Everyone did.

Darcy could chart the port calls in her unbroken voyage of screwing-over: the college financial aid officer who told an eighteen-year-old Darcy that she'd get plenty of loans even if her parents had already wrecked her credit by putting their utility bills in her name. The Navy recruiter who promised a nineteen-year-old Darcy that she'd learn a ton of marketable skills in uniform. The Park Service contractor who guaranteed a twenty-seven-year-old Darcy a permanent position in forestry if she just got her foot in the door doing hospitality work. Finally the Goederts, who'd pitched *this* job as involving a lot more wilderness education and a lot less property maintenance.

Coming to the end of another seasonal gig always made Darcy punchy as she scrambled to figure out housing, transportation, and other logistics for her next move, but something about this transition was really rubbing her face in her failure to live her life in anything more than ninety-day increments.

In October, Rachel would close the ranch up until the next May. October was shoulder season, and without a car, Darcy wasn't sure what she could do until it snowed, even if she wanted to spend another winter babysitting tourists in Yellowstone. Thirty-year-old aspiring rangers who couldn't seem to finish a bachelor's degree were not in high demand.

She rested her forehead against the wall, granting herself sixty more seconds to be angry before she got back to work.

She heard the motor of the blender from the kitchen next to Rachel's office and looked at the clock—almost snack time for the guests. She glared at the telephone one last time, daring Travis to call her back without the promise of the delivery of her car, then headed to the kitchen to collect the afternoon smoothies.

Kristin, the only other live-in staffer besides Darcy, was tossing produce into the blender at random. Darcy nodded companionably at her sturdy, purple-haired, and heavily tattooed coworker and began pulling mason jars out of the dishwasher. The guests ate that stuff up—the implication that someone might be pickling their own vegetables using the same glasses they drank their smoothies out of. High-priced authenticity.

Darcy couldn't tell if Rachel actually, sincerely, in her true heart of hearts believed that the guests at the wellness retreat were benefitting from the organic food, the essential oils, the guided meditation, and all the other vaguely New Age crap she pushed on them. A reasonable person couldn't really, right? Darcy did not believe in it. So she didn't press Rachel on whether she did either. Darcy was sure the guests benefitted from being out in the woods where they couldn't drink or do drugs, and that was enough to assuage her conscience about her participation in what might otherwise be considered an elaborate health scam. Darcy kept her mouth shut about the ridiculous aspects of her job, like the smoothie served after Midafternoon Mindfulness.

She scanned Rachel's instructions for the day, trying to make sense of what the woman was saying about immune support and glycemic load, as though Rachel was a certified nutritionist, rather than a former LA yoga mom with a big Instagram following for her perfectly lit breakfast photos where she posed with ancient grain oatmeal in her underwear.

"Any luck with your ex?" Kristin asked as she tossed beets into the juicer.

"He's not my ex," Darcy insisted. "He was just a . . . horny mistake."

"Irregardless, are you going to get your car back?"

Darcy scowled. "Probably not."

When she ran the critique on this situation, Darcy was going to have to accept that letting her hormones get the better of her a couple times had probably contributed to her ex-roommate's belief that he could get away with her car. Lessons learned. Better to make horny mistakes outside the home than inside them.

"That sucks," Kristin pointed out unnecessarily. "So, where are you gonna go after this, then?"

Kristin had pulled out several bunches of kale, so Darcy started washing them in the prep sink. Beet-kale-turmeric-huckleberry juice was a staple here.

"Somewhere with no commute, I guess," Darcy said un-happily. She had no good ideas. "I heard that those off-shore oil platforms always need to hire people to cook and clean," she mused, thinking out loud. "You go out for ninety-day contracts, and they pay really well." Maybe she'd be able to save enough for a second car after a couple of those gigs. Maybe she'd have more time to study than she did here— she was only taking eight hours online, and at that rate she was never going to graduate. But it sounded pretty thin, even inside her head.

The list of accomplishments she could reasonably expect to garner with her life kept shrinking. She was basically down to finishing her degree and getting a job in forestry, but those goals were looking more remote by the year.

Kristin stopped her work and stared at her. "Darcy, the first time they spilled oil on, like, *one* duck, you'd start pushing your coworkers into the ocean."

"Maybe they wouldn't spill any oil if I was in charge."

"I don't think they'd put you in charge, at least not at first."

"Well, they should," Darcy said.

Kristin silently nodded agreement to that proposition until Darcy tipped her head back and laughed. Nobody was going to put her in charge of anything bigger than a warming hut.

"Maybe I'll stay in Montana," Darcy said. "When's rodeo season? I could be a clown."

"Mmm, I'm not sure whether the rodeo is seasonal," Kristin said. "But I don't think rodeo clowning pays as much as bull riding. Is that oppressive to bulls, or would you consider it?"

"Seems like the bull's on equal footing with the rider, so maybe? Do you think it's hard?"

"A lot of guys at my high school in Butte did it, so it can't be *that* hard," Kristin said. "You don't skip leg day, do you?"

"Never," Darcy said, looking down at the limbs in question. "I could crush a walnut between these babies."

"Now *that's* an idea. OnlyFans. One girl, one walnut. You could come with me to Bozeman and be a cam girl. Or, you know, work with me at the vegan caterer's."

They looked at each other again, Darcy appreciating that there was an actual offer behind the joking suggestion. Kristin might be lazy. She did zero work at the wellness retreat unless Rachel or Darcy was standing right over her. But as far as Darcy had been able to discern that summer, laziness was Kristin's sole besetting sin. She was genuine and nice and pretty funny. Darcy could do worse for a roommate, even if she was sure she'd end up doing all the cleaning.

But moving in with Kristin and taking the kind of job she could have gotten at eighteen was as good as admitting that Darcy hadn't been—oh, smart enough, capable enough, strong enough—for college or the Navy or the Park Service. And that she had nothing at all to show for the past decade and more of her life: no degree, no pension, no career, not even a fucking car.

"I want to have my own bedroom again," Darcy said, gently declining Kristin's offer. "I'm going to start sleeping naked. Rachel said it's healthier. I overheard her telling one of the guests yesterday that she does it."

"Gross," Kristin said, cackling. "Though I bet Dr. Goodhair appreciates that."

"I bet it was his scientific suggestion," Darcy agreed. "Just like our uniforms." She gestured to their cutoff shorts, and Kristin snorted. Whether Dr. Goedert was a good psychologist or just another pervy grifter was outside of Darcy's area of responsibility. If the Navy had taught her anything (aside from not very useful things like auxiliary engine maintenance and how to pee in a hole with deadly accuracy), it was that worrying about the overall mission was wasted effort. *Worry about your own job, Albano.*

"Anyway," Darcy said, looking at the two remaining mason jars, "what are you serving the new guys?"

"Mr. and Mrs. Van Zijl?"

"I don't think they're married?" The two new guests didn't fit the usual profile. Darcy had seen some interesting people come through the retreat—B-list actors, musicians, an actual European royal—but these two seemed both younger and less colorful than most guests.

Kristin laughed. "The guy brought his kid with him to rehab?"

"No, I think she's like, his sister or something."

"Weird. Well . . . do they have any allergies?"

Darcy grabbed the latest guest register and passed it to Kristin. "Take a look."

Kristin scanned Rachel's notes, pretending to take into account her detailed instructions regarding the balance of anti-inflammatory and immune-optimizing ingredients.

"Okay," she said. "I'm feeling inspired. Their immune systems are getting *boosted*."

"You are an artist with a blender," said Darcy.

Kristin began rustling through the refrigerator and cupboards, pulling more ingredients out haphazardly. Rachel bought the weirdest shit for these smoothies: fruits and vegetables and herbal supplements Darcy had never heard of before, because Darcy found peanut butter and Oreos to be a very satisfactory and cruelty-free diet when she was planning her own meals. The ranch's clientele, by contrast, were of the sort that would eat *anything* if it was blended with ice and pitched as a health food.

Kristin tossed everything into the industrial-sized blender, pulsed and pureed, then grabbed spoons for them both.

"I call this the Fighting Farmer," Kristin declared, dipping a spoon into the mush and handing it over to Darcy for her approval. "Apple juice, beet puree, carrots, arugula, garlic powder, and"—she winked at Darcy—"bee pollen."

Darcy took a tiny taste off the spoon. It was awful. Kristin had truly outdone herself this time.

"You know, I think it needs a little something else," she said, pretending to think very hard about it.

"Oh? More beet, maybe?"

Darcy tapped her chin. "No." She scanned the piles of produce. "I think it needs some rutabaga."

Kristin took her own wincing sip of the smoothie and nodded, impressed. "You are so right."

"I'm always right," Darcy said, grabbing the root vegetable and beginning to peel it. She scraped a little into the blender, then pulsed it again, followed by the ice that convinced their guests that the beverage was a treat, not a punishment.

Kristin poured the smoothie into two mason jars for Teagan and Sloane Van Zijl, then loaded the rest of the smoothie-filled jars into a basket with a handful of stainless-steel straws for transport to the meditation deck. Darcy checked the clock again. Still running on schedule.

"Darcy?" Kristin asked.

"Yeah?"

"Why don't you tell Rachel you don't have a job lined up? Maybe she or Dr. Goedert could find you a job in Bozeman. Like at his practice or something?"

Darcy kept her face carefully blank. The Goederts thought she was an illiterate knuckle-dragger. They wouldn't hire her to do anything in an office besides clean it.

"Yeah, maybe I'll do that," she lied, grabbing the basket. "Thanks."

Darcy was just in time for the end of the session, approaching as Rachel rang the crystal bell that signaled the end of meditation free time. There were about a dozen guests participating, most of them clad in expensive activewear or vaguely bohemian natural fibers. Darcy handed out the smoothies, finishing with the Van Zijl girl, a skinny slip of a thing with a trendy layered haircut.

There was one smoothie left in her basket.

"I think this goes to your . . . guy . . ." Darcy let her voice trail off as she passed the beet-based beverage to the girl. Sloane Van Zijl looked almost a decade younger than Darcy, which was really young for a guest. Most people were trying to get over entire lifetimes of bad habits.

"Brother," said Sloane, rolling her eyes. "Teagan's not here. He went on a hike by himself after lunch. He didn't want to do the guided visualizations."

Darcy glanced over at Rachel. It was after three. It wasn't like Rachel to let one of her baby ducklings wander off by himself for so long. Darcy did her best to check the luggage as it came in, but addicts were very skilled at squirreling things away for the second or third day of rehab, when withdrawal really started to hit. Sometimes she found them out in the forest, high as giraffe balls.

"Is your brother a big hiker?" Darcy asked.

Sloane dramatically frowned.

"Teagan? He lives in Manhattan. The last time he embraced the wilderness was the day a pigeon got into his condo."

Darcy sighed. "Which way did he go?" she asked. She'd bring him back for painting or pottery or basket weaving or whatever Rachel had planned for art class today. Sometimes this job was a lot like being a preschool teacher. Sit down. Eat your snack. Don't put that in your mouth; it's poison.

Sloane pointed toward the waterfall trail. It was a five-mile loop, with a fair amount of elevation gain. Not a good trail for beginners, especially not alone.

"Ah, goats," Darcy swore. She kept a hiking backpack

ready to go in her room, but retrieving it and the lost bumblefuck hiker would use up her time cushion for the rest of the day. She'd hoped to free up enough time before dinner to study for her final exams for once. "I'll have to go find him."

"Is it not safe?" Sloane asked anxiously.

Darcy gave her a reassuring smile, covering her own annoyance. "He's fine," she said. "Kristin and I climb that trail every week. You just have to keep an eye out for bears."

three

TEAGAN FELT BETTER AND BETTER ON THE PATH UP
the mountain, but that brief sensation of well-being did not
last through the descent. One of the other guests—a record
executive from LA, two months sober—had told him the
trail was five miles long, and that had sounded just perfect
to Teagan. He regularly ran five miles on the treadmill at
the gym, sometimes with an incline. And walking the trail
sounded much more restorative than another round of yoga
or meditation.

The goal of Teagan's typical exercise regimen was "enough
cardio to let me sleep tonight," not the development of strength,
endurance, or—most relevant to the yoga—flexibility. He'd
winced through the entire uncomfortable hour-long session,
worried that his ass was hanging out of his loose sweatpants,
the most appropriate clothing he possessed here.

Sloane hadn't done a terrible job at packing his clothes, but
his gym clothes were all he owned that were even vaguely
suitable to the ranch lifestyle, and they weren't very suitable.
His body wasn't suitable either. His hips didn't flex. His back
didn't bend. His knees pointed nearly at the sky when they
sat cross-legged for the five minutes of meditation that concluded the hour of poses.

And the meditation was a whole other thing. Teagan was

pretty sure being left alone with his thoughts was what had gotten him into this situation—sitting and dwelling on how awful he felt was probably the opposite of productive, if the goal was to return from Montana as a functional human being. So when it had come time for Midafternoon Meditation (Rachel's cheerful pronouncement suggested capital letters), Teagan did a thing he had never done during school: played hooky.

The waterfall at the top of the trail had been breathtaking. Well worth the hike. He hoped Sloane made it up here with him before they left, although his sister was usually thrifty with her energy when it came to long walks. If he'd been allowed his phone, he would have snapped a picture to send to his friends and colleagues to reassure them that he was doing well. Even without one, he did his best to appreciate the scenery. It was beautiful here, though Teagan shouldn't have been on a glorified vacation in the first place when he had so much to do back in New York.

Now he was teasing his way down the mountain in his running shoes, which he'd purchased with pavement in mind, not hillside. Going up the mountain had alerted him that hiking used some muscles he wasn't activating at the gym, but on his way downhill, new parts of his body were protesting, and mental fatigue was setting in as well.

He'd managed a solid seven hours of sleep the night before, but he was still tired. On Lexapro, sleep was like cat fur. It clung to him as he tried to brush it off, fuzzed the world's colors, and softened the edges of his thinking. The benzodiazepines he was tapering off probably did not help either. He supposed he'd better get used to the feeling, because detached was decidedly preferable to lying awake in a cold sweat every night.

Teagan's calves started to cramp as he came around a switchback and saw a wide expanse of wild raspberry brambles. He wasn't a botanist, but he remembered eating handfuls of wild black raspberries in Vermont as a child.

All the food at the ranch was vegan. That wasn't a problem in and of itself, but one small square of wild mushroom lasagna with cashew cheese and nondairy béchamel had really not cut it in terms of lunch. He was hungry. The sweatshirt he wore—the logo said "Yale School of Management," which made him feel like a douchebag, wearing it out in public—had a front pouch pocket. He decided it was time to do some gathering. A few minutes of berry picking would give his calves time to get with the program and stop complaining, and Sloane would be happy if he brought some back to treat her. She'd loved raspberry-jam sandwiches as a toddler.

Teagan waded into the bushes, eyes on his feet to avoid getting stuck on the brambles. He picked whole clusters of berries, dividing them between his pocket and his mouth. They exploded in little starbursts of flavor on his tongue, the taste sour but somehow fruitier than the kind you could buy at the store.

This is so wholesome, he thought to himself. He imagined explaining it to Rose—in this fantasy, she hadn't told anyone else where he'd been—saying, "Yes, I think the past couple of years just caught up to me. So sorry for the lack of notice. I just needed a quick break. It's wonderful up there, anyway, you should go—I went hiking, picked wild raspberries, slept with the tent open to see the stars. Highly recommend it for your next vacation. Now, what was the return this month on the international equities portfolio?" Nobody would remember that he'd abruptly disappeared in the middle of a work week.

It was with that thought foremost in his mind that he took a long step to skirt a clump of white-barked trees and approach a particularly promising hedge of raspberry bushes. His eyes were on his feet, and so it wasn't his eyes that alerted him but his ears, which registered only a single guttural *HRRMPH.*

Teagan had spent most of his life within the boundaries of the Greater New York metropolitan area, but some primeval part of his malfunctioning brain recognized that sound and sent a wave of adrenaline coursing through his body. He looked up from his feet and nearly met the bear eye to eye.

A grizzly bear. An absolutely enormous, brown-furred, humped and clawed and growling grizzly bear. It was halfway crouched on its back legs, head higher than his own, even though Teagan was a tall man. He'd interrupted it raiding the same cluster of berry bushes he'd targeted. It was hungry too. It also liked berry bushes. He'd interrupted a hungry bear in the berry bushes.

Teagan's mind, which had not been at all helpful for days now, began hanging—distant, removed—on the realization that *oh shit* was probably the last thing that most people thought before they died.

Oh shit, Teagan thought. *Oh shit.*

The bear growled or snorted again and reached out with an almost casual swipe of its dinner plate-sized paw. More of a *fuck off, I was here first* gesture than a serious attack, but as the paw was attached to a nine-hundred-pound apex predator, it sent Teagan reeling backward when it made contact with his hip. Sharp, tearing pain radiated through his left side.

His body began moving without his conscious control, twisting to avoid landing in the bushes, yelling a garbled string of nonsense to the effect of "NO! BEAR! STOP! BEAR! NO!" and kicking with desperate effort as his feet scrambled for purchase. This unfortunately sent dirt flying at the bear, which snorted in alarm.

He was going to die. For the second time in a week, he believed he was going to die. He had met Death in Big Sky after fleeing him at the Metro-North platform.

Teagan managed to get his feet back underneath him and began scooting backward as fast as he could, given the uneven terrain and the berry brambles pulling on his clothing and tearing into his legs. The bear followed him, still huffing and growling.

He recalled hearing advice to fall down and play dead if confronted by a bear. Also advice to flap his jacket and make himself as intimidating as possible. These two pieces of advice seemed directly contradictory, not to mention somewhat implausible. Falling down and playing dead was practically asking to be eaten, and flapping his arms at the bear seemed like a challenge he couldn't possibly win.

Teagan heard shouting. He wasn't sure if it was coming out of his own throat, but just in case it wasn't, he shouted back: "BEAR! BEAR! BEAR!"

He was nearly back to the trail now, and the bear still hadn't bitten his head off, but that situation could change at any minute, as the ground was most level immediately next to the switchback he'd stepped off of.

He could run faster back up the trail. He needed to run. His legs were probably longer than the bear's; maybe he'd make it. But terror was making his muscles stiff and slow, and his knee turned just as he stepped into the pea gravel of the trail. He slipped, knocking his head against the hillside as he fell. *Oh shit*, again—this was it. He'd somehow materialized his end.

From opposite directions, he heard a woman's yell and the bear's definitive roar, both very close. Stunned on the ground, Teagan tried to crane his neck backward to see who was yelling but noticed only the great spray of something orange and liquid approaching him and the bear. His sinuses caught a bare moment's whiff of pepper before his nose and eyes and mouth were seared by the bear spray, and he lost the ability to sense anything from those parts of his body except blistering heat and pain.

Someone seized him under the arms and hauled him up. His feet dragged in the dirt for a couple of yards before he got them underneath him for a second time. His left leg wasn't working very well; that was the side the bear had swiped and the side where his knee had twisted. But after a moment, his unknown rescuer stuck her head under his left arm and pushed her hip against his so that he could hobble forward. They were going back up the mountain. They stumbled together for what felt like a dozen yards, Teagan's rescuer pulling him back to his feet every time he put a foot awry and tripped.

"Come on, come on," the woman puffed. She supported most of his weight on the inside curve of the switchback, but somehow, she held him upright. Teagan couldn't speak, because almost everything hurt. His eyes, his nose, his chest from the spray, and also his knee and the slash on his hip. He gritted his teeth against whimpering, but he still wheezed as his throat burned.

They reached a level section, and she dropped his arm to take his hand. Tugging him at first, she urged him into a stumbling run. He clenched her fingers tightly as he picked up speed, trusting that she wouldn't lead him off the cliff. Together, they ran. He couldn't see a thing. For all he knew, the bear was right behind them. He wanted to yell at the top of his lungs just to expel something from his body: fear, pain, desperation. It all felt stuck inside him.

After maybe ten minutes of lurching uphill, his rescuer gradually slowed until she stopped, still holding his hand.

"It's gone," she said.

Teagan sagged in relief. He wavered on his feet until his rescuer pushed him up against a broad tree trunk, finally releasing him.

"Okay, you can sit," she panted. "Let's look at you."

Teagan slid down until his ass was on the ground, his legs splayed in front of him. Some of the bear spray had gone down his throat, and he coughed and hacked to get the burning taste out of his mouth.

The woman crouched over his knees, straddling him. She adjusted her position until she was comfortable on his thighs. He heard a lid being unscrewed. His rescuer wiped his face with what felt like the lower hem of her T-shirt and then, as he blinked, poured water directly into his eyes to flush them out. He'd kept his eyes screwed shut against the pain as he climbed, but he tried to clear them enough to squint at the woman who'd saved him.

Her features were very fuzzy at first. He was facing southwest, and the sun had dipped to backlight his rescuer. His clearing eyesight gave her a halo that his giddy relief mentally seconded. She was his age or a little younger, cheeks flushed with exertion over olive skin. Her long, wavy chestnut hair was caught in a high ponytail, with little tufts escaping to stick to her temples and neck. The sun had bleached it golden at the tips and around the perfect oval of her face. Large chocolate-brown eyes regarded him with concern, and full berry-red lips were pursed under a dramatically arched nose. She looked like a pre-Raphaelite angel. Like an altarpiece.

"Are you going to be all right?" she asked from her perch over his knees.

Teagan took stock of his injuries. Nothing fatal, probably.

"Yes, I think so," he said, his abused throat making his voice hoarse and gravelly. He tried to wipe more water and tears off his face. His hands were shaking.

His rescuer shifted her seat on his legs, letting more weight fall on them. He heard her breathing begin to slow. She must have run when she heard him start yelling, and she had a large backpack that she'd carried up the hill in addition to most of his body weight.

They locked eyes again, and Teagan felt his heart clench in his chest. She was *beautiful*.

His rescuer exhaled, shoulders relaxing. Some of the fear and desperation began to trickle out of Teagan's body too. He was going to live, actually. He did not get eaten by the bear. He did not die alone on the mountain.

"Yes, thank you," he said, gathering himself. "I'm okay." He forced his eyes to open and his mind to focus so that he could catch her next words. She leaned in, fists resting gently on his torso.

"Mother*fucker*," said the angel, with feeling.

four

TEAGAN VAN ZIJL'S EYES, WHICH HAD STARTED OUT rather shocky and unfocused, went round and impressed as Darcy began to bawl him out. She'd learned critique from a truly gifted chief petty officer, and although her current job offered few opportunities to practice that particular skill, she was alight with an incendiary mix of anger, fear, and disgust.

"Do you know how close you came to being bear chow?" she yelled directly into the man's dazed face. His features were fine and patrician, mostly sharp angles around his chin and cheekbones, but decorated with incongruously thick eyelashes and a plush, full mouth, now hanging open in slack-jawed surprise.

"Did you wake up this morning and decide you were going to make the worst decisions possible, or was this an impulse thing? Did you think, 'Damn, Darcy doesn't have enough to do today. I should go hiking. By myself. In bear country. In July. With no fucking bear spray. That'll do the trick!'"

"Are you Darcy?" he tried to interject, wiping again at his wet face and only managing to smear more dirt across it.

She smacked him in the chest with one palm. The big dork was dressed like he was going to use the elliptical machine for twenty minutes at the 24 Hour Fitness. He didn't even have a water bottle with him, let alone bear spray or an emergency beacon.

"Yes, I'm fucking Darcy. The woman who is asking you what the hell you were thinking?!"

"I thought—"

"Did you really? *Did* you think?" she demanded.

Teagan's throat moved as he swallowed.

"I guess I wasn't thinking," he said faintly.

No, Chief, I wasn't thinking.

"Do you know what would have happened if you got yourself killed up here? Do you know what a shitstorm that would have been for everyone? Me? The Goederts? The bear?"

Teagan coughed. "The *bear*?" he asked, a little incredulously.

Darcy smacked his chest again. "Yes, the bear! A bunch of jackbooted assholes from Montana Fish and Wildlife would have come up here and *murdered* that bear. Did you think about that?"

Every year, some brainless hiker got himself mauled because he tried to take selfies with bear cubs or store his leftover hot dogs in his tent. And what happened to the innocent bear, just protecting its cubs or grabbing a midnight snack? Death penalty!

"No, I did not think about what would happen to the bear after it ate me," Teagan admitted, shifting uncomfortably beneath her.

"Yeah, that's what I thought," Darcy said with disgust. "You people never think about anyone but yourselves."

God, this job would be so much easier if it weren't for the frigging guests. Rich jerks who left their trash all over the place, complained constantly about the beautiful wilderness they were despoiling, and spent their time feeling sad they weren't allowed to do all the drugs they wanted.

The coyotes kept me up all night. Could you do anything about that?

What do you mean there's no coffee? Could I just get a drip cup?

The floor of my tent is dirty. Could someone vacuum it while I'm on my trail ride?

But this guy had just climbed the hierarchy of useless jerks: a lost little gym bunny who'd never bothered to ask whether a bear shit in the woods.

Not that he was so little. Unfortunately, he was tall and broad-shouldered for how slender he was, which probably meant he looked good when dressed in something other than his gym clothes but was really going to suck for Darcy when she had to carry him back to camp.

"I'm sorry that my mauling has ruined your day," Teagan said. His tone was appropriately contrite, but his words made her squint suspiciously at his deadpan expression to check whether he had dared to sass her. "How can I make it up to you?"

"You're not mauled," she scoffed. "Just a little banged up." She'd show *him* mauled if this made the wildlife officials start sniffing around Rachel's outfit.

"I think I'm bleeding, actually," he said with an apologetic wince.

Darcy looked down sharply. She hadn't noticed that. Hadn't checked for it either.

Guess nobody was thinking today, Chief. There was a spreading red stain across the left side of his body.

"Christ," she breathed. "Do *not* die on me up here; everyone will think I killed you." She scrabbled for her backpack, which had a basic first aid kit somewhere.

"I don't think it's that bad," Teagan said, but his judgment was obviously not to be trusted.

"Take off your shirt so I can see if your guts are falling out, jackass," Darcy growled at him, hands rattling on the box of bandages. It had been more than a decade since her first-aid training, and Darcy had been on the noncombatant training arc, so that hadn't amounted to much in the first place. Her confidence that this rescue mission would be successful and casualty-free dipped. What if he died? What if she'd just yelled at him for getting killed, and then he *died*?

Darcy jerked Teagan's sweatshirt up, revealing a pale, muscular—and unmauled—stomach. She mentally revised her opinion of his workout routine. He was spending plenty of time at the gym.

"Where's the blood coming from?" she asked, confused.

Teagan looked down at the red mess on his sweatshirt. "I think most of that is raspberries," he said, although his face was a little pinched. He stuck a finger in it, then put his finger in his mouth. "Yeah, raspberries."

She smacked him one more time in the shoulder for good measure. "Jesus Christ! Are you the most annoying person in the entire world? Where are you bleeding?"

Teagan pointed at his hip.

"Then take off your damn pants," Darcy said, reaching for the waistband of his sweats.

Teagan intercepted her hands.

"Maybe I could buy you dinner first?" he said, pushing back against her wrists.

Darcy dramatically rolled her eyes. "If you're not wearing

underwear, I promise I will never tell a soul what your junk looks like."

"I'm wearing underwear, but—"

"Oh my God! Why are you being so precious about this, then? Take off your pants!"

He hesitated. But he complied. Still looking very peaked, Teagan reluctantly slid his pants down. Darcy then understood his objection.

"So, my sister packed my clothes—"

"Please spare me the Folgers commercial plot of your sister's involvement in your Cookie Monster briefs," Darcy said, struggling to keep her expression straight.

His underwear said "om nom nom" on the waistband. The bear would have been *embarrassed* to eat this man.

Teagan put both palms over his face.

"You know what, why don't you go back without me. I'll get down by myself, and we can just never discuss this again," he mumbled.

"You'd like that, wouldn't you," Darcy said, amused despite her best efforts.

She got off his lightly furred thighs and pushed him over to his side so she could look at the long bloody scratches that had cut through the fabric on his hip. It wasn't as bad as she'd feared, but it was still a mess.

"Dammit," she said, patting the area with gauze. She had enough tape and bandages to cover the wound, but some actual professional was going to need to be involved. *You are delinquent in necessary qualifications, Machinist's Mate Albano.* "I have to take you to an emergency room. These need to be cleaned out, maybe stitched up." There went her evening.

"I can drive myself if you had plans," he offered.

"Of course I had plans."

"Then I'll just take myself—"

"No. Before *we* get to the ER, we are going to come up with an explanation for how this happened that does not involve that poor bear."

"The poor bear," Teagan repeated.

"Yes, the poor bear. Who was just minding his own damn business before some asshole wandered off the trail and interrupted his dinner, and then some other asshole sprayed him with mace—"

Teagan looked up at her through thick blonde eyelashes. His soft, shining hair was a pale, nearly white-blonde color that Darcy would have assumed he'd paid dearly for if he was a woman but was curling over his ears and forehead in a way that suggested he didn't pay much attention to it.

"You just saved my life. I don't think you're an asshole," he said seriously.

"Well, the bear does," Darcy replied, waving her hands in the air. "And you are not going to put him on a hit list. You are going to tell the doctor that you tripped and fell over your own hideous finance bro sneakers." She hoped her expression impressed him with the seriousness of this command.

Those full lips of his thinned in a stubborn line. "Won't the doctor need to know what happened to clean out these cuts? Don't bear claws have . . . bacteria or something?"

Darcy glared at him. "Tell the doctor you fell in bear shit, then."

"I tripped on my own shoes and fell in bear shit," Teagan repeated incredulously.

"Yes," Darcy insisted.

"And I am doing this so the bear is not unjustly accused of mauling me?"

"You *should*, but if not for the bear, do it because I am

telling you to, and I am the one who is going to be carrying your carcass down the mountain."

That got a reaction.

"You most certainly will not. I can walk," Teagan said fervently, his bloodshot hazel eyes flashing with panic. He began struggling as though he intended to stand. Darcy leaned one palm against his chest to hold him down.

"Barely. You're limping."

"And there's no way you can carry me."

"Of course I can. What do you weigh, a buck sixty? I could do that piggyback, even."

"More like one eighty-five—"

"With your boots on, maybe," Darcy said skeptically. Teagan was over six feet tall, but thin and wiry despite the breadth of his shoulders and chest, like a soldier who'd just come off campaign. The chiseled line of his jaw appeared painfully sharp. "I had to lift a guy who weighed over two hundred during basic, so it'll be fine."

"You absolutely cannot," Teagan said.

"Your misogyny is showing."

"I don't mean you can't—I'm saying *no*. If you were a very, very manly man, I would have the same objection to being carried down on your shoulders."

Darcy narrowed her eyes at him, wondering if she could conk him over the head with a stone or something to carry him down in peace.

Teagan must have guessed what she was thinking, because he held his hands out in a pacifying manner.

"Look," he said after a deep breath, "I apologize sincerely for all the trouble to you . . . and to the bear."

"Did you know that there are fewer than eight hundred bears left in the whole Yellowstone ecosystem?"

"I did not. But I appreciate that."

"Do you?" she said skeptically. "Do you really? Because it doesn't seem like you're worried about the bear."

"I am. I promise I am. I won't narc on the bear. I just—" He sighed. "You must see a lot of people at rock bottom here, right?"

Nobody who had *really* hit rock bottom could afford to stay at the wellness retreat, but Darcy had seen a lot of people miserably sweating things out of their systems and regretting their life choices.

"Sure," she said.

"Consider this mine. Can we please make a deal? I won't tell anyone here that I was even hurt. And you'll let me just crawl down the mountain. Please? It's been a hell of a week." His gaze was frank and vulnerable, much more direct than she was accustomed to receiving.

Darcy wrinkled her nose at her messy, raspberry-juice-and-blood-smeared problem in his Cookie Monster briefs and gym clothes. Rachel would have a cat if she saw him, probably ask why Darcy hadn't remediated the bear infestation prior to camp opening.

He looked so distressed that she felt a wave of unwelcome sympathy swamp her determination to get back to her lecture. She was such a sucker.

"Oh, fine. Deal," Darcy said reluctantly. She stood up and offered him her hand. With her help, he got to his feet well enough, even though he kept one hand pressed against his hip and favored his other leg. At his full height he loomed over her, his broad shoulders filling out the space despite his slender build. It was like someone had designed a big hunk of a man and then failed to equip him with the bulk he was supposed to wear.

"Thank you," he said gravely. "Thank you for saving my life, Darcy."

Darcy felt heat suffuse her face. She shook the words off. The critique would say she shouldn't have loitered while he still needed medical attention. Somehow, she was sure this would turn out to be her fault.

five

GETTING DOWN THE MOUNTAIN FELT LIKE THE EASY
part. Getting from the trailhead to the camp's pickup truck
while oozing blood and raspberry puree—all unnoticed by
Sloane and the other guests, who were painting watercolors
of the lake vista on the meditation deck—was more difficult. The adrenaline and endorphins of the bear attack and
escape had ebbed from Teagan's body by the time he crawled
into the passenger seat of the ranch pickup truck. Darcy
curtly forbade him to bleed on the upholstery.

She drove them for an hour east to Bozeman's regional
hospital. The ER was crowded when they arrived: asthma
attacks, chest pains, and a couple of car crashes bumped Teagan to the back of the line. "I tripped over my own hideous
finance bro sneakers," Teagan dutifully told the triage nurse
when he pointed out the gash in his hip. Darcy didn't even
crack a smile. She'd barely spoken to him the entire way there.

Possibly she doesn't like you very much was his gloomy assessment as he kept pressure on his scratches and waited his turn
to be called. This somehow seemed just as unfortunate as
being stuck in the Montana hinterlands with his sister or being a little bit mauled. Of course, she'd just seen him lose a
fight with a grizzly bear and need to be evacuated down two

miles of steep trail, so there was probably not a lot he was going to be able to do to change that impression.

He snuck a glance at her out of the corner of his eye. She was sitting next to him, but as soon as they sat down in the waiting room, she had put her headphones on, stretched her long, bare legs out in front of her, and appeared to go to sleep. Teagan shifted in his seat. His side ached and was starting to stiffen up. The chairs were bare plastic—probably so they could be easily hosed down and disinfected. He didn't know how she could possibly be comfortable enough to sleep there.

As he squirmed, Darcy's eyes popped open. She raked them over his injuries.

"You hanging in there, Bear Bait?" she asked with more concern than he'd expected.

He wasn't sure what the alternative was, but he said, "I'm fine," anyway. He was tacky with dried panic-sweat, raspberries, and gore, everything in his entire body hurt, and he had claw marks down his hip, but someone would presumably call his name and start fixing that when his turn was up. "You can leave if you need to get back. I'll call a cab when I'm done."

She snorted inelegantly. "I'm not ditching you at the ER," she said, and now he'd offended her again. "I'll stay till they release you."

"Okay," he said, striving for the same tone of neutrality, one that he hoped would convey neither that he wished she'd stay and perhaps stop calling him names nor that he wished she'd go and no longer observe him in the basest state of his life.

Darcy regarded him for a moment longer, then stood and crossed the room to the intake window. When she reached it, her face transformed, becoming open and beguiling. She leaned forward to prop herself on her elbows and cross her delicate ankles.

Darcy was built like a comic book superhero: dramatic curves and sharp, muscular lines, all of it contained in a tight T-shirt and cutoff shorts. The triage nurse looked just as impressed by it as Teagan had been. He instantly blossomed under Darcy's attention, harried frown dissolving.

Darcy smiled and tucked a loose strand of her glorious hair behind her ear as she struck up a conversation with the bedazzled man, and while Teagan was too far away to catch every word, he gathered that she was telling the triage nurse a funny and highly fictionalized story . . . of how Teagan fell down a hill and landed in bear shit. She gestured at her side, pantomiming big geysers of blood, then finished with a beseeching clasp of her two hands together. The triage nurse leaned out of his window to get a better look at Teagan.

Teagan didn't try to look any more miserable than he actually felt, but he must have still managed to look pretty bad, because after another minute of typing, the triage nurse came around, opened the door to the ER, and led Teagan and Darcy to an examination room deeper inside the hospital. Darcy turned her head just long enough to wink at Teagan, her expression self-satisfied.

She took the only chair in the examination room, leaving Teagan to perch on the paper-covered bench, his legs dangling awkwardly over the side.

He wracked his brain for some natural topic of conversation that did not relate to her employment, his injuries, or his stay at the wellness retreat.

"Have you ever been here before?" he asked her.

Come here a lot? To the hospital? Well done, Teagan. No wonder you're single.

"No. I'm careful when I go hiking," she said, one eyebrow arched judgmentally. Then she put her headphones back on.

Teagan lay back on the examination bench and closed his eyes. They sat in painfully persistent silence for the next ten minutes.

"No opiates," Darcy casually told the doctor who came to scrub out Teagan's scrapes and stitch them shut. "He's in recovery."

"Good for you," said the doctor before Teagan could object to that characterization. Like the triage nurse, the doctor was also favorably impressed by the shape of Darcy's chest, if the direction of his gaze at the same time he was supposed to be putting five stitches in Teagan's hip was any clue. "Would you like some ibuprofen?"

"I—okay, fine. Sure." Teagan nearly demanded the real stuff—he'd never taken anything stronger than aspirin in his life, so he was willing to run the risk of getting hooked on a single dose of Tylenol #3. But then he wondered whether opiates mixed well with his antidepressants. Rather than recite his recent medical history in front of Darcy, he sighed and accepted an eighty-dollar tab of Advil. He tried his best to look manfully stoic as he was patched up, but he didn't think he managed very well.

Nobody mentioned Teagan's underwear, which was a very small blessing. An ex-girlfriend had bought them as a joke almost four years ago, and Sloane had for some reason decided to pack them in lieu of an entire drawer full of white boxer briefs.

"Don't get your stitches wet," said the young doctor when he was done with the stitches. "They'll dissolve on their own. Change the bandages every other day." He passed a packet of discharge papers to Darcy, who handed them back to Teagan.

"Can I shower, at least?" Teagan asked.

"Not for a week," said the doctor. He looked at Darcy and raised his eyebrows. "Maybe you can convince your girlfriend to give you a sponge bath."

Darcy dropped her head back and laughed so loudly that people turned their heads all the way out at the nurse's station. She slapped Teagan on the back.

"Yeah, sure. Maybe you'd like a blowjob and a foot rub while I'm at it?"

Some part of Teagan thought *Well, that sounds nice*, but that part was subsumed by a fervent wish that the ground would swallow him up, that he could throw himself out a window, that he could go back in time a week and decline medical treatment so that he would not be in this position. No such relief occurred, and Teagan managed to smile and nod and not look anyone else in the eye. He wasn't sure where he got the strength to do it, except from long practice.

It was a late gray twilight when they finally emerged from the hospital. Teagan was dizzy from hunger and fatigue, his head and his side aching in tandem. He paused at the edge of the parking lot and laced his fingers behind his neck, closing his eyes and trying to take stock of what he had to do.

He should have gone home as soon as he got the news that he had no cardiac issues. Then he'd be sleeping—or not sleeping—in his own bed. He'd be at work, instead of his second hospital in a week. None of the women in his life would have observed him completely buckle under a weight he should have been able to carry.

He heard Darcy's footsteps behind him.

"All better?" she asked.

He coughed out a laugh. "Yeah, sure. Good as new."

Darcy paused. "Thanks for not diming out the bear."

"Well, I said I wouldn't." Teagan turned to look at her, hands still behind his head. Her attitude seemed to have softened now that there was no risk of vengeful wildlife officials becoming involved in today's fiasco. "Thanks for staying."

"Well, I said I would." She tossed the pickup's keys in the air and neatly caught them. "Ready to get back to rehabbing?"

"Can you drop me off at the airport?" Teagan asked, not sure whether he was joking or not.

"Yeah, they're not letting you on the plane looking like that," Darcy said, eyeing him in his grime.

Teagan tugged on the hair at the back of his head. "Could you take me to Walmart, *then* the airport?"

"I guess," she said doubtfully. "What about your sister though?"

A lance of guilt shot through him that he'd barely thought about Sloane for the past few hours. What *was* he going to do about her? Would she leave if he did? She might insist on coming with him, and he couldn't keep an eye on her while he was at the office. He didn't even have a good place for her to stay. His condo was a studio. His mother's house felt haunted.

"I'm not sure what to do about her," Teagan sighed. "She's the one who actually needs rehab. But what can I do to help?"

"You know," Darcy said slowly. "I think it's pretty cool, actually, that you're here with her. More families ought to figure out their substance issues together. God knows they're usually the place people learned them."

Teagan shook his head. "No, you don't understand. I don't do drugs. I'm not an alcoholic."

"I've heard that before," she replied, patently disbelieving. "Look, you wouldn't be the first person to bounce on rehab after the first day. But you'll probably feel better about it if you explain it to your sister, rather than me. What's she going to say?"

"This was her idea in the first place. She thought we'd just . . . feel better out here. We haven't been doing well since our mother died." It didn't seem right to use a euphemism like *passed*. Her death had been sudden and violent and more disappointing than surprising. And even if his life felt uncontrollable now, that had less to do with her absence in Teagan's life than his presence in what had been hers.

"Ah, damn. Sorry to hear that," Darcy said, raising her eyebrows. "No wonder you two are in it. I'd drink a *lot* if one of my parents died, and I haven't seen them in a long time."

That sounded like an excuse. Like sympathy he didn't deserve. It had been two years, and even before her death, *close* had been more of a description of their physical proximity than their emotional connection. Teagan shook it off.

"So you don't think you'll feel better out here?" Darcy pressed, hands on round hips. "In the most beautiful place in the world, where other people bring your food and clean your room and all you have to do is go to group and pet the horses?"

Teagan wordlessly gestured to his battered self. She tossed her head, still unimpressed, and gave him an insistent look. She was going to make him explain why he was bailing out of rehab, even when he didn't need it in the first place. He stared down at his feet.

"This just isn't the right kind of program for me," he finally said. "The very last thing in the world I would like to do is sit around and think right now. All I can think of is everything else I should be doing back home."

"You don't have to go to meditation. Nobody's gonna

make you," Darcy said. "If you want to stay too busy to think about the sauce, Rachel's got all sorts of stuff for you to do."

"Clearing my toxins with healing crystals?" Teagan said skeptically.

Darcy snorted. "Yeah, no," she said. "The crystals are bullshit. But it doesn't really matter what you do, right? It could be anything, as long as you aren't drinking. And if Rachel can't find you something you like to do, I will. There's a whole giant wilderness to play in. You know, you could even help me clear out a different trail to the waterfall, because there's a fucking *bear* on the one we've been using."

He laughed, even though it sent a wave of discomfort through his side.

"Your real agenda is revealed," he said.

"Yep," said Darcy, warm brown eyes softer than her words. "In fact, you could say you owe it to me, because this is your fault to begin with, and it wasn't like *I* was dying of too much free time on my hands."

He was fairly certain she was joking, since she wasn't trying to hustle him back into the truck, and her tone was gentle. Teagan scrunched up his face tightly, buffeted by conflicting impulses. His mother couldn't have done more damage to the foundation if she'd tried, but she hadn't tried at all when it came to Sloane.

Poor Sloane. Teagan had been so tied up in knots with his work, he hadn't even noticed her struggling.

He couldn't leave Sloane out here alone.

"No, you're right, you're right," he told Darcy. "I'm sure my sister's wondering where I am already."

Darcy reached out and patted his shoulder again, a gesture that seemed comforting this time. Teagan wanted to lean into the small touch, but he was afraid he'd topple over if he did.

"You're finally making good choices. I'll take you back." She smiled brightly, the pleased expression on her beautiful face the first hopeful thing Teagan had seen in weeks. "We can listen to a podcast on bear country safety on the way."

six

GROUP THERAPY WAS FIRST THING IN THE MORN-
ing to accommodate Dr. Goedert's practice in Bozeman.
It was clear and chilly, and the dew lingered on the grass
and wooden Adirondack chairs arranged around the fire pit
set a few dozen yards back from the residence. Teagan and
the other guests huddled under thick woolen blankets that
smelled of woodsmoke, hands clutching steaming paper cups
of cinnamon-bark-and-ginger water they were allowed in
lieu of caffeinated beverages. This morning, the still thin
peace of the scene was punctuated by the drone of the riding mower with which Darcy was cutting the camp's grass.
Teagan's eyes tracked her as she buzzed from the woods to
the lake in long, straight rows.

Hi, Darcy, he began to mentally compose for the next
time they spoke. *Hi, Darcy*, because he hadn't managed to
say anything more intelligent to her in the week since they
made mutual acquaintance under the jaws of furry death.
He ought to use this time to think of something else he
could say to her. Any of the typical things he might say to
her after *Hi, Darcy*—*do you want to get a coffee, do you want to
get a drink, can I buy you dinner, can I perform normalcy for you*—
were off the table out in Big Sky. He didn't know what

came after *Hi, Darcy* out here, so all he got back was *Hey, Bear Bait* and the teasing flip of her ponytail as she kept on walking.

"Do you have anything you'd like to add, Teagan?" Dr. Goedert called.

"No, I'm just thinking," Teagan replied, which was true, although he was thinking about the curvaceous figure of the woman on the mower, not the group therapy agenda.

He squirmed in his seat, owing as much to the topic as to his stitches, which were scabbed over and starting to itch.

The discussion topic of the day was *fathers, relationship with*. While *fathers* was a slightly less fraught topic than *mothers*, in his book at least, Teagan stared down at his bark water and tensed as Sloane's turn to speak approached.

Group therapy was the only mandatory activity at the retreat, but it was the one he most wished he could opt out of. Everyone else at the wellness retreat was in recovery from some type of substance abuse. Some of them had been very ill; some of them had lost jobs and relationships and children over their struggles. But Teagan had no idea what he could say that could possibly be insightful, and he shifted uncomfortably through every day's session, trying not to draw attention to himself.

"So, my father," Sloane said from the chair next to him. The wind caught her short brown hair and pinked her cheeks. She was probably freezing in her cotton sundress. "That's a complicated question. My family tree forks a lot. Too much extramarital forking, you know?"

The others chuckled—Sloane was by far the youngest person at the wellness retreat. Teagan kept a suspicious eye on the other adult men in the group, but so far they'd shown an inclination only to baby her and laugh at her jokes.

Sloane held up one finger until she was sure everyone's attention was on her.

"Legally speaking, my dad was Teagan's dad. Arnold Van Zijl. It was in the divorce decree and everything. He didn't ever ask for a paternity test, because oh my God would that have been embarrassing for him. But, you know, I didn't think of him as my dad."

Teagan looked away. Darcy was methodically making her way closer. She occasionally turned her head to look at the group but was surely too far away to hear anything over the noise of the mower, which was a faint blessing.

"Biologically speaking"—Sloane held up a second finger—"my father was a Danish artist showing at the Whitney Biennial. Married. Not to my mom, sadly. I haven't seen him since my conception."

Everyone laughed politely, excluding Teagan, who winced. God. Get him out of this therapy session. He didn't see how talking about old, painful drama made anyone want to drink *less*.

"I guess in, like, every way that matters"—Sloane held up a third finger—"my dad was Teagan?" She ducked her head to her chest as though unsure how he'd respond.

There was a round of soft, appreciative chuckles, more eyes now on Teagan. Discomfort squirmed through his stomach. He'd give anything not to have this talk in front of a dozen strangers.

"Yeah, in every photo until I'm, like, *five*, Teagan's wearing me in a Baby Bjorn," Sloane followed, mouth curling up when he didn't object to the characterization. "I don't know how I learned to walk."

It wasn't the first time someone had praised him for acting like her dad, and for a few years, *so good with the baby* had been an accomplishment he'd been happy to wear pinned to his chest, like perfect grades or sports trophies. But what he'd long since realized was that there was a reason that nature did not turn twelve-year-old boys into parents: he'd done a terrible job of it. Look at him! Look at her! He'd never gotten married or had his own kids, and Sloane was in rehab before she'd even graduated from college.

Teagan glanced over his shoulder at the tall grass Darcy had not yet reached. He entertained a momentary fantasy of causing a diversion and army crawling away from the conversation. If he was Sloane, he'd be angry. At the men who'd declined the opportunity to be her father. At their mother, who'd barely tried to replace them. And at Teagan, for failing to fill that gap.

Dr. Goedert steepled his fingers in his lap and leaned in, eyes sparking with interest.

"We haven't discussed parentification yet. That's a dynamic where a parent will encourage an older child to take on an outsized responsibility for rearing a younger one. Teagan, do you feel like your parents forced you to raise your sister?"

"No, not at all," Teagan lied, trying to convey to the psychologist with his expression that the question was a terrible one. What did he expect Teagan to say, right there in front of Sloane? No, he hadn't volunteered to be responsible for an entire other person. At twelve he'd wanted a puppy—he remembered monitoring the widening girth of the neighbor's Irish setter, who was rumored to be in trouble via an adventuresome poodle-schnauzer mix—not a baby sister. But that wasn't Sloane's fault. Teagan tried to smile at her. "Good thing you were a cute baby."

"I was, wasn't I?" Sloane said contentedly. She turned to

her indulgent audience. "We never fought. Some of my friends had dads who were, like, super mean, or who yelled or took their phones away for stupid stuff, but Teagan was the opposite. People thought he was this tragically young teen dad who was somehow stepping up."

"Because your mother wasn't present?" Dr. Goedert asked.

"Oh no, Teagan was the one who came to field hockey games and stuff like that, especially once he'd graduated college and came back to New York. Mom was always busy at the foundation or doing events."

The psychologist narrowed his eyes at Teagan. "Did you feel like there was anyone you could go to for help with Sloane while you were growing up? What about now?" he pressed.

Teagan would rather have fought another bear than admit to Sloane and a dozen strangers that he'd floundered through it all. How did that help her? Sloane needed to know he was there for her, not wonder if he was seething with secret resentment. Teagan suspected that the bullshit in this program didn't end with Rachel's healing crystals.

"It wasn't like our mother was never there," Teagan protested. She'd been there. Usually passed out in her bedroom with the door locked, but home most nights. "Now Sloane's in college. And self-aware enough to check herself in here."

Teagan looked away at Darcy again. She was driving closer, nearly drowning out the noise of the conversation. Or maybe that was the buzzing in his own ears. He wanted away from this.

"And whatever Sloane needs when she gets out of here, I'll make sure she gets it," he said when it appeared that Dr. Goedert was still waiting for more of an answer. The other members of the group smiled and nodded.

"Thanks, Pops," Sloane said, squinting at him.

Teagan exhaled, thinking that momentary crisis was averted, but Dr. Goedert held up a hand to forestall the next speaker.

"Teagan, you're very good at deflecting attention from your own needs to those of others," he remarked. "That's common with children of alcoholics."

"Thank you," Teagan said modestly.

"That wasn't necessarily a compliment—" The rest of his words were cut off by Darcy's approach. Like a World War I ace on a slow-motion bombing run, she leaned in to scrape the edges of the fire pit area, showering Dr. Goedert with grass clippings. It could have been unintentional, but Teagan saw the smirk she cast back over her shoulder as she rumbled off toward the woods again as well as the decisive swing of the braided pigtails she'd caught her hair in today.

Teagan took a long swig of hot bark water to cover his own smirk as the psychologist sputtered and brushed himself off. She'd rescued him a second time.

"Excuse me," Dr. Goedert said, standing and glowering at Darcy's retreating back on the mower. "Let me tell her to do that after lunch—"

"I've got it," Teagan said, seizing the opportunity to escape like a rope tossed to a drowning sailor. He jumped to his feet.

The therapist opened his mouth to object, but Teagan couldn't hear him on account of the mower, and also on account of walking away very quickly. The gap between his shoulder blades itched as he imagined people staring at him, but he took big strides that carried him away from the circle. He escaped.

Darcy was a good distance ahead of him, but the mower didn't move that fast. He began to close the distance between them, calling her name. She had noise protection earmuffs on, though, and the white wires of her ever-present headphones dangled down below them. Teagan broke into a jog until he caught up alongside her. His side ached, but he ignored it. It would heal eventually.

Darcy turned her head, saw him running, and broke into a grin. The brightness of her smile sent a feeling like homesickness coursing through his chest. Darcy was fully awake and alive in the early morning light, and Teagan couldn't remember the last time he'd felt like that.

She nudged a lever at her knee, and the motor of the lawnmower revved to full power. She leaned over the steering wheel as if racing him down the freeway.

A laugh bubbled out of his throat. "That thing can't go more than five miles an hour!" he yelled over the roar, jogging faster. He didn't think she could hear him.

"Race you!" she called, pointing to the trees.

"Stop!" he called, even though he wanted to laugh.

"Man versus machine," she yelled back.

"Darcy, come on," he tried, feeling breathless as he jogged alongside her in the world's slowest chase scene, his stitches aching in earnest.

He was at least a hundred meters away from the therapy group now though. Possibly that meant he was done for the day.

That would be great.

He poured on some speed to pull ahead of the mower and loped to the end of the wide grassy meadow. He waited at the edge of the clearing, holding his side and trying to slow his breathing as Darcy rumbled up. She hit the brakes mere inches from his knees, killed the engine, and slipped her earmuffs around her neck.

Despite the morning's chill, she wore only a black T-shirt over cutoff shorts and hiking boots. The T-shirt was printed with an airbrushed picture of three wolves howling at the moon. Teagan squinted. Her two fuzzy, dangling braids obscured some of the design, but it appeared that the wolves were armed with laser rifles and launching an assault on the moon, which was emblazoned with the logo of the Montana Department of Fish, Wildlife, and Parks.

He jerked his eyes up to her rosy cheeks when he realized that he probably appeared to be engaged in a lengthy study of her chest. She was waiting for him to speak, an amused expression gracing her red lips.

"Hi, Darcy," he said, because it seemed that he still couldn't get any further than that.

"Looks like you're healing up nicely," she said when the silence stretched out.

Teagan nodded vigorously, because the last time she inquired about his bear wound, she'd nearly pantsed him in the dining hall to check if his stitches were infected. She eyed his belt buckle as though in contemplation of doing it again. He put two protective hands on his waistband.

"Stitches are dissolving. Bruises fading. Good as new," he said.

"Can I see?"

"No, I swear they're better," he said.

Then he said nothing else.

Darcy waited expectantly. Teagan's brain did not deliver the clever opening he wanted that would allow them to discuss something unrelated to his mauling or treatment for diseases he did not have.

"Did you just literally run away from therapy?" she asked when he came up empty.

"I guess I did," he admitted.

"Doc running short on insight this morning?"

"He wanted to talk about my relationship with my dead parents," he said, keeping his expression straight to make it clear that this was not a bid for sympathy.

"Oh, ew," Darcy said. "Keep that shit deep down inside where it belongs, right?"

"Right. Never ever talk about it. Generations of my WASP ancestors can't be wrong."

"About a single thing, obviously," Darcy agreed, smothering a giggle before she tilted her head back and laughed. "Anyway"—she finally looked down at her phone to pause her music and take her earbuds out—"what's up?"

"Ah," Teagan said, abruptly remembering why he'd gone running after her. "The doctor was wondering if it might be possible for you to mow at another time."

"What?" Darcy demanded, her engaging smile abruptly shuttering.

"It was a little loud. During group. Dr. Goedert asked if you might possibly mow the grass after lunch."

Darcy wheeled around to stare back at the fire pit, beautiful face crumpling into a scowl. Her look at Dr. Goedert was angry enough to strip paint off metal. Her fists curled as though she were contemplating a physical reply against the person of the psychologist.

"No, I might possibly *not*," she said. "I have things to do after lunch. I *told* him I needed this afternoon off."

"I think they'll be done with group in another half hour. Maybe then?" Teagan suggested, taking a step backward.

Darcy swung a leg over the side of the mower and hopped down, stalking over to Teagan. She poked him in the chest. "I have things to do in half an hour *too*. I have things to do all damn day today. You can tell him that if he wanted to decide when the lawn gets mowed, he shouldn't have fired the lawn crew!"

"Why'd he fire the lawn crew?" Teagan asked, leaning away from Darcy's accusatory finger.

"Because he figured I could do it for free if he bought a big mower," Darcy growled.

Teagan closed his lips over the observation that it wasn't fair. She knew that, obviously.

They stared at each other for a few tense seconds.

Then Darcy cursed, tossed her earmuffs to the ground, and stalked off toward the residence without a word of farewell.

Well. He'd said more than *Hi, Darcy*, at least. He'd also managed to piss her off.

Teagan stared wistfully at her retreating figure. He supposed that was his cue to go back to group therapy, except that he very passionately did not want to, and Darcy had promised that there would be trail breaking and other woodland adventures if he stayed, but all week long she'd only told him to rest and recuperate when he tried to raise the subject.

He stood in the field for too long before hurrying after her. Her mood looked incendiary, but he felt compelled to follow and ask about the other programming she'd mentioned.

He searched for her inside the residence until he located her in Rachel's office, bent over a laptop.

"Oh, there's Wi-Fi?" Teagan blurted. He'd been unable to connect his work laptop, which was the only device Darcy hadn't confiscated upon his arrival.

"Not for guests," Darcy said, glancing over her shoulder at him. She turned back to the keyboard, hunting and pecking for the keys she wanted. "If we gave you internet access, you'd use it to order hookers and blow."

"Can you get hookers and blow delivered to Big Sky?" he wondered out loud. He'd assumed this area was too remote to even buy her flowers to thank her for saving his life.

"See, that kind of thinking is what landed you in rehab," she said, finally spinning around in the chair and folding her hands across her muscular stomach. "So don't even think about it. You can't use the internet unless Rachel's monitoring you. Why don't you go back to therapy instead?"

Teagan grimaced. He didn't want anything nefarious. He only wanted to check his email and voice messages, because he was sure his directors were going nuts after his sudden disappearance. God only knew what Rose had told them.

"I believe I've had enough therapy for the day. Is there anything else I could be doing right now?" he asked. *Something with you.*

Darcy pursed her lips thoughtfully and flicked her eyes at the window. "It's a gorgeous day outside. If I were you, I'd get a canoe and a book and paddle out to the middle of the lake. Odds are nobody will bother you till dinner if you do that."

"I just—what do you have planned, if you're not mowing this morning?"

She wrinkled her nose. "Oh me? Very exciting plans. I'm going to watch a YouTube video *in German*, which I don't speak, about how to fix the diesel generator. Then I'm going to fix the diesel generator. I'm going to swear a lot probably. Then I'll watch the video again. Repeat as necessary."

"Oh," Teagan said inanely. "Do you . . . need any help?"

"Do you know how to repair a diesel generator?"

"No."

"Do you speak German?"

"No."

"Do you know any curse words I don't? Remember, I was in the Navy."

"Definitely no," Teagan sighed, feeling completely useless, mourning a wasted life that left him so lacking in any skills which might be of use to Darcy. "Um . . . what about this afternoon?"

"I'm doing computer stuff this afternoon," she said, looking at him askance. "By myself. Do you need something? I'm free after dinner—well, after dinner and the mowing—if you need a ride to the store or—"

"No, no, I'm fine, I just thought you were in charge of wilderness education here, since you were talking about the woods—never mind. I just didn't know if you might have something planned for today."

Darcy frowned, lower lip curling over her teeth in an appealing way. "I am in charge of wilderness education," she said with a little uncertainty, as though she expected him to dispute it.

Teagan had been waiting less than patiently for the daily schedule to reflect some activity led by Darcy, but the only item bearing her name had been supply runs into town.

"You mentioned working on the waterfall trail," he said. "Which sounded . . . fun. Or hiking. I like hiking." He thought he'd like hiking with Darcy and without bears, anyway.

And despite his hope that he'd played the conversation straight, Darcy's answering smirk was knowing. Her eyelashes dipped as she considered him in his oxford and chinos.

"You're having pastoral fantasies, huh? You wanna go have a frolic in the woods?"

Teagan blushed. "I'm not sure I frolic, as a habit—"

"I bet you'd surprise yourself," Darcy said. Then she checked her watch. "You know what? No. Yeah. Let's do some wilderness education. Fuck this. Yeah. Yeah. Come on." She stood up directly into his personal space, just long enough for him to reckon with the coiled energy implied in her body and the obvious strength of her arms and bare legs. Then she flipped into quick, decisive motion.

Teagan had to walk fast to keep up with her as she led him to the storage shed at the back of the residence. She glanced around as though expecting opposition or an ambush along the way, but they saw nobody.

In the storage shed, Darcy loaded him down with lopping shears and a bow saw, then fetched her trail backpack and a battery-powered portable speaker.

"Come on, come on, don't let Rachel catch me doing something fun," she said, striding briskly through the freshly mown grass behind the residence. The area between the residence and the lake was mown, leaving the fields sloping up toward the hills still undone.

"Where are we going?" he asked.

"The old trail. It needs to be cleared out, because it hasn't been used in a few years. It goes up to the same waterfall you saw last week."

They approached a featureless clump of bushes at the rear of the lawn that Darcy had already mown. Darcy dropped her backpack, face softening with anticipation, while Teagan eyed the thick underbrush with suspicion, scanning it for ursine threat.

"Here we go," Darcy said in a very satisfied way. Teagan was glad to be some minor cause of that state, but he couldn't tell what she was looking at.

"Where's the trailhead?" Teagan asked.

"You don't see it?"

"No?" Teagan said. All he saw were trees. Big, potentially bear-infested trees.

Darcy waded into the thicket and pointed up at the stub of a branch that had been cut away between the two trees closest to the lake. Then another. Now he could see them—old cuts framing a way up the hill. There was vegetation growing over the break, but a space about five feet wide was level and free of rocks.

"You can see where the branches were cut back before to leave a corridor. That's what you're going to do today—cut back the new limbs," Darcy told him authoritatively.

Teagan abruptly calmed, because that sounded very tangible and achievable. Here was a thing he could do, for once.

When he quit his quiet, boring job trading municipal bonds to take over the family charitable foundation, he'd imagined that he'd only stay six months or so—just until the finances were straightened out and under control. Two years in, it was difficult to tell if he'd accomplished anything more than understanding the scope of the problems. Spending had to increase every year to keep up with the growing number of kids who needed summer programming, but he wasn't raising enough money to keep up with the spending. Unlike every other problem in his life, it seemed completely immune to effort. He didn't even know what he was doing wrong.

But this? Yes. He could cut the branches with Darcy. And then there would be a trail.

Darcy's attitude became very relaxed as they got into the trees as well, and Teagan cautiously allowed himself to look forward to a morning spent doing pleasant, industrious tree things with Darcy. The look she gave him as he hefted the clippers was approving, and he wanted to wallow in it.

"Better than meditation, right?" she said, her smile like light through the forest canopy. "Everyone comes out to Montana to touch grass, but Rachel has them sitting on that deck all day long communing with a bunch of rocks she bought at the visitor center gift shop."

"This is better," Teagan agreed. This was great.

Darcy was a good teacher. She showed him how to prune the new growth on the trees outside the bark collar. How to make two cuts on thicker branches with the bow saw to remove the branch without harming the tree. Where willow was sprouting and would soon cover the trail if it wasn't dug up.

Darcy's voice changed when she was telling him how to do something. The usual note of caution fell away, replaced with actual interest. She cared, not just that he pruned each branch correctly, but that he knew how to do it for all the trees he was bound to prune in the future, and that he understood why he was cutting each branch at the correct angle for the safety of both hiker and tree. Teagan smiled at her as she sternly forbade him to cut his toes off by dropping his tools on them.

"Aye aye, captain," he said, not quite daring a salute.

She caught his look and paused, a little flustered. "You always do what you're told, huh?"

"Not a lot of people have tried, honestly," he replied. It might have been easier to feel that he was doing what he was supposed to do, he reflected, if anyone else had ever cared enough to lay out their expectations.

Darcy snorted. "That must be nice," she said, expression darkening as she tucked her chin, mind somewhere else. She shook it off and looked up the hill. "It's about three-quarters of a mile before this trail intersects the one you tried to die on, but it'll take you a few days," she said.

Teagan blinked at her, thrown by the apparent change in subject.

"Wait, what?" he asked as Darcy dusted her hands on her tattered shorts. She was leaving?

She raised her eyebrows at him.

"What do you mean, what? Do you have any other questions?"

"I—no. You're going?"

"Yeah, I told you I've got a lot of stuff to do today," she said, expression confused. She picked up the stereo. "Look, I'll leave you with my phone and all my podcasts"—she flipped the power switch, and a static-filled voice began to hiss out of the dusty machine—"so the bears won't bother you. And if they do"—she picked up her backpack and tapped the bear spray fastened to one of the straps—"you're prepared this time. I put a bottle of water and a sandwich in the backpack. Anything else?"

Teagan made a wordless noise of disagreement in the back of his throat, feeling abruptly whipsawed. He shook his head.

Darcy took a step toward the lake, then paused. "You don't have to do it," she said. "If you'd rather meet the crowd for yoga. This'll wait. Till next year, even."

He shook his head again.

Darcy took another step away, face still guarded as she looked over her shoulder in departure. In another couple of steps, she'd be out of earshot.

"Am I being punished for something?" he blurted out before he could stop himself.

Darcy turned halfway around and crossed her arms. "Punished?" she asked incredulously.

"You're leaving me alone in the woods," he said.

"Are you worried about bears? I promise, no bear is going to come near while you're blasting Animal Radio."

"No, I just—I thought you were staying."

Darcy's face was mobile as she processed that.

"Oh. You didn't actually want to learn about conservation. You just wanted to spend some time hitting on me outdoors," she concluded, face falling into disappointment.

Teagan looked down at his chest, wondering if a direct verbal shot to the gut could cause him to bleed out. How'd she pick that up from *Hi, Darcy*?

God, what was wrong with him? She worked here. She probably thought he'd just wasted an hour of her time.

"No, I actually did, but—okay. I'm sorry if I—if I made you feel uncomfortable," Teagan said, shoulders slumping. "I'll stop."

She sighed and shook her head. "You're not making me uncomfortable. I don't care if you hit on me. Go ahead and take your best shot, Bear Bait. But just buy me flowers or something, because this isn't punishment." She gestured to the woods around them. "Don't you dare pout about this. This is the good shit."

Teagan didn't understand, but every time he'd opened his mouth, he'd stuck his foot in it, so he remained silent.

Darcy huffed in aggravation. "Look, *you* get to spend the day in these beautiful woods, listening to podcasts and getting a little light exercise. You understand? That's what I'd rather be doing. That's what I was *supposed* to be doing."

"Supposed to?"

"That's what Dr. Goodhair and Rachel hired me to do," she said, upper lip curling. "I thought I was going to be teaching everyone ecology and botany and leading daily trail hikes." She snorted. "I even practiced my lectures. You were going to learn all about rewilding and the aspen population of the Gallatin range."

"But I'd like to hear the aspen lecture," Teagan said slowly. It was the most personal thing she'd ever told him, and he was greedy for more details about the woman he only knew for being brave and funny and not interested in him. "I really do. Completely irrespective of any opportunity to, um, make an idiot of myself—"

"It's fine. Flirt with me indoors next time though. I'm on a schedule," Darcy said, shrugging it off, though the lingering disappointment on her face made Teagan's chest hurt for having put it there.

"No, really. If you've got time, tell me about the trees."

She sighed again. "I don't. I wish I did, truly, but I don't. You can go back. I won't hold it against you."

Teagan looked at the clippers. "No, I'll keep working," he said. "No worries."

"You say that, and it's like I start thinking of how I should be worried. Is this a bad idea? Are you going to brew moonshine from the wild raspberries or stab yourself with the clippers?" she asked, frowning at him.

"I'm fine," he said. "I'm set for the rest of the day."

Darcy gave him a long look, as though she doubted his ability to remain safe without her supervision, but after a moment she patted the bear spray on the backpack in farewell and left, walking off in the direction of the residence, just short of a jog. He watched the sway of her round hips as she went, wishing he could look away.

seven

DARCY LEANED FORWARD AND PUT HER NOSE SIX inches away from the screen of Rachel's laptop. It didn't help. She read the last sentence of the third exam question again, her lips moving as she attempted to wrest meaning from the shotgun blasts of unfamiliar words.

She was going to fail this exam.

The exam format was timed, closed book, short answer. A worse format could not have possibly been devised—not least because the exam software didn't have a screen reader. Darcy had just ten minutes left, and she was only on the third of the five questions. There were little red squiggles under many of the words in her answers, but she couldn't tell whether she'd misspelled them or if the program simply didn't recognize *heterozygosity*.

Darcy entertained the modest plan of hurling the laptop out the window, stripping naked, and running into the woods to eat grubs and tubers with the bears. It was as good a career plan as she'd managed so far.

She was going to fail this exam, in this required course, which meant she wasn't going to have enough credits to graduate for at least another year and a half.

A growl bubbled up in her throat around the spiky lump of shame and embarrassment that had formed as she fought with the test questions. She probably knew the answers. She knew them! If anyone had sat down and asked her what was the fundamental driver of biodiversity in isolated populations, she thought she could have explained it very succinctly and conversationally. But she doubted any professor at OSU even knew her name, let alone that she might not have failed Ecological Genetics if they'd given a different sort of test.

At some point soon, she was going to need to accept that this degree was never going to happen. She was wasting taxpayer dollars. Maybe the government would reallocate some money to wilderness conservation if they didn't have to keep paying GI Bill funds to OSU for classes Darcy was going to fail anyway.

She imagined her senator twirling his mustache: "Can we afford to reintroduce gray wolves to the Southern Rockies? Oh, no, looks like Darcy Albano still needs eight hours in Vertebrate Biology after all these years. Let's build a highway that we'll name after some dead asshole who voted against civil rights instead."

Eight minutes left. The fourth question refused to divulge its meaning to Darcy even as she forced her eyes to march sequentially through each of the words.

She could have spent the day bossing Teagan around in the woods. That would have been a more productive use of time, or at least one that left her feeling competent and desirable.

Darcy heard someone coming down the hall. Probably Rachel or Dr. Goedert, there to inquire when Darcy was going to finish the mowing. She prepped a really nasty rejoinder—one that would specify an anatomically unlikely place where they might store the mower in the future—then swallowed it down. If she wasn't ever going to finish her degree, she couldn't afford to piss off next year's potential employer.

When the door opened, it instead admitted the willowy perfumed figure of Sloane Van Zijl. She was wearing a long floral maxi dress under an oversized knit sweater, and she looked more put together than Darcy ever had in her life, despite Sloane's two weeks' residence in a tent.

"Oh," Sloane said, apparently surprised to see Darcy in front of the computer. "Hey. Are you busy?"

Darcy checked the time. Five minutes left. She hadn't started the fourth question. It was a lost cause. She'd failed the exam.

"I'm done," she said unhappily. She closed the laptop so hard the screen rattled. "What do you need?" The girl looked a little taken aback, and Darcy made a conscious effort to put her customer service face on. If she never finished college and made her way into a conservation job, she was going to need to get a lot better at keeping tourists happy if she wanted to stay in Yellowstone. "Can I help you?" Darcy asked in a more conciliatory voice.

"I was just seeing if you knew where Teagan was," Sloane said. "He didn't come to pottery class."

Darcy reflexively looked out the window, but she couldn't see the trailhead from her vantage point.

"I provided some alternative programming," Darcy said, trying to sound authoritative. "He's doing trail maintenance. Wilderness therapy. He's a hard case, but I've got it under control."

Sloane chewed the inside of her cheek. "Wilderness therapy is good for him, right?"

"I'm sure it's at least as good as pottery class at curing alcoholism," Darcy said.

Sloane gave a small roll of her eyes. Darcy knew Sloane was in her early twenties, but she looked younger, and the expression was pure teenage brattiness. Sloane curled and uncurled her fists, dissatisfied with Darcy's reassurances.

"Okay, but Teagan hasn't gone to any of the art classes, and he blew off group therapy this morning, and after Rachel told him he can't eat tropical fruit anymore because he's a Virgo and he's prone to inflammation, he went off and ate an entire mango for breakfast," Sloane said earnestly.

"I wouldn't worry about that," Darcy said. "I doubt the mangoes are going to make or break his recovery."

Teagan hardly seemed to be bad off, for the people who came through the camp. He was too skinny, but he didn't have that sallow glow that accompanied real damage from substance abuse. He looked pretty good, in fact. He looked like a guy she would have seen jogging on the trail with his dogs—purebreds, probably, he looked like a sighthound kind of guy—and thought, *I'd like one of those. One of each. Maybe if I ever have my life together.*

Teagan would sober up, switch to Shirley Temples, and be some nice woman's normcore fantasy by the end of the year, she thought with a tinge of wistfulness.

Sloane made a frustrated noise. "Sure, that's what it seems like, but I thought he was just a little overworked before, and then he ended up in the hospital."

Darcy shrank back defensively. "Well, he knows about bear safety now."

"Bear safety? What bear?" Sloane asked, cocking her head.

"The bear that put him in the hospital?"

"What?"

They stared at each other in mutual confusion.

"Teagan was . . . in the hospital," Darcy said slowly. A different hospital? For non-bear reasons?

"Are you listening? Yes! I brought him straight here from the hospital."

Darcy swallowed. "Well, I didn't know that."

"Uh, yeah. Nobody knows," Sloane said. "My mom, when she drove into the tree, that was no big surprise. You drive home drunk, eventually you're going to hit something. Teagan spent years trying to wrestle her car keys away. But nobody had any idea anything was wrong with *him* until I got a call from the hospital."

"Holy shit," Darcy said, eyes widening. That must have been one hell of a bender. She would never have guessed Teagan's drinking problem was that severe. She'd figured he was one of those martini-lunch guys who figured out they were spending a thousand dollars a week on hard liquor and decided to dry out before moving on to a new expensive hobby. "Well, Teagan's safe out here," she told Sloane. "No booze, no drugs, nothing but sunshine and healthy living."

"You think that'll do it?" Sloane asked, face skeptical. "That'll fix him?"

"He's doing okay here, isn't he?" Darcy asked. It was alarming that Teagan had never told her how deep his problems ran, but he'd shown no signs of wanting to leave and get back to bad habits since the day of the bear attack.

"Okay, but that's why I'm worried! When mom died, everyone was all like, 'She should have taken an Uber,' as if the real problem was that she didn't keep her phone charged. No! The problem was that she was an alcoholic. So even if Teagan seems fine out here, he's gonna go home someday, right? I'm already screening calls from a bunch of jerks who

want him to go back to work. He's not going to do anything different. He's not addressing his problems."

"You're worried he's not taking his recovery seriously,"
Darcy said, frowning.

"He's totally not," Sloane said. "He thinks the Goederts
are full of it."

Darcy could understand why he thought that. But that
didn't mean that Teagan couldn't use this opportunity to
turn his life around.

Sloane had her narrow hands twisted together in front of
her, pretty face full of concern. For the second time in the
day, a Van Zijl was looking at Darcy like she had all the
answers. This wasn't the reaction Darcy typically elicited in
others—the Goederts, for example, treated her like a poorly
housebroken foster pet—and she was taken with Sloane's
assumption that she could do something to help with Teagan's recovery.

"You know what?" Darcy said, filled with sudden resolve.
If the Goederts weren't reaching him, that meant it was up
to her. She'd screwed up at a lot of jobs, but it was never for
lack of trying. There was nothing about this one she couldn't
handle, if given a chance. "I'll talk to him."

"Uh, the doctor already tried to talk to him."

"No, like, more than talk," Darcy vowed. "I'll take over
his schedule. Plan stuff he'll actually do. Real wilderness therapy, not Rachel's vibey-wibey homeopathic bullshit."

"Okay," Sloane said, looking only mildly reassured. "That's
where he's been all day?"

"All day?" Darcy asked. She checked her watch. It had
been almost seven hours since she last saw Teagan. She'd
repaired the generator, cleaned up all the breakfast dishes,
then taken her test. She felt a pang of foreboding.

"Yeah, he wasn't there at lunch," Sloane said.

"Um, he is probably still out on the trail," Darcy said, scrunching up her face. She hadn't meant that he needed to clear out the whole trail *today*.

Sloane made an alarmed noise in the back of her throat. "See! This is what I meant. You have to tell him when to stop, or he'll do dumb shit like work through lunch."

"Yeah, I'll go, I'll go," Darcy said guiltily, standing up and looking out the window again. "I'll have him back for dinner."

Teagan! His sister was obviously terrified for him, and no wonder, if their mother had died from the family curse. And now he had Darcy picking up the pace as she jogged down the stairs and toward the woods, afraid that he'd somehow managed to lure the bears right into the retreat by sheer propensity for disaster.

Maybe he hadn't been hitting on her. Maybe he needed her help, but she was so jaded by years of fending off adulterous tourists and bored dockworkers that she couldn't recognize honest vulnerability when she saw it. Maybe his fragile sobriety depended on Darcy's intervention.

She could do this. This wasn't a written test.

Trail clearing. Some bird-spotting—they could collect data to send to the Audubon Society. A couple of botany lectures. Basics of fire suppression. And a *lot* of alcoholism podcasts. She could keep him too busy to think about drinking.

It was a surprisingly appealing plan. The Goederts didn't know how lucky they were to have her on staff. The Van Zijls didn't know how lucky they were to have her on staff.

She shoved down that hurt which was her third run at Ecological Genetics and shoveled over it with this opportunity to actually succeed at something.

Her bad mood from failing her test had kindled into determination. Darcy hustled past the lake, mind brimming with ideas. Rachel Goedert lured vulnerable people to this place with the promise of healing out in nature and then sat them on yoga mats to lecture them about their auras. Darcy could do way better than that.

Darcy expected Teagan to be only a few paces into the woods, given the level of overgrowth on the trail. He had hung the stereo from a high branch of the tree marking the start of the trail, and the staticky newscast of the Bozeman NPR station filled the empty woods. But although she saw evidence that he'd cut back branches for a while, Teagan was nowhere to be seen.

She called his name, to no answer. Perhaps he'd gone back? But everyone else was now on the porch outside of the residence for pottery—she would have seen him. And there were muddy athletic-shoe tracks leading up the hill past the point where the branches had been cut back.

Jesus. This guy *would* manage to get attacked by a bear twice in one rehab stint. Darcy picked up speed and sprinted up the hill, shouting again until she heard Teagan call back from the direction of the waterfall, sounding unmauled for a change.

She found him at the base of the waterfall, standing in the shallows. The stream was fed by snowmelt and freezing even in July, but Teagan had rolled up his chinos and waded into the water to wash off his face and arms. His oxford was tied around his narrow hips, despite the mildness of the day, leaving his long calves and forearms bare. Darcy's backpack and tools were piled neatly on the stream bank.

Teagan spun around as she approached, a crooked smile blooming across his face at the sight of her. He had a dimple in his left cheek, and the lopsidedness of his mouth made it appear that he was holding half a smile in reserve rather than fully committing to the expression. His golden hair was wild with sweat and pine sap, giving the impression he'd been working very hard, despite the lack of much effect on the clearing of the trail.

"Hi, Darcy," he said, and then he engaged the last bit of smile he'd withheld.

All her worry melted away like the last bit of ice in spring under the force of that tentative smile. It was boyish, hopeful. Totally charming.

Darcy resisted the urge to smirk right back at the mess of him, because he obviously needed some strong handling in light of his lackadaisical approach to his very serious issues. He probably got away with everything by flashing that dimple. No more! From here on out, Darcy was in charge.

She put her hands on her hips and kept her face stern by biting down hard on her inner lip, which wanted to curve into a matching grin. "This is not very good progress, Teagan," she announced. "You should have been able to get a lot further. Have you just been hiding out here and listening to the radio?" she demanded.

"No?" he said, blinking those sweetly confused eyes at her. "I worked."

She would not be charmed! No, she was stronger than that, even though she had the impulse to pat his arm and tell him he'd done an okay job and he'd do better tomorrow.

"You can't just fuck off from therapy and mindfulness and do nothing all day." He had a dead mom and a worried sister and a potentially lethal substance abuse disorder. He needed to *think* about how he was going to put his life together after he left, otherwise he seemed destined to be eaten by some kind of bear, of the figurative if not literal variety. "The whole point of this place is that you need to learn how to do stuff sober—"

"I mowed the lawn," he interjected, eyes widening.

Darcy paused, taken aback. "What?"

"I went back and mowed the lawn. After group was over."

Darcy blinked hard at him. The lawn was several disappointments ago. She'd totally forgotten about the lawn, except in the sense that she'd thought she'd have to do it before she could eat dinner.

"But . . . why?"

Teagan rubbed a hand through his hair, leaving new furrows in the blonde waves. "You seemed like you had a lot on your plate today. So I finished mowing the lawn."

Her stomach seemed to bounce against her ribs.

"All of it?"

"I think so? It took a while for me to figure out the turns, so some of the places are a little, ah, over-mowed." He seemed concerned that she might disagree. "I think the grass will grow back. I'm not a botanist though."

He pressed his lips together in hesitation as Darcy reeled on her feet. He blurted, "I also got you flowers."

"What?" Darcy said again, belatedly realizing that she hadn't said anything intelligent in a couple of minutes now. "Flowers? How?"

He gestured down the hill. "The purple ones. Over there. I transplanted them from the bottom of the hill, since it's hard to see the trailhead otherwise—"

Alarmingly, Darcy felt the hot prickle of tears behind her nose. She hadn't noticed when she arrived, but he'd replanted two big clumps of vivid purple fireweed to flank the two trees that marked the second route down from the waterfall.

He'd cleared all the other vegetation around their base and watered the dirt with his canteen. There were crescents of dirt under each of his fingernails, which he'd been cleaning in the stream when she arrived.

She guessed this was what she got for telling him that he was free to hit on her. Except that she couldn't recall, in nearly two decades of being hit on, anyone hitting on her in a way that struck home quite so precisely.

She had told him to take his best shot. This was a pretty good one.

Darcy sniffled loudly, praying that it would just look like she had allergies. She wiped her nose on her arm.

She should have told him to think about sobriety instead. All this did was make her feel—well, not quite better, because maybe he hadn't been pursuing her for help with his sobriety after all, but not *worse*. It made her feel. That wasn't going to help either of them.

"Yeah, okay. Thanks," she said, cursing the little wobble in her voice. Teagan politely averted his eyes.

Oh, no wonder nobody had ever taken Teagan in hand before he ended up in the hospital. Darcy could barely remember the lecture she'd planned to deliver about abstinence and effort and focus.

"Did you finish everything else you needed to do?" he asked with a hopeful note in his voice, gaze resting on the equipment he'd piled next to the stream.

"If the lawn's done, I guess I did," Darcy said, wishing she sounded more casual.

"Do you want to work on the trail with me for a while, then?" he asked, failing to conceal his interest in her answer. "If you've got time, you could give me the aspen lecture. I haven't seen any around here. They're the white ones, right?"

Darcy wavered on her feet, looking up at the man who was probably going to disappoint her in all sorts of ways that she just couldn't manage to anticipate at this exact moment. He shouldn't be hitting on her—or anyone. He was already good at that, obviously; what he needed to work on was his sober living skills.

They both needed to refocus on the job at hand. Regardless of what the Goederts thought of her or whether she would ever finish her degree, Darcy was responsible for wilderness education in *this* job. And regardless of whether Teagan was interested in rehab, that's where he was.

"Your sister said you missed lunch. Did you eat?" Darcy asked Teagan. "There was a sandwich in the backpack."

"I . . . did not. I thought that was your lunch."

"It was, but you were the one outside working all day. You can't work through lunch. You'll get sick."

"I thought you might come back for it."

"It's a really good sandwich. Peanut butter and banana on raisin bread," Darcy said, plastering up her vulnerability with a delinquency she could address. "You should eat it." She rustled in the backpack until she found the sandwich and unwrapped it from its wax paper.

She took a step toward Teagan, sandwich extended.

Teagan began to refuse, hands waving ineffectually to ward her off. "I'm fine, really, I had—"

Darcy pulled him to the edge of the stream and stuffed the cut edge of the sandwich directly into his ridiculous mouth. He couldn't even manage to keep himself fed. She shouldn't have left him alone in the woods all day.

He knew how to make an effort; he just didn't know how to direct it toward the things that mattered. That part would have to be up to Darcy.

"I bet we can clear the way to the first switchback before dinner," she told an unprotesting Teagan. She had one hand holding the sandwich in his mouth, but the other was pressed to his chest, just over his heart. Even through the T-shirt, she could feel it fluttering against her palm, heat boiling off his skin and bleeding through the fabric. "And maybe you can talk to *me* about your mother's accident."

After a moment, Teagan nodded and took a big bite. Darcy watched the muscles in his throat move to be sure he swallowed.

eight

IF DARCY HAD WORRIED THAT THE GOEDERTS
might object to the expansion of her job duties to match her
job description, she escaped their notice over the next two
weeks. Dr. Goedert only cared that Teagan showed up for
group therapy. Rachel only cared that his checks cleared the
bank. It was a really good thing he had Darcy on top of things.

It was only Kristin who expressed any misgivings about
Darcy's new project, and then not until Darcy skipped
down to the kitchen to pick up snacks on the day that they
were to finish grading the portion of the waterfall loop
which had washed out that spring. They'd discussed the necessity of water bars that morning, and this afternoon they
were going to split some treated lumber left over from the
new fence. Darcy wanted to get extra provisions for that
work.

Although Kristin's only responsibilities were related to
cooking, the kitchen was still a disaster three hours before
dinner, with dirty smoothie jars still piled in the sink.

"Bitch, you live like this?" Darcy asked.

Kristin flipped her the bird without taking her eyes off
her phone. Darcy was surprised she'd even gotten the smooth-

ies out without Darcy there to prod her. Darcy had been off in the woods with Teagan most of the day.

"Can you make me two more smoothies?" Darcy asked.

"I could, but why would I?"

"Because you love me," Darcy said winningly.

"I do," Kristin acknowledged, but she still didn't look up from her phone.

"And I'll clean this all up tonight?"

Darcy would end up doing that anyway, but the chance that Kristin might clean up was a polite fiction that she and Kristin maintained. Kristin popped her head from side to side, considering. "Yeah, okay. What do you want in it?"

"That one you make with bananas, peanut butter, spinach, and two scoops of protein powder."

"Ah, yes, the Chunky Monkey Hiding in the Shrubbery." Kristin's face softened in a proud smile. It was one of her favorite creations. A couple thousand calories in a jar.

"Yeah. Put extra immune stuff in it. Vitamins, whatever."

"Sure. Who's it for?"

"Teagan."

Kristin put her phone down, round blue eyes narrowing on Darcy. "Who?"

"Teagan. Van Zijl. You know who he is. He's been here for weeks."

"What's he look like, again?" Kristin asked.

Darcy considered it, summoning the man in her mind. The messy blonde hair and big sad golden eyes. *He looked like a grown-up version of the little boy prince who lived on an asteroid with a fox and a flower*, she thought.

She couldn't say that.

"I don't know. Tall, I guess?"

"Oh yeah, I know the one. Pretty good-looking, isn't he?" asked Kristin, who was as sapphic as the trees were tall.

Darcy elaborately shrugged, feeling judged. Probably there were some women who liked their men tall, blonde, and rich, but she wasn't shallow like that. It was hurtful that Kristin would imply anything to the contrary. Darcy's motives were very pure.

"I haven't noticed," she lied.

"But you noticed he needed a smoothie."

"He had a rough time before he got out here. And he's been working hard," Darcy said, still studiedly casual. For all the yard work and forestry he'd been doing with Darcy, he needed more calories in his diet than the spa food Rachel ordered from the vegan caterer in Bozeman.

Darcy caught herself studying the sharp edges of his cheekbones sometimes, worrying that she was working him too hard, trying to picture what he might look like after he recovered.

"Darcy."

"What?" she replied innocently.

"You know *what*. No horny mistakes with the guests. It's wrong."

"How would it be *wrong*? I'm basically the maintenance guy! That's an entire category of porn," Darcy protested, even though she had in fact parsed this fine ethical dilemma herself, without coming to a definitive answer. Not that it mattered. She hadn't been doing anything with Teagan but forestry, and she wasn't going to.

Kristin gave her an arched eyebrow. "Of course. Porn would never steer you wrong, morally. Hey, you'll never guess what I'm giving my hot stepsister for Christmas."

"Not gross porn," Darcy objected. "I'm talking about

porn that's like—" Darcy put on her best leer and wiggled her shoulders. She dropped her voice an octave. "Hey. I'm here to have a look at your pipe. Oh no, I see what the problem is. I'm gonna need a *lot* more caulk. Bam, bam, bam."

Kristin snickered but relented, opening the blender to toss in the pea protein. "1975 called. It wants its erotic energy back."

Darcy scoffed in faux outrage, sticking her thumbs through her imaginary belt loops and swiveling her hips. Teagan should be so lucky. He wouldn't be.

"You've got the wrong idea," Darcy said. "Teagan is not a horny mistake. I am not going to lay his pipe, even though I *totally could*, and that would probably fix all his substance abuse issues, add five years to his life, and show him the very face of God. No. I'm helping him. *Therapeutically.*"

Kristin bit her lip as she poured the smoothie into a mason jar. She shook her head, face turning more serious.

"Don't you think he should be doing, like, real therapy? Because it kind of looks like you're just messing around in the woods all day."

"We've got wilderness education and forest bathing right in the brochures!" Darcy insisted. "It is real therapy. And he goes to group."

She didn't see how it could be any less effective than watercolors or rock gardening. And Teagan was doing better every day. Sloane had said so too.

Kristin gave her a dour look until Darcy broke first and looked at her feet.

"I know, I know," Darcy said. "I'm being careful with him, I swear."

"You be careful with yourself too," Kristin warned her. "These guys aren't reliable, and I don't want to be telling you I told you so when he goes back to Drunktown. You have the world's worst taste in men, I swear to God."

"What? I don't need to be careful. I'm good at my job. I *could* be good at this job, if the Goederts would give me half a break. I'm not planning a threesome with a guy in a long-term relationship with Johnnie Walker Blue. I'm a professional."

"Okay, lady," said Kristin, passing her the finished drink with a roll of her eyes. "You know best."

Darcy let the note of sarcasm fly off her starboard bow and nodded conclusively. She took the smoothies and marched back down to the woodpile where she'd left Teagan, pleasantly anticipating several more hours on the trail before she had to get started on her long list of places that needed cleaning and repair.

nine

SLEEP WAS THE BEST AMENITY AT THE RETREAT. For the first time since college, Teagan slept eight hours a night. When he went to bed, his body ached from the effort of hauling sacks of pea gravel up the mountain, from cutting limbs, and from digging out roots, but the ache was pleasant. He was glad to fall asleep. He was glad to wake up the next day. He didn't know whether it was the drugs, the labor, or the bolster of Darcy's direct attention, but he felt better than he had in years.

Part of it was the sheer absence of the hours spent lying awake in bed, thinking about things he'd done wrong that day. He'd hated the empty, twitchy hours in the middle of the night, and now those hours were gone. He slept. This was real luxury: he went to sleep when he was tired, and when he woke up, there was daylight. Every day he reveled in the sybaritic pleasure of his cheek against the linen pillowcase and the contrast between the cool morning air and his warm blankets. It was so gentle an ascent into wakefulness that he couldn't remember his dreams, which had previously been of the sort where he was accidentally naked in public or taking a test he had forgotten to study for.

But today he dreamed of falling. He *was* falling. He fell off the bed and landed on the synthetic sheepskin rug of his tent, as confused about where he was and what he was doing as in those banished bad dreams. It took several flailing, jumbled moments to realize that he'd fallen because Darcy had pulled the sheets off the bed with his body still tangled up in them.

She stood over him in the faint blue predawn light, looking at his unclothed form with frank appraisal and what he hoped was a small degree of approval.

"Not bad, Bear Bait," she said, hands on her hips as she critically assessed the stomach that was still taut with panic at its abrupt descent. "Looking good, actually! We'll have you back up to your fighting weight in no time."

Teagan reflexively jerked the duvet off the bed and over his hips to cover himself, but his antidepressants had more or less eliminated the risk of untoward morning wood incidents. Nothing to see here. Please move along.

"Hi, Darcy," he managed, choking back a sludge of embarrassment and surprise.

"Good morning," she said with solid cheer. "You're a heavy sleeper, huh?"

"Only recently."

Darcy looked different today, and his rebooting brain slowly grasped for the details: her hair was down and blown straight so that it hung nearly all the way down her back. Instead of her customary T-shirt and cutoffs, she wore fitted jeans and a button-down black shirt. Carved silver hoop earrings dangled alongside the curve of her cheeks, the first jewelry he'd ever seen her wear. *She's so pretty*, his barely conscious mind mumbled.

Darcy nodded in satisfaction. "That's what honest work will do for you! Do you have any plans today?"

Darcy made his plans every day. Or rather, his plan every day was *Hi, Darcy*, and she told him what she wanted him to do. For two weeks, it had been a good program.

He wordlessly shook his head.

"Great. It's my day off," she said, face expectant.

"Oh," he replied. "Did you . . . want to go do something?"

He barely dared to hope. It was not at all apparent to him that Darcy was organizing his days out of anything more than professional obligation or the usefulness of his manual labor. He didn't mind. *Use me, please.*

"I do!" she said cheerfully. "Would you like to see a beaver?"

"Beaver?"

"Beaver," she confirmed.

Teagan didn't know what was going on half the time that he was here, and that proportion only increased when Darcy was speaking to him. Possibly Darcy was delivering the least charming proposition he'd ever received. More likely there was an actual giant rodent sighting in his immediate future.

"Sure," he said from the floor. Either way, sure.

"Fantastic!" she said, although she didn't seem to have doubted his answer. "Hurry up and get dressed—Yellowstone is a three-hour drive from here."

Ah. The toothy kind of beavers it was, then.

Darcy pulled his folded clothes off the chair by the bed and tossed them over to him. She bounced on her heels while Teagan pulled on his pants, eyes fixed awkwardly on the ceiling as he did up the fly on his chinos. She did all but physically hustle him out into the bracing chill of the early morning.

"I got you breakfast already," she said when he looked at the residence building. "You can drink it on the way. And we'll get lunch in Mammoth Hot Springs." She took his arm and began to drag him along with her to increase their pace.

"Wait, wait, I should ask Sloane if she wants to go," he

said, leaning back on his heels and looking at his sister's tent. He wasn't totally awake yet.

Darcy halted. Her face flashed with a few emotions, faster than he could follow: surprise, wariness, then a shade of judgment. "You want to bring your sister along?"

Teagan flushed as he realized that yes, objectively speaking, he was cockblocking himself. He nodded rather than backpedal.

"Okay, go on, then, be quick," Darcy said. "There's a line outside the tollbooth by nine."

This was the little dance he and Darcy did: he acted like a teenage boy with his first crush, and she graciously pretended not to notice. He remained keenly aware that she had used most of her words ever uttered in his presence to convey that he was a disaster, and he was only deluding himself if he thought that uninterrupted time with Darcy would do anything to change her mind about him. Despite that conclusion, he still generated a small pearl of regret as he veered off the main path and over to his sister's tent. A long ride alone with Darcy might have been nice.

"Sloane?" he warily called from the mosquito-netted entrance. He ducked inside. "Sloane, could you wake up for a second?" Sloane went off like a parcel bomb if disturbed in her sleep, and he carefully stayed out of striking range. She didn't move from under her mound of fluffy pillows. "Sloane?"

"Mrf," she finally grunted, tossing the uppermost pillow aside. "Are you dying again?"

"No," he quickly reassured her. "Nothing's wrong."

"Thenfugoff," Sloane moaned, reaching for her pillow again.

"Sloane," he insisted, grabbing the pillow away. "Hold

on. I'm just checking if you want to go to Yellowstone to-day. On a hike. To see beavers."

"*No*, I don't want to get up and see beavers, have you met me?" she snapped, lunging for the pillow to wave it with menace in his general direction.

"I have, yes, but also, you dragged me out here. So I thought you might be interested in hiking now," Teagan said, planting his feet.

"I'm not."

"Okay," Teagan said, a little relieved despite his best intentions.

"Wait," Sloane called when he took a step back. "You're going though? Is Darcy taking you?"

"Yeah," he said, rubbing the back of his neck, hoping he looked blasé about the topic. "You're still welcome though."

Sloane snorted her disagreement to that proposition. "You're so dumb, Tiggie."

He sighed. "So I'm often told. You're sure you don't want to come? Who knows when you'll ever see Yellowstone if you don't."

"I can live with that," she muttered sleepily. "But you and Darcy have a *very nice time*, okay?"

He wondered what he was missing that Sloane was engaging in subtext.

"It's not like that. I'm like her . . . rescue pet. That she's fostering. She doesn't like me."

"God, wish I could meet someone hot who dislikes me the same way she does you. You've been spending, like, every waking hour with her for the last two weeks—do you realize that?"

"I'm sorry," Teagan immediately said. Had he been neglecting Sloane? That was the entire reason he was at this glorified summer camp. "I don't have to go either. Do you want me to stay? We could do something together today."

Sloane made an annoyed sound in the back of her throat. "No, I *do not* want you to stay. Go see beavers with the hot maintenance girl. Live a little. Jesus. Ask about *her* beaver."

"Sloane!" he objected in horror. She might be twenty-two, but he preferred to maintain the illusion that his baby sister had never heard of sex.

"What? Good for you. You both should have some fun."

Teagan hesitated. "Do you really think so?"

Sloane growled and hurled her pillow at him. "Get out of my fucking tent, Tiggie! I'm going back to sleep. You're *so* dumb about this stuff."

"Okay, okay," he said, replacing her pillows on the bed and backing away from her. "See you tonight, I guess?"

He assumed he'd be back tonight. But he knew there were hotels in Yellowstone, and if it was three hours away and Darcy's day off, maybe she'd want to stay there?

"Teagan?" Sloane called when he was almost out of the tent.

"Yeah?"

"I *am* happy you're going. You look really happy."

As Teagan walked through the wet grass to the rumbling pickup truck emblazoned with the wellness retreat's logo, where Darcy waited with visible impatience, he was surprised to realize that was true. He probably should have gotten on antidepressants years ago. Or taken time off. He'd taken vacations since business school, of course, but most of them had revolved around other people's weddings and bachelor parties and life milestones, and he hadn't found them particularly relaxing.

This trip was relaxing, in a different way from running

on a treadmill until endorphins made his brain stop screaming. He felt quiet and whole after a day spent clearing trail
with Darcy. Maybe it was Darcy. Maybe he just needed to
spend time with someone whose demands on him were
tangibly achievable. And maybe she was coming around on
him. Maybe he was just too out of practice to realize it.

It had been a couple of years since he'd been in a relationship. If anything, he'd seemed to get *worse* at dating as he got
older, and conversations that had moved easily when he was
in his twenties had grown superficial and stilted. Women still
asked him out from time to time—he didn't think he was
such a catch, but he was aware that just being single, gain-
fully employed, and interested in women his own age guaranteed a baseline level of marketability in Manhattan—but
nothing had gotten serious for a long time.

Not that this could either, since he'd be gone in a couple
of weeks, but it felt important anyway.

Teagan was full of optimism when they departed the
wellness retreat for the first time in his three-week stay.
"Jack and the Giant Tree Stalk," Darcy said as she thrust a
thirty-two ounce smoothie at Teagan's chest and jerked the
truck into reverse. "Jackfruit, kale, and lots of coconut cream."

She'd made him drink worse things, so Teagan obediently
put the straw in his mouth and settled into the passenger seat,
as pleased to go on a morning car ride as a hunting dog who
saw the game bag in the truck bed.

Nature! Scenery! A beautiful woman in the driver's seat!
Somehow, he'd thought his adult life would look a lot more
like this, back when he was a teenager.

Darcy plugged her phone into the center console and

fumbled with it, eyes mostly on the narrow unpaved road back to the highway. The phone connected, and a tinny artificial voice slowly and phonetically recited that the sea otter was a keystone species in Pacific Northwest kelp forests because it regulated the sea urchin population.

"Shit," Darcy said, fumbling again with her phone and propping it on the steering wheel.

Teagan covertly put one hand on the bottom of the wheel as Darcy thumbed through her phone screen at forty-five miles an hour around a switchback.

"Can I help?" Teagan asked, glad that he couldn't really manage *terror* as an emotion through the SSRIs.

"Finish your smoothie. I had to wake Kristin up to make it," she said. She found what she wanted on her podcasts app and plugged her phone back into the truck.

The podcast that began to play was professionally produced, with slick background music. Darcy turned up the volume and settled back in her seat as they hit I-90.

"The first step," the mellow-voiced narrator recited through the truck's stereo, quoting the Twelve Steps. "'We admitted we were powerless over alcohol—that our lives had become unmanageable.'"

Teagan looked over at Darcy. She kept her eyes on the road this time, but she smiled with closed lips.

"So what does that mean to us?" the narrator asked. "The first step looks different to everyone I've ever met, because alcoholism looks different on every person."

"Darcy," Teagan said, abruptly full of foreboding for the rest of the car ride.

Darcy didn't look back at him.

"Bear Bait," she replied.

"Can we listen to music instead?" Teagan asked.

"No," said Darcy. "I always listen to podcasts on long drives. This is *Sober Sam's Sobriety Podcast*. It's very highly rated. Five stars."

"Does it have to be this one?" he asked, polite yet firm. "We can listen to the otter talk."

"No, that was for school. This one's for you."

"Darcy. I'm not an alcoholic," Teagan insisted. "I barely drink. I'm not lying."

"See, that's why we're listening to Step One," she said with professional cheer. "You need to work on that one, obviously."

"I would admit it if I was an alcoholic. My mother was an alcoholic. My sister abused pills. Everyone else out here has some kind of substance abuse problem, and they're all nice people. But I don't have a drinking problem."

"Uh huh," Darcy said, patently unconvinced. "You know, your sister told me you were hospitalized before she brought you out here."

Teagan froze, the distant shame that had circled him from far out in space now visible in orbit for the first time in days. He looked at it in alarm, willing it to go back out where he didn't have to think about it. The fluorescent lights of Gracie Square were so foreign to the experience of cutting back branches in the woods with Darcy that it sometimes seemed like he'd hallucinated the experience. "I was," he warily admitted.

"Yeah, and *you* never mentioned the hospital to me. Or to anyone else, right? Nobody knows."

Teagan exhaled. He didn't want to think about it. It was a beautiful morning in Montana, and everything else was very far away. It was going to be a very nice drive.

"So?" he asked. So what else was he supposed to do? He'd

done everything his doctor had told him to do. There weren't twelve steps for having a panic disorder. There wasn't some duty to announce it to everyone he knew. He took his medications every day. It was even possible he'd never have another panic attack, so *that time he had a nervous breakdown* did not need to be part of his biography.

"*So*, we're listening to the podcast," Darcy said. "Unless you want to talk about why you landed in the hospital? I get why you wouldn't talk about it with Rachel or the doctor. They suck. But you've also had two weeks to talk about it with me, and you haven't. Do you wanna?"

Her expression said that this was a challenge she was certain he would not meet. She was right. Besides, there was nothing really to talk about, nothing relevant to the woman, the car, the scenery. That was one bad week, one which would not recur.

Teagan shut his mouth and sat back for the long, winding road through the mountain valleys as Sober Sam encouraged them to take stock of everything drinking had cost them. Darcy turned up the volume even higher so that she could crack the windows and get a heady stream of cool air as they sped down the highway.

Teagan's enthusiasm for the trip was only slightly diminished by the price of admission. The weather in the park couldn't have been better, and Darcy was probably the best person in the world to visit it with. She'd worked here before, she'd mentioned that. She seemed to know more about it than most guidebooks.

And God, anywhere he looked, the view was amazing.

They passed sprawling mansions and log-cabin shacks, herds of cattle and new-construction horse ranches. The hills and raw rock cliff faces gleamed gold and silver in the morning light. Bits of wind from the cracked windows caught at Darcy's loose hair and teased it around her face. Her fingers tapped on the steering wheel as they drove at exactly ten miles an hour over the posted speed limit.

As they turned off I-90, the podcast fell silent with the conclusion of Sober Sam's thoughts on the first step. To cover the absence, Darcy began to sing an endless marching cadence:

I wanna be a forest ranger
Wild squirrels are my only danger

The sun was now coming right through the windshield and into their eyes. Darcy pulled an elastic from her wrist and tied back hair lit to the color of fresh embers by the angle of the light, then took a pair of knockoff Ray-Bans from the sun visor and tipped them over the arch of her nose. She was so beautiful his chest ached like he'd pulled a muscle there.

Darcy caught him looking at her and shoved his arm, laughing because she thought his expression was about her singing.

"Episode two," she said, and turned on more Sober Sam.

Teagan would have preferred her singing, even though she couldn't find half the notes she was looking for.

Darcy straightened up as they passed the tollbooth to Yellowstone and fiddled with her hair in the rearview mirror when they reached the first intersection.

"Which way to the beavers?" Teagan asked, scrutinizing the park map she'd shoved in his lap.

Darcy finally, blessedly, turned off the podcast and looked at him out of the corner of her eye as she took the turn toward Mammoth Hot Springs.

"Okay, so, full disclosure," she said. "Beavers are actually crepuscular."

"Crep—"

"Active at dawn and dusk. So. It's almost eight thirty. The beavers are probably going to sleep right now."

The road she chose was the one that led to the visitor center, not the turn toward the northern lake trails. Teagan began to feel confused again, not certain any longer why he'd been lured out of bed before dawn and promised beavers, only to be subjected to a podcast about alcoholism and interrogated about bad habits he didn't actually have.

"Are we not actually going to see beavers?" he asked, looking down the busy road ahead of them, full of summer park tourists.

"I mean, I can never promise you'll see any animals here. They're wildlife. Wild. They have their own agendas. *But*, if you're willing to wait while I run a couple of errands in Mammoth Hot Springs, I can ask the rangers what's out today, then we can go see the bison, maybe some elk, whatever . . . and we'll catch the beavers at dusk. Does that sound like a plan?"

Darcy said it all very quickly, as though she were hoping to gain his agreement without a great deal of thought on his part.

"What kind of errands?" he asked, not sure whether he was supposed to be suspicious.

"Some stuff for my job," she said evasively.

"Doing what?"

"Does it matter?" she asked.

"Well, yeah, do you need any help? Anything I can do to get it done faster?"

"No," she said firmly. "You've helped plenty. Just hang out, all right?"

"For how long?"

"I'm not sure. Maybe a couple of hours?" she said, tone tight.

Teagan stared at her.

Darcy's jaw clenched as she kept her eyes fixed on the road ahead of her. "I'll give you my phone. You can keep listening to the podcast while you wait."

Oh, to hell with *that*.

"Did you seriously just bring me out here to make me listen to alcoholism podcasts?" Teagan demanded, annoyance beginning to rise after three hours of Steps One and Two.

Now who's dumb, Sloane? She'd halfway convinced him this was going to be a date.

"No," Darcy snapped, face shuttering. "I brought you out here because it's my only day off for two weeks and I need to interview for winter park positions, but Rachel's planning some appropriative sweat lodge bullshit today where you choke on steam and talk to your ancestors. She had me up and stacking firewood before dawn."

At that explanation, Teagan sat back hard in his seat. Of course it was something like that. He should have known better.

She didn't like him.

Stop showing your ass, Teagan.

"Seemed like talking to your ancestors in particular was the kind of thing that could set you back to day zero," Darcy said, voice still defensive.

She didn't like him. She didn't like him for very good, understandable reasons. She thought it was her job to help him, and she was trying her best, but he needed to stop expecting anything more than that.

Beavers.

Darcy fidgeted again with her hair and the collar of her shirt, which had been ironed and starched within an inch of its life.

"I didn't find out about the postings until last night or the sweat lodge stuff until this morning, so I didn't have a chance to plan anything else for you." Her tone was apologetic now.

"Sure," Teagan said. "I get why you needed to be here." Why *he* was here was not apparent.

"I'll try to be quick," Darcy repeated. She now sounded openly guilty. "I really will take you on the wildlife tour after that." She snuck a look over at him as she slicked on some cherry Chapstick, the closest thing to makeup he'd seen on her yet.

Teagan shook his head. She probably had things to do back at the camp. Things she wanted to do on her day off.

"You don't have to babysit me," he said. "You could have just warned me about the sweat lodge plans."

They arrived in a cluster of old, federal-style buildings looming over a few gift shops and cafes.

Darcy's lips pursed as she parked the car, hand tight and nervous on the gears.

"Well, I couldn't leave you to your own devices all day if you didn't want to come, could I?" she asked.

Teagan sighed and unclipped his seatbelt. She seemed to think he'd spent most of his previous three and a half decades passed out in a gutter somewhere.

"I would have been fine," he said.

He mentally shook himself, afraid that he sounded like a brat. He gathered his composure, which he'd scattered all over a train platform several weeks ago and never quite recovered. He smoothed his face and gentled his posture.

"I'm sorry Rachel treats you the way she does," he said, meeting her eyes. "But it's actually not your job to take care of me."

Darcy visibly flinched.

He didn't want to be her job. He wanted—well, nothing he could picture actually happening, but he didn't want her to look at him and see another giant mess she had to clean up.

Despite her frown, he got out of the truck. There was a restaurant on the other side of the parking lot. Maybe it had Wi-Fi. Or coffee. Or bacon.

"Look," Darcy said, grabbing him by the elbow and drawing his attention to a trailer at the base of the hill. "I'll be in there, okay? I don't think the restaurant serves alcohol this early, but don't order any. Don't go near the elk. They bite." She nodded at some large, somnolent creatures grazing on the nearby lawn to the delight of a crowd of tourists. "After I'm done, I promise we'll go hiking, and I'll find you a beaver if I have to swim into the goddamn pond myself. Okay? Sound good?" Teagan didn't know why she was still asking. It's not like he had a choice but to wait.

Teagan eased her hand off his arm and ignored her worried frown. "You don't need to worry about me," he said. "Thanks. Good luck with your interview."

ten

IT TOOK LESS THAN AN HOUR. THAT WAS THE ONLY thing that went as planned.

Darcy trudged across the parking lot, dodging RVs and minivans full of frazzled vacationers in search of restrooms and hot food. She thought about turning onto one of the trails so that she could scream alone in the woods for a few minutes, but she already felt like a jerk for wasting Teagan's entire morning now that she wasn't even going to have anything to show for it.

She found Teagan in the largest cafe, seated next to the window. She wasn't sure whether the stiff, defensive look he sent her was about her phone against his ear, the big spread of animal protein in front of him, or his palpable disappointment that they were not, at this moment, frolicking hand in hand through a woodland meadow, but he didn't look happy.

Me too, buddy, she thought.

She took the seat catty-corner to him so that she didn't have to smell his bison burger. On closer examination, Teagan looked even worse. He had a little wrinkle in his forehead as he listened to whoever was speaking on the phone, and the muscles in his jaw were tight. He turned his head toward the window and spoke:

"Hi, yes, still waiting. I understand. Look, I know she's very scary, but she doesn't actually have the authority to fire you, and also, technically, I do. No. No, I am not firing you. I just—No. I'm sorry I said that. You're not getting fired. No, I'm sorry. Right. I just want access to my email—"

Darcy propped her elbows on the table. Since she hadn't slept much the night before, the downward momentum carried her all the way to her head buried between her biceps. She closed her eyes and slumped on the table.

"I'll call you back," Teagan said.

She heard him put the phone on the table. After a moment, there were quiet eating noises. He had a cheeseburger, fries, and a soda. All that shit was going to hit his system like broken glass after three weeks of Rachel's wild rice and kale regimen.

"Can I have some fries please?" Darcy mumbled without lifting her head.

Teagan didn't respond, but after a couple of seconds, fries were put in her outstretched hand. She didn't open her eyes as she shoveled them to her mouth. She put her hand back out, willing Teagan to pay attention to her. She spread her fingers imploringly and more fries were provided.

"You didn't get the job?" Teagan asked, voice guarded.

"They wouldn't even let me apply," she said bitterly, mouth full of fries. She scraped herself into a sitting position and surveyed the rest of Teagan's food. He had a pickle spear on his plate. She eyed it with sad interest until Teagan rolled it onto a side plate and pushed it across the table to her.

"Why not?" he asked.

"They said they had to advertise all the positions online this year, so they're using some big recruiter to screen all the candidates. They *know* me, but they want me to go through the portal and upload a resume and send a cover letter and . . ."

She put her head back down. She'd rather climb a sheer cliff face carrying fifty pounds of gear.

"I think that's what most big employers do now, yeah," Teagan said.

"Well, it fucking sucks," Darcy growled. "I parked snow-mobiles all last winter. There's no reason to assume that there's some other person out there who they'd rather hire this year because they parked snowmobiles at Yale or some shit."

Teagan didn't deserve that dig, but Darcy had a wild creature's instinctive fear of showing vulnerability, and the idea of Teagan watching her land flat on her ass had her lashing out.

"If I had a snowmobile that needed parking, I'd definitely hire you over someone like me," Teagan replied, and Darcy curled her lip in anger that he wouldn't even get into a proper fight with her about it, when she longed to fight with *someone* about this.

Darcy didn't know how long to count to stop being angry that she couldn't get her last job back. If she had to sculpt flowers out of root vegetables this winter in Bozeman with Kristin because she didn't have a car and she couldn't even manage to apply for a hospitality gig in Yellowstone, she wasn't sure she'd manage to stop being angry until spring.

She started counting anyway, and she'd gotten to forty-six before Teagan cleared his throat and began to read aloud, "Park Ranger. GS 7 scale. Yellowstone. Develops and presents a variety of natural history programs including geyser walks, ecology walks, lectures, campfire programs—"

Darcy turned her head over to look at him. He was read-ing off her phone. "Are you on the National Park Service page?" she asked.

"Yeah. This position opened last week. Is this the one you wanted?"

"No. I was applying with a contractor. Those Park Ser-vice jobs all want a four-year degree."

Teagan blinked as though it had never occurred to him that she might not have finished college or potentially not gone to college at all.

"You don't have one?"

"Nope. Hence the lawn mowing. And the generator re-pair. And the schlepping and hauling and—"

"But why don't you have one?"

Darcy huffed in pained annoyance. "Maybe I'm just not that smart." That's what she worried sometimes, because there was no good reason why she couldn't pass Ecological Ge-netics or navigate a hiring portal or figure out when job boards opened, except that she just couldn't, no matter how hard she tried.

Teagan shook his head in embarrassment. "That's obvi-ously not it. I thought the Navy paid for college, I meant."

"It does. But I've been enrolled at Oregon State since I was eighteen. I still need twenty-eight more credits to graduate."

Teagan looked back down at the phone in consternation, scrolling more. "Well, there are some jobs here that say you can substitute experience—"

Darcy interrupted him. "The Park Service won't hire me to do anything good, whatever the listing says. I tried two years ago."

The jut of Teagan's jaw said he didn't believe her. He kept scrolling. She leaned across the table and tugged at a lock of golden hair that had fallen over his forehead to get his attention and change the subject from her recurring life failures. He'd looked stressed.

"Hey. Who were you talking to on the phone? Better not have been your horse tranquilizer guy."

Teagan's eyebrows quirked ironically. "IT. And they can't even get me access to my email, much less fun drugs. Rose, my CIO, got all my messages forwarded to her account, and she told IT not to give them back to me."

"Wow, someone's leading a coup against you?" Darcy asked, startled at the idea, even though she was vaguely aware that people outside of her own industry could suck too.

"Maybe. Rose is the only one who knows where I am. The board chair left me a bunch of voice messages asking what the hell I'm doing out of the office this long. I guess the official word is that I'm out sick."

"You are out sick," Darcy said, taking the last of his fries. If he had sick leave stored up, he ought to use it for this.

Teagan once again refused to argue his contrary opinion, looking down at the phone screen instead and changing the subject back to Darcy's persistent failures.

"I bet I can find a job you're qualified for. Do you want me to edit your resume? I can rewrite it so it looks like you're the perfect candidate. I'll find the buzzwords in the post and copy them into the skills field. That's all the screening software checks for."

"It's not a person who looks at it?"

"No, not on the first screening, usually," he said, face nonjudgmental.

This news took Darcy aback. How could she possibly have known that? Not only had she not known that, nobody else had ever edited her resume, which meant it was probably a mess.

"I guess you could look at it," she admitted, even though she winced to imagine him finding all her misspellings. "If it's not too big a hassle." She turned her face into her arms and put her hands over her head. This sucked the most.

She'd been nothing but bitchy to him all day long, and he'd been nothing but understanding in response. It was just one more reason to be angry at herself. One man in the entire world treated her with respect, treated her like she knew what she was doing, and she was doing her best to change his mind on that.

Teagan paused again. "Do you want me to do it right now? I can download Word to your phone."

"I thought you wanted to go hiking," Darcy deflected, face still hidden.

"Not as much as you want a better job though, right?" he asked gently.

Darcy swallowed hard.

"Okay," she muttered.

When she didn't reach for her phone, Teagan pulled his mouth to the side, considering. "Do you want me to just make you a resume from scratch? I've done all the hiring at the foundation for the last two years, so I've seen a lot of them."

That prickly feeling had returned to her nose and throat. Jesus, no guy had ever worked this hard to get her out of her clothes, assuming that's what he wanted. That was what men usually wanted when they were nice to her on a sustained basis, though Teagan had been slow to work himself up to the proposition.

She could wish they'd met under different circumstances,

if that's what he wanted, because she knew what she would have done. Two years from now, when he was good and sober and spending a week at the Lake Yellowstone Hotel to catch the bird migration and Darcy had somehow found work in forestry, that would have been a nice time to meet him. She wouldn't have minded a little proposition then. Would have enjoyed watching him sweat over how to palm her a room key after the fireside lecture. Would have been in a position to drag him out into the woods with a quilt and six-pack of O'Doul's.

The more troubling possibility, in fact, was that he was just like this. Sweet. Kind. She had no idea what she'd do about that, under any circumstances.

"Yeah, please," she said, eyes still closed. "I can send you my DD-214 from the Navy. It's got most of what I know how to do listed on it."

D arcy ate a second basket of fries as Teagan copied and pasted on her phone. He doubted that she was really impressed at his knowledge of shortcuts on Word for iOS, but that painfully defeated expression on her face had eased, either from the food or his promise to work on her job application materials. This small, solvable problem was a welcome distraction from the meeting request he'd found in his personal email.

For the past three weeks, Rose had responded to his every call checking in with some variation on "Everything is fine/get off the phone and go sit in the woods/don't you think I can do my job without your micromanagement?"

But today in his personal email inbox, Nora, the chair of

the board of directors, had forwarded a calendar request for 9:00 a.m. Eastern on the following Friday. Teagan was invited to join by phone, but it appeared that the other members of the foundation's leadership would attend in person. Rose had scheduled the meeting. The agenda was vaguely and ominously described as *Foundation Strategy*. Teagan had left a polite message with Rose asking about the purpose of the meeting, but she had not responded while Teagan was seated at the diner. So he played with the formatting on Darcy's new resume as he waited for Rose to call him back on Darcy's phone.

Darcy licked salt off her fingers, momentarily distracting him from his weighty choice between Times New Roman and Palatino. She caught him staring at her mouth and gave him a tight smile, though she thankfully didn't seem to notice the flash of an obscene thought across the barest surface of his mind.

She wanted her resume to stress her ability to lift seventy-five pounds and operate a variety of motor vehicles, but if she wanted to be a park ranger someday, Teagan thought he might also make her resume look a little more managerial class.

Darcy's phone chirped with a notification. She startled with interest.

She immediately snatched the phone away from him to look at the screen. Then she made a wonderful noise. A breathy growl of pleasure and surprise deep in her throat, a noise that hit Teagan right in his gut and sparked immediate jealousy of whatever had caused that noise. Her face lit up with joy.

Before he could ask what had occurred to put that

blessed look on her face, Darcy thrust her phone back into his face.

"Look!" she said, dropping it into his confused hands before he could focus on the screen. "We gotta go right now."

Teagan barely managed to pull out his wallet and drop an indeterminate number of bills on the table before Darcy began physically dragging him from the cafe. She wrapped a hand around his bicep and tugged when he didn't move fast enough, then slid her hand down to his own palm and laced her fingers with his as she pulled him toward the parking lot.

"Where are we going?" he asked, digging in his heels. The last two times someone had hauled him off to an unknown destination, he'd been taken to rehab and then to someone else's job interview. Twice was bad enough, but three times would make a really unfortunate pattern.

"Junction Butte pack brought down an elk by First Meadow. We can see them from Slough Creek Trail. *If* we hustle."

"We need to see a dead elk?"

"*Wolves*, Teagan," she said, beaming at his bemusement when he did not join in her excited squeals.

Teagan had just recently recovered from his last encounter with the top of the food chain, and he was only able to muster a halfhearted smile.

"I promised you something good!" Darcy crowed, even though she had made no such promise, and had in fact dragged him out here primarily to pursue a job she still didn't have an application for. "Even better than beavers."

"But I—" The unanswered message to Rose nagged him. Something was going on at the foundation, and nobody was telling him what it was. And if positions had opened today for the winter jobs Darcy wanted, she ought to apply for them today. HR managers often went straight down the list of applicants in the order received. There wasn't cell service outside of the park headquarters and most of the way back to Big Sky, so this was his last chance to work on them until tonight. "I actually ought to stay here while you go," he said. "I can finish your application. And I'm waiting on a couple of calls."

Darcy halted, eyes widening. She turned to stare at him, face utterly appalled.

"You want to stay in the cafe and work instead of seeing wolves," she repeated in disbelief.

"Well, I don't *want* to, I—"

"Give me my phone back," Darcy demanded, hand outstretched, palm up.

Teagan put a protective hand over his back pocket and took a step away from her.

"If I didn't say it earlier, you don't owe me the animal tour or anything else, if you need to work on your applications—"

"Give me my goddamn phone," she said, more insistently.

"Hold on," he said, taking another step back, natural stubbornness rising to the forefront of his mind. Five unanswered messages, Nora had left him. If he wasn't there when she called him back, she'd think he was blowing her off. "I can't quit doing my job just because I'm out in Yellowstone, and you—"

Darcy lunged. She knocked into him shoulder first, trapping him up against the side of a weather-beaten Ford Bronco. He had at least six inches on her, but she was packing a lot of muscle on her frame, and she got him pinned before he could sputter out a protest.

"Your. Fucking. Job. Can. Suck it," Darcy grunted as

she wrestled for the phone. She wrapped her arms around his midsection and thrust her hands in his back pockets, fishing for it.

He yelped her name, but she ignored him.

"Give up!" she panted. "This could be your only chance in your whole joyless life to see this."

Her breasts were jammed up against his chest as she determinedly groped him in furtherance of her goal, but for once, *don't get a hard-on* actually worked as a mantra. His knees sagged, and she plucked the phone from his pocket. She backed away with it raised victorious in the air.

"You are unbelievable, do you know that?" he gritted out as Darcy stuffed her phone into her bra, giving him an eyeful of pale skin and electric blue satin. He couldn't decide whether he was annoyed, embarrassed, turned on, or some heady combination of the three.

"That's what every boyfriend has said before and *after* dating me, so yeah, I do know," Darcy said, oblivious to the discomfort her reference to other, more fortunate men engendered in Teagan. She pointed to the truck. "We're wasting time if we wanna be there before they finish lunch! Hut hut."

Darcy had the keys turned in the ignition before he had finished buckling his seat belt. She tossed the phone back to him as she hit the accelerator, and they took off for the east exit of the park headquarters in a squeal of tires and a cloud of dust. Teagan glared at her, because he was going to lose signal as soon as they got a hundred yards away from the visitor center.

"This is happening, Teagan," Darcy insisted. "No more work today. It's Saturday, and we're gonna see some awesome wolves, and you are gonna be glad you did."

I'm so sorry, Nora, Teagan imagined apologizing to the board chair. *I've been kidnapped. Let's talk in two weeks instead, okay?* That's what his mother would have said. Of course, his mother wouldn't have worried about meeting fundraising targets in the first place; she'd had some knack for it that he had not inherited.

This was all going to crash down on him as soon as he got back. The world didn't go away if you ignored it. But what was he going to do, walk back alone? He gritted his jaw.

"Do you even like your job?" Darcy burst out as they pulled onto the main road when he still hadn't responded.

Teagan opened his mouth to automatically respond that yes, of course he liked his job, he sent seven thousand underprivileged kids to art programs last year, this was a dream gig—but he found that he was unable to lie.

"I'm happy to be making a difference," he answered instead, but Darcy wasn't fooled.

"You're not. You get this pissed-off look on your face like you just got orders for Diego Garcia every time you think about work."

"Diego Garcia?"

"A shitty base in the middle of the Indian Ocean. Anyway, it's really weird that you stay in this job you hate."

"I don't *hate* it," he said, even though he wasn't sure that was true. "And even if I did, I haven't finished the restructuring I started after my mom died."

He didn't know when he'd be finished. Putting the family foundation back on course had seemed like a thing he could do when Nora had brought it up. At his mother's funeral, he remembered with a frown.

But he should have been able to do it. He had an MBA.

His last name was on the front door. He hadn't expected that two years in, the foundation would still be doing the corporate equivalent of living paycheck to paycheck: the endowment only supported about half the grants it made every year. It was still precariously reliant on his monthly fundraising—a job he was definitely not doing from Montana. Teagan hunched his shoulders at that unwelcome thought, but it couldn't inspire the kind of fear it had three weeks ago.

"You know what I mean. Your *job*'s never going to fuck you," Darcy said.

Teagan shot her an arched-eyebrow look, because she seemed to think that someone else was going to volunteer for that task, and he wondered who she had in mind.

"Your job's not going to ever love you back," she amended.

"I don't expect it to."

"You're purposefully misunderstanding me," she said grumpily. "If I had all the credentials in the world, all the money in the world, all the choices in the world, the way you do, I'd do something I loved. You could go get any job. Someone else could do yours."

"I should be the one doing this one. The foundation is eighty years old, it's founded on my great-grandfather's dirty sweatshop money, and it's basically the only good thing anyone in my family has ever done. My mother nearly ran it into the ground, and I had to go in and save it from being dissolved when she died."

"You really think you have to do it for her?" Darcy demanded. "She's dead. She doesn't care."

"I think I have to do what I said I was going to do," Teagan replied, and that, at least, felt honest. He heard Darcy swallow. It seemed she didn't have an argument against that.

The stereo was blessedly silent as they drove through the heavily forested roads of the park. When they turned into a side road, Darcy tapped her phone.

"Will you copy the GPS coordinates? From Ranger Ralph's DM."

Teagan gingerly pulled up Darcy's Twitter app, not sure what to expect. It was open to a message from an account whose profile picture was an elderly man holding a very large fish, the message consisting of a simple string of numbers and letters. Teagan dutifully copied the coordinates to the truck's console, then very accidentally clicked out of Darcy's messages to look at her account's home page. Her profile consisted of a photograph of a fat opossum climbing out of an unsecured dumpster, the description blank.

He blinked in surprise when he scanned the rest of the home screen.

"Why do you have six thousand followers?" he asked.

Darcy took her eyes off the road long enough to leer in his direction.

"Sometimes I feel insecure, and I post thirst traps," she said.

Teagan choked as his thumb moved, as of its own accord, to the media tab of her account.

"No, really," he said before he could click on it. There wasn't any signal out here anyway. Nothing would load. He put the phone in the cupholder and folded his hands in his lap.

"The Twitter account's just for my wolf photos," Darcy said, eyes intent on the road. "Last winter I checked all the snowmobile trails first thing in the morning, so I'd run into the wolves a lot. I posted some pretty awesome shots. You'll see. This is going to make the whole day worth it. The whole trip."

She shifted the truck into higher gear as the pavement turned to gravel, and her restored confidence made it impossible to doubt her.

"This is going to change your life," she promised.

Eleven

"IS THAT MELANISTIC YEARLING ONE OF 317F's?"
Ranger Ralph asked Darcy, passing his binoculars over to
her and sweeping stringy gray hair out of his face.

Ralph had not actually been a park ranger before retiring, but he'd lived in West Yellowstone for thirty years, and
he could usually be found wherever the wolves were. He and
half a dozen other wolf enthusiasts were clustered at the top
of the rise over First Meadow, watching the Junction Butte
pack feast on the unfortunate elk a few hundred yards away.
One actual uniformed park ranger—a new hire, Darcy didn't
know him—kept a watchful eye on the wolf-watchers lest
they try to take selfies with the wildlife or otherwise do something inadvisable off-trail.

"No, I think he was one of 1094F's last litter before the
Phantom Lake pack was exterminated this spring. Looks
healthy though," Darcy said, squinting at the distant black
shape and speaking into her phone.

The Junction Butte pack was viewable from this trail
several times a week, but this chance to watch their feeding
behavior—with the juveniles, no less!—was a rare treat. The
other wolf-watchers were humming with satisfaction as they
recorded video and photographs. This might make the news.

Darcy pointed for Teagan, who was quietly watching the pack through Darcy's binoculars. "See that one? His whole family was wiped out by baited traps in Montana, just off park boundaries."

"That's awful," Teagan murmured. Darcy gave him a sharp look under the assumption that he was just saying what she wanted to hear, but he kept the binoculars up. He hadn't fought her for the rest of the ride to the trailhead, and he'd jogged two miles up the trail at the speed Darcy demanded. He'd been quiet the whole time.

She didn't know what she'd expected. That he'd get down the trail, get an eyeful of the wolves, and have an epiphany? *Oh, wow. I am awestruck by the majesty and strangeness of the wilderness, and I perceive how small and unimportant my own mistakes are when viewed against the size of the world. I'm cured! Thank you. You changed my life. I'm sober, quitting my terrible job, and moving to Montana to raise money for wolf protection causes.*

She hadn't really thought through how bringing him out to watch the wolves would aid in his recovery. She'd just wanted to do something . . . big. Something meaningful, with a lasting impact. She'd already saved him from a bear, she supposed. That was pretty permanent. But Teagan kept looking at her like he thought she had the answers to all his problems, and she unexpectedly expected more from herself.

Was this good for him? He looked good here—broad shoulders relaxed, the wind ruffling his hair and his sleeves casually shoved up to his elbows—but making voice notes on wolf behavior was Darcy's idea of a good time, probably nobody else's.

"Feeling better?" Teagan asked. He let the binoculars dangle from his wrist and gave her a soft, searching look.

"Me?" she stuttered. "I got you wolves!"

Maybe this had been a selfish impulse. Of course she wanted Teagan along while she did her favorite thing in the world, because bringing along someone handsome and attentive made any activity more enjoyable, but she was supposed to be supporting him, not the other way around.

But she did feel better.

"Was this not what you wanted to do today?" she asked, feeling flustered. "This was probably a bad idea. I can take you back."

"No," he said, straightening. "This is amazing. Give me the lecture."

"What lecture?"

"The wolf lecture. I can tell you have one. Tell me what I ought to know about these wolves."

Darcy looked around. There were still half a dozen other people there, including the park ranger.

"Go ask the park ranger," she said, feeling conspicuous now. "That's his job."

Teagan barely glanced at the ranger. "That guy? His uncle is the secretary of the interior. He got his job through political patronage."

Darcy laughed. "The secretary of the interior is a woman. And not known for nepotism."

"Well, I want to hear your lecture anyway. Please?" Teagan said. He put a beseeching expression on his face.

Darcy ought to have been stronger against that, or so she thought. When he made big golden eyes at her, she felt compelled to do whatever he wanted, even if she didn't think it was the right thing to do.

She sighed in a put-upon way, trying desperately to pretend

that she wasn't desperate to tell him all about it. Like she hadn't imagined standing here in her own set of Park Service chinos, knowledgeable and respected.

"Okay, so, you see the puppies?" Darcy asked, putting her shoulder against his. She turned him until he saw the three gray fluff balls nearly hidden in the sagebrush, falling over each other in a pile of wagging tails. "I hope this litter makes it. I'm worried about genetic bottlenecks in the Yellowstone wolves. There were only thirty-one founders when they were reintroduced to the park in 1995—you know they were extirpated in the twenties, right?"

"Of course," Teagan said, and she looked at him suspiciously, but his face was very respectful.

"The wolves do their best to avoid inbreeding, but now they've been culled down to below a hundred individuals. The surrounding states plan to wipe out their wolves in the next few years if the feds don't intervene, so you have a recipe for genetic stagnation, because there won't be any exchanges with the Canadian gray wolf population."

"There aren't enough in Yellowstone?" he asked.

"It's not just Yellowstone that needs wolves. Every wilderness needs wolves. The wolves are a keystone species. Without wolves, the elk overgraze the aspen and the willows. Then the beavers don't have material to build their dams. If the beavers don't build ponds, you don't have wetlands to support waterfowl or pools for trout. And wolf-kill carrion is a big support to ravens, eagles, and bears."

"Ah," Teagan said, sounding satisfied. "There it is. It all comes back to the bears."

Darcy snorted. "It is not *all* about the bears."

"You don't have to say any more. I am convinced. We need

to save the wolves, because that will help the bears, and as you know, I am deeply, deeply devoted to the safety of the bears." A honey-sweet, crooked smile hung off his lips, even better than a pile of wolf pups for Darcy's mood.

Teagan didn't make jokes often. And only ever at his own expense.

She grabbed his arm to wrap her own around it. She tugged him tight to her side, knocking him off balance until his hip was flush against her own. She felt a surge of protectiveness, even if the only person Teagan needed to be protected from was himself. She squeezed him, heart suddenly full and tight.

He did look better than he did when she first saw him, even accounting for the mauling. A little more weight on his frame, a little more presence in his eyes, a few more smiles. She had to be doing something right.

"Yeah, you are," she said, shaking his arm. "Because bears are awesome. You just don't let them eat *you*, all right? Because you're probably full of all sorts of toxins from your New York lifestyle. Perfluoroalkyl substances and other forever chemicals."

He chuckled. "I won't let the bears eat me. For their sake, if not mine."

The wolves had stripped the choicest bits off the elk and were heading back into the tree cover to nap. The ravens were circling, soon descending to take their shot at the carcass. The wolf-watchers started to pack up their equipment.

Darcy squinted up at the sun to gauge the time, then turned to Teagan.

"So, how are you feeling, big guy? You up for the beavers too? We could make it to Beaver Pond Trail before sunset."

"Yes," he said definitively. "We can do the beavers next."

She grinned at the enthusiasm of his response.

They bade farewell to Ranger Ralph and took more time on the hike back to the truck. Darcy's step was buoyant with victory. She'd done what she set out to do, for once. Maybe the Goederts had been lying about the job when they hired her, and maybe Darcy hadn't been qualified to work with people with substance abuse problems when she started, but she'd figured it out anyway.

"This was good for you," she told Teagan decisively as they reached the trailhead. "I knew it. Wilderness therapy really does work. I bet you didn't think about drinking the whole time you were out there, huh?"

"I couldn't possibly think about anything else while trying to commit so many important facts about wolves to memory," he said, but his smile was warm and lingering as he looked directly at her.

Darcy ducked her head, her cheeks suddenly heated. She peeked at him sideways to be sure he wasn't making fun of her—she'd toss him right out of the truck if he was—but instead his face was contemplative.

"This is what you should do," Teagan said. "This. You shouldn't be fixing generators. You should be doing this."

"Yeah, I *know*," Darcy said. "That was the entire idea of my job with the Goederts. I just got screwed over when it was too late to find something else for the summer."

"You should quit your job. Go to school full time. I looked up the GI Bill—you get a stipend. Finish your degree and get that park ranger job. You'd be good at it."

Darcy laughed at how he assumed the world worked. That all the bills got paid, that she passed all her classes, that all the government benefits arrived right on time. "You should quit *your* job," she said.

"I can't. Or I can't yet, anyway. But there's nothing stopping you."

She snorted again. "Okay, well, first of all, I don't have a car, I don't have savings, and if I tried to go to school full time, I'd just flunk out again."

"You wouldn't flunk out."

"I already *did*. When I was twenty. I lost my scholarship, had to drop out of the ROTC program, went and enlisted just to pay the Navy back." She decided not to mention that she was failing out again right now.

"You'd probably take it more seriously now than when you were twenty," Teagan said.

Darcy thought she'd taken it pretty seriously the first time around too, but she was buoyed by his assumption that she was smart enough to finish her degree, and she thought she'd just roll in that for a little while rather than disabusing him of the notion. When she failed her summer classes, it was going to be hard enough to reregister for the fall.

"Maybe I should just run off naked into the woods to live with the wolves," she suggested after a minute.

Teagan gave a stutter of a laugh. "That's a . . . career plan for sure."

"I'd be good at *that*."

"Hard to fail at naked in the woods with the wolves," he replied. "Though the vegan diet might be difficult to accommodate."

"I'm not a vegan," Darcy said heatedly. "I eat honey. And eggs, if I know the situation with the chicken."

"What's the situation with the chickens of the Yellowstone woods, then? Acceptable?"

"Mmm, good point. I'd probably have to eat meat, wouldn't I? I guess that would be okay if I ran down the game myself."

"I'm getting such a mental picture of this," Teagan said, and he turned his head to smile at her again. She had a sensation like riding her bicycle down a hill and taking her hands off the handlebars when she made her next suggestion.

"I'm not sure I could kill the moose or whatever though," she admitted. "Pretty sure I couldn't. You should come too, after you quit your job. You can do that part."

"Kill the moose?" he said, voice rich and full of laughter. "I've worked in an office building my entire adult life. I couldn't even cook the moose."

"I bet *you're* related to Teddy Roosevelt. You can handle the moose."

"Only on my mother's side," he said with that wide, crooked grin. "Distant cousin."

"Well that settles it," Darcy said, feeling ridiculously as though something had in fact been settled. "We quit our terrible jobs, quit everything, and live off the land here in Yellowstone."

It was hard to keep her eyes on the road as she waited for Teagan to reply. Because of course it was a joke. But she wanted him to be in on it with her. She wanted him to agree that this was the good stuff, much better than whatever was waiting for him when he went back to New York.

She wanted him to admit she'd been good for him.

"It'll make packing easy the next time I come back here," Teagan said, and it sounded like a promise.

The light lingered even in August, this far north, so it was barely sunset by the time they reached Livingston, the nearest large town outside of the park. Darcy turned onto a long stretch of two-lane highway lined by strip malls with faux Old West facades over casinos, gift shops, and bars, then pulled into a gas station. The tank was still almost half full.

Teagan wondered if she was as reluctant to let the day end as he was. They had not found any beavers, in the end, but Darcy had pointed out a muskrat and an endangered water bird. She seemed very pleased with their visual haul.

He got out of the truck when she did and tried not to ogle her when she bent to stretch her legs after the two-hour drive out of the park, even though her jeans clung to her ass in a really wonderful way. He looked away down the street before she caught him.

"Do you want to get dinner? Since we've already stopped?" he asked. Her stomach had been audibly growling for the last half hour, and he couldn't recall seeing her eat anything but French fries and half a pickle spear all day.

He wanted to buy Darcy dinner. He wanted to sit across a table from her and ask her questions about her life and pretend that today had been a date, pretend that at the end of the evening he'd kiss her under the stars and that tomorrow he'd do it again.

For a few hours today, he'd felt both awake and happy, and the confluence of those two feelings was so unusual over the past two years that he wanted to stretch today until it became tomorrow.

"I doubt there's much I can eat here," she replied off-handedly. "And I've already had French fries today."

"Oh, of course, sorry," Teagan said in automatic response. This place probably wasn't big enough to support a vegan restaurant.

"I think Kristin was making tempeh-stuffed peppers

today. We'll be in time for dinner back at the camp," she said, flicking a strand of hair behind her ear as she punched buttons on the gas pump.

"Sounds great," Teagan lied.

Darcy glanced up from the gas pump. "Do you not like stuffed peppers?"

"Who doesn't like stuffed peppers?" Teagan said, wishing he was better at lying.

Darcy's full lips pursed as she considered him and his stoic face. She looked away at the convenience store.

"Yeah, you're right, stuffed peppers suck. If you'll go buy some peanut butter crackers, we can stop in Bozeman and eat them on Pete's Hill while we watch the dog-walkers. Do you want to do that for dinner instead?"

"I'm fine, really. I'm not going to let you eat crackers for dinner."

Darcy laughed. "Wouldn't be the first time. I didn't become a vegetarian because I liked *vegetables*. Pop Tarts and peanut butter crackers were, like, a staple of my diet for years."

"You deserve better than peanut butter crackers for dinner," Teagan said before he thought about the judgment implied in that statement. It was true though. Darcy deserved many things she didn't seem to have. At a minimum, he thought Darcy ought to have at least one person who bought her plant-based dinners and told her she was wonderful on a regular basis, and the lack of a crowd of applicants for the position was mystifying to him.

Undeterred, Darcy briefly patted his chest as she walked past him to the windshield cleaning bin. "Get me Takis too, then."

Teagan nodded slowly, unhappy that he couldn't arrange

some big Nepalese spread like he might have done in New York but content at the thought of the rest of the evening with her. He had taken two steps away before Darcy looked up the windshield.

"Teagan," she said with a small frown. "You should try asking for the things you want sometimes."

"Of course," he said. Lying again. Why wouldn't he spare her the inconvenience of telling him no?

Thinking about Darcy had been a wonderful distraction from dwelling on his present in rehab with his baby sister and his past and future begging strangers to give him money, but he needed to remember to keep it at the thinking level. Too many men mistook the professional politeness of women in service jobs for interest, and even if *polite* rarely described Darcy, the last thing he wanted to do was make her job harder. But he could do what she asked him to do, at least, and that was a good line to toe.

He went into the convenience store, vowing to purchase every terrible nondairy snack food in the place. He loaded his arms with Oreos and potato chips of various textures. He hadn't seen Darcy drink anything but water, but he picked up a couple of bottles of flavored iced tea in the event that she wanted something sugary to wash down the pounds of sodium they were about to consume. He was in line to check out when he happened to look out the window and notice that Darcy had left the truck with the gas nozzle still in the tank. He looked behind him to check that she hadn't slipped into the store, then back out the window.

He was beginning to feel faintly alarmed when he spotted her all the way across the parking lot, in front of one of the bars. She was peering into the back window of a dusty red Subaru Outback. She straightened, fists curled at her sides.

Teagan had never seen a grown woman literally stomp her foot on the ground in anger before. Her angry cursing was audible even from inside the convenience mart. Darcy spun on her heel and marched into the bar behind her, fists curled at her sides.

"Excuse me," Teagan told the startled clerk, dropping his armload of snacks on a case of bottled water and dashing for the exit.

twelve

TRAVIS WAS SEATED AT THE BAR WATCHING THE game, blissfully unaware that he was the worst man in the world. He was a big cornfed farm boy from eastern Washington in a sheepskin-lined jacket and Mariners hat, and he had a friend with him, nearly a duplicate but with perhaps ten extra years and a few hundred more cans of Skoal behind him. Neither noticed Darcy come in. They were absorbed in the game and the pitcher of beer in front of them.

Darcy wedged herself between Travis and the empty stool next to him, kicking his boot as she did. He was slow to respond to her, and when he did, he lurched in that high-momentum way of very drunk people. The pitcher of beer in front of him was still half full, but the game was in extra innings; he must have been there all afternoon.

"Darcy! Hey, babe. What are you doing here?" he asked when he finally found his focus, blinking bloodshot blue eyes at her. He turned to his companion, knocking him with an elbow. "Jared. Jared, look, it's the girl I lived with last winter."

Travis let a big obnoxious grin spread across his face, as though Darcy had not been leaving voicemails threatening increasingly creative vengeance upon him for the past month.

"Hello, Travis," she managed to get out in a conversational tone of voice. *Catch more flies with honey, et cetera*, she thought.

Jared leaned down the bar, giving Darcy a once-over and an appreciative leer. "Damn, Travis," he whistled. "Can you hook me up with that?"

Travis smirked, eyes flicking over her. "Yeah, you look nice. Always thought you'd clean up okay. You wanna get a seat?"

Darcy growled deep in her throat, counting to ten in her mind. She just needed the car. She just needed the car, and then she could leave. If Travis gave her the car, they were fair and square, and she wouldn't have to carve all the weeks of aggravation he'd given her out of his carcass.

She stuck out her palm. "I assume you came to drop off my car?" she gritted out. "I can take it right now."

Travis drew a very apologetic look over his face as he patted his jacket pocket. "Oh, hey, I was going to call you about that tomorrow. The logging gig fell through, actually, so I'm headed to interview for another snowmobile rental job in the park."

"Fine," Darcy said, hand still out. "I don't care. Give me the keys."

Travis fixed her with a look of mild contempt, as though she were the one who didn't understand what was happening. "No, but that means I need the car this winter. I can't sell it to you."

Darcy felt cold fury creeping up her body, twining around her ankles. Another ten count. "You mean you're going to give me my money back?" she asked, words precise.

Travis snorted. "Babe, that's like ten thousand dollars. I don't have ten thousand dollars. I'll have to pay ya back. Are you working in the park again this winter? If you want to shack up again, that'll help save on rent."

Darcy slammed her fist down on the bar, hard enough to make the pitchers of beer vibrate. "No, I don't want to live within a hundred miles of you, ever again. I want *my car*. The one you already sold me!"

Travis's friend Jared chuckled loudly. "Christ, your girl is spicy, bud."

"I know, right? Why is it that hot girls are always off the crazy curve too?" His finger spun a casual circle next to his head, like he'd lowered himself for her, like he hadn't been absolutely panting for her before she got lonely and vulnerable on the weekend of her thirtieth birthday.

"The keys. To my car," Darcy insisted, feeling her control fray to a slender thread.

"Darcy," he said, turning back to her and speaking as though to a small child. "I didn't sell you jack shit. I didn't sign jack shit. You've got jack shit in writing, so you're just gonna have to chill out and wait till I have the cash to pay you back."

"The hell you didn't!" Darcy spat, jabbing a finger at Travis's chest. "We had a deal, you fucking weasel. I'm going to call the finance company—"

"And tell them what, you want your money back? Good fuckin' luck," Travis said, his wide pink face turning mean.

Rage dimmed her vision to a hazy red as visions of knocking over the bar stool danced through her head. Darcy found that she had taken a grip on Travis's jacket when abruptly Teagan was there, shoving the two of them apart. She hadn't even noticed him come into the bar.

"Hey," Teagan said in a very calm voice, tone soothing

and tranquil as he looked between Darcy and Travis. "Hey, let's talk for a minute. We'll take a lap, and then we'll talk."

Darcy sputtered as Travis drunkenly craned his neck back to assess the newcomer.

"The fuck are you?" Travis demanded, instinctively suspicious of a new male in his space. Then he took in Teagan's running shoes, Yale sweatshirt, and chinos, and he guffawed, dismissing him. "Damn, girl, you must be pretty hard up if you're fucking tourists these days," he sneered to Darcy. "Well, if you change your mind about this winter, you know I can fix that for you too."

That volley snapped Darcy's last thread of control. She grabbed the pitcher of beer, mind quickly evaluating the variable satisfaction of dumping it over Travis's head and clocking him with it, but just as she'd tentatively decided on the first option, strong arms encircled her from behind and lifted. Beer splashed all over her stomach as she dropped the pitcher.

Darcy instinctively threw her head back and kicked with her legs. Teagan cursed when the back of her head connected with his chin, but he didn't drop her. He picked her up in a tight bear hug and staggered backward to the door, Darcy still swearing and flailing to get free. Travis and Jared cracked up at the sight, pounding on the bar from the joy of watching Darcy hauled outside.

She was going to kill them. Both of them. Teagan too. Teagan *especially*, the traitor.

Teagan was stronger than she'd thought, because even though she was fighting like a cat in a sack, Teagan got her most of the way across the parking lot before he set her down on her feet. He jumped backward like he'd just pulled the pin out of a grenade and held out his arms defensively.

"Darcy, listen for one second," he said in that same gentle little voice as before.

"He stole my car!" Darcy yelled, pointing at the bar.

"I heard. I know he stole your car—"

Darcy snarled at Teagan for talking to her like *she* was the irrational one.

"Get out of my way. *Get.* I need to deal with this," she gritted through closed teeth.

Teagan took a step to put himself between Darcy and the bar.

"Okay, two things though. First, that guy is bigger than me and *definitely* bigger than you. Please do not get me beaten to a pulp tonight? It's been a good day."

"Then stay outside," Darcy snapped, trying to sidestep Teagan. She had no time for misplaced chivalry, and she could take care of herself.

"I really can't," Teagan said. "It's a guy thing. If you go back in there, I have to go back in there, and he's going to kick my ass. I can't even make a fist. See?"

He held up one hand with the thumb tucked under his fingers.

Darcy halted, the absurdity making her snort-laugh despite herself.

"I'll protect you," she said, even though a little of her anger had already trickled out. "I'll get our bear spray from the truck."

"Good plan, good plan, good thinking," Teagan said, still soothing. He opened his big golden eyes wider. "But listen to my second point."

Darcy scuffed one boot in the pavement, thinking about how much she wanted to rub beer into Travis's eyes. "Yeah?"

"Are these the car keys you needed?" Teagan asked, shaking a set out of his sleeve.

He held a Jesus-fish-shaped bottle opener attached to a Subaru key. He pressed the lock button to make the headlights of the car flash. It worked. They had the keys.

Darcy gasped. "Oh my God. Oh my *God*. How did you get these?"

Teagan shrugged, a small smile twisting the corners of his mouth. "Taking car keys from drunk people is a breakout skill of mine."

The cascade of emotions over such a short time period had made Darcy's knees almost wobbly. Anger was totally gone. Embarrassment was beginning to creep in. Gratitude and relief were warring for top position. She compensated for it by jumping to lock her arms around Teagan's neck. He staggered back in surprise but got a leg planted and an arm around her waist to hold her up. She buried her face in the side of his neck. "Thank you," she whispered. *"Thank you!"*

Even after a day in the woods, he still smelled so nice, like shaving cream and expensive cologne. While Darcy was wearing half a pitcher of beer. But he didn't try to wiggle away, so she held on and swayed back and forth. After a full month of feeling like a mark because Travis had duped her, after three months of feeling like a sucker because the Goederts had duped her, after years of dead-end jobs, after, after, after, any triumph was a heady shot of victory.

She found one more emotion in the stack and grabbed on to it. She went up on her toes, slid one hand down to Teagan's cheek to turn his head, and pressed her lips to his.

She meant the kiss to be brief. She thought it would be, anyway.

It wasn't brief.

Darcy sometimes wondered whether she had a lower back tattoo, obtained during some forgotten, inebriated shore leave, that instructed anyone in a position to see it to slap her ass and call her names. That's how men typically proceeded when she gave them the opportunity, or even if she really hadn't.

She didn't mind rough stuff too much, and God knew she was Built Ford Tough and all that, but it had given her certain expectations. She expected Teagan to slip her some tongue and haul her against the side of the nearest pickup truck. Which would have been fine. She would have given him a couple of seconds to enjoy the standard kissing-Darcy-in-a-parking-lot experience, then punched him in the shoulder and called him her hero to bring things to a close.

Instead Teagan went very still, too long to be from mere shock. And his lips were soft on hers, not stiff from surprise. He'd realized he was kissing her, but he was being wonderfully, unexpectedly careful about it. He brought his arms around her but let his hands just barely frame her back, one fisted and resting against the curve and the other sweeping up to gently tangle in her hair. Darcy half wanted to break away and laugh about Teagan kissing her like a Disney prince while she was damp with stale beer, but she couldn't, because it was *working* on her.

She sighed and parted her lips, and Teagan pulled her closer and closer until she was balanced against his chest, fingertips caught in the downy hair at the back of his neck, tongue in *his* mouth. He kissed her the way she wanted kissing to be: its own destination, not a trail marker on the way to some place he'd rather end up. Only when she started to feel dizzy from not breathing properly did she pull back, still tingly and aware of the long line of his body.

Teagan immediately released her, and she braced for him

to say something to ruin it, because beautiful, delicate moments like this never lasted. But he only beamed at her under half-lidded eyes.

"Wow," he said, voice barely audible through his long exhale.

Darcy's cheeks hurt from grinning at him. For once, everything had broken in her favor. For once, the bread had fallen margarine-up.

She wobbled there against him, struck with amazement that Teagan knew how to kiss like that; Teagan no doubt stuck in place with amazement that she'd let him.

She had to say something. They'd be there forever if she didn't.

"Do you wanna . . . go get a drink or something?" she asked.

Teagan cleared his throat, cheeks turning pale pink. "I'd . . . probably better not."

Oh, right. Darcy flushed, because she'd completely forgotten.

"That was a test," she lied. "Um, good job. Very good job."

First rule of rehab, probably: don't buy drinks for the alcoholics.

Teagan gave her a tight smile, then tossed the car keys in his hand. "So, which one do you want me to drive back? Probably better get away before that guy realizes he's keyless."

Darcy realized that she still had two hands on Teagan's chest. She gingerly slid them off, feeling absurdly disoriented, because she'd forgotten about the car too.

"Um," she said intelligently. She took the keys from Teagan's hand to give herself a moment. She stuffed them into her pocket. "So, I can't drive it away right now," she said with reluctance. "I don't have anything saying that I own it. Travis is probably not enough of an asshole to call the cops, but I didn't think he was enough of one to keep the car in the first place, so . . ." She thought hard. Maybe she ought to just key the car and toss the fob into the sewer. No, be smart for once, Darcy. "Maybe I can get something from the finance company, and if the car is still here in a couple days, I can drive it away then." Travis might not have the cash for a locksmith.

Teagan's grin widened. "Let me just move the car to the VIP parking in front of the casino. There's a tow truck lurking across the street. You'll have to pay to get your car out of the tow lot, but at least you'll know where it is."

Darcy gasped in delight at the plan. She shook his arm in agreement and then, thinking better of it, grabbed him by the sweatshirt. As she yanked him closer to kiss him a second time, she ruefully thought that Kristin had been right.

Darcy was definitely going to make some mistakes with Teagan.

thirteen

TEAGAN FELT BUZZED, LIKE HE'D SPLIT A WHOLE bottle of wine with his date and now the waiter was coming around with the dessert menu. His face was warm. His hands were heavy and loose where they rested on Darcy's hips. He could only faintly remember feeling this good, but it wasn't owing to any intoxicants.

The passenger door of the pickup truck was open, and the cab interior light was on, because when Darcy pulled into the wellness retreat's front drive and killed the engine, he'd thought the evening was over. But when he'd moved to go, Darcy had wordlessly swung a leg over the center console, landed in his lap, and kissed him breathless for so long that he thought the truck's battery would soon give out.

When Darcy untucked her shirt from her jeans, he broke lip contact for a moment and cast a worried glance at the residence. Anyone could look out and see them, and he didn't want Darcy to catch hell from her employer.

"Um," he said, thumbs reflexively smoothing across the bare skin exposed by her movement. She was nothing but silk and muscle to his touch. Darcy pressed into the caress, leaning forward until his hand slipped up her ribcage to rest against the lower curve of her breast.

"This okay?" she asked, running the tip of her tongue over her lower lip. His gaze snagged on the sight.

"Oh, yeah, yeah it is," Teagan said fervently, if not very articulately. "But, um—"

He jerked his chin at the lit windows even as his breath swelled in his chest.

Darcy followed his glance at the building.

"Who cares," she said, sweeping her hair back over her shoulders. "I'm off duty till tomorrow at noon."

"But I'm—" He cut off. He didn't want to remind her why he was here, or even why she thought he was here. He wanted *here* to be limited to the cab of this truck, the points of contact where her breast was in his hand and her hips were flush against his own.

"Right now you're just this hot guy I picked up at a lumberjack bar," Darcy finished for him, grinning even though he was the one who'd carried *her* out. She pressed another leisurely kiss against his mouth in a slow twist that somehow managed to make him aware of the promise of both her slick tongue and sharp teeth.

Teagan thought that was his cue to make a wood joke, but his mind wasn't really working on a verbal level. He buried his face against her exposed throat instead, and Darcy made an appreciative noise when his lips brushed the dip in her collarbone.

If lumberjacks got picked up in bars by women like Darcy, he was going to rethink both his drinking habits and his career choices. As soon as he could think again.

"Unless—this isn't bad for your sobriety, is it?" Darcy asked, voice suddenly concerned.

"I'm not an alcoholic," Teagan said directly into her skin.

Darcy made a noise of disagreement.

"And I can't drink while you kiss me," Teagan quickly suggested, feeling he'd made a brave and insightful point.

Darcy nodded, throat still against his mouth, and indicated her apparent concurrence by reaching for the buttons at the neck of her shirt. Teagan's eyes widened.

This surely couldn't go much further tonight, he told himself, both in reassurance and warning. *But perhaps just a little further.* He caught another glimpse of blue satin and slid further down in the passenger seat.

He was about to pull the door closed to save both the battery powering the interior cab light and Darcy's modesty when they froze at the sound of a window sliding open.

"Darcy!" someone hissed. "What are you *doing?*"

Teagan lifted his hands off Darcy.

"Shit," Darcy said, sliding off his lap and through the cracked passenger door. Her boots landed on the gravel of the drive a moment later.

Teagan looked back at the building, thankfully recognizing the appalled face of the camp's cook in the upstairs window, not that of Darcy's boss.

He took a brief moment to mourn the loss of Darcy's warm weight from his lap, assessed that there was no awkward lumber situation going on there (small blessings from the SSRIs), and followed Darcy out of the pickup truck.

He glanced around the front yard. Kristin was gone from the window. Darcy was already circling around the back of the residence toward the kitchen. She shook her head at him when he moved to pursue her, inclining it instead at the front door. He halted.

"Good night," he said, as loudly as he dared.

Darcy looked back and smiled but didn't respond, and in another moment, she was gone.

Teagan took a little sidestep on the gravel drive and linked his fingers over the top of his head. He let out all his breath in a long whistling sigh. The day had ended as abruptly as it had begun. Falling out of bed to nearly falling out of a truck.

At no point since nearly passing out on the subway platform almost a month previous had he known what would happen to him next. Even today was supposed to have been an ordeal in the sauna and then stuffed peppers, and instead he'd been swept away on a small adventure involving gray wolves, a bar fight, and getting to first base in front of a bingo hall. Then second in a pickup truck.

What would happen tomorrow? There had been an implication in her backward glance that Darcy would have lingered if she could, and that made him excited to see what the next day would bring. He had absolutely no idea what that would be, and the thought was energizing.

Good things rarely made it to his calendar. His calendar usually held the things that he would rather have avoided, like silent auctions and awards luncheons. Tiny electronic markers of misery. His calendar didn't hold anything he looked forward to.

Well, he could do his best to clear that calendar so that Darcy was free to make additional plans, regardless of whether they involved wildness or wildlife. Teagan would spend tonight resolving the mystery conference call scheduled for Monday morning, and he'd tell Nora and Rose he'd be out here for at least another couple of weeks. Anything else was up to Darcy.

He decided to sneak into Rachel's office to see if the CIO had responded to his messages. Sneaking in to use the computer was a mild offense, but he wouldn't order hookers and blow. He'd listen to his messages, and then he would finish Darcy's applications. He smiled, imagining her face tomorrow morning when he reported that it was all taken care of.

He climbed the stairs, alert to avoid detection by any of the staff, but from the other side of the building he could hear Rachel loudly informing Darcy of the presence of an angry raccoon in the yoga shed, so he supposed that the raccoon situation had everyone else occupied. He quietly let himself into Rachel's office.

To his surprise, Sloane was seated at the desk there, most of her hair swept up into a topknot and secured in place with a pair of mechanical pencils. Her harassed look at the opening door was replaced with a familiar guilty grimace when she saw it was him. This was the look Sloane wore when he caught her doing something she wasn't supposed to do, like forging his signature on her report card or sneaking out of the house in their mother's vintage Gucci boots.

Before he could speak, she preempted him.

"Oh hey! How was your day?"

"Good," Teagan said, undistracted. "What are you—"

"Did you see beavers?"

"They weren't out," Teagan said, noticing how she minimized her email account on the computer. "But we saw some wolves."

"Wolves! That's awesome. I've always wanted to pet one. Do you think they feel more like corgis or like shelties?"

"Sloane. What are you doing in here?"

His sister screwed up her face defensively. "Emails."

Sloane, like most others of her generation, had the communication habits of a crime lord under FBI scrutiny—no phone calls or email.

"What about," he said casually, leaning into the door frame.

"Some work stuff."

"Work stuff? I didn't think you had a job."

"I mean, I don't, really. It's not a big deal."

Teagan looked at her suspiciously. Sloane took no longer to crack than she had at age five on the subject of *what happened to the rug*. She wasn't good at keeping secrets.

"So, you know how you've been asking me if I wanted to start working at the foundation," she said.

Teagan had to go months back in his memory, but he had suggested that Sloane might enjoy earning money at one of the summer programs the foundation sponsored rather than take another unpaid internship shadowing entertainment executives of questionable morality back in LA. Prepping paper-mache animals, he'd meant, or making sack lunches.

"Yes," he said, eyes narrowing.

"I started talking to Rose about what I could do from here, and she's had me make some fundraising calls." Her face reflected a bit of fragile pride. "Like, I got over fifty K this week just by calling up some of Mom's friends."

"What?" he exploded. "Since when? Why didn't you tell me? Why didn't *Rose* tell me?"

Setting aside the issue of his sister being an art history student and not a professional, their mother's friends were a collection of aging socialites pickled in vodka and hardened by decades of debauchery. Teagan didn't want Sloane anywhere near that mess, especially while she was dealing with her own substance issues.

"Since you've been *here* and not *there*, and you're not *supposed* to be working, according to your *doctors*, I asked Rose

if there was anything I could do to help, and I've been working with her. She says I've done a good job, and I have a talent
for it, and if I wanted to, she'd bring me on full time this fall."

Teagan stared at her. "You're going back to school this
fall," he said, focusing on the most urgent of the unpleasant
disclosures she'd just made.

"I already missed the first week. I'm going to take the
semester off, and this way I'll be there in New York when
you get back, and I can help with fundraising. Like, I went
to high school with June Marino's daughter, and I know
she's got her name on the wall at the symphony—"

"June Marino! I found her and Mom passed out in our
jacuzzi at six on a Sunday morning once. And still she tried
to cry all over me at Mom's funeral and say she never saw it
coming."

Sloane shrugged dramatically. "So she probably feels guilty,
right? That's worth at least twenty grand in blood money.
For the kids, you know. Remember them? Little cherubs who
want to go to pottery class instead of watching TV alone all
summer? According to Rose, you need the cash."

"I don't want you involved in making fundraising calls.
This is serious—"

"Of course it's serious!" she snapped at him. "It was serious enough that you nearly gave yourself a freaking heart
attack over it. And I am serious about it. I can be a very serious person!"

Teagan dragged his fingers through his hair, trying to
gather the words to warn Sloane off the disaster that had ruined his life—no, wait, where had that come from? He was
lucky to have his job. Surely he ought to be happy Sloane was
interested in a real job—without putting her efforts down.

He finally settled on, "Rose doesn't actually have hiring

authority. We'd have to go through normal channels." And Teagan did all the hiring. That would do it.

"She seemed like she knew what she was talking about. She thought I'd get the job." Sloane's face dared him to contradict either of them.

Teagan didn't usually contradict Rose. Nora, the board chair, had made him hire Rose when he started as CEO, because he was nothing but a municipal bond trader with a slightly dusty MBA, and Rose had worked in wealth management for most of her career. But Rose had never previously tried to undercut him or acted with anything but icy professionalism.

Of course, he'd never had to call her while having a psychiatric episode before, so perhaps this was what he ought to expect from here on out.

Teagan sat down in the chair in the corner and bent until his elbows hit his knees, trying not to imagine things getting *worse* at the office when he returned.

"It's not that I think you wouldn't be good at it. I don't want you uprooting your life any more than you already have. I just want things to go back to normal when I get out of here," he said.

Sloane snorted. "Don't sound so eager to leave your comfy tent and your hot maintenance girl. Your normal life gave you panic attacks."

"You know what I mean," Teagan said, although he wasn't sure he did.

"Yeah," Sloane said, face still skeptical. She spun her chair and kicked the sole of his shoe with her own. "Wouldn't you be glad to get me away from the LA party scene, anyway?"

"Not really. I've heard that it is also possible to purchase cocaine in New York."

"Oh, well, fine. I guess I'll follow career plan B. Model for a few years, marry rich, then become someone's muse," Sloane said in an airy tone.

Teagan stared at her in consternation, because she didn't really sound like she was joking.

She snorted. "Fundraising it is, then. Okay, so when *we* get back to New York, I won't do coke anymore, and you'll take it easy, all right? Deal?"

Teagan couldn't imagine what that meant for him. He wasn't doing any more than the things he'd committed to doing. But he was feeling a lot better for a month in the woods, and he hoped that the long break was all he'd really needed.

"Deal," Teagan said, standing up. "For now, though, you're done. And I need the computer."

Sloane pursed her lips. "Does Darcy know you're using the computer?"

"Yes. It's for her."

Sloane waggled her eyebrows at him. "So you had a *nice time*, huh?"

"Good *night*, Sloane," he said, pulling her chair away from the computer desk. "I'll see you tomorrow."

"So you're actually coming to something?" Sloane asked, stalling, eyebrows raised. "Papermaking? Yoga?"

"Breakfast, at least," he said. Who knew what Darcy had planned for the next day, but he couldn't wait to find out.

Sloane finally relented and released custody of the computer. She squeezed Teagan's shoulder when she passed him on her way out the door though, which was as good as a bear hug for their family's typical level of demonstration.

Once alone with the computer, Teagan cracked his knuckles and dove into the triple-redundant portal for seasonal park hiring. He uploaded Darcy's new resume, entered the exact same information on the resume line by line into the series of radial prompts, and then confirmed the same information on the specific pages for a half dozen positions that might offer Darcy the opportunity to drop some wolf knowledge on the park visitors. It took a couple of hours, but it was before midnight when he finished. Almost two a.m. in New York. Nothing from Rose still when he checked his messages, which was unusual, even for a Saturday night. She was usually more responsive than that. He'd have to check again tomorrow.

The rush of cool air when he left the building was steadying. It reminded him of where he was and where he wasn't. The camp closed in three weeks. That would get Sloane well past thirty days of sobriety and Teagan as well rested and grounded as it was possible for him to be. People took sabbaticals around his age, didn't they? He would never have scheduled one in the middle of a fundraising shortfall, but it sounded like Rose was on top of that, at least.

So there were three weeks left with Darcy. He'd never set out to have a short-term romance before—he dated women one at a time, with the idea that it *could* get serious until it *didn't*—but he didn't see how it could be bad for either of them, so long as he didn't do anything indiscreet to affect her job. And then she'd be off to her next gig, a better one if he could help it. Maybe she'd send him wolf pictures when he was back in New York. Maybe he'd come back to the park as a visitor this winter, and she'd want to see him.

These were unexpectedly peaceful thoughts as he reached his cabin. The bed was still unmade from tumbling out of it this morning, but someone had come in and left a tray with a smoothie in front of his bed. It was the same thick sludge of indeterminate color that he'd come to expect, but to-night he'd merited an extra dollop of whipped coconut cream and half a fresh Rainier cherry on top of it. Some-how, he knew Darcy had been responsible for the upgrade, and he grinned.

He sat on the edge of the bed to toe off his sneakers, and his eyes fell on a new pile of paper on top of the dresser. Mail. Rose hadn't seen fit to give him his emails back, but he'd called his building manager to get his mail forwarded from his condo as soon as he got here. This was the first batch to arrive.

He stripped to his boxer briefs and got ready for bed, took a wincing gulp of the smoothie, and sat back down to sort through the pile. Some men's health magazines—ha, should have made more time to read those—alumni fundraising ap-peals, invitations to charity events, junk, junk—one envelope bearing the foundation's seal, stuffed to over-bursting.

Teagan tore that one open one-handed, metal straw bal-anced in his lips as he began to read. Mostly monthly finan-cials. Their cash position was getting really bad, but he'd known that before he ended up here. There was also a note on the chairman's letterhead tossed in loose behind all the printouts. The letter was dated a week previous and penned in Nora's artistic, looping scrawl.

Dear TVZ—

> *Haven't been able to get good intelligence on how long you're planning to be out. Heard from Rose that U R very ill. So sorry to hear that!!*
> *Asking the Board 2 tee up some asset sales to free cash this fall. Hard assets = art portfolio. Need you back next*

week to discuss, or I'm recommending 2 Board we put Rose in as CEO.

Understand if you can't make it. Your health comes first!!

XOXOXO, Nora

He recognized an ultimatum when he saw one—come back now or watch Nora liquidate the foundation.

Shit.

Oh shit.

The straw fell out from between his lips to the unfinished pine boards of the floor, where, by the time Teagan found it, the kale and cherry juice had already stained the wood. He'd been too busy packing to notice.

fourteen

MANY RUSHED FOOTSTEPS DOWNSTAIRS STAR-
tled Darcy long before she wanted to leave the bedroom she
shared with Kristin. She'd been up until nearly two in the
morning dealing with the raccoon and then laundering
towels, since Rachel had *forgotten* to do it and several guests
were out of fresh linens.

But at just after seven in the morning, Darcy pulled out
her earbuds, turned off her favorite geology podcast, and
went downstairs to see what the commotion was. It took
a few long syrupy seconds to make sense of the scene: Teagan and his sister in Rachel's glass-walled office with both
of the Goederts. Teagan was the only one dressed in street
clothes—Sloane was in bird-print pajamas, Dr. Goedert
in sweats, and Rachel was wearing an oversized terry-cloth
robe over God knew what—but the crowd was arguing
vigorously with each other. There was a stack of paperwork on the desk and a pair of suitcases at the entrance to
the room.

Oh. Teagan was leaving.

Anger immediately kindled, like a spark on dry wood, because what was he thinking? He couldn't leave! He couldn't even admit he had a problem yet! He didn't have any kind of plan for how he was going to stay sober once he went home. If he was bailing on rehab this impulsively, he was definitely going to fall right back into his old habits as soon as he got home. Darcy went stiff, nearly incandescent with anger, because didn't he realize this was how people died?

She looked right at that bright, burning anger on his behalf, because if she looked away from it, she'd have to see how angry she was at herself for expecting anything more from him.

Kristin had warned her, even. These guys weren't reliable.

Darcy stood in the stairwell with her fists curled, trying to pick up her feet and go back to her bedroom. As though sensing her disapproval, Teagan turned his head and saw her watching them. His expression changed from annoyance to one of quiet regret. That only made her angrier, because that meant he knew he was wrong to leave. Leave rehab. Leave her.

She'd known better than to think he'd do anything but disappoint her.

Darcy spun on her heel, ready to make herself scarce until after he'd gone. She didn't know whether he'd planned to say goodbye before he left, but she'd take some spiteful satisfaction in denying him the opportunity. She started back up the stairs, but Sloane had seen her too. The girl pushed the glass office door open and rushed out, calling Darcy's name. She caught up to Darcy halfway back to the landing.

"Wait. Help. Help me," Sloane said, grabbing the sleeve of Darcy's thermal knit shirt. "Help me convince him to stay."

"I'm off duty till noon," Darcy snapped.

Sloane tensed her shoulders nearly to her ears. She looked back at her brother, face full of worry, then back up at Darcy. "Help me anyway, please?"

"What makes you think he'd listen to me?"

If the guy wasn't even going to stick around to see if she'd sleep with him, she didn't see why Teagan would be moved by Darcy's less-than-legendary powers of persuasion.

She'd thought he liked her. She'd thought he *really* liked her.

"He's pissed at me," Sloane said, looking teary and harassed. "Because I didn't tell him about this stupid board meeting."

"He's quitting rehab to go to a meeting?" Darcy asked incredulously. No. That had to be an excuse. Addicts quit rehab to go back to their addictions.

Teagan had followed Sloane to the foot of the stairs. He stood there silently, hands on his hips.

Sloane turned around. "I'm coming with you," she said. "I'll get my stuff."

"You are *not*," Teagan said, breaking out a very *dad* kind of voice. "You are going to stay here and finish rehab." It didn't work on Sloane, and it only straightened Darcy's back, because if he could see that his sister needed to stay and work on her substance issues, why couldn't he see that he did too?

Darcy brushed past Sloane and marched down the stairs.

"You're making a mistake," she told Teagan, poking him in the chest. "You'll be back to square zero in a month."

He shook his head, but he didn't argue with her. "I'm sorry" was all he said.

That only made her angrier. "No you're not, because if you were sorry, you wouldn't do it."

"I meant, I'm sorry I won't be here to help you finish clearing the new trail. I finished your job applications though. The password for the account is on a red sticky note by the computer."

Because you always do what you said you'd do, Darcy thought with a sharp throb of pain. And he'd said he'd help her apply to a better job in Yellowstone, but he'd never said he'd stay and pursue whatever small sweet thing they'd been building, no matter what it had *felt* like he was promising when she kissed him.

"As if that even matters. Do you want to end up in the hospital again?"

"I have to go. The board is going to fire me if I'm not back this week, and they'll be right to do it, because our cash position—"

"Rose said she has a proposal for the board," Sloane interjected. "She said she was handling it. She said you *don't* have to go."

"Rose is the one gunning for my job," Teagan said, his voice rising in volume. "And the chair told me to get back to work." He looked exhausted, now that Darcy examined him more closely. His hair was damp from the shower, and he had a little cut on his neck from shaving, but he had bags under his eyes and lines of fatigue around his mouth like he hadn't slept since she last saw him.

Darcy wanted to shake him, and she also wanted to wrap her arms around his neck and hold on, because at some level he obviously knew he was making the wrong choice.

"Is someone going to show up and arrest you if you're not there? Are they going to send security to drag you back? Who is *making* you go? I'll fight them for you," Darcy said.

Teagan exhaled in aggravation, hands shoved in his pockets. "I've spent the last two years trying to rescue this organization—"

"Like *you* can't get another job," she said scornfully. "Mr. Yale sweatshirt."

He bit down on the side of that full lower lip, face hurt and conflicted.

"You can't think that anything is going to be different when you get back to New York," Darcy said, internally alarmed by how thick her voice had gotten. He was wandering off into the woods without bear spray again, and Darcy wasn't going to be there to save his ass this time. "We hadn't even gotten through all of the third step on the podcast."

"I have to go anyway," he said. He gave a little twitch of his shoulders like half a shrug. "I'm sorry, Darcy," he said again. "I didn't find out about this until last night. I wish the timing had been different, obviously."

Darcy didn't know whether he was wishing yesterday away or just saying that his worthless meeting shouldn't be next week, but she opened her mouth to yell at him regardless.

"You should come with us," Sloane said from behind her, her voice that of a woman who had finally had a good idea.

"What?" Teagan asked.

"What?" said Darcy.

Sloane licked her lips, glancing between Darcy and her brother. "Teagan should stay here. In the program. But if he doesn't, you could, you know, come along and keep doing whatever you're doing—"

"Didn't work," Darcy said bitterly. "Look, he's going."

"No, no, but you've been great! He's doing a lot better. It has to be because of all the stuff he's doing for you. You could do all that tree programming you've done for Teagan, but, like, in New York instead of here—" Sloane said, eyes wide and insistent.

Darcy frowned at her. "But I don't know if the wilderness education would work if we're not actually in the woods," she said. "And we only just started getting into his alcohol abuse yesterday."

Sloane stared back, face going blank. "You've been treating Teagan like he's an alcoholic," she said slowly.

"Well, of course I have," Darcy said. "That's why he's here, right? But we're only on episode three of *Sober Sam's Sobriety Podcast*."

The girl blinked several times. "And you think he needs to finish that."

"I don't," Teagan said, ignored by both Darcy and Sloane.

"He's feeling better because he's eating well, exercising, and not drinking. But he needs to think about his sober lifestyle before he goes back to his real life," Darcy said, shooting Teagan another insistent look.

"Okay. Yes. That's it. You should come with us and make him," Sloane said, nodding emphatically.

"Like a sober companion?" Darcy asked, finally catching on.

"A what?" Teagan asked but was again ignored by the two women.

Some of the guests who came through the wellness retreat

left with sober companions provided by their employers. The idea, as best Darcy understood it, was that someone had to follow the recovering addicts around and make sure they didn't fall back into bad habits when they went home. Easy work, Darcy had thought, client depending.

Sloane's attitude was nervous, as she was obviously thinking very hard under pressure. "Yes," she said. "Like a sober companion."

"I don't need a sober companion," Teagan said. "I'm not—"

"Shh, be quiet, Step One," Darcy said, sticking her hand out behind her, palm out. This was something to be negotiated with Sloane, apparently. He *needed* to stay in rehab. But if he wouldn't stay in rehab, could rehab go home with him?

Darcy licked her lips, thinking hard and fast herself. She'd quit this terrible job for half a bag of stale Takis. And the only part of the job she'd ever *liked* was the wilderness education angle, the sole beneficiary of which was folding his arms across his chest in misery behind her.

She just had to remain alert to pitfalls. Run the traps on this. This situation wasn't Teagan's fault, not really— he'd come here for help. It was Darcy's fault for forgetting that he needed her help first and foremost, for getting her expectations up, for losing track of how this would inevitably end.

Maybe it didn't have to end just yet though.

"For how long are we talking about?" Darcy asked Sloane.

Sloane rubbed the back of her neck. "Whatever's typical, I guess?"

Darcy had no idea what was typical. "Ninety days after rehab, I think?" That would get her to the winter season in Yellowstone, if she could swing this. The winds of her

mood had begun to shift again. Ninety days sounded perfect. She'd never even had a relationship last ninety days, so
the odds were she'd be ready for a new job by then.

"You can't just drop everything for me," Teagan said, but
he'd been making so little sense that morning that Darcy
lifted her hand a little further and plopped it right over his
mouth. Darcy would have immediately stuck out her tongue
in his position, but he just went shocked and still.

So dense. He'd been the one telling her to quit her job
yesterday. This seemed like a wonderful opportunity to do
that.

"Yeah, that sounds about right," Sloane said, scrunching
up her nose meaningfully at her brother.

"And does this position pay?" Darcy followed up. "More
than room and board," she amended, just to set a floor for
her expectations.

"I mean, of course, yeah," Sloane said, looking a little
green. "Um. Who usually pays?"

"Employers," Darcy said. "At least, record labels and
production companies do. Or insurance, maybe?"

"Right," Sloane said, on more secure footing now. "Teagan's got good insurance. And even if he didn't, I'm sure the
foundation would pay. Since he is, you know, the CEO. And
a Van Zijl. And he needs to be sober to *do his job*, if that's so
important." She glared at him over Darcy's shoulder.

Darcy nodded slowly.

She was already shoveling dirt over the hurt she'd felt
when she saw him ready to leave. Because she'd known better than to get attached. Like Kristin said, these guys weren't
reliable. Expecting Teagan to sweep her off her feet was
asking for disappointment.

But there was the other piece still, where she'd thought she was making a difference in his life. Helping him. That her job had some meaning to it.

This didn't change that. If anything, Teagan's overconfidence in his sobriety spoke to her abilities. She'd probably be decent as a sober companion, maybe even good at it. After all, she'd seen Teagan in a bar fight. She could keep the booze out of his hands by main force, if necessary.

"Okay," Darcy said, having thought it through. "That sounds good to me. I can do that." She dropped her hand from Teagan's mouth and turned to see how much longer she and Sloane were going to have to argue with him.

He didn't immediately say anything. He was pale except for two bright spots of pink over his cheekbones, lips now pressed hard together. He looked between Darcy and Sloane, then back at Darcy, gaze hanging on her own.

"Give us a minute?" Darcy asked Sloane, who nodded vigorously.

"Cool, I'm gonna go pack," the girl said, squeezing past Darcy on the stairs.

Teagan's expression shifted, and Darcy thought he might try to object. So she grabbed him by the front of his sweatshirt, squaring up with him.

"Do you agree with this plan?" Darcy demanded.

Teagan's mouth flexed again as he unclenched his jaw muscles.

"You really want to go to New York?" he asked when he'd gathered himself, voice very soft.

Darcy nearly shrugged, because she was neutral at best on New York. What she wanted was to go with him and finish what they'd started.

"We don't have to go to New York," she said. "August's also the great wildebeest migration in Masai Mara. We could go see that instead. Would be more fun."

Teagan exhaled in faint amusement. "I have to go home. I meant, do you really want to come with me?"

Darcy narrowed her eyes at him.

"So, that depends," she said. "Are you serious about your sobriety? I'm not coming along to watch your downward spiral."

"I . . . am going to stay sober," Teagan said, sounding evasive.

"For how long?"

"Indefinitely?" When he answered, it still sounded like a question. Darcy frowned.

"I meant, forever," he quickly added. "That's fine. I know I can't drink. But. Ah. You're going to stay in my house?"

"Well, yeah," Darcy said. "I can't do my job remotely. And room and board are included, remember. So I'll go wherever you go, for the next ninety days."

"Right, of course," he said, getting even paler, if that was possible.

Darcy shook him by the handful of his sweatshirt she had in her fist.

"Listen. Here are my other conditions for coming along. You can check out of rehab. But you are going to listen to the whole twelve steps. You are going to listen to *me*. You are going to get all the alcohol out of your house and office and anywhere else you go. You aren't going to drink *ever again*, because you are an *alcoholic*." She tried to express with her tone how very seriously she took this charge.

Darcy, in accordance with her rank and duties, had very

rarely been put in command of anything. But that didn't mean she'd ever taken her responsibilities less than seriously. This disease killed people, and Teagan was not dying on her watch.

"Okay? You agree?" she prodded Teagan. "Use your words."

She watched the muscles move in Teagan's throat move as he swallowed. His eyes were as round and golden as a burrowing owl's.

"Okay," he said, faintly but without blinking, gaze fixed on her face. "I'm an alcoholic."

The mood in the residence was tense and tumultuous. Sloane was rushing back and forth between her tent and the office, signing discharge paperwork and hauling bags. Dr. Goedert, displeased to be losing two patients and an employee in one morning, was bouncing among the three of them, alternately pleading for reconsideration and dispensing advice. Kristin, appalled at Darcy for following a presumed alcoholic home (or potentially concerned that some of Darcy's duties would now fall on her shoulders) was standing in the middle of the entryway as though she could block the exit.

And Teagan was propped against a wall, face hidden in his phone screen. Theoretically he was adding Darcy to his flight. In reality he was staring at a blank glass rectangle, mind sputtering like one of Yellowstone's thermal features, erupting with incoherent bursts of *oh Christ oh shit what now oh fuck*.

Because, like the saying went, inside of him were two wolves. One was smugly pleased that the most surprising, fascinating, beautiful woman he'd ever met was coming home with him. The other was incoherently panicking that he was taking that same dangerously unpredictable woman, perfectly suited to her Western wilderness . . . to his white-collar job in New York. To address his nonexistent drinking problem. And when she inevitably figured out that he was a very different species of hot mess than she'd signed up to deal with, *his* species would be endangered.

Only Darcy was cheerful in the chaos. She had her ear-buds in to better ignore all extraneous demands put upon her, and she was hauling green canvas sea bags full of her worldly possessions out to the parking lot with a literal smile on her face and a song on her lips. Actually, when she next passed him, Teagan discerned that she was repeating not song lyrics but several of the twelve steps. She had to be listening to that cursed alcoholism podcast again.

So he had that to look forward to when he got home, in addition to whatever trials Nora put him through.

Teagan pulled his thoughts away from his imminent doom and bought the additional ticket.

"Can I use your printer?" he asked Dr. Goedert the next time the man turned to him.

Dr. Goedert's thick dark hair was matted in some places and sticking up in others. This wasn't how he thought his morning would go, Teagan supposed. "Yes," the man said, eyes focusing on Teagan. "Come into my office."

Teagan followed him up to the finished attic, the room crowded with bookshelves and file cabinets. He hadn't been here before; group therapy was bad enough, so he'd brushed off all offers of individual counseling. Teagan ignored the therapist's scrutiny as he connected his phone and printed Darcy's ticket. His heart was hammering in his chest, and he could feel a cold sweat breaking out across the back of his neck, but by long practice, he kept his face smooth.

He'd better get good at keeping himself together. Darcy was expecting him to get better, not decompensate.

He could nearly taste the bear spray in the back of his throat. That's probably how Darcy would kill him, if she figured out he'd lied.

Dr. Goedert closed the door behind them.

"Teagan," Dr. Goedert said as he collected the papers from the printer. "I've read your medical records from Gracie Square, you know."

Teagan vaguely recalled signing releases on the first day, and he'd never thought about it either way since then.

He made an uninterested and noncommittal noise as he plucked the paperwork from Dr. Goedert's hands, satisfied that they weren't visibly shaking.

"I wasn't sure if you'd realized. And I thought after a little more time, you'd open up with me and the group about your actual diagnosis—your panic disorder—and your experience with an alcoholic parent," Dr. Goedert continued.

"Well, I'm leaving," Teagan pointed out. So that wouldn't be happening.

"We haven't addressed your crisis before arriving here *at all*," Dr. Goedert said, voice distinctly stressed. "Can't you delay your flight, even for a day, and make a plan with me for what you are going to do when you go back to your routine?"

"I have a plan," Teagan said.

He meant his bottle of antidepressants, his second bottle of Xanax to be taken as needed—now felt like a good time—and the reassuring knowledge that just because his heart felt like it was going to rip out of his chest, that didn't actually mean he was having a heart attack, but Dr. Goedert took him a different way.

"Taking our handyman with you is not a plan. Darcy doesn't have a single therapeutic credential. Or any training," the therapist snapped. "Or instincts," he muttered, in a lower voice.

"Interesting that you hired her to be a wilderness educator here, then," Teagan said offhandedly. He edged toward the door. *Oh God oh shit.*

Dr. Goedert's eyes narrowed. "I need you to sign a release so that I can discuss your treatment with her," he said, "if you're going to do this against my advice. You have a serious mental health condition."

"No," Teagan said pleasantly, even though he felt like he was going to throw up.

"No?" The therapist acted like he'd misheard.

"No, I won't sign the release."

Teagan had been in business long enough to realize the power of simply telling people no and refusing to explain himself. No. Dr. Goedert was not going to tell Darcy anything about him, let alone that Teagan was not a recovering alcoholic but a nervous wreck with a lifetime prognosis of the same.

"I need to at least explain to her that she's not qualified to treat you for alcoholism," Dr. Goedert insisted, forehead creasing in consternation. "Not that you'd benefit from it, in any event."

"I think the only thing you need to explain to her is that she's entitled to quite a bit of overtime and back pay for the hours you've been having her work," Teagan said, voice coming out unperturbed. "She seemed to think she wasn't entitled to it just because she was on salary."

The two men stared at each other.

Teagan put a polite smile on his face and dug his nails into his palms. He stood there, face still over the internal churning as he waited to see if Dr. Goedert would call his bluff. He could go right out there and tell Darcy that Teagan had come to Montana straight from the psych ward, not the drunk tank. *Oh no oh crap.*

"I'll . . . look at Darcy's pay stubs," Dr. Goedert said after a moment. "Should I send her final check to the address in your file?"

"Thank you," Teagan said gravely.

He went back down to the lobby, his feet curiously weightless where they were attached to his legs. He thought he might just float away, or maybe pass out. Darcy stood in the middle of the swirl of activity, hands on her hips, Teagan's luggage at her feet. She'd put those big aviator sunglasses back on and changed into a traveling outfit consisting of her least-shredded pair of jean shorts, hiking boots, and an oversized orange T-shirt depicting the bug-eyed beaver mascot of Oregon State University standing victorious over the prone and bloodied figure of a defeated rival duck. She favored him with a conspiratorial grin as she picked up his backpack and slung it over her shoulder.

That was her. That was the one. That was the only woman for him. If his board tried to fire him, she'd probably help him set a trash can fire under the building's smoke alarm before they could finish signing the resolutions.

Seeing him halt to take her in, Darcy crossed the room and put her hand back on his chest.

"You worried?" she asked.

Teagan nodded. He was very worried. The odds he could pull this off for three months seemed low.

"Don't be worried," Darcy said. "I've got this, I promise. I've been listening to Sober Sam for two weeks."

Teagan smiled despite himself. Darcy grinned in answer, then went up on her toes and kissed him lingeringly, mouth closed over his lower lip. When Teagan hesitated a moment in light of the other distressed people coming in and out of the room, Darcy pulled back.

"Should I not do that? If I'm your sober companion?" she asked.

"I'm sure it's fine," Teagan hastened to reassure her. If Darcy ended up murdering him when she figured out he was a liar, he might as well enjoy his short remaining life. "No reason why you shouldn't."

Her face still had a trace of doubt on it.

"It's not like you're my sponsor, after all," he said, discovering hitherto unnecessary and unused reserves of bullshit. "Or my therapist."

Darcy's face cleared. "That's right. It would be different if I were your *sponsor*," she reasoned.

They both nodded, in perfect agreement on that score, even though Teagan did not really know what a sponsor did, and a sober companion even less. But he'd be damned before he'd put a single obstacle in front of Darcy kissing him whenever she felt like it.

Rachel, still not looking as flawlessly groomed as typical, stomped up the stairs from the basement. Her lineless, wrinkle-free face still managed to convey harassment.

"Darcy," she snapped. "You need to get the towels out

to the tents before you leave. I'm going to have to pay the housekeeping service to come out today and clean the residence as it is."

Darcy's dark brown eyes sparkled with glee as she unhurriedly pressed another kiss to the corner of Teagan's mouth. He'd barely slept in more than twenty-four hours now, but he was feeling better by the minute.

"I already called a taxi," Darcy whispered to Teagan. Without even turning her head, she extended one arm and one finger in Rachel's direction.

"Bitch, I quit," she said.

fifteen

TEAGAN SLEPT ON THE RIDE TO THE AIRPORT. HE fell asleep again when their plane lifted off. Darcy let him have the window seat, but his eyes were closed before the shrinking peaks of the Gallatin range filled the little porthole.

Even asleep, with his mouth hanging slightly open and his hair falling over his forehead, his expression was tense. Every half hour or so he'd jolt awake and look around in confusion, then settle back down when he reoriented himself. Darcy would have teased him about it if his expression hadn't been so wide-eyed and incredulous when it landed on her. Like he expected her to bail out of the arrangement while they were cruising over Ohio. Like she'd call the flight attendant back and say that actually, Teagan was allowed to drink whatever he wanted, she didn't care. Instead, she proficiently ordered him an apple juice and some mini-pretzels, draped him with her hoodie, and told him she had hours of topical podcasts saved for her own education and entertainment if he wanted to sleep the rest of the way. He did.

Darcy, by contrast, was brimming with energy. She had fifty-seven new bookmarks saved on her phone to review. She had plans to make. She was riding an exhilarating wave of agency and competency as much as the jet stream as they flew east. She might be good at this job, she thought. Years later, Teagan might reflect that he was lucky to have had her.

She did not really think about where, exactly, she and Teagan were going beyond *to New York*, and she was so unfamiliar with the area that she did not even realize their Newark airport taxi was taking them away from the city until they were on the highway headed north and the Manhattan skyline was illuminating the rear window.

Darcy couldn't figure out where they were relative to the city until they crossed the Hudson just as the sun finished setting. The woody hills flanking the river valley were still verdant and misty in the light rain at this time in the early autumn, and Darcy pressed her nose against the window as they slowed for suburban traffic. Teagan was a tense, curled-in shape on the other side of the backseat, gaze fixed on the blur of headlights from the oncoming traffic.

"It's going to be okay," Darcy said, turning away from the window and patting his knee. Her importance to this venture straightened her spine, and she strove to sound authoritative as she reassured him. "I won't let you fuck up your recovery." Teagan startled, looking first at the hand, then at the rest of her, like he'd momentarily forgotten that she was with him.

He cleared his throat. "Thank you," he said in a rusty voice. He put his hand down next to hers, little finger just brushing her own as she anchored him from wherever his mind had gone. "I know that."

"You just looked worried about it, is all," Darcy said. He barely looked better rested for having slept all day.

"I'm worried about Sloane, actually. I shouldn't have let

her go back to California to pack up on her own. I should have asked her to come with us, bought her new stuff," he said.

"She's twenty-two," Darcy pointed out. At twenty-two, Darcy had been on her second enlistment contract and second deployment. "And her issue was just a little coke? She can probably keep her nose clean for a couple days, at least."

"No, I mean—I wish I'd asked her to come with me," he said.

Darcy looked at him in confusion. Sloane had muttered a few things about third-wheeling it, and Darcy understood that concern. Teagan turned his face to the window.

"Okay, this will sound dumb," he muttered. "But when Sloane was about four, she was going through a rough stage. It was hard to drop her off at preschool. She'd cry and cling to me and yell so loud that sometimes the teachers would just send her home."

"She didn't seem worried about going alone for a few days," Darcy pointed out.

"Yes, but it's the principle of the thing. About asking her. Because I didn't know what to do back then. The tantrums went on for weeks, and it was just turning into more and more of a production every day."

"You did the drop-off every day?"

"I did, on my way to school. Anyway, I tried bribing her, I tried sneaking away, I tried putting my foot down. Eventually I started reading parenting books. One of the books said that I couldn't teach her that I'd come back for her at the end of the day by leaving. I couldn't just leave. If she was holding on, I had to hold on harder. So if she wouldn't go to preschool, I brought her with me to my high school. It only took two days of precalculus before she decided she'd rather do arts and crafts with the other kids than come with me. But, you know, it made it her decision."

Darcy felt her chest squeeze at the image of baby Teagan with even more baby Sloane, then cursed herself as a repeat sucker for the single dad schtick. That was just her hormones talking, and they rarely wanted what was best for her.

"You didn't catch hell from the other kids?" she said, trying to push the feeling away.

"No? Why would I?" Teagan asked, face honestly confused.

Darcy snorted, because his high school must have been much more accommodating of personal differences among its students than the three she'd attended.

Teagan looked away again. "Everyone was always very impressed with me for taking care of Sloane." He paused. "And then later my mother too, I guess."

"It's not your worst quality," Darcy said drily. Of course everyone had cooed over the teenage boy with his parenting books. It was all she could do not to go misty about it herself. Steady, girl.

She shoved him with her shoulder. "Sloane's not going to feel abandoned because you let her spend a couple days packing up on her own. She knows you care."

Teagan put on that familiar half smile, the one she now knew to be directed mostly at himself. "Knowing that something is real or isn't doesn't always help."

That was a good and sound observation, something Darcy needed to keep in mind herself, but he looked so worried that Darcy had a sudden pang of misgiving.

"It's not too late to change your mind on going home,"

she said, nodding out the window at the suburbs. "We could tell the driver to take us right back to the airport. Or anywhere else. It's honey harvesting season upstate. I watched a YouTube video on beekeeping a while ago, so I'm basically an expert in it already. How does your sister feel about agricultural work? She could come too."

"Sloane's afraid of bugs," Teagan reported, the second corner of his mouth now engaged.

"I'll keep thinking, then," Darcy promised. She needed to work out a backup plan in case Teagan bailed on sobriety before the ninety days were up.

From the bridge, they traveled another ten minutes north until the taxi disgorged them, minus a truly astronomical sum of money, at a low-slung yet sprawling house constructed of poured concrete forms on a large lot high over the valley. It was dark by then, but bits of the landscape were illuminated by lights in the bushes and tall, mature trees. The place was huge.

Darcy had expected anything up to and including a castle with turrets and a moat around it, but Teagan's house was beautiful in a tasteful way, like something out of an architecture magazine. The grass was mowed and the landscaping immaculate, but Teagan had to fiddle with a lockbox on the front door to get the key.

"This is theoretically for sale," he said by way of explanation as he opened the big square front door and admitted them to a terrazzo-tiled foyer. "It was my mother's house. But since I wanted Sloane to have somewhere she could come home to during school breaks, I haven't tried very hard to sell it."

He flipped on the lights, illuminating the vast interior.

"You don't live here?" Darcy asked, eyebrows shooting up as she took in the space, full of raw stone, warm wood, and complicated midcentury furniture. Why wouldn't he live here if he was allowed to? It was gorgeous. She was nearly bouncing on her toes with excitement that she got to live here for the next three months.

"Not since I was in college. Now only when Sloane is here. I have a condo in Midtown, but it's just a studio, and . . ." He didn't finish that thought, but his cheeks turned a little pink.

Darcy felt her mouth curl up in a wide smirk. "You didn't want to get me there and announce, 'Oh no, only one bed, what to do?'"

Teagan pressed his lips together, not quite returning the expression. "I didn't think I could pull that off, no."

He might have done better than he thought, but there was no sense in inflating his ego just yet. Darcy looked around the open floor plan. There was a kitchen at one end, a bar at the other, and a big living area in between. A hallway between the kitchen and living room led off to the back of the house.

Rachel had decorated the wellness retreat's big residence complex, and it had all been nice and matching and all that, but this house was flawlessly arranged, every fixture and item of furniture fitting the space as though designed with this room in mind. For all Darcy knew, it had been.

And there was art on every wall—real art, where you could see the artist's brushstrokes and their signature in the bottom corner.

Darcy dropped her bags and started pacing the exterior, searching in vain for some photographs of Teagan or other members of his family. The only photographs were black and white, weird angular shots of people writing on their hands or smoking unfiltered cigarettes through bad haircuts. Probably not captured during Van Zijl family vacations.

Teagan went straight to the fridge to fetch bottled water out of a drawer apparently maintained for that purpose, so Darcy continued her snooping. She marked the location of the wet bar, spotted two cabinets full of wine on built-in racks, and critically noted a stack of mirrored drink coasters on a glass coffee table that must have been staged specifically for doing lines. She added them to her to-do list.

Her gaze was eventually drawn to a huge portrait hanging next to the bar. It was so exaggerated as to be almost cartoonish, but it depicted a young woman with her dress falling off her breasts, bright pink nipples lovingly detailed.

"Um," Darcy said, stifling a laugh, because she hadn't really anticipated Teagan having tits-out art in his living room, even if she'd braced for all the drinking and drug paraphernalia.

"Oh, yeah, that's a John Currin," Teagan said, following her expression and wrinkling his nose. "Mom was a big collector. I think it's kind of ugly, but I haven't taken anything down. It technically belongs to the foundation."

Darcy walked up to take a closer look at the painting. It had the expensive layered quality of museum art, but the subject matter overwhelmed the technique. "Is this a painting of your mom?"

"What?" Teagan asked, mouth falling open in shock. The idea had obviously never occurred to him. "No, John Currin is famous. He does lots of these."

"Your mom never met him? Because the lady kinda looks like Sloane . . ." Darcy trailed off.

"I—she probably did. But she never said—Jesus."

Teagan's face went through several shades of horror. Darcy guessed that she would also have been horrified if she found out she'd been eating breakfast under the watchful gaze of her mother's tits for over a decade.

She looked at the painting longer. Definitely looked like Sloane.

"God. Now I'm never going to be able to unsee it," Teagan said, staring at the artwork in dismay, hands on his hips.

Darcy laughed at how stuck he seemed. There was a simple fix. "Let's just take her down, then."

When he didn't object, Darcy lifted the painting off its nail and turned it so that it faced the wall. "See? Easy enough. Show some modesty, Ma."

Teagan blinked in agreement. "Maybe I'll let Nora sell just this one," he muttered, putting one hand over his mouth.

Darcy nodded to encourage him. Maybe he could put some vacation photos up instead. Make it a little homier. This place could be perfect with just a few updates.

"So, where should I put my stuff?" she asked, hooking a thumb at the hallway, trying to project the nonchalance of someone accustomed to standing in houses like this. Probably never again. This was probably her only opportunity to live the lifestyle of the rich and famous. She wondered whether there was such a thing as vegan marabou heels. If so, she wanted to order some and walk around in them, liven up Teagan's life a little. Let her own tits hang out.

Teagan grabbed her sea bag and set it over his shoulder despite her abortive grab for the strap. "Sloane's room is pretty nice; she redecorated a couple of years ago. Queen bed. The guest room smells a little bit like cedar because that's where my mother kept her furs—they're gone, don't worry. And the primary's been cleared out too, but . . ."

He obviously didn't want to vocalize any objections to Darcy taking his mother's bedroom, but the mere thought sounded like a buzzkill.

"What about your room?" she asked lightly, waggling her eyebrows to dislodge his unhappy thoughts.

She had an idea of what Teagan was like in bed, and it was already playing through her mind in high production values. She imagined their hands clasped together, the muscles of Teagan's shoulders rippling as he moved, curtains rustling. None of the windows in this house had curtains, but somehow, curtains were rustling.

Teagan ducked his chin and smiled between closed lips. "Twin beds," he said. "And all my water polo trophies."

"You hiding some stuffed animals, champ?"

Darcy was going to be disappointed if he didn't make even a tiny pass at her while they talked about sleeping arrangements.

"That's what the second bed is for," he said, dimple not quite popping out.

She edged close enough to wrap her hand around the inside of his arm and slide her bag onto her own shoulder. She could feel the tension vibrating through his body. His mind was still somewhere else.

"I'm not picky," Darcy said. "My first deployment, I had to hot rack on a stack of Tomahawk missiles."

"You're welcome to whichever one you like best," Teagan said, still not picking up what she was laying down. "I think all the sheets are clean."

Coming home from rehab was supposed to be very hard. One of the most fraught events in recovery, according to the podcasts she'd been listening to all day. The temptation to fall back into bad habits would be overwhelming. Darcy set her shoulders back, shaking off her amusement at how oblivious he was. She was here to work, after all.

Well, time to start earning her keep.

"I'll take the guest bedroom, then," she said, releasing his arm. "Then I'll get started on the bar."

sixteen

AFTER FOUR WEEKS OFF THE GRID, TEAGAN SEEMED to have already lost his ability to concentrate on his laptop screen. He'd been up most of the previous night packing and finishing Darcy's job applications, but he'd slept all day. So he ought to feel more rested.

It was the Xanax, or the Lexapro. They made him tired, and he needed to be able to think.

There were 8,573 new email messages that had accrued in Teagan's inbox since the previous evening, when he'd left a message for Rose that promised that if he still had a job at the foundation past the next week, she would *not* unless she released her hold on his emails. Her written reply, if any, was lost in the vast sea of fundraising pleas from other charities, spam, and routine office correspondence, but he supposed she'd blinked first.

Teagan sat down at the tulip-shaped breakfast table, intending to drill into the most recent weekly reports, but it was hard to concentrate past Darcy's flurry of activity in his peripheral vision. She'd satisfied herself that the fridge and freezer contained no controlled substances, pronounced his bedroom clear in the style of a bomb disposal technician, and then moved on to the bar.

Unlike Teagan, she shone with the righteous energy of the productively engaged.

Teagan tried to force his eyes to remain on his inbox. But they kept drifting over to the woman who made up most of the color and movement in his life. She'd hopped up on the counter at the other end of the living room, and she was systematically emptying the contents of the liquor cabinets into the wet bar sink.

Darcy made occasional judgmental comments as she worked.

"Peach schnapps, Teagan, *really*?"

"What do you even make with spiced rum?"

"Why do you have three different types of orange-flavored stuff?"

It was all untouched since his mother's death. Teagan wouldn't be surprised if some of it was decades old, moved from their house in Greenwich after his parents' divorce. His mother had preferred the elegant simplicity of vodka on the rocks, and there was no vodka left in the house now. Teagan had never been able to stand the smell of it.

He stared blankly at his laptop screen. He ought to be working. He ought to be doing something. But his mind steadfastly refused to absorb any information as he clicked through four weeks of messages.

He wished he had even half the determination Darcy exuded as she finished dragging trash sacks of empty liquor bottles out to the curb and started removing the wine collection.

Stop, he wanted to tell her.

You don't have to do all this.

Open one up and come sit with me instead.

But that would only lead to Darcy clocking him over the

head with one of those pretentious bottles of Montrachet before taking a taxi back to the airport.

Her expression was solemn with purpose as she marched in and out of the house, her ponytail flying behind her like a flag. However misplaced that purpose was, Teagan keenly missed the feeling that he was in the right place, doing the right thing, which had slowly dwindled to a trickle over the past two years.

Lying to her wasn't going to help with that. It seemed pretty likely to make him feel like shit, in fact. And once she rendered his home alcohol free, what was he even supposed to do with her? Was he going to have to invent relapse crises? Pretend an urgent need to hit up bars? God, what was he even going to feed her? He and Sloane usually just ordered sushi or ate frozen Trader Joe's entrees cooked in the toaster oven.

With that thought, Teagan found his priorities clear. He had to provision the house, because Darcy needed to eat. He could accomplish that much, at least.

He pulled up a grocery delivery page and began adding food to the cart. Flax milk. Forbidden rice. Spaghetti squash. Things he remembered eating in Montana.

He was hesitating on silken tofu versus firm when Darcy's warm, sweet weight unexpectedly descended into his lap. He grunted and wrapped an arm around her waist to keep the chair from toppling over, steadying himself as she nonchalantly perched across his knees and looped her arm around the back of his neck for balance.

"Hi," she said.

"Hello," he said, muting his surprise.

"What are you doing?"

"Buying groceries."

"Oh. Your expression looked a lot more dire than that." She squinted at his face, then at his screen. "Wait, who's gonna cook all that tofu?"

"Um," Teagan said intelligently, because he'd assumed she would. "You could tell me how, and I'll do it, I guess?"

"I don't know how to cook," Darcy said after investigating his face again. When Teagan sighed, she squirmed a little, wedging a hip against some important bits of his anatomy and finally achieving what appeared to be a more comfortable seat against his chest. "You can just buy me a couple of those eighty ounce jars of peanut butter and some bananas. I'm easy."

Teagan opened his mouth to argue that he'd buy and cook Darcy whatever she actually wanted, but she reached out and closed the laptop, seeming to consider the matter decided. The movement brushed her ponytail against the side of his neck, and he shivered.

Darcy settled in, her back against his chest, his heartbeat thudding against the solidity of her shoulder.

"So," she said. "I gave the wine away to your neighbors. They were pretty happy about that."

"I'll bet," Teagan said. There had been some really nice bottles in there, gifted to his mother over the years. They'd accumulated since she'd always said she wasn't wasting the calories on anything less than fifty proof.

Darcy began to count on her fingers. "I got rid of all the liquor in the bar."

"Thank you."

"And the mouthwash in the bathrooms."

"Um, thank you for that too."

"Do you have any hand sanitizer?"

"Why?"

"It's got alcohol in it, I heard."

"But I like having clean hands," he protested. "And a little nip of hand sanitizer right before I go to bed."

Darcy lightly pinched his stomach, making him jolt and nearly dislodging her from his lap. He got a hold on one of her bare thighs, just above the knee, to keep her in place.

"It was in a video. Stuff alcoholics might try to drink," she said defensively.

"Pretty sure I'd try driving to a liquor store before hand sanitizer," Teagan said.

Darcy looked so concerned by that statement that he wrapped his arms more firmly around her. "I won't," he promised.

She exhaled and curled a hand around his wrist, rubbing her thumb against it. "I haven't been able to find the manual on sober companioning yet," she said. "Like a YouTube instructional video. Or a podcast. Everything's directed at the actual drinkers. So I'm not sure if I'm doing it right. I'm making it up as I go along."

"I think you're doing a great job," Teagan said honestly. If he'd actually been inclined to drink, clearing out all the booze and then sitting on him seemed like thorough preventative measures.

"Yeah?" Darcy asked, and it took Teagan a long moment to parse the cautious note in her voice as vulnerability.

He leaned forward enough to press his nose against her shoulder. "Yeah. I'm . . . really glad you're here."

"I guess it would have been pretty overwhelming to come back here alone," Darcy suggested.

"No, it's more than that," he said. "I'm glad *you're* here. I'm glad I've been with you. Everything that felt loud and overwhelming just got . . . quiet and still."

Darcy laughed. "Nobody's ever called me quiet."

"It got quieter in my head, at least," Teagan said. "I think it's because whenever you're around, all I can think about is you."

Darcy craned her head around so she could meet his eyes. Her expression was skeptical, but it shifted to pleasure as he stood behind the words. Had he not said it yet? He ought to remember to say it every day.

"Really?" she asked, a bit of swagger entering her voice.

"Really," he reassured her. "It's like trying to see anything else after looking right at the sun."

The expression of delight that bloomed across her face warmed him all the way down to his toes. Darcy's nose crinkled in a wonderful way before she leaned in to kiss him, slowly and thoroughly. How could he think of anything beyond the woman in his arms? Everything else faded away.

This. This. This. This was worth all of it, the four weeks away, the embarrassment and shame, the *lying*—

It was an awkward position, with Darcy's feet dangling and his legs braced to keep them from toppling over, but Teagan made an instinctive sound of objection when Darcy slid off his lap and stood up. He wasn't done with Darcy sitting in his lap and kissing him. He could have done with a lot more of that.

She grinned and grabbed his arm to pull him up too, tucking it against her body when he unwillingly got out of the chair.

"I want to hear about the house. Give me the grand tour," she said, waving her other arm.

"You've probably seen it all already," Teagan said, looking wistfully back at the chair.

Darcy dragged him a few feet out of the kitchen. "I mean the amenities."

"Amenities?"

"I saw the pool," she said in tones of deep satisfaction.

"Oh, yeah. I need to clean it out, probably, but I can do that for you tomorrow. There's also a jacuzzi."

"Amazing," she singsonged. "This place is amazing."

"I'm glad you like it," Teagan said, because he hadn't been sure she would, or if she'd want to pitch a tent in the backyard to protest the energy inefficiency of the original 1960s windows.

"Do you know what's the best thing about this house though?" Darcy asked, pointing to the front living room.

"The fireplace?" he guessed, following her glance.

"Wrong! It's the sex couch," she said, face spreading into a Cheshire cat grin. It took Teagan a few seconds to follow where she indicated.

"You mean the conversation pit," he said when he identified her area of interest as the sunken space with built-in seating, padded with red felt cushions and bolsters around a low, marble table. "They were popular in the sixties and seventies. For entertaining."

Darcy dropped his arm and positioned herself between Teagan and the furniture in question, giving it a thorough inspection.

"*Naked* entertaining," she said decisively. "Why else would you make the seats that wide? Or the back bolster so low?"

"I think that's how they all are."

Darcy shook her head knowingly, her long ponytail bouncing. "They're all like that so that people can fuck on them."

Teagan laughed. "I promise you, no sex has been had on that couch. Look, it's in full view of the entire house. And the front windows."

Darcy took a step closer to him, her hands resting on her hips.

"You're sure about that?"

"I mean, yeah," Teagan said. This house was all the way up in Irvington; his mother had rarely even had dinner guests over, let alone men she was dating, and few of Sloane or Teagan's school friends had cared to make the trip either. "Sloane or I have lived here for more than twenty years now, and—"

A thought occurred to stop him while he was speaking, a thought which coincided with Darcy closing the distance between them and curling two fingers into the gap between the lowest buttons on his shirt. A wonderful, compelling, implausible thought about what Darcy was really asking. She tilted her head to the side and looked up at him through her dark eyelashes, a small smile playing around the corners of her full, red mouth.

"It's not a sex couch?" she pressed.

Teagan was abruptly unsure about that. Perhaps he'd spoken too soon.

"It's hard to say," he temporized. He watched the pink tip of her tongue curl delicately between her lips before she spoke again. The heel of her palm was pressed against his stomach just above his waistband. His heartbeat was probably audible, echoing off the terrazzo.

"Well, could it be?" Darcy asked.

God, he was really dumb sometimes.

He opened his mouth to reply that of course it could be, the conversation pit or any other architectural feature of his house was more than suitable for sex, no worry about that, in fact, the floor or walls would do in a pinch—

But the rational side of his mind abruptly chimed in to

inform him that he shouldn't make any promises he wouldn't be able to keep, and he just stared at her wordlessly.

Darcy closed her eyes and pressed her mouth to his loose lower lip, no doubt interpreting his hesitation as amazement that he could be getting lucky tonight. He kissed her back, trying to compose an explanation that wouldn't make him sound like a completely worthless excuse for a man, but a graceful description of the circumstances eluded him. Her hands got busy on the buttons of his shirt.

Teagan chased Darcy's mouth as she focused on divesting him of his clothes. He tried to convince himself that if he just didn't *think* about anything, maybe his body would cooperate and do what it always had before. He wanted her. He wanted to touch every inch of her, taste every texture and color on her body. But where that wanting would have filled up the hollows in his body before, it was fighting for space with a damping fog that made him feel distant even from this moment.

He couldn't feel that wanting outside of his head.

Darcy backed away, casually ripping off her top and tossing it to the ground. She wore the same electric blue bra he'd so briefly glimpsed—was it really only yesterday?—but he registered it only for a moment before she bent her arms behind her to unhook it, then tossed it away as well.

Teagan made an incoherent noise at the unfairness of it all. Darcy registered that as appropriate respect for the glory of her bare breasts, hanging round and full, tipped with dark brown nipples, and she grinned at him. He hadn't yet moved.

"Come on, Teagan," she said, in the same impatient tone of voice she'd used to urge him faster up Slough Creek trail, and she pulled him by the hand toward the couch.

Moving mostly via muscle memory rather than conscious

intent, he ended up braced over her, one hand supporting himself, the other cupped around the soft swell of her breast. The places she was soft were delightful to him. He'd seen a lot of her hard edges already. The sharp jut of her chin when she was angry. The muscular line of her calves as she climbed a trail in front of him. But her round hips, the curve of her stomach, the satiny skin under his fingers—these were equally precious.

He worked to lose himself in the sensation. Maybe more time would do it. Circling her nipple with his thumb was an endeavor he was willing to devote the next ten minutes to, at least, and if that didn't get him there, he'd try worrying it between his lips.

This tentative plan seemed to conflict with Darcy's orders, however, because she was working hard to render them both naked in short order.

"Wait, wait," he gasped into her mouth when her hand dipped to the waistband of his pants.

"I have condoms," she said reassuringly as her fingers closed around the top button of his fly.

Of course she did. Darcy never went hiking without bear spray, and of course she had not offered to try out the sex couch without protection. But that wasn't the issue. She pulled down his zipper.

"No, I mean—" He disentangled himself from her, pulled back to a kneeling position. She followed, hands dipping perilously close to his groin. He grabbed her wrists just as she cupped him, panic spiking.

"Wait," he said again, but too late.

Her eyebrows shot up in surprise. At what she wasn't feeling, presumably.

"I'm on, um, medication," he said as she slowly pulled her hands away.

Her expression was uncomprehending.

"Antidepressants," he said, feeling his cheeks burn.

She still didn't get it.

"They have, I think, side effects," he said, willing a meteor to target Irvington, New York, and put him out of this conversation.

Darcy's face was still a muddle.

"So . . . do you not want to . . . ?" she said slowly, as though saying something that didn't make any sense. And it didn't make any sense. Of course he wanted to sleep with her. She was a dream. He literally dreamed about her. But if he'd thought about wanting to sleep with her—and it wasn't like the idea *hadn't* occurred to him—it was in the same abstract way that he'd thought about wanting to take her to that little Ethiopian restaurant in East Williamsburg or to bury his face in her loose hair, because desire was one of those emotions that he could only halfway feel now. He wanted to do everything with her. He hadn't planned to do anything at all.

He pulled all the way away, so they were no longer touching. "I'm saying I probably can't. I don't know. I was in the hospital when I was put on this stuff, so I don't remember the whole spiel, but—yeah. I can't sleep with you. I literally can't." His voice was rougher than he wanted, and Darcy jerked back at his tone, but hot shame was clogging his throat.

Her eyebrows flexed as she processed that. Teagan looked away, down at his feet. He didn't even have his shoes off. Not that that was a strict prerequisite to sex, he supposed, unlike a functioning cock.

"I didn't know they gave out antidepressants for alcoholism," Darcy said after a minute.

"I don't know. I'm not a doctor," he snapped, the deception burning worse than the embarrassment now. Maybe it didn't really matter either way. He leaned forward and covered his face with his palms.

He heard Darcy shift closer to him. She leaned up against the side of his body.

"Sorry. I was just surprised. *My dick doesn't work* isn't a line I've heard before."

Teagan managed a self-pitying laugh. "Christ. It's not a line. Believe me, I wish . . ." He wished he could be more than half hard when the most beautiful woman he'd ever seen was half naked in his arms. He wished he really was an alcoholic instead of someone with a psychiatric disorder, because then he wouldn't be lying to Darcy, and he could just stop drinking and go on with his life. He wished he'd been eaten by a bear so he'd never had to have this conversation. "I wish I could," he hesitantly finished. He forced himself to open his eyes and look at her, because if he never got any more than this, he at least wanted to be able to remember what she looked like.

Darcy's expression had moved past confusion now. And she showed no signs of getting up and putting her clothes back on, which was what he'd expected she'd do. Instead, she looked . . . thoughtful. Like she was considering a diesel generator error code.

"I can work with that," she said, mostly to herself. She stretched and flicked her hair back over her shoulders. She nodded.

"Work with what?"

"You. Who cares about your dick, anyway? Not me,"

she said brightly. "You know, it's not like it matters to me whether *you* come." Then she was back in motion, pushing at his shoulder until he slumped over onto his back in surprise. She leaned over him, smile showing many sharp teeth. "And I wouldn't even *expect* you to while I'm sitting on your face."

A confused laugh tangled in his throat. "What?" he asked again.

She'd gathered both confidence and momentum, and her hands were back on her clothing. "I'm asking if you eat pussy, Teagan," she said, a cheerful note entering her voice.

"I—on occasion," he said, mind struggling to keep up with his rapid change in fortune. He did. Not too badly, he thought. A great wash of relief began to flow through him.

"You're not one of those *birthdays and anniversaries* guys, are you?" she said, judgmental for the first time since their clothes had started to come off. But she undid her own fly anyway.

"No, I mean—when the opportunity presents itself," he said, trying to convey his sincerity.

That cracked her up. "Oh man, this opportunity is going to be *presenting*," she chortled. She shoved her underwear down over her hips, shimmying them off. "Do you want me to do a little dance, like a bird? Or some alluring poses, like a cat in heat?"

Maybe this situation was salvageable.

"I would *love* to see your little dance," Teagan said, but the remainder of his smart remarks were cut off by Darcy's tongue in his mouth, and he supposed he ought to start putting his own to more productive use.

seventeen

HER TRICEPS BURNED FROM THE EFFORT OF BRAC-ing herself. Big words aside, Darcy hadn't actually tried this position before—or more precisely, no man had trusted her in a position where slightly less core strength on her part would cut off his oxygen supply.

But oh my God, she thought. *OHMYGOD*. This was a fantastic place to be: knees around Teagan's ears, feet on his chest, hands propped on the upholstered back of the couch. His lips exactly where she wanted them.

That had been the happy thought she'd gone to bed with the night before, like a twenty-dollar bill in her pocket to spend at the commissary: Teagan would do whatever she wanted. Or rather, whatever she asked him to do. Most of the men she'd ever been with had probably *thought* they were doing what she wanted in bed; they just had brain rot from too much porn.

But this one had actually listened.

Darcy gasped as he pulled her hips forward so he could lick along the entire seam of her body. His hands were spread along her ass, and even if he wasn't supporting much of her weight, he was holding her tight enough to leave an inter-esting constellation of fingertip bruises there. She grinned, imagining his blush as she walked past him in her smallest pair of underwear tomorrow. He had really good blushes for a guy who was eating her out like there was a scheduled critique afterward.

Darcy thought she could have gotten off no matter what Teagan did; she had all the leverage, and she could just rub against that full lower lip until she saw fireworks. But Teagan was trying to show off or earn a new rank in oral sex or something, and the sideswipe of his tongue against her clit was making her arms tremble every time a wave of sensation crashed through her.

"Oh hell," she moaned when he rolled her clit between his lips. "I'm actually going to come. Keep doing that."

She wasn't sure he could hear her with her thighs around his ears, but either her command or the urgency with which she rocked against him made an impression. He redoubled his efforts, lips hard and tight around her most intimate spaces.

Tension was gathering, winding up her thighs and tightening her nipples. Darcy closed her eyes to the beautiful, empty room and tried to picture how the two of them must look: decadent. Indulgent. Darcy so rarely got exactly what she wanted, when she wanted it—in sex, in anything—that she wanted to be able to summon this moment the next time someone told her she had to accept a substitution for what had been promised to her.

That person wouldn't be Teagan. He did what he said he would. That's why she was naked and rocking against his mouth.

There was always that one terrifying moment right before she came, when she lost balance and control. The inevitability of climax would feel perilous and unsteady, like stepping off the edge of a cliff. That instant of vulnerability, where she felt like she was falling, was the reason she didn't have a lot of sex. She wasn't even sure what she was afraid might happen in that split second of uncertainty, but she knew there was no risk of it with Teagan's arms wrapped around the lower half of her body. She wasn't going to fall.

The thread of tension broke through her body, sending a shimmering wave of sparks out along her limbs. She gasped as her body tensed and released, every sensation suddenly heightened and compelling: the air against her bare breasts, the softness of Teagan's hair against her thighs, the wetness of his mouth still moving against her.

The pleasure quickly shifted into oversensitivity, and she jerked upright. Teagan instinctively moved with her, and she had to grab for his hair to stop him. She tipped his head back, eyeing his unfocused, glazed expression with satisfaction.

"You doing okay, big guy?" she asked. "You had enough air?"

Teagan licked his red, swollen lips before answering.

"Yep. I'm great," he said thickly.

"I was a little afraid I'd accidentally kill you," she confessed.

He gave a small huff of a laugh. "What a way to go though," he said, hands smoothing appreciatively over her ass, pulling her back down like he intended to get right back to work. Darcy grinned as she carefully rolled away to kneel next to him on the couch.

She was dizzy with delight. So very pleased with herself, with him. The perks of this job were fantastic.

"Where are you going?" he complained, pulling her back. "I'm fine." He cuddled her against his body, where he was giving off heat like a furnace.

"I'm good for now," she said, patting his chest through the white cotton of his undershirt. She hadn't managed to get him very undressed. "You can chug some water and take a lap." She rubbed the firm muscle under the fabric. Maybe she'd just grope him for a bit then get back into it, if he was up for it. She gleefully pressed her face into his neck. This was so good. This was going to be the best three months of her life.

Teagan made a noise of disagreement and hauled her back into his lap. He cupped her chin and kissed her messily, wet mouth restless against her own. Darcy squirmed with satisfaction at the tight pressure of his arms around her. He definitely wasn't thinking about his emails or the liquor store's worth of booze she'd carried out now. Instead, his eyelids were heavy with arousal, and shoulders had relaxed with renewed confidence.

Darcy shifted in his lap, pleasantly considering her immediate future. Her workload was going to crater. She was going to get caught up on all of her classes. She was going to have a lot of sex. Like, *a lot* a lot, even if his dick wasn't part of the equation. This house had a hot tub, a pool, a sex couch, and *four* bedrooms, and she was going to get it in all those places.

She'd eventually convince Teagan to tell her what he actually wanted, what he was afraid to ask her for, because there was no way he didn't want something. She could feel the hard-on he'd said he wasn't capable of pressed firmly against her thigh, and from the shape of it, he didn't have anything to be modest about.

"Um, so," she said, letting a hand drape down his chest and settle at the open fly of his trousers. She scooted toward his knees to give herself more room to work. "I feel like I could do something with this."

Teagan's eyelids fluttered in surprise, like he hadn't even

noticed the erection tenting his pants, and he looked down in wary confusion.

"Oh, I"—his lips pressed together as he hesitated—"I don't know."

His eyes dipped again to her breasts. He didn't move to do up his pants or to push her away though, so Darcy decided to continue troubleshooting.

"What are you afraid is going to happen?" she asked.

One corner of his mouth pulled to the side. "Nothing. I'm afraid nothing is going to happen."

Darcy snorted in disapproval. That didn't sound so terrifying. That was the same risk every woman bore whenever she hooked up with someone new.

"Well, I'm not. Because, like I said, I don't really care if you come."

That got a hint of a wry smile out of him. Encouraged by the expression, Darcy slid down over Teagan's knees, landing on the upholstered floor of the conversation pit. She cupped him again through the fabric, letting her thumb brush the bottom curve.

He drew a nervous hand through his hair as he took in her new position in front of him.

"I think," Darcy said, curling her fingers under the waistband of his underwear, "you would like my mouth on you." She thought that was fairly universal, and if he was also interested in, say, clowns or hardcore bondage, they'd just work up to that admission.

"Yes," Teagan said, worry mixing with rapt focus on the distance between her lips and his lap. "I would. I just—" His voice broke off, and he bit down hard on his inner lip, apparently determining not to ruin this for himself.

Darcy carefully pulled the fabric down tense thighs covered in light blonde fur, easing the elastic over the healing claw marks on his hip. Moving slowly, she looked up at him through her eyelashes and let him anticipate the first moment of contact between the rounded tip of her tongue and the bottom of his cock. She exhaled just before she touched him so that he felt the damp heat of her breath first. He jerked against her mouth as she closed lips around the crown, his sharp intake of breath audible.

She liked this. The way the muscles in Teagan's thighs shifted when he forgot to hold his body tightly together. The taste of his skin. The slip of him over her tongue. The rasp of his breathing. The control it implied for her, the pleasure in his face.

After some minutes—long minutes, quiet minutes—Teagan began to shift in his seat.

"I swear I'm not trying to drag this out," he said.

Darcy hadn't thought he was, but she hummed in appreciation of that promise.

"And this feels fantastic," he quickly added, tone apologetic.

Darcy didn't think *apologetic* was how Teagan probably sounded when he was having a really good time, so she took that as her cue to try to get fancy in terms of what she was doing with her tongue and hands. Break out all the stops. She was rewarded with a slightly shocked inhale of breath from above her, but no further developments.

Her jaw was starting to ache. She thought she was covert about the way she rubbed a palm against it, but Teagan caught her.

"Stop. Don't hurt yourself," Teagan said glumly, hand reaching out to cup her face. "You can just—call it. No heroic efforts needed."

"What if you stood up?" she asked. "Or I bent over from the side—"

He shook his head. "No, no, this isn't your fault." His abruptly tragic expression said he was dramatically overestimating the portion of Darcy's self-worth tied up in her cock-sucking abilities.

"No worries," Darcy said. "I know I'm awesome at this. Pretty sure I could turn pro if I didn't have this sweet sober companion gig going already."

That got a real laugh out of him, but he sat up more, hands reaching for his pants.

Darcy protectively wrapped two hands around the base of his cock to halt him.

"Have you really not been able to come at all for the last month?" she asked him with sincere concern. She would have called a doctor or something, if that had been her.

Teagan's flaming cheeks said that he would prefer not to discuss it, but he reluctantly said, "Pretty much. I mean, once in the shower, but it took so long that afterward I just gave up."

She leaned in and smirked at him, mind readily giving her the image. "Were you thinking about me?"

It was a tease, just a chance to let him use a good line, but if anything he turned redder, lips tightening over white teeth.

"I was, yeah," he admitted.

Darcy pulled her hand down his shaft, tightened it, and stroked back the other direction.

"What were you thinking about?" she asked.

He licked his lips, and for a moment she thought he wasn't going to tell her. But she stroked him again, and he bit out like a guilty admission, "You. This. You, on your knees. Your mouth on my cock."

Darcy blinked up at him in startled gratification, though that didn't give her much different she could do. But maybe if—

She stood up. "Come on," she said again, grabbing him by the arm.

There was a big bathroom attached to her room, with a walk-in shower. Plenty of room for two.

"Where are we going?"

"The shower," she said, trying to convey happy determination. She could recreate those conditions in captivity, no problem.

Teagan made one more abortive grab for his clothes, but she muscled him away from them.

"Darcy, really, it's okay—"

"No reason not to use the equipment you've been supplied," Darcy said, hauling him upright.

He made a few more halfhearted protests as she hustled him into the bathroom and turned on the hot water.

"You don't have to do this," he said unnecessarily as they waited for it to steam up the bathroom. Darcy tested the water with one foot but kept both hands on Teagan's body to keep him from fleeing. "This is . . . probably the most awkward situation of my entire life."

Darcy looked at him skeptically, because in her experience, sex often involved someone's ribs getting bumped by the gearshift or her roommate coming home too early or the wall-to-wall carpet giving her rug burn in a sensitive spot.

"No one gets laid gracefully. Haven't you ever watched a nature documentary? There are always weird noises and lots of flapping."

The water was hot now. She got in and pulled Teagan after her, smiling at the water pressure. Like everything else in this house, it was excellent. She put his back to the spray, then pressed her naked body up against his. She knew he wanted her. Did Teagan get to have so many things that he wanted in his life that he'd just pass this up?

He sighed and bent his cheek against the top of her head, arms loosely around her. And even though his erection was still poking her in the stomach, she could tell he thought she'd given up.

Darcy considered the various bottles on the floor of the shower before picking up someone's conditioner. For sensitive skin, that was appropriate. Teagan didn't catch on to her plan until she'd poured it into both palms.

"Jesus Christ," he said, covering both eyes with his own hands.

"Is that a no? I assumed you didn't have lube here."

"It's not a no, it's—Darcy, I'm sorry I'm terrible at this."

"You're not terrible at this," Darcy said, rubbing her slick palms along his shaft. "If you mean sex. Do you remember me coming all over your face earlier? That was pretty great."

"*That* part I'm going to remember until the day I die. This part—"

"Are you saying this isn't a memorable hand job?" she demanded, pretending to be insulted. She tightened her grip and increased her speed.

That small, crooked grin briefly reappeared on his face. He ruefully lowered his hands to brace himself against the tile behind him.

"Top five, for sure," he said, a beat too late, but Darcy laughed anyway.

It took a long time.

Teagan's face said he knew it was taking a long time, and that was killing him, and that was at least one reason *why* it was taking a long time, regardless of whatever drugs he was taking. But when he finally gave a stuttered gasp and came across her fist, Darcy immediately stuck both arms in the air and gave a loud victory whoop.

She clasped her messy hands together like a prizefighter and shook them above her head, dizzy with the thrill of success.

"Oh my God, I'm incredible!" she said as Teagan sputtered and tried to pull away. "Is this how men feel when they actually get a woman off? I want a medal. I want a write-up. Put this on my resume!"

She wanted to be praised now. She wanted Teagan to kiss her all over her face and tell her she'd done a good job again. *This is the good life*, she wanted to crow at him. Take the wins you get.

He laughed, but he wouldn't meet her eye.

"I'm sorry that took—"

Darcy made a chiding noise in the back of her throat and wrapped her arms around his neck. She leaned forward so their bellies were pressed together and she could feel the fluttering beat of his heart against her chest and his softening cock against her stomach.

"Don't be sorry," she told him fiercely. "It's just like spending the day in the park. You're never guaranteed to see beavers."

"Up to a month ago, a few things were pretty guaranteed, would have been pretty guaranteed if you did even half of that," Teagan said.

Darcy rubbed her face into the wet blonde down below his collarbones. "A month ago, you hadn't decided to get sober. So a lot of things are going to change. Is it so bad if it's always like this?"

He was quiet for a long minute, and Darcy was glad for

the background noise of the shower. He slid his hand along the curve of her lower back, fingers skidding on damp skin. She was more aware now of the different textures of his skin against her own, the hair and muscle of him. It was almost more intimate than what they'd just done, without the rush of desire or the pounding of her pulse to sweep her away. She looked down at her bare feet framed by his, finding the image oddly compelling.

"I wouldn't mind if it was always like this," he said, voice lower than a moment before. His hands pulled her more tightly against him for a moment before he seemed to catch himself, smoothing them almost apologetically away.

He probably didn't mean how that had sounded. Men said a lot of things they didn't mean right after they got laid, anyway, so Darcy just nodded, despite the weighty feeling in her chest, somewhere in the district of her heart.

She let go of Teagan and reached down to investigate the labels of the shampoo bottles, ready to interrogate Teagan about their animal testing guarantees and nonvegan ingredients.

"Okay, good," she said, striving to make her tone businesslike. "Might wanna buy some carbon offsets if we're gonna spend this much time in the shower though."

When she next looked up, Teagan's expression had turned so soft that Darcy wondered whether he really was still thinking about the sex they were going to have, or whether he'd meant it a different way after all.

But all he said was, "Okay, I'll do that."

Teagan was a sucker for a woman wearing nothing but one of his old T-shirts after sex. Had to be one of his favorite looks. Hot. Simple. Darcy, however, hadn't bothered to put on even that much and was wandering around the house in nothing but her socks.

Teagan decided that was the very best look on a woman. Bar none. Utterly beguiling to him and any late-evening dog-walkers who happened to pass the open front windows.

Maybe she was a nudist. Maybe he could expect this to be his view every single day that she was in the house. Maybe she'd eat breakfast and brush her hair and study her textbooks in nothing but her skin.

Maybe she'd stay.

That thought was so ungrounded yet unexpectedly hopeful that it hurt when he perceived it. He immediately pushed it away lest his mind begin to list all the reasons why she would not.

Teagan went to the thermostat to check that it was programmed to keep the heat at a level that would accommodate any naturalist tendencies on Darcy's part.

She had not yet unpacked, but she'd helped herself to the toothbrush she found in his bathroom, and it stuck out of her mouth as she padded up next to him. She brushed his hand off the thermostat and turned it until the little leaf symbol for ecological efficiency appeared on the dial. She looked him over. He'd put on plaid cotton pajama pants, and he felt overdressed.

"I bet you're one of those guys who wants to cuddle all night after sex, huh," she said around the toothbrush, dark brown eyes judging his apparel. She had toothpaste foam on her lips.

Teagan was willing to try to be whatever kind of guy she wanted in that moment, as the past month had rewritten his idea of the kind of guy he actually was. He studied her very casual expression, trying to guess the right answer to that inquiry.

"I . . . am, yes." He went with honesty when he couldn't decide what she wanted to hear. Yes, he wanted Darcy to fall asleep on his chest, preferably without putting anything else on, and if he woke up in the night, he wanted her feet tangled up with his and her hair in his face.

Darcy swung that hair back over a bare shoulder. "That's fine. I was in the Navy. I can sleep anywhere. If you wanna spoon, though, you better move your stuff to the big bed in the guest room."

That wasn't quite an invitation. He didn't want to impose, if she wanted her space.

How did people do this? He'd never had casual sex in his entire life, if that's what this was. He didn't think he was strong enough to decline, but he could already imagine how it would hurt if nothing else changed about their relationship.

But he said nothing and grabbed his shaving kit to follow Darcy back to the guest bathroom. Darcy spat out toothpaste and unself-consciously began rifling through the drawers of the sink console for floss and face wash.

Maybe things would change. Maybe she'd stay.

Teagan opened his shaving kit and took out a new toothbrush for himself. His prescription medicine bottles were wedged behind a bottle of shaving cream and a half-used packet of Benadryl. He zipped the kit back up and stowed it under the sink. He brushed his teeth. He put his old toothbrush on the stand next to his new one. He took a step backward.

"I've been thinking about quitting the Lexapro," he announced, very proud of the nonchalant tone he managed to impart to that statement.

Darcy was propped on her elbows at the other end of the console, taking off mascara with a wet tissue. She paused and looked over her shoulder at him.

"Because of the dick side effects?" she asked.

"The side effects, yeah," he said. "And the doctor said I might not need it forever, anyway. I feel fine now." His heart rate picked up as he waited for her response.

Darcy toweled her face off and tossed it in the bowl. "I'm here to keep you off the sauce, so it doesn't matter if you quit the pills—is that what you mean?"

"That was my thinking," Teagan said, relieved. Darcy thought about it longer.

"Don't do it on my account," she ultimately responded, sinking his heart into his gut before she amended, "I could order one of those harnesses with the double-ended strap-on attachment. We'd have more dick than you or I would know what to do with. *Plenty* of it, anyway."

"I—" Teagan froze, eyes widening. He wasn't sure if she was serious. She probably was. She was usually both literal and serious about her plans. "Homemade is probably more environmentally friendly?" he suggested, mouth going dry with excited terror.

Darcy slid past him, patting his ass familiarly as she went, which wasn't quite an answer.

After he picked up the living room and checked the locks on the doors, he found her in the guest bedroom, already drowsy-eyed in the dead center of the bed. She scooted perhaps an inch to the left to make room for him, and he slid in next to her. Darcy authoritatively arranged him on his back and pressed her face into his pectorals as she curled around him.

"I'll order something made of recycled materials just in case you change your mind," she mumbled.

Teagan grunted in what he hoped was a noncommittal fashion. He could quit the Lexapro. He was better now.

Darcy nuzzled in closer, wrapping both arms around his bicep. It didn't feel casual.

She was asleep and drooling into his shoulder within less than a minute. It took Teagan a few hours longer, but he didn't regret any of them.

eighteen

DARCY WAS AN EARLY RISER AS A MATTER OF BOTH habit and preference, but Teagan was up before her. He was already showered and buttoning a white dress shirt before Darcy blinked into alertness and realized he was preparing to leave the house.

Darcy sat bolt upright, startled to be both naked and apparently late, and began to rub her hair out of her face.

"Oh shit, sorry, what time is it?" she asked before she wondered whether she ought to be the one apologizing, actually.

After correctly intuiting that Teagan was the kind of guy who was willing to spoon all night if his world was sufficiently rocked, she'd banked on him *also* being the kind of guy who got up and made breakfast to butter her up for round two. She'd been looking forward to the morning. She hadn't expected him to be sneaking out.

Teagan jolted at her voice. He wheeled from the mirror, looked at her, blushed, turned around, realized he could still see her in the mirror, blushed harder, then completed the circuit.

"Sorry," he matched her words. "I didn't want to wake you up. I have to go."

"Then don't I have to go too?" Darcy said, trying not to sound accusatory.

"You don't have to come with me," Teagan said, casting a regretful glance over her mostly bare form, still tangled in the sheets. "It's a long commute, and I'm going to stay late catching up on work."

Darcy wrinkled her nose, reorienting herself to what she was doing here. Shore leave was canceled. Back to the boat. Primary mission objective was to keep Teagan from wandering off to a three-martini lunch.

"I *also* have work," she retorted, which made him frown. "Wherever you are."

He sat down next to her, making the mattress dip under his weight. He trailed the back of his knuckles along the curve of her hip, the movement at once tentative and soothing. Darcy leaned into it. If he'd get back into bed, she was sure she could wipe that tight expression off his face.

"You don't have to do anything today," he said, voice careful. "I'm just going to be in the office. Mount Beacon is supposed to be a nice hike, or if you drop me off at the station and take the car, you could check out some of the state parks toward the Catskills—"

"We could do that instead of going into the city," Darcy suggested.

Teagan's mouth twisted, and he looked away.

Well, she'd tried.

"I can get ready in five minutes," Darcy promised, pushing them both out of bed.

By the time Darcy had thrown on the clothes at the top of her suitcase and brushed her hair into submission, Teagan was knotting an aggressively boring blue tie in the bathroom mirror, his movements short and tense.

"Do you wear a suit every day?" Darcy asked, curious. She came up behind him and wrapped arms around his torso to take the fabric out of his hands. She pretended to know how to tie it, folding the fabric in a running knot instead.

"Only on days where I have board meetings or I'm coming back from a month at rehab," he said ruefully. He realized that she was just playing with the tie and pulled it away from her hands to fix it.

In Darcy's life, she'd only seen men wearing suits for church ceremonies or the senior prom. Teagan's face said it was a funeral. She leaned her cheek against his broad back and squeezed him before she let him go. He was missing signals again, his head off somewhere other than next to her.

They drove an ancient Mercedes sedan to the station, then took the Hudson line into the city. The sun was just coming up when they pulled away from the platform, but the train was crowded with other commuters in work clothes. Teagan used his shoulders to push through the crowd and get them two seats together, yielding the window seat to Darcy.

It was oddly domestic. Here they were, going to work together, as though this was something they did every day. Darcy had the awkward sensation that she was playing dress-up in someone else's clothes. That she hadn't read the mission brief again.

"Do you mind?" Teagan asked, pulling out his laptop as soon as they were underway. "I usually work on the train."

She shook her head and rummaged in her backpack for her headphones. "I have plenty to do," she said.

"Not the alcoholism podcast," he immediately objected.

"Not that one." She was already up to Step Ten and planned to wait until Teagan caught up a little more before listening to the last few episodes. "I have my reading for class."

Teagan looked over at her phone. "That must be convenient," he ventured. "I don't think they had audio versions of all my textbooks when I was in college."

Darcy hid her expression. It wasn't convenient. The audiobooks couldn't be purchased used, so they were always exorbitantly expensive. And often there wasn't an audio version available at all now that she was taking very specialized classes for her major, and she'd have to get or make PDFs, then convert them to text, then export the files to a screen reader app, errors and all.

"Sure," she said, slipping her headphones on and resolving to enjoy the ride as she listened to unmodulated mechanical sentences and bursts of static.

Almost an hour later, they emerged in Grand Central Station. Teagan guided them briskly through the teeming crowds and into the smelly, humid streets of the city. Darcy had been here once before, for Fleet Week, but she'd been so blitzed the entire time that she could barely remember it. She decided that discretion was not telling Teagan about her own drunken escapades, and she pretended to be impressed by the skyscrapers and rush of taxis and buses through the busy Midtown streets as they walked a few blocks west to the middling-tall building that housed Teagan's office.

Some people liked New York. She'd heard that. Some people loved living in the city: the crowds, the energy, the variety. Teagan's expression said he wasn't one of them. His face was set with grim determination as they rode to the twenty-fifth floor and emerged in a very corporate-looking lobby, with walnut paneling on the walls and cool cream stone on the floors that made every footstep echo, even Darcy's boots.

In the lobby there was a knot of three women examining a large piece of art hanging to the left of the reception desk. It was another one of those grotesque naked women like the painting from Teagan's living room, though this one was a cotton-candy blonde holding a slice of cake. The three women were appraising it with the coolly judgmental faces of grocery store shoppers browsing a stack of April peaches.

Teagan took a deep breath when he spotted them, paused, squared his shoulders, and turned in their direction.

Two of the women in the group were short and round and dressed in professional attire like Teagan. The third, a tall, slender brunette like Sloane but a couple of decades older, broke away to approach him first, face consciously assuming a bright, artificial smile. The woman wore flowing camel-colored trousers with a matching cropped sweater and carried a large leather tote bag that Darcy suspected of costing more than her car.

As Darcy grimaced suspiciously, the brunette kiss-kissed Teagan's cheeks and drew back to examine him.

"Well, you look fantastic! I think you've gotten a tan!" she announced, flicking an imaginary strand of hair away from a perfectly made-up face. "How are you feeling?"

"Great," Teagan said unconvincingly. He tried again. "I'm doing very well. It's good to see you, Nora." He looked past her to the other two women. "Rose, Modeline . . . good morning."

All three women seemed to register Darcy's presence at the same time. They shifted to face her, and Darcy looked back at them, putting Rose's name, at least, with a face. Teagan's office nemesis was barely five feet tall and had a cloud of black ringlets around bright pink cheeks. The five-inch block heels and polite scowl she wore, however, matched her reputation.

Darcy flicked her eyes at Teagan and cleared her throat, because she wasn't sure how he planned to introduce her or explain what she was doing there.

Teagan's jaw worked before he spoke.

"Darcy, this is Nora, chair of our board of directors," he said, indicating the tall woman with several carats worth of diamonds in her earlobes. "You've heard me mention Rose, the chief investment officer, who's been running things in my absence. And this is Modeline, the programs officer." The last was a Black woman in her fifties with an elegant fall of tiny braids running down her back, the only one whose look at Teagan bore any hint of sympathy.

"Hi," said Darcy.

After a long blink, Rose took a step around Teagan and shook Darcy's hand with her own small manicured one.

"Nice to meet you," said Rose, seemingly prepared to let Teagan avoid any explanation of Darcy's presence.

After a beat, Modeline did the same, smiling at Darcy with more welcome. Bemused, Darcy shook her hand as well.

Nora tilted her head and examined Darcy from muddy boots to messy ponytail.

"Are you interning at the foundation this fall?" Nora pointedly asked Darcy, expression a trifle dismayed as she took in Darcy's jean shorts.

"No," Darcy said, suppressing an eye roll. "I'm not."

Everyone looked at Teagan again.

He briefly closed his eyes.

"Darcy is . . . my sober companion," he said after nobody changed the subject.

"Your what?" asked Rose.

Even the receptionist was now paying close attention to Teagan. Darcy had the sudden urge to take Teagan's arm, just to help hold him up, because he looked almost grayish under the florescent lights of the lobby. They probably should have walked through this. If he'd stayed at rehab as long as he was supposed to, they would have gone over reentry.

Modeline's eyebrows lifted in surprise. "All Rose told us was that you were out sick."

Teagan's mouth tightened as he shot an angry glance at Rose before addressing the group again. "I was in rehab, actually. For alcohol abuse," he said in a rush. "So. Darcy is my sober companion. She'll be here for the next . . . a few months, at least."

All three women goggled at him, but Darcy was so proud she wanted to burst. That was the first step! That was a huge deal! As far as she knew, that was the first time he'd ever admitted it to anyone but her.

"Oh my God!" Nora said, laying a dramatic hand to her chest. "I had no idea you were an alcoholic. Just like Margaret."

"Yes," Teagan said, more smoothly now. "Just like my mother."

"I never noticed that you had a drinking problem." Nora's expression was rapt and interested. "Oh my God, you poor thing."

Teagan's admission seemed to have settled him, and his shoulders visibly relaxed. "I do. Or rather, I did. But as of today, I'm back full time." He gave all three women a cautious professional smile. "I'm looking forward to getting back to work."

"I'm glad to hear that," Modeline said, sounding sincere. "And I'm happy to hear you're getting help." She looked over at Darcy. "Welcome. My assistant manages the office assignments, so if you need one to work out of, just speak to him."

"Thank you," said Darcy. This was going as well as she could have possibly imagined.

"Wait, this makes sense, actually," Nora said, still processing, thumb tapping her lips. "Is that why you snuck out of that reception at the Whitney last month? Because there wasn't an open bar?"

Teagan looked at a spot on the wall, his cheeks turning pink. "I don't think that's related, actually. I didn't even notice. I just had to leave early."

"I'm sure things must have come to a crisis for you to consider rehab. Your mother never did, you know."

"I know," Teagan said stubbornly. "But I wasn't drinking at . . . work events."

Nora's face was smoothly skeptical. "Of course not."

"I didn't." Teagan raised his voice, looked over at the receptionist, then back at the trio. "I don't know what the message has been while I've been gone, but let's get this straight. I would never do anything to put the foundation's mission at risk, and I am going to do everything to mitigate my situation's effect on my work."

"I'm sure this is a lot on your first day back. We can talk tomorrow," Nora said, unperturbed.

"I'm fine," Teagan said, tone insistent. "We can talk now, since you're here. Any questions you have, either about the foundation or my ability to work, I'm happy to answer them."

Maybe this was closer to what Darcy had imagined. She edged toward Teagan, wondering if she needed to extract him.

"Oh, you're so sweet, but I'm just happy to see you're do-ing better," Nora said.

Rose had recovered from her surprise, but her expression was displeased. She crossed her arms and squinted up at Tea-gan, mouth twisting pensively.

Teagan registered the look but purposefully disregarded it, keeping his attention on Nora instead. "What brought you to the office today though?" he asked.

"I had a breakfast meeting with the ladies," Nora said, inclining her head at Rose and Modeline. "Looking at our cash needs for the next fiscal year. Reviewing some of the illiquid assets."

"I see," Teagan said, eyes flicking to Rose in a moment of anger. "I would have met you for it if it had been on my calendar. I got back last night."

"We scheduled this meeting two weeks ago," Rose said defensively, arms not budging.

"No need to worry," Nora said airily. "We can catch up for dinner some night this week. Just text me. I actually have to run right now. I have to get up to MoMA. Second donor affinity group meeting on acquisitions this month, if you can believe it. Busy, busy," She waited for murmurs of due appreciation.

"I'll be in the office all week," Teagan said. "Just call my extension. Happy to talk at any time."

Nora smiled noncommittally. She bid everyone farewell, then kiss-kissed on Teagan's cheeks for the second time. "So sorry to hear about the alcoholism. I'm glad to see you look-ing well though."

She didn't look at Darcy again. Darcy decided she didn't like her.

Darcy wasn't looking forward to meeting the woman again at dinner, if that happened.

Was she going to be invited to this dinner?

Of course she was. Teagan couldn't go off somewhere where alcohol was served without her.

Having spent a moment working through it, Darcy decided that every job had its hazards, and socialites were less dangerous than bears. She resolved to wear makeup and something more professional than her "Coronado is for Lovers" T-shirt when the dinner happened.

As soon as Nora's elevator was gone, Teagan looked at Rose, expression stormy. "If we could talk for a moment in my office?" he asked, tone excruciatingly polite but redolent of icy fury.

Darcy stiffened, because she'd never seen him take that tone toward anyone. From the look on Rose's face, she wasn't familiar with it either.

"Of course," Rose said, not cowed.

Teagan gave Darcy a tight smile before he turned toward the lobby's exit. "I'll check in with you in a few," he said. "Just ask Modeline's assistant, Kevin, if you need something."

Darcy hadn't expected to be dismissed almost immediately after their arrival, so she went back on her heels as Teagan stalked off, Rose following him. She'd wanted to congratulate him for telling his coworkers about his alcoholism. He'd need support after Darcy was gone, even if he didn't seem particularly close to Rose or Modeline.

That last thought gave her some concern. Someone would have to be here for him, since Darcy's podcast talked about recovery in terms of months and years. Maybe Sloane would do it. Maybe he'd get an actual sponsor. Maybe he'd get a girlfriend.

Wouldn't that just take the cake? Darcy would do all the hard work drying him out, then some snotty New York lady could move in when Teagan's biggest remaining issue was holding onto his mother's bedroom furniture. That seemed very unfair.

Darcy frowned at the door where Teagan and Rose had exited. She wasn't sure what her objection was, exactly, but she abruptly felt like she ought to go sit in to keep an eye on the man.

"Maybe I should," she began, taking one step toward the door.

Modeline shook her head. "Let them have it out," she advised. "If I hear screaming, I'll let you know to rescue him."

Darcy let Modeline lead her back into the warren of cubicles in the office's interior, where she pointed out the break room, the executive suites, and her assistant's desk before excusing herself and shutting the door to her own office.

It was eight thirty in the morning, and everyone was at their desks, wearing headsets and polo shirts. The office air smelled like plastic carpet and burnt coffee. There was a low background hum of overhead lights, clacking keyboards, and computer notifications.

Darcy felt a wave of dislocation wash through her stomach. She'd never been in a place like this in her entire life, and it was hard to immediately summon what she was supposed to be doing here, surrounded by office workers. Was everyone else looking at her or was that her imagination?

Wrinkling her nose, Darcy rustled in her backpack for her headphones. Her hands steadied as she pulled up her podcasts on her phone and plugged in for the next couple of hours. She supposed she'd check whether there was any booze in the break room fridge, then ask about her office.

She'd always said she wanted to be in charge. And if nobody had told her what to do, that had to mean she was.

Someone had come in to empty the trash since he'd last been in his office, but motes of dust spun in the air and caught in the morning light breaking through the venetian blinds. Teagan flipped on the overhead lights and shut the door behind Rose as she followed him inside.

This had been his mother's office. The angular white furniture and bright blue Persian carpet were too feminine for his tastes, but it hadn't seemed appropriate to spend the foundation's money on redecorating in light of the dire state of its finances when he took over, and then he had just learned to live with it.

He gestured for Rose to take a seat in one of the clear acrylic chairs in front of his desk, but she walked to the bank of windows instead. There was a gilt bar cart with an untouched crystal decanter full of God knew what, also inherited from his mother. Rose got a wry look on her face as she gazed down at the tray of Baccarat glasses.

Teagan grimaced at this latest act of defiance and slumped into the armchair behind the desk. It was a good thing that he'd learned that the tightness in his chest and the painful quickness of his heartbeat were caused by nothing more than his anxious mind; otherwise, he would still have been worried.

"I should fire you," he said. Cutting him off from communications was one thing, but getting between him and Nora was another.

Rose did all but roll her eyes, making him grit his jaw. Even if Nora hadn't told him to hire her, she'd been the best-qualified person for her job—better-qualified than Teagan when he started, honestly. He thought he'd always treated her with respect. They'd never gotten close, but that hadn't bothered him until now.

"You've never fired anyone in your entire life," Rose said, sounding crisply unperturbed by his threat. "You couldn't even fire that network admin who lied about knowing DNS configuration. Modeline had to do it."

"I think I'm working myself up to it," Teagan said darkly.

Rose turned and assessed him again, looking him over.

"You look a little better," she said. "But you didn't need to come back just to make Nora happy. Modeline and I have things well in hand."

"Do you think I'm stupid?" he snapped, "Nora told me she was going to hand you my job."

"On an interim basis only," Rose said. "I don't want your job. I make more money than you."

His self-preservation instinct was barely functioning, but he managed not to point out that Rose could presumably ask for a raise if she got promoted.

"Well, it's not happening regardless," Teagan said. "Which means you can call off whatever you're doing with Nora too. We aren't selling the art. Don't waste any time on it."

Rose picked up one of the crystal tumblers and peered into it. She rubbed it against her sleeve and wrinkled her nose at the dust.

"What's going on with you, Teagan?" she asked in a tone of bland curiosity, completely ignoring his last instruction. Her deadpan and thick Boston accent made her observations even more cutting. "You called me from an ambulance and said you were having a heart attack. When I tracked down your sister for an update on you being maybe dead, she said you'd had some kind of nervous breakdown. Is that what this is?"

"As it turns out, I am an alcoholic," Teagan said through gritted teeth. How many times was he going to have to do this?

"Hmm. I can't recall ever seeing you drunk," Rose said. "And your sister said you needed some time off from work, not from drinking."

"That's another thing," Teagan said, showing that he could dodge questions just as well as she could. "Keep my sister out of this. She's a college student. She needs to focus on school."

"Your sister raised more money in the past three weeks than you did in the entire last quarter. She's pretty good at it, which you aren't."

Rose's words hit him right in his vulnerabilities. He knew he wasn't good at it. He didn't know what to do about that though.

"I've had a lot of other priorities here," he excused himself. "If Nora's worried about our cash position, I'll focus on fundraising."

"I've seen you make donor calls. You listen to them blather about their knee surgeries and their kids' college admissions, and half the time you don't even ask them for money."

Teagan curled his hands into the loose fabric of his trousers. "If you have suggestions for improvement, I'm sure we have a box for that somewhere."

"How about this? You literally do the work of three people. You know how I know that? Because I had to assign all your work, and it took three people to do it. We need to hire a controller, a director of HR, and an executive assistant for you. Don't handle the fundraising. Let someone else do it."

"You want to increase headcount while we're running out of cash?" he groaned.

"No, I want to increase headcount and improve our cash position. Which is why we need to start selling off the art. It doesn't generate any liquidity, and we can sell the pieces that aren't even accreting value."

"I didn't take this job to just liquidate the endowment," Teagan said, even though it was hard to remember what he'd really thought he'd be able to accomplish. Today, this year, this entire job.

"Your mother sold art almost every year she ran this place. And took in new in-kind donations to replace it," Rose pointed out. "Which we haven't done in two years."

"We are *not* going to do things the way my mother did," Teagan said, standing up and leaning over his desk.

Most of the people who worked at the foundation pre-dated his tenure here. They remembered his mother. They certainly remembered her irregular hours and erratic behavior, and nobody could possibly forget how she'd died. If he'd disappeared for a month and came back with the announcement that he was an alcoholic, that meant he had to try harder than ever to impress upon everyone else that he was not her.

"The art donations are a scam, did you know that?" Teagan said, hand against the desk for emphasis. "It's basically a tax shelter. My mother's friends got inflated valuations on the art, the foundation held it for three years, pretended to use it for educational purposes, then sold it at a huge loss. And Nora got a piece too, when she brokered the sales."

"Of course it's a tax shelter! This is a family foundation, what did you think you were doing?" Rose said, dark eyebrows condensing skeptically.

"I'm running a children's charity!"

She scoffed. "There are hundreds of these things in New York alone, and they only exist to avoid estate taxes and provide full employment for the progeny of the obnoxiously rich with delusions of dynasty. Funding art camps for children is basically a side effect."

"If you really think that, what are you doing here?" Teagan demanded.

Rose shrugged. "I'm an investment manager. It's better than working at Deutsche Bank. Or, you know, selling fentanyl on the street. What I'm saying is, it's not worth killing yourself about whether you're doing a good job or not. We could just liquidate the entire endowment and give the money out to poor kids; we'd probably have the same positive effect."

"Are you *trying* to get fired—"

Teagan was cut off by two loud raps on his closed door.

Both of them turned and watched it open. Darcy peered in warily.

"Inside voices," she admonished them. "You'll scare away all the wildlife."

Once she'd established that Teagan and Rose were not actually at each other's throats, she let herself into the office, surveying the space. Her eyes landed on the crystal decanter.

Making a chiding noise, she scooped it up with a stern glance at Teagan.

"Don't worry," Rose said in a dry voice. "I've been watching him. He hasn't had any of it."

"Good," said Darcy. "I already took care of the beer in

the break room fridge. Do you think there's anything else in the office?"

"I keep a bottle of Jameson in my desk drawer for days when my boss is being unreasonable, but I can lock the drawer," Rose said, glaring at Teagan.

"Ah," Darcy said, eyes flicking to him. "Well, maybe let me work on the boss."

Rose was happy to take that excuse to go, even if Teagan was not entirely happy to leave it like that. He didn't want to continue the conversation in front of Darcy though, so he waved Rose off. She shut the door behind her.

Darcy tucked the decanter under an arm and came to perch on the corner of Teagan's desk.

"That was just for show," she stage-whispered. "If you want to take her to mast for insubordination, I'll help you put her in the brig. Are you allowed to put people in the brig here?"

Teagan couldn't quite manage a laugh, but he leaned forward and propped his head in his hands, then dragged his fingertips through his hair, trying to brush it back behind his ears. He hadn't had a haircut in weeks; he probably looked like a college student.

"I think that would be bad for morale," he said, trying to pull himself together. Arguing with anyone always knocked him back and put his stomach into knots. He looked at Darcy's booted feet, dangling incongruously against the side of the white desk.

He had a sudden burst of longing to be back in the woods, clippers in his hands, some simple solvable task in front of him.

"Do you want to go for a walk? There's supposed to be a red-tailed hawk nest a few blocks away," he said, scraping for some reason they might both get out of this office and away from the dozens of people who were right now find-ing out where he'd been.

Darcy's face was doubtful. "You want to go for a nature hike in Midtown Manhattan?" she asked, gesturing out the window to the other skyscrapers crowding close around them.

"It's there. It was on the news," Teagan said, even though he sensed this was not a great inducement. "I saw a video clip of it feeding a rat to its babies."

Yes, Darcy, stay with me, your life can be this exciting.

"No, I know," she replied, gracefully forbearing from criticism of his idea of a good time. "That species adapted well to urban environments. But it's August. The nestlings would already be fledged and gone."

"Right," Teagan said, like he'd known that.

Darcy ran an affectionate hand over his shoulder. "Be-sides, I have stuff to do, and I'm sure you do too. I was just checking in. Today I'm going to take that resume you made me and send it to the contractors for a couple of other na-tional parks. Hedge my bets, you know."

"Right," he said again, gritting his teeth at the idea. He wished she'd stay, instead.

He'd block his calendar to spend a half an hour today looking at job listings for the state parks around New York.

"If you suddenly get a feeling like you're gonna rush out of here and hit the gin, just call me first," she said. "I'll check in on you later." She patted his shoulder as she left with the decanter of bourbon, and it was like half the air in the room went with her.

There was more than enough work to be done. It would take him days to dig out from under the email alone, even if Rose or Modeline seemed to have responded to everything from external partners.

But his head felt like a mason jar full of fireflies—little flashes of light as winged insects tapped against the glass. He couldn't call any donors while he felt like this.

He couldn't concentrate on anything until he moved his inquiry into nearby jobs that might interest Darcy to the top of his to-do list.

Half an hour of work only produced a running list of nearby state park websites and a note to email a donor who'd also supported the Audubon Society, but he could see the shape of the project taking form. It was a little thread of hope to hold on to before he turned his attention back to the business of the foundation as expressed in the email backlog.

At lunchtime, he went to the break room, but he did not find Darcy there. Someone had ordered in cold cut sandwiches for lunch for the office. Under the curious looks of the gathered staff, Teagan did a stiff circuit of the room, shoved half a sandwich onto a paper plate, and quickly retreated to his office, feeling like all eyes were on him.

He checked his phone, finding a voice text from Darcy indicating that she'd gone out for a couple of hours.

Which of course she could do. He couldn't reasonably think she'd be with him twenty-four hours a day. Who'd want to?

He ate his sandwich over his keyboard as he checked the performance of the foundation's asset portfolio over the past month, then moved on to Modeline's reports on grant spending. This part of his job he did not mind. The paperwork was nonjudgmental, the numbers asked little of him, and together the two told a story about the real-world impact of this venture: actual children enjoying their lives.

Once absorbed in the finances, he did not look back up until the lights went out at six p.m. Teagan automatically waved his arms to catch the sensor's attention and make them come back on—this happened to him several times every evening here—then realized that he hadn't seen Darcy all day. He checked his phone. No new messages.

A little worried, Teagan went back out into the open office. Most of the staff were gathering purses and backpacks and shutting down their computers. He looked through the break room and cubicles until he found Darcy working on an old laptop in an empty conference room. Much relieved to see her there, he grabbed a fistful of menus out of the break room with a view to dinner.

"Quitting time?" Darcy said eagerly when he came in, reaching for her backpack.

"Oh, I—we can leave," Teagan said. He usually worked a few hours longer so as to avoid rush hour congestion on the train if he was going back to Irvington.

"No, no, let's keep it as close to your usual schedule as we can," Darcy said, even though her face said she was unimpressed with his office hours. "I'm fine here."

"Did you get your job applications done?" Teagan asked, hoping the answer was no.

Darcy popped her neck from side to side.

"I found one place that wants a fucking *essay* from me on my commitment to customer service," she said darkly. "So I'll work on that tomorrow."

"An essay?"

"A cover letter. Same deal." She paused. "I might ask you to look at it before I send it in. Just, you know. Spelling and stuff."

Teagan nodded and held out the stack of paper menus to her. He usually went out for lunch but ordered something up to the office for dinner for himself and anyone else who was working late.

Darcy took the top menu—the Chinese restaurant in the lobby—and looked at it blankly for a few seconds. Then she passed it back to him.

"You pick. Just something not too heavy on mushrooms," she asked, not sounding too interested.

"I could take you out to dinner," he said, hopes rising again. Darcy back here in his office was good, but Darcy tucked into some cozy booth with him and a bowl of chana masala would be much better. "What would you like? Indian, maybe? There's a good place near my condo."

At that, Darcy perked up. "Your condo! That's a good point. Do you have some time to go over that right now?"

"Time for . . . my condo?" he asked, confused.

"Yes. Where is it?"

"Midtown West."

"I couldn't find that on the map. Is it not in Manhattan?"

"Realtors invented Midtown West to sell condos," he admitted. "It's Hell's Kitchen, really."

Darcy nodded thoughtfully, then reached into her backpack. She pulled out a map, the giant foldout kind that newsstands sold to tourists to mark them as people who ought to be pickpocketed or robbed. She unfolded it over the conference room table and peremptorily gestured at Teagan to come stand next to her.

The map was covered in black pen marks, checks and crosses, and Darcy had drawn a thick, highlighted route from his office to Grand Central Station. The route was far from direct—it zigged and zagged circuitously around a number of blocks, nearly doubling the distance between the two destinations. He couldn't figure out what it was meant to capture.

"Show me on this map where your condo is?" Darcy asked, frowning at the center.

Teagan tapped 47th Street.

Darcy scanned the area. "Okay, I didn't get that far north today. I'll look tomorrow."

"Look for what?"

She grinned, glancing over at him with just a quick flash of curving red lips.

"So, this is how you get to the train without passing any bars," she said, tapping the thick black line with her finger. "There are a couple of restaurants *here*"—she indicated a black check mark—"and *here* that look like they have bars in them, but if you keep to the south side of the street, you won't walk right by them. We'll practice tonight on the way home."

Teagan inhaled, his chest tightening until it felt like a vibrating string between his heart and his throat. She must have spent hours today methodically mapping the local watering holes. It didn't matter that it wouldn't help him if she were gone. She'd done it to keep him safe.

Teagan had always thought about love in terms of want and need. He'd been in love. He'd felt loved before. He'd seen it expressed in words and embraces and gifts. The austerity of Darcy's kind of care had made it hard for him to recognize—it wasn't a way he'd been loved before. But Darcy mapping his way home was a kind of love too, so tangible that he'd never be able to tell himself even on his worst day that he'd imagined it.

She squeaked when he reached out and roughly pulled her

to him. He wrapped his arms around her and buried his nose against her scalp to breathe in the sweet smell of her hair.

"This is really good work," he told her, because he didn't know if she wanted to hear him say *I think I'm in love with you*. He still had three months to show her.

"Well, thank you," Darcy said, crushed against his chest, sounding a little flustered. "I'll get to your condo tomorrow. And then we can talk about everywhere else you go."

Nowhere without her, Teagan hoped, mentally resolving to spend twice as much time with the state parks department's job board tomorrow.

nineteen

FOR ALL THAT TEAGAN WAS THEORETICALLY EAGER to get back to his typical social schedule of benefit luncheons, dinners, and balls, he made several attempts to abort the mission on the evening when Darcy finally cleared him to stress-test his sobriety under typical field conditions.

"We could go out to dinner instead," he offered as they exited his office building. He kept trying to take her to restaurants, which was baffling to Darcy, since she had already slept with him. "And I should have reminded you to bring something to change into. We could go to the St. Jude's gala tomorrow, see most of the same people."

He wore a suit but no tie. Darcy was wearing a button-down white shirt tucked into black slacks. They weren't dressed very differently, she didn't think. She'd helped Kristin cater plenty of fancy parties in this outfit, last spring.

"This is the nicest outfit I own," she said. She owned dresses, but they were all of the kind that she put on mostly for the taking off, and she didn't think that was the vibe of a party to benefit the Feldman Visual Arts Academy. "Unless you count my dress blues. You wanna see me in a dixie cup hat?"

He didn't, it seemed. His expression was morose as they

walked further through Midtown. The sun was still bright on the pavement and bags of uncollected garbage.

"You're not going to enjoy this," Teagan warned her.

"It can't be much worse than escorting oil tankers through the Straits of Hormuz," she said. "Petrochemicals. Iranian go-fasts. Sea snakes, if you fall in."

"Do you think?" Teagan asked, eyes rounding with concern.

Darcy laughed and smacked him in the chest. "Of course not. It's a seated dinner. At worst, it'll be like that time a squirrel died under Rachel's porch, and I had to dig it out with a broom."

"In this metaphor, am I the dead squirrel?" He tilted his chin away in faux outrage as Darcy giggled at him.

Darcy didn't think she'd mind the evening as much as he seemed to think. For all Teagan was twitchy and subdued, he looked very handsome in his charcoal suit, and Darcy wasn't above feeling up on herself for arriving at this fancy rich-person function on his arm.

"Don't ask me to identify metaphors. I'm a wildlife science major," she said grandly.

That was a thing she felt comfortable saying because she'd spent four solid hours catching up on homework this morning while Teagan listened to conference calls on his headset and ripped Post-it notes into little piles on his desk. Then this afternoon she'd marked half a dozen cafes without liquor licenses within a few blocks of Teagan's office while she listened to Carrie Fisher's memoir. It felt like years since she'd had the time to listen to anything for pleasure. Fully employed, progressing in her class, and engaged in leisure activities? Yes! That was her!

She beamed at her charge, willing his miserable expression

to lighten. She'd show him. They'd make it through this evening free and clear if she had to personally tackle a cater-waiter to keep the cocktails out of his hands.

"Would you usually drink at one of these things?" Darcy asked, trying to suss out what his issue was. A fundraiser really didn't sound too terrible of an ordeal, but Teagan's face was taut with stress.

Darcy had yet to get a good feel for where the crisis points were likely to be in Teagan's life, since it didn't seem like he'd made a habit of drinking at either his mother's house or the office. He never talked about it.

"I would probably have a drink or two, yes," he said. "There's a cocktail hour before the banquet, and then they serve wine at dinner."

She nodded. "Okay, so what's your plan, then?"

"I'm going to imagine that I'm back in Yellowstone, and everyone else is a gray wolf, but they're actually two hundred meters away from me, and the park ranger is standing by with a gun."

Darcy rolled her eyes. "I mean about the drinking."

"Oh. I guess . . . I'll order a club soda," he said, eyes flicking to her for approval.

"That's good," she said approvingly. Teagan didn't look reassured though. She tried again. "Gray wolves use social grooming to show pack allegiance. If you're at a loss for what to do without a drink in your hand, try nibbling gently on the fur around one of the other guests' scent glands."

He snorted faintly. "That's a good way to get invited to less of these things, at least."

They reached the lobby of the Westin and followed the signs promoting the event to the ballroom, where dozens of people were milling in front of a bar. There was a stage against one wall, round tables set for dinner in the middle, and long rectangular tables set against all the other walls bearing wrapped gift baskets, stuffed envelopes, paintings and bits of sculpture, and various crates and bottles of liquor.

Off on the other side of the room, there were a dozen or so middle school–aged kids stuffed into matching polo shirts being minded by nearly as many teachers, all milling around in front of some felt partitions on which their colorful watercolor paintings had been hung.

Teagan halted at the entrance of the room, his expression softening when he saw the huddle of bored preteens. "I forgot this is one of the ones where the kids come and talk about their art. We help fund this school's summer camp."

"All the stuff you do is for children's art charities, right?" Darcy asked.

"That's what's in the foundation's charter, yes," Teagan said, absently wandering toward the bar, smiling at last. "I went to a summer program at this school when I was a kid."

"Do you paint?" Darcy asked, suddenly curious about what Teagan actually ever did for fun.

"Not anymore. I wasn't any good at painting. But I could make a perfectly serviceable ashtray," he said, the corner of his mouth pulling out that lopsided dimple.

"Teagan!" came a woman's voice from across the room, and Teagan froze like a rabbit who'd just heard a hawk's cry.

At first Darcy thought it was Sloane, who was supposed to be in attendance tonight. But the slender brunette in a gray hammered-silk jumpsuit who swished to Teagan's side was his chairperson, Nora.

She kissed his cheek and smeared it with red gloss.

"I didn't know if you'd come! And I'm so glad you made it in time for cocktail hour," Nora said, winking like she'd made a clever joke. She gestured with the big glass of white wine in her hand. "This must be like going to Bâtard while you're on a diet. Oh! But of course you brought your helper with you."

Darcy showed Nora the white points of her teeth.

"Cocktail hour is my specialty," Darcy said. "It's like demining without the risk of death."

Nora laughed in a way that mimed huge amusement without much volume.

"Good! Very good," she said, somehow implying the opposite. "I'm sure you take very good care of Teagan."

"We were just going to get a club soda," Teagan said, edging away. "And then see the kids' art."

"Oh, of course! I love to see the little babies' paintings too. So cute. But actually, can I borrow you for a minute first? Patricia Hausauer said she was dying to catch up with you. And she collects Cindy Sherman, just like your mother did. You must remember Patricia, right? You picked up your mother from her birthday party out in West Hampton a few years ago."

"Yes," Teagan said. "I remember."

Darcy had begun to recognize a certain sludgy quality to Teagan's voice when he was agreeing to something he didn't want to do, so she told Nora, "I'll bring him by after we've got our drinks."

"He'll be fine!" Nora said breezily. "I promise I'll keep an eye on him."

Without waiting for Darcy's response, Nora grabbed onto Teagan's arm and turned to wave at an older woman in a flashy pink skirt suit on the other side of the room.

"Well, I—" Darcy began to object. She didn't think she

should let Teagan out of reach at his first event where alcohol was served.

"Save yourself," Teagan muttered despondently, sotto voce, as he was dragged away.

Darcy hesitated until he was already gone. Nora all but frog marched him to a group of women near the bar, several of whom pantomimed great excitement to see him, an emotion Teagan overtly did not return.

Darcy was left alone in the middle of the entryway. She felt slightly less optimistic than she had on the way over. She'd imagined standing next to Teagan for the entirety of the evening, batting away cocktails and whispering judgmental observations into his ear to make him laugh.

She should have said something, Darcy decided. Next time she'd make a scene. She didn't really mind making a scene, and she sensed that the women at this event would consider it a tragedy if the entire evening passed and nobody made a scene. It might as well be Darcy. Next time she'd fight Nora off.

Her stomach sank as nobody else looked her way. Shit, what was she supposed to do now? What did people do at parties if they couldn't drink or dance or flirt with strangers?

At loose ends now, she edged back over to the tables of junk. Most of the people present were talking with other people they seemed to know, but there was one man standing by himself, a tall man with dark auburn hair and a bored attitude. He and Darcy made brief eye contact as he desultorily browsed the items on display. His thousand-yard stare and the death grip he had on his glass of red wine gave her the impression that he was just as happy to be here as Teagan.

He glanced over at the crowd around the bar as Darcy

approached him, so she assumed he belonged to one of the well-dressed women catching up with their friends there.

"This is a silent auction?" Darcy asked to open the conversation.

The redhead looked down at the clipboards arrayed along the table. He gave Darcy a long look down his very aristocratic nose before he answered.

"Yes. Have you never been to one before?"

Darcy shook her head. She wasn't ashamed that her life had been more interesting than this.

"All of the things on the table were donated to the event. People come and write down the amount they bid to buy them. You can see what the current bids are and what the reserve price is. At the end of the evening, the proceeds go to the charity," he said, his explanation very neutral.

Darcy hummed and browsed a little further down the table. There were spa packages, vacation rentals, ski lessons—all the stuff rich people liked, she guessed. She came to a large painting and stopped.

The style was semiabstract, and the colors were gray and chilly. The subject was a riderless horse in the woods, fully saddled and bridled but rearing in alarm.

Darcy didn't know anything about art, but she didn't think she liked it.

Nobody had bid yet. She looked down at the reserve.

"Holy shit, thirty-five hundred dollars?" she yelped.

The redhead wandered over.

"Do you think that's too high or too low?" he asked, sounding interested for the first time.

Darcy snorted. "Who's going to pay three months' rent to own a painting you can't even hang over your couch?"

"I believe some people hang paintings in other locations from time to time," he said. "But why can't this one go over your couch?"

"I don't like the message it sends," she replied, trying and failing to imagine the painting in Teagan's living room in the place of his mother's tits.

"Too grim?"

"No, the painting says *I've never seen a horse before*," she said.

The redheaded man coughed like he was covering a laugh, expression sharpening.

"Why do you say that?" he asked.

"Well, just look at it. The eyes are too big, the nostrils are too small, and a horse's jaw doesn't even open that far."

They both considered the painting for a few moments more.

"Perhaps the artist was anthropomorphizing the animal to increase the viewer's sympathy with it," the redhead suggested.

Darcy squinted at the painting. "No, no. I think they just didn't bother to Google *horses* before they started drawing."

"I doubt that, but I suppose all reactions to art are valid under several schools of criticism," Darcy's new friend said, but his expression also said that he did not belong to one of those schools.

"You think they did it on purpose?" Darcy asked.

"I do," he said, expression very stiff.

"Why?"

He took a sip from his glass of red wine. "I painted it."

Darcy was so surprised that she snorted the club soda she'd been drinking, managing to spray the poor man as she coughed and sputtered. *I have a drinking problem too*, she'd tell Teagan, who loved a dad joke.

When she recovered, the artist's appalled expression was nearly enough to send her into hysterical laughter. She'd gone and made a scene after all. A few heads were turning to see whether anything fun was happening. No, not yet.

"Oh my God, I'm sorry," Darcy said. "I'm just uncultured. I'm sure the actual guests will like the horse. This perfectly normal, accurate, ordinary-looking . . . horse." She strove for sincerity, but she could barely get the words out past her giggles.

The artist hesitated like he was considering just walking away, but he ultimately brushed his face off with his sleeve and put his hand out. His shoulders slumped as though he'd decided to take his lumps.

"Adrian Landry," he introduced himself. "An artist who has definitely seen many horses."

"Darcy Albano. Horse enthusiast." They shook on it.

Darcy expected him to excuse himself after that bit of awkwardness, but he shot a cautious glance at the group of people Teagan and Nora were speaking with and stuck his hands into his pockets instead. She supposed he didn't have anyone to talk to at this thing either.

Adrian gestured with his head for Darcy to follow him to the exhibition space for the kids' artwork. They examined paintings of cats, rainbows, tennis shoes, and superheroes in general silence as each of them waited in vain to be retrieved.

"You're here with Teagan Van Zijl?" Adrian finally asked.

"Yes—do you know him?"

"I know—or knew—all the Van Zijls, actually. Nora has been my gallerist for most of my career, and of course she's very involved in the foundation. She brought Margaret Van Zijl to one of my first shows—she bought two of my paintings."

"Teagan's mother? What was she like?"

Adrian considered the question. "She was a very beautiful woman. Good taste in art. Not very much like her son though."

"How's that?"

He smiled in rueful amusement. "Teagan seems like a nice guy. The first time I met Margaret, she asked if I wanted to fly off for a romantic weekend in Iceland together."

Darcy laughed. Adrian was a very pretty man, and he looked like he was about her age. She could just imagine an older version of Sloane making a sloppy pass at the uptight artist.

"You have a problem with cougars, huh?" she teased him.

"No, it wasn't that. My fiancée is a few years older than me, in fact. But that fiancée had just introduced me to Margaret, so . . ." His voice trailed off. "Teagan's easier to talk to."

Darcy raised her eyebrows in commiseration. The crowd of women around Teagan certainly seemed to think so too. He hadn't even looked over at her since she walked off with Adrian. Not that she'd been checking.

"You must go to a lot of these things with them," Darcy said, grateful for an outsider perspective. She opened her mouth to ask him what Teagan had been like while he was drinking.

She nearly toppled over as a big weight struck her in the back. She stumbled, nearly knocking Adrian's wine out of his hands as someone dropped an arm around her shoulders.

The big weight resolved into Sloane, dressed in a short

black dress with outlandishly puffy sleeves. The girl squealed and hugged her, a little champagne sloshing out of her glass.

"Darcy!" she said. "You're here!"

Darcy got Sloane steadied on her high heels and more gently returned the sentiment.

"But what are you *wearing*?" Sloane immediately demanded, raking her blue eyes down Darcy's outfit. "You look like you're working tonight."

"I *am* working tonight," Darcy reminded her. She didn't need to feel abandoned by Teagan, or underdressed, or like an ignorant rube. She firmly reminded herself that this evening was not about her, or even her and Teagan. She was here to do a job, and she was doing it.

"I know, but it looks like you're going to clear tables. You should have borrowed something from me. Something with a little sex appeal. Oh my God, do you like Alaïa? You'd look great in Alaïa. I'll find something in my closet with room for your boobs."

"I could wear a little vest like a guide dog," Darcy said in exasperation, gesturing to her shirt. "You could embroider 'Sober companion, do not pet' on it."

Adrian tilted his jaw. "You're not Teagan's date?" he asked in surprise, taking the most minute of steps back.

"I mean, sort of," Darcy said, abruptly flustered. She didn't want Adrian to get the impression that she'd been hitting on him, because she hadn't been.

She also didn't want him to get the impression that Teagan was her date but he'd ditched her. Teagan didn't have to take care of her. She was here to take care of him.

Sloane turned to Adrian, sizing him up with evident interest.

"Adrian," Sloane trilled. "I haven't seen you in forever! You and Nora are both in town? We should all go out for drinks somewhere." She beamed at the redhead, who continued to edge away. His expression grew wary and hunted.

Darcy smirked at the change in dynamics. Served him right for not saying right off the bat that he'd painted the ugly horse.

Sloane launched into a stream of meaningless small talk with the ease of long practice. She looked like she belonged in this room. Not like Darcy—also not like Teagan, who was still standing ramrod straight in the center of a crowd.

"I want to hear all about your new series," Sloane said to Adrian, her words just a little thick. Darcy eyed the champagne glass in her hand with concern. "My mother used to buy and sell so much art for the foundation. And if Teagan won't do it, seems like I ought to, you know? I could buy one of your paintings."

"Sloane," Darcy interrupted her. "Should you be drinking?"

Sloane rolled her eyes, briefly tearing them away from Adrian. "It's fine. I didn't have a drinking problem. I had a coke problem. If you see me trying to put this stuff up my nose, you can totally stop me then. Anyway," she turned back to the artist.

"I don't think it works like that," Darcy said before Sloane could get started a second time.

"Ugh. Like anyone can make it through this sober," Sloane said, tilting her face to the ceiling with a martyred expression. "Look at Teagan. He *hates* these things. He wants to die right now."

All three of them craned their heads to locate Teagan halfway across the room. He was surrounded by women ranging from sleek socialites his own age to tiny old ladies with white hair and too many diamonds. Nora had a death grip on his bicep, her wine waving in her other hand. Teagan indeed looked like he wanted to disappear. His color was not great, and he had knees locked as Nora tried to keep him engaged in the conversation.

"What does she even want with him?" Darcy said before she could stop herself. She didn't know why Nora and Teagan were at odds about selling paintings, but she knew when Teagan was unhappy to be somewhere.

"Her gallery used to sell a lot of the art donated through the foundation," Adrian began to explain, but Sloane's snort cut them off.

Sloane balanced her empty glass in the crook of her arm and covertly made a very rude gesture with her thumb thrusting into the circle of her other hand.

"That's what she wants with him," she announced. "Like, for years. She made him take her to the prom, and he was only a *freshman*."

"Um, no," said Darcy, and Adrian scrunched up his face in disgust.

"I know, right?" Sloane said. "Like, he just got out of the hospital. Leave him alone."

"Exactly. He's not in shape to date anyone," Darcy responded without thinking first. Then she grimaced and looked down at her glass.

Maybe that wasn't quite right. Maybe he could date someone who didn't suck. But his first priority needed to be sobriety anyway, so this shouldn't be encouraged.

Sloane gave her a knowing glance as Adrian continued to frown.

Teagan would make someone a great partner someday.

He was a brick house of a man, complete with a white picket fence. A little bit of a fixer-upper, sure, but great bones. Shame about the location. Shame that Darcy wasn't in a position to buy.

"Nora's not flirting with him," Adrian said authoritatively. "She's like that with everyone."

"Nora's not like that with *me*," Sloane said.

Adrian's pouty lower lip tightened. "They've known each other for years. Their mothers were best friends. Teagan's obviously uncomfortable to be back from rehab. She's trying to put him at ease."

They all watched Nora run her hand over Teagan's back, basically groping him. Teagan looked decidedly *not* at ease.

"Hooker," Darcy said decisively, and Sloane nodded.

Adrian made an exasperated noise. "You know we're engaged now, right?"

"Sucks to be you, then," Darcy said to Adrian absently. He reared back in dismay, ready to retort and defend Nora again, but Darcy held up a peremptory hand. She'd spotted a potential issue. Her eyes narrowed.

Darcy lifted her fingers to her mouth and whistled. She could be heard over open water at a range of almost five hundred meters, and easily on the other side of this ballroom. Sloane lifted her hands to her ears. Adrian jolted. Everyone else turned to identify the noise, including the waiter who'd been carrying a laden tray full of champagne flutes in Teagan's direction.

Darcy tried to catch the waiter's eye, shaking her head and waving her arms vigorously, but the startled man kept walking toward Teagan and Nora's group.

"Excuse me," Darcy said, pushing her club soda glass into Adrian's hands.

She moved quickly to get to Teagan before the waiter did, catching him just before he was offered a drink. Everyone was staring at Darcy now, instead of Teagan. Which was fine—Teagan didn't look like he had much enjoyed being the center of attention, and Darcy wasn't going to see any of these people after November.

"I need him back now," Darcy said brightly to Nora. She fixed Teagan with a chiding look and tossed her head in the opposite direction.

Teagan quickly excused himself from the huddle of women he'd been speaking to. Or who had been speaking at him, really. Still, he looked very peaked as he trailed Darcy back to a vacant spot near the silent auction area.

"I wasn't going to take one of those drinks," he said when they stopped.

"Oh, I know," Darcy said. She hadn't *really* been worried. Just a little worried. "But I got tired of standing around and decided that you'd talked with them long enough."

She wasn't sure how Teagan would react to that, but thankfully, his shoulders slumped in a mixture of relief and amusement.

He quickly ran both hands over his face, knees bending and then straightening as he gathered himself.

"I talked with them long enough," he agreed. "God. Who thinks it's a good idea to tell a recovering alcoholic stories about all the parties they went to with my mother?"

"Motherfuckers," Darcy said, glaring at the women, who were still goggling curiously at the two of them. "Do you want to go?"

"Yes. No. No, I can't. Nora bought the table we're sitting at. We have to stay."

"No we don't. I can take her," Darcy said. "Especially in

those heels she's wearing. You run out first, and I'll lay down some cover fire."

Teagan sighed again, briefly closing his eyes. "We have to stay, or everyone will wonder where I went. But we can go see the kids before dinner, at least. I like hearing them talk about their paintings."

Darcy looked over at the gallery area. It was empty now.

"I think they already went home," Darcy said.

Teagan's face fell.

"Are you sure you don't want to leave?" she asked again. "No shame in a strategic retreat."

Teagan's eyes flicked to the empty gallery, the bar, the people gossiping about him.

"I'm sure," he said, and Darcy was equally certain he was lying.

twenty

TEAGAN HAD CALLED AHEAD TO CONFIRM THERE would be a vegan option for dinner, but this vegan option turned out to consist of an undressed green salad and a second helping of seven-grain dinner rolls with margarine.

Darcy had calmly retrieved some trail mix from her purse to supplement her meager rations, but stewing on his inability to even provide proper food for her gave Teagan something to think about beyond the press of the attention of a dozen other people at their table.

He hadn't thought through how he'd respond to everyone who wanted to know about his drinking problem, his stay in rehab, his new sober companion. He hadn't realized how interested people would be, or how free they'd feel to ask him all kinds of intrusive questions.

If he actually had possessed any interesting drinking stories, perhaps he would have wanted to talk about the things he would never do again. Since he didn't, his only options were lying through his teeth or adopting a haunted expression and muttering that it was still difficult to talk about his *journey*, as one friend of his mother's put it.

Hearing how proud everyone was of him, when he had done exactly nothing heroic, was possibly even harder than it would have been to state that he'd skipped town for a month over some garden-variety anxiety.

Everyone had anxiety. Everyone was stressed. This was New York. He wasn't special.

But that was the whole point of his ridiculous charade, wasn't it? Recovering alcoholics got welcomed back to their jobs and their friendships. Nobody called you a hero when you got discharged from inpatient psychiatric treatment.

"When did you *know* you'd hit rock bottom?" asked Patricia Hausauer, who'd once donated a pair of Peter Max sketches that his mother later consigned to Nora's gallery at half the price they'd appraised for.

Teagan poked at his salmon in Bearnaise sauce, wondering where the fire alarm was and how many people would be inconvenienced if he pulled it.

"You know, it's a misconception that an alcoholic has to hit rock bottom before seeking help," Darcy leaned in to answer for him.

She'd done a lot of that this evening. Redirecting. She had an endless supply of stories about rowdy sailors, rabid opossums, and lost yuppies that she shoehorned into conversation whenever Nora tried to bring up her art contact at Sotheby's or one of his mother's friends tried to pin him down on serving on a new planning committee for a different fundraiser. Teagan wanted to kiss her for it, except that he was sorry he'd put her through this evening at all.

"All you really have to do is recognize you want help with your drinking. That's where you start," Darcy added, swallowing a bite of dry arugula.

Most of the people at the table looked very impressed with that answer, but Nora leaned over Teagan to guilelessly ask where Darcy had trained as a sober companion, a certain steely glint in her eye.

"Is it a difficult job?" Nora pressed.

Darcy recognized what Nora was doing and narrowed her eyes. Teagan would put all his money on Darcy in a proper fight, but Nora had spent her whole life training in the dark arts of Manhattan snobbery. Darcy looked around the table uncomfortably before answering.

"I started by working with a psychologist at a wellness retreat—"

"Oh, but you aren't a psychologist yourself?" Nora asked sweetly.

Darcy flushed.

"No, but—"

"What did you study, then?" Nora asked. "And where?"

Teagan unobtrusively hooked Darcy's ankle with his own, hoping to get a little warning before she started flipping tables. *Where did you go to school, again?* could be considered fighting words if the subject hadn't attended an Ivy.

"Darcy's studying wildlife sciences," he said, hoping to preempt the need to carry Darcy away from the banquet. "So her approach has been wilderness therapy. Lots of work outdoors, nature lectures, mindfulness."

"Oh really?" Mrs. Hausauer leaned in to ask, sounding interested. "How are the two connected?"

Teagan was stumped on that, but Darcy took a long draught from her water glass, wiped her mouth on her sleeve, and slowly answered. "Well, it's just like when you release rehabbed wildlife. After you've finished the veterinary assessment, you have to ask yourself, is this a suitable habitat? Does the animal have the necessary skills to thrive? Is it going to disrupt a stable population in the area? But, you know, with Teagan instead."

Teagan thought Darcy's approach had been based more on physical interception of any possible sources of alcohol, but what she said had sounded very plausible.

"Fascinating," Mrs. Hausauer said. "And that's been effective for you?"

"I think so," Darcy said, shooting him an only slightly dubious look.

"Darcy's done a great job," Teagan said more forcefully, casting a warning glare at Nora. "I can't imagine doing this without her."

That smear of pink on Darcy's cheeks spread to her ears. She looked down at her greens, avoiding Mrs. Hausauer's speculative look as the older woman shook her head.

"You know, my son, Jamie, had a little too much fun during his year abroad in Barcelona. He's been blowing off his classes at NYU. I wish he had someone to help him reacclimate to the real world," she said.

Teagan felt a drop of inspiration fall on his head: an idea about Darcy working in Manhattan, in a job that didn't depend on Teagan's alleged alcohol dependency.

"Are you interested in a sober companion for Jamie?" he asked.

"Well, maybe," Mrs. Hausauer said, looking again at Darcy. "If she's not already fully booked with you."

"I am though," Darcy said immediately.

"Only through November. Or even sooner, potentially," Teagan said.

"Definitely through the end of November," Darcy said, frowning at him.

Teagan cut his eyes at Darcy, trying to silently urge her to consider a job that could keep her in Manhattan for several more months. She screwed up her mouth in distaste.

"Do you have a card?" Mrs. Hausauer asked, oblivious to the sudden tension.

"Take mine," Teagan said, pulling one out of his wallet despite Darcy's look of consternation. Darcy feinted as though she was going to intercept it, but then her eyes landed on Sloane, at Teagan's left, who'd been playing with her phone while drinking champagne since they sat down. Darcy reached across Teagan's lap and lifted Sloane's two wine glasses to put them toward the elaborate floral centerpiece, making the silverware rattle.

"Hey! That's your third," Darcy stage-whispered to Sloane. "You're cut off now."

"I'm taking a taxi home," Sloane protested.

"I don't care. It's not your birthday. Three's plenty," Darcy said, in a tone that brooked no disputes.

The entire twelve-seat table had gone silent to watch the interaction.

"The technique in action! That's a free sample, I suppose," Nora said to her stone-faced fiancé, not very quietly. Everyone at the table lifted their eyebrows at Darcy's breach of table etiquette, and Sloane scowled, but it occurred to Teagan that if anyone had been willing to risk a little social unrest to take his mother's drinks—or at least her car keys—out of her hands, she'd be here tonight instead of Teagan.

"Thank you," Teagan said to Darcy. Then he set his shoulders and looked at Mrs. Hausauer. "I'll call you when I get the all-clear to talk about your son."

As was typical at these fundraisers, there was a series of speeches. While they ate, the speakers introduced each other.

The director of community giving introduced the chair of the board, who thanked him for introducing her. They then thanked each other. The chair introduced an art teacher, who thanked the chair and also the director. They agreed that they had all done a good job and worked very hard on the evening's event. Additional thanks were exchanged.

After the guests were served coffee and tiny slices of cheesecake, the crowd dispersed to look over the silent auction again.

Darcy stood up as soon as the first person left their table, her body radiating agitation. Teagan tossed his napkin over his place and chased after her, catching her by the fire exit. It was alarmed; he steered her toward the main doors.

"Can we go *now*?" she snapped at him. "Or do you need to spend more time sucking up to Nora while she fondles you in front of her fiancé?"

"It's not on my schedule. It wasn't on my schedule. And you don't want to talk to Patricia Hausauer about her son?" he asked, even though the answer seemed to be, unfortunately, no.

"No! No, I do not want to apply to babysit some snotty-nosed college brat."

"Okay, well, what if it was someone else? Someone older? I can ask around, put the word out—"

"Jesus! Are you trying to get rid of me already?" Darcy burst out.

"No," Teagan said immediately, but Darcy ignored him. "You're going to need another job soon. You said you liked this one. I thought I could help—"

"Sorry that I'm cramping your style. You're just going to have to accept sobriety until December," she said, walking faster.

They passed through the lobby and into the cool air of the Midtown night, redolent of exhaust and hot trash.

"No," he said again. "No, no, no, wait. I'm not trying to—I'm glad you're helping me. I just thought, maybe you'd like to line up another job, and I could be flexible on the timing."

I just thought you might like a reason to stay nearby.

"I have a job until December," Darcy repeated stubbornly. "And I have plenty of applications in to do real work after that."

He wished he had a good argument for why she was wrong.

"This is a one-time deal. This is not a skill set I'm interested in developing. These people suck, and so do their parties. I can tell everyone thought my job was bullshit," she continued, stalking down the street.

"It doesn't matter what they think," Teagan said, trying to keep up with her. "Half of them could probably use a hard think about their own drinking."

"Well, I'm not the girl to make them," Darcy said sourly. "You know what? Just don't even tell them what I do. I don't want to talk to anyone about it. Just say I'm your girl-friend."

Teagan stopped dead in his tracks.

"Is that what you are?" he asked, surprised and suddenly light-headed. He hadn't thought that. He hadn't dated anyone seriously in a couple of years, but he hadn't ever been under the impression that a relationship firmed up just because you'd seen someone naked a few times. But he was often wrong about what Darcy thought, and he was willing to be told he was wrong about this too.

Darcy turned around and put her hands on her hips.

"Oh I—I just meant that was something you could tell people," she said, face clouding with confusion.

"Right," Teagan said, feeling very foolish. "Never mind."

He clenched his jaw and began walking again. Darcy had never said a thing about wanting to know him past the time she decided that he was sober for good. And since he already was, he was on borrowed time anyway.

"Teagan," Darcy said from feet behind him.

"What," he said, not slowing.

Darcy caught up to him.

"You didn't think—"

"No."

"Teagan," she said again, and her voice was guarded but so gentle that this time he did stop. "Look, I don't even know where I'm going to be living next—and you know long distance doesn't ever work."

"I don't know that," Teagan said, even though he hadn't until this moment considered that possibility with Darcy, as focused on the idea of finding her a job near New York as he'd been. "How do you know that?"

"I was in the Navy for seven years. I saw everything from a guy who came back from a six-month deployment to find his wife three months pregnant to a girl who checked her credit card bill from Bahrain and found out her boyfriend was tipping strippers with her combat pay."

"I wouldn't do that," Teagan immediately said. "You can't think I would do anything like that."

"You're so sure I wouldn't either?" Darcy said, crossing her arms.

Teagan paused and thought about everything he knew

about Darcy. He couldn't imagine it. She was impulsive and she made mistakes, but he'd yet to see her do anything she ever thought was *wrong*.

Not like him.

"You wouldn't either," he said, even as guilt wiped out his building anger at her disinterest in being part of his life.

Darcy's mouth twisted to the side. "Okay, maybe you're right, and maybe I wouldn't. Shit, I don't know. Nobody's ever stuck it out long enough to even give me the opportunity. But you hadn't even thought about it before tonight either. So why don't you think about it first before you start making any more promises you have to keep?"

That was more of an opening than he'd ever gotten so far.

"It wouldn't be hard to keep that promise," he said. "And I did. Think about it. Or at least, I was thinking about you and me. I think about you all the time. That wouldn't change if you moved somewhere else."

Darcy ducked her chin to her chest. She twisted away to the side, as unspeaking as she ever was whenever he got brave enough to tell her the smallest part of how he felt about her. He got the sense that she would have pulled her hair over her face to hide if they hadn't been in the middle of the sidewalk. It took her long seconds to speak, and she didn't look at him when she did.

"You know I'm not going anywhere until you're well, right?" she offered. "I won't bail out on you while you're still in recovery."

Teagan briefly closed his eyes, not really reassured. He wasn't ever going to be recovered. He was going to feel like this the rest of his life. And if Darcy really left in December, he didn't think he'd recover from *that*, maybe not ever.

But he still had most of three months to work on it.

"I know that," he said simply.

Darcy twisted back to lean against him. The weight of his body was anchoring.

She tugged on his tie and pressed her knuckles into his stomach, her teeth cutting into her lower lip.

"I'm tired of this place," she mumbled into his chest. "I don't know why anyone lives in the city."

"I was born here," he said. "I guess I never really thought about living anywhere else."

He wished he could picture it. He wished he could imagine anything other than this.

Darcy looked up at him through her thick, dark eyelashes.

"Hey, here's another idea. You know those little frozen fruits that are stuffed with fruit sorbet?"

"Yeah?" Teagan asked, wrapping an arm around her shoulders and pushing his face against her temple. He loved hearing Darcy's escape plans, even if he'd realized that part of what she was escaping was any thought of permanency, with him or otherwise.

"They have a factory in Florida. We can rent a house on the water, work in the sorbet factory, and eat mangoes on the beach," she said, tone conveying utter sincerity.

"Hmm. Florida," he said. "My hair doesn't handle the humidity well. It sticks straight up, and I look like a muppet."

Darcy heaved a sigh. "All right, so that's out. I'll keep pondering."

"Please do," Teagan said. He kissed her forehead, then turned back to the street. It was well after rush hour. Taxis streaked by at high speed, and the lingering pedestrians were rushing past them in the cool dark. He thought about Darcy's map, which way she'd want to head for the station.

Darcy tugged on his tie again. "Hey. I have a plan for tonight, at least," she said. A predatory smile spread across her face. "You wanna go home and screw around in the hot tub? It probably works just like a shower."

Teagan laughed. It wasn't half of what he wanted from her. But that did sound amazing.

"God, yes," he said. "Let's take a cab."

twenty-one

TEAGAN COULDN'T REMEMBER EVER SLEEPING well. Even when he was a kid, he'd been prone to waking up in the middle of the night, especially if his parents had gone into the city for the evening. He'd pad down the hall to the living room and turn on the TV, put on a sitcom and turn the volume down low. Sometimes he'd go back to sleep on the couch, and sometimes he'd just wait for his parents to come home. After Sloane was born, Teagan was usually the one to get up and feed her if she woke up after midnight. He'd get her bottle mixed and prop her in the crook of his arm so they could watch *Frazier* reruns together. They'd both liked that. But she got better at sleeping through the night, eventually, and he never did.

When he got older, he started to worry about being tired the next day. He acquired more responsibilities, and he thought about them while he was awake at night. He tried harder to go back to sleep when he woke up, which was usually counterproductive. Lying in bed and wishing he could sleep was not a pleasant way to pass the time, so he started taking melatonin, dialing up his cardio routine, and investing in a mattress that advertised a number of ulti-mately specious health claims. Nothing had really worked.

Then there had been that month on Lexapro where he'd wanted to sleep *all the time*. That was weeks past now.

Now he woke up in the night again, but he didn't mind it at all. He'd roll out of bed silently to avoid jostling Darcy, then go back down the hall without turning on any lights. The big windows in the front of the house admitted plenty of light from outside, even in the middle of the night. Teagan would get a glass of water and admire what he saw: Darcy's boots tossed carelessly in the middle of the entryway. A peanut butter-covered spoon in the sink. Her jacket draped across a kitchen chair.

When he went down the hall to the bathroom, there were two toothbrushes in the stand and a hairbrush next to the mirror. The air smelled like her conditioner. It looked like two people lived there. He liked how it looked.

When he felt tired enough to go back to sleep, Teagan would return to the guest bedroom. Darcy's laundry was tossed in with his in the hamper and her clean clothes were strewn across the dresser. Darcy herself would be asleep in the center of the bed, spread out like a starfish, sleeping the guiltless slumber of the innocent. When he slowly shuffled back under the covers and shifted an arm or a leg to make a little room for himself, she'd roll toward him and curl her warm body into his side, making a little smacking noise with her lips as she dreamed on. If she stayed, he thought, this was what the rest of his life would look like, every night.

Teagan didn't mind being awake now, because there wasn't a thing he would change about what his world looked like at night. There were eight hours out of every twenty-four that looked just perfect to him, and wasn't that more than there had ever been before?

twenty-two

"WHAT ABOUT THIS ONE?" TEAGAN ASKED, SPINNING his laptop screen around toward Darcy.

Darcy flexed her stomach muscles to sit up and see it.

She was drinking her coffee at his desk while watching a movie on her phone, her boots resting on a stack of loose correspondence. He'd given her a mild look of reproof but said nothing, probably in consideration of the many improvements she'd made to his office that week.

Her first step had been to take out the big white dupioni silk curtains. They'd been ugly and collecting dust, and now the morning light streamed into Teagan's office. Then she'd swapped the uncomfortable plastic seating for the pair of upholstered armchairs going unused in a corner by the women's restroom. Finally, she'd put the bar cart out on the curb and requisitioned a mini-fridge to store sodas in.

It was harder than she'd imagined to keep busy. She'd been through the full backlist of Sober Sam episodes, and new ones only dropped once a week. She was caught up with her reading for class. She'd identified every alcohol-serving establishment north of 14th Street.

For the first time in her life, Darcy didn't have anything

to do. Or rather, she didn't know what to do, specifically. She was supposed to be supporting Teagan in his sobriety, but she was at a loss for what else she might do on that account. She was beginning to wish she'd read the manual on this first, because as the days went by, the tight set of Teagan's mouth only seemed to worsen.

She'd promised she'd help him, but she wasn't sure that's what she was doing anymore.

Darcy took out her earbuds to focus on his computer screen.

It was a job listing for the New York State Parks Department. She squinted at the title: PARK MANAGER, BEAR MOUNTAIN STATE PARK. She thought, anyway. Below it was an impenetrable block of text. She gritted her teeth and tried to parse it, hanging up on the second sentence.

"They want a bachelor's degree," she said, looking away from the screen.

"Or equivalent experience," Teagan corrected her.

Teagan spun the computer back around and began to read out loud.

"Primary duties include managing operations of park facilities, communicating with other park branches, managing park maintenance, educating park visitors, reviewing reports of operations—"

"Are you actually working this morning, or are you just looking at jobs I'm not qualified for?" Darcy interrupted him. She expected him to back off at the suggestion he was slacking on the clock, but he dug in.

"Isn't that the kind of job you want?" he asked.

"I wanted to be a park ranger."

"I think the person in this job does everything a park ranger does, and look, it pays more—"

Darcy scoffed. "Yeah, because they also want you to do a bunch of other stuff."

"So why couldn't you do this one?" he asked.

"I can't do a single one of those things you just read," she said.

"What do you mean? Operations? Education? Maintenance? You could do all of that. You were doing all of that in Montana," Teagan insisted.

"Not for that kind of job," Darcy said. "There's probably tons of paperwork. Admin. Fifty different monthly reports. No."

Teagan frowned down at the screen.

Darcy put her headphones back in, hoping that was the end of it.

"Darcy . . ." Teagan unexpectedly spoke again, his voice very hesitant. "Even if you can't read the reports, I bet they could—"

Darcy sat bolt upright, sliding her feet off Teagan's desk and sending papers fluttering to the floor. She pulled out her earbuds and tossed them back in her purse.

"Of course I can read," Darcy snapped. "When did I ever say I can't read?"

Teagan didn't respond, big hazel eyes wide and watchful.

She grimaced. She hadn't realized that he'd noticed anything. But of course he wouldn't have said anything at the time, because Teagan was unfailingly kind, and now she'd bitten his head off.

Of course he'd noticed. It wasn't like Teagan wouldn't notice the same issues that had caused her to fail half a dozen college courses, doomed her Navy career, and gotten her demoted from wilderness educator to handyman at Rachel's wellness retreat.

Teagan's face was nothing but concerned for her.

What a jerk—it made it impossible to argue with him when he just wouldn't fight.

"It's not that I can't read."

"Okay," he said gently.

He didn't even ask what the problem was. He'd sit there waiting all afternoon, and he'd never ask. How was she expected to stomp off if he didn't give her an opening to do that?

Fuck. She was just going to have to talk about it.

She wrinkled her nose at her coffee.

"I can't read very fast," she amended in what she hoped was a calmer tone. "Writing's a bigger problem, actually. I could probably handle reading the reports, if they were the same stuff every week. But I can't write anything unless the software has spellcheck and will read it back to me."

Rachel had demanded a written agenda for Darcy's proposed educational hikes. On fancy paper, so it could be pinned to the corkboard at breakfast and fit with the desired aesthetic. Darcy's big mistake had been trying to do it by hand. But all her spelling mistakes had convinced Rachel that Darcy couldn't possibly be an authority on the actual content she'd planned to deliver, and her exciting job opportunity in wilderness therapy had turned into nothing but manual labor.

"You're dyslexic?" Teagan asked.

"Yeah, I mean, I assume so," Darcy said uncomfortably. She'd never said that out loud before. Mostly because nobody had asked, and she'd kept her own conclusions to herself.

"You never got tested for it?"

She shook her head. "My mom kept moving us all up and down the West Coast, a new school every time she broke up with a boyfriend or got evicted, so I was never in any one school long enough for anyone to notice."

By the time she'd made it to high school, she'd figured out how to cope. There had been audio versions of all the textbooks in the library for the students with low vision. Her English scores were never great, but she'd kept up her GPA with math and science electives.

Her grades had been good enough to get into college, but when her professors stopped working from textbooks and started assigning handouts and journal articles, she just hadn't been able to work fast enough.

"But lots of people are dyslexic, in any job you can think of. And especially for a government job, you'd think they'd accommodate you, get you whatever software you need—"

Darcy forced herself to remain calm. He meant well. He had no idea what the real world was like, having never lived there.

In the real world, nobody helps you. If you can't pass the test, you fail. If you're bad at your job, you get fired.

"I'd rather just have a job I'm good at to start with," she said.

"You'd be good at this job, Darcy. Someone else can handle the paperwork," he insisted.

"It's all theoretical, isn't it? Because I don't have equivalent experience, and I don't have a degree," she said.

"How many hours do you still need?" Teagan asked. "Maybe you could just say *degree expected*."

"Twenty-eight."

Teagan blinked a few times, no doubt doing the math about how long Darcy had been enrolled in college. She could have been a doctor after twelve years. Doctors went to school for less time than she had.

"Okay, but that's—you could do that in one year, if you went full time," he said.

Darcy twisted in her seat, feeling itchy and exposed. They were really playing the greatest hits of all her life's failures this morning, weren't they? Maybe he'd like to talk about her dating history next or ask why she hadn't been promoted to petty officer second class.

"I'm only taking four hours right now," she said. "I tried to take eight this summer, but I failed one of my classes, and if I fail another one, I can't graduate in my major."

A wrinkle formed between Teagan's eyebrows.

"You should take more than four hours. You could take a full course load right now. What can I do? I could take dictation. Or record your course materials for you."

Darcy laughed and looked down at the ground. He sounded so sincere. He probably meant it, even. He would probably make her all sorts of promises if she let him. She couldn't let him, she reminded herself.

When this inevitably ended, one of the things she wanted to remember about this was that Teagan hadn't ever broken any promises to her. Or it could get even worse, if he kept them, and he didn't want to. It was going to hurt like a shipwreck when she had to leave anyway, she could see that already, but she never wanted to be one more thing Teagan felt trapped into taking care of. He had too many of those things in his life already, and she didn't want to be here when he stopped looking at her like she had all the answers and started seeing her for the trash fire she usually was.

"Thanks. But exams are in December, and I probably won't be here," she said.

Teagan did that little jerk backward that he did whenever Darcy mentioned her departure date, like she'd called him a name. Whatever progress they'd made in the month she'd been in New York, it hadn't convinced him that he'd be just fine without Darcy here to help him.

His mouth flexed as he worked on a response.

"But you might be," he said slowly. "If you had a job here."

Darcy scrunched up her nose in reluctant assent. "I haven't applied to any jobs here. I haven't even heard from anywhere in Yellowstone yet."

"I'm working on that," he immediately said.

That was too close to a promise for her liking, and Darcy instinctively tightened her shoulders.

"You can't pimp me out to your drinking buddies as a sober companion," she warned him.

"My . . . okay, sure. No drinking buddies."

"And I'm not working at an art camp. I can't draw."

"Okay," he agreed again. "Only things in your field, I promise."

Even though she'd done all but bite his head off this morning, Teagan gave her a slow smile, sweet and encouraging.

Darcy felt her face suffusing with blood, and she put her feet back on his desk so that he couldn't see her expression.

It was like a whole spoonful of sugar sliding into her cup, his confidence that she'd finish her degree and land the kind of job she'd wanted since she was eighteen, repeated failures to do that notwithstanding. It hit her right in her feelings, when she should have dodged.

Darcy bent over her phone to hide more, tempted to wrap her arms around the emotion and catch it for later study.

She knew better than this. Disappointment always hurt worse than brutal honesty would have.

Darcy heard him start typing.

"If you get an interview with the New York parks department, I'll help you practice questions about what you'd actually be doing day-to-day," he said.

"You're seriously putting in an application with the bear place?" she asked.

"Yes?"

He looked at her with mild challenge over the rim of the computer. Darcy had that teetering-on-the-edge sensation again. Experience counseled that this was a trap, and she'd end up mopping staterooms on the way to Diego Garcia.

It was a nice daydream though. Being in charge of some little state park. Coming out of her own office to meet school buses full of cabin-feverish kids who'd listen to ten minutes of bear facts before sprinting for the rocks.

Was Teagan imagining it too? Was he able to imagine a life where he was sober and unafraid, with Darcy still in it? If so, could he please tell her how that worked? Could he read the manual to her?

"Suit yourself," she said, trying to play it off like it wasn't something she wanted, because wanting things very rarely had anything to do with having them.

"I will," Teagan said, undeterred.

Darcy braced her feet on the floor, wishing she ever knew what was happening in her life more than a few days in advance. He didn't say anything else though, and the reeling sensation had faded by the time that someone knocked a few minutes later.

Rose opened the cracked door and peered into the room.

Darcy eyed her clothing with interest: a jewel-toned sheath dress, small pearl earrings, high block heels. Rose had one of those figures that was as hard as Darcy's to dress professionally—lots of chest, lots of hips and stomach—yet she always looked like she was ready to present the nightly news, not a hair out of place. It was easier for Darcy to imagine herself dressed like that than poufy and feminine like Sloane.

"Nora's here," Rose said, one accusatory eyebrow delicately arched. "With a guy from Sotheby's. She said they want to inventory the whole collection, everything not out on loan."

"What?" Teagan said, face stating that this was an unpleasant surprise.

"Was this on your calendar?" Rose asked.

"No. Was it on yours?" Teagan said.

"No."

Teagan gave her a stern look.

"No!" Rose reiterated, tossing her small pink hands in the air. "No, Teagan, I am not scheduling meetings with our directors behind your back."

"I didn't say you were," Teagan said, and the two of them stared off like rival alley cats.

"Do you want me to come to the meeting?" Rose asked.

"No, I'll handle it," Teagan said, standing up and pulling his jacket off the back of his chair. He took a red tie out of his desk drawer and began rolling it on.

Rose made a frustrated sound in the back of her throat and spun on her heel, stalking off.

"You know, if you think she's out to get you, you probably need to fire her before she starts setting leg traps in the hall," Darcy said. She wasn't sure the other woman really was out to get Teagan though. It seemed like Rose might consider that beneath her dignity.

"I can't fire her. Nora likes her. Besides, she's not required to like me," Teagan said.

He paused in the doorway on his way out of his office,

visibly gathering his courage. Darcy didn't know what could really go terribly wrong in a high-rise conference room, but Teagan's face said that he was contemplating several different disaster scenarios.

"Hey," Darcy said. "Do you want *me* to come to the meeting?" Her hands itched to wrap themselves around Teagan's chest, but this was the middle of the workplace, and she thought he might consider that inappropriate.

He shook his head. "I'll handle it," he said again. Then he left.

Darcy waited alone in Teagan's office for a few minutes afterward, but she found that she was unable to concentrate on her movie. So she got up and wandered out to the lobby.

She wasn't surprised to see Rose pacing there, nor Adrian, Nora's redheaded artist fiancé. But she was surprised to see them speaking with each other—she supposed they knew each other through the foundation. Adrian was pretending to leaf through a glossy home design magazine as Rose vented to him.

"I will get with the strategy—I don't even *care* what the strategy is, just let's have a strategy, you know?" Rose said, arms animated. Her high heels clicked on the tile as she turned in place.

Adrian grunted without much interest, but they both turned to look at Darcy as she entered the room. The receptionist was off bringing refreshments to the boardroom, and the lobby was otherwise empty.

Rose spun to focus on Darcy.

"What's Teagan's issue with selling the art?" she demanded. "We don't have to sell anything that's hanging at his house."

"No, I think he's fine with selling some of that stuff," Darcy said, thinking of the titty painting in the living room.

"He won't tell me what he's willing to let go of," Rose said, grimacing at the boardroom.

"Letting go is . . . not Teagan's strong suit," Darcy admitted.

Rose twisted her mouth in consternation. She took a step closer to Darcy and pitched her voice so as not to carry quite so far. "Is it just the issue with using Nora's gallery? Because we could use an independent broker. We don't have to let Nora do the sales."

Darcy lifted her palms in supplication.

"Look, I don't know—whatever you want to know. If Teagan ever told me, I overwrote the space with bird facts."

Rose squinted at her suspiciously.

"Do you want me to find out?" Darcy asked. "Teagan's not really the secret plan type."

The other woman sighed. "We're spending more on programs than we're bringing in via donations or investments. So either we need to raise more money or Teagan's going to eventually liquidate the endowment. And either would be fine with me. But it's not fine with the board, which raises fiduciary concerns—"

"I don't really know what any of those words mean," Darcy said. "But I'm sorry? Or glad? Which is right?"

Adrian made a muffled noise like he'd stifled a laugh but snorted instead. Rose glared at him.

"I don't suppose *you* know what the board wants to do about cash flow," she said.

"No. I am also very careful not to pay attention when Nora's talking business," he said, perfect features unruffled.

Rose rubbed her face. "Where was I the day they were handing out rich partners?" she mumbled to herself. "I could have expensive hobbies. I could paint. I like birds."

"It was your choice to study something frivolous like accounting," Adrian said, delicately flipping through pages of antidepressant ads, eyes still on his magazine. "I knew I wanted the flexibility of a career as a kept woman when I got my MFA in studio art."

Rose closed her eyes and tipped her head back. "That wasn't a dig," she groaned. Her eyes flicked to Darcy. "At either of you. I'm jealous, honestly."

Darcy wondered whether she needed to reinforce that she wasn't actually Teagan's girlfriend. If Teagan did in fact settle into sobriety and thank her for her time at the end of three months, Darcy wanted the dignity of considering herself not dumped.

But there was a part of her—maybe not the best part, sure, but a new part—that preened at the idea that she'd secured the bag, that she had a life someone else wanted, that she had her shit together. Nobody had ever thought Darcy had her shit together.

"So, I am happy to talk about my career path as a sober companion," she began to say, but the door to the interior conference room where Teagan had gone with Nora flew open so hard it banged into the opposite wall.

Teagan flew out of it, at a pace just short of a run, and ducked into the restroom a few steps away.

Adrian and Rose both looked at Darcy, their eyes rounded with alarm. This was apparently not expected behavior in the Van Zijl Foundation workplace.

Oh shit.

"Excuse me," Darcy said brightly, trying to project the confidence of a person who definitely knew what was going on. "I'll go handle that."

· · · · ·

I am not having a heart attack.

I am not having a heart attack.

Teagan repeated that to himself, even as every instinct shrieked that he was dying. Fear raced along every nerve at the speed of lightning, collecting in an aching pool in his chest. Everything was wrong. He was breathing wrong. His heart was beating wrong. He was going to fall, he was going to throw up, he was going to pass out.

He was not having a heart attack.

This would pass. He told himself things that he'd learned intellectually, even as the corner of his mind that could still think intellectually was overwhelmed by the animal core that could do nothing but fear and shriek of shame and danger. This would pass, because there wasn't actually anything wrong with him, and this was all in his head.

Thank God there wasn't anyone else in the bathroom. He leaned against the door, his entire body shaking.

This will pass. This is all in my head. This isn't really happening.

"Teagan?" He heard Darcy's voice through the bathroom door. She knocked. "Teagan? Are you okay?"

He was breathing too hard to answer. He couldn't make his voice work. After another syrupy, painful ten seconds, she pushed against the door to open it. Teagan pushed back to keep it closed, then pushed the lock closed with trembling fingers.

"Jesus Christ!" Darcy snapped when she discovered that the door was now locked. "Teagan, tell me what's going on."

He managed to force out, "I'm fine." He knew he didn't

sound fine. He probably hadn't looked fine to anyone in the conference room. They were probably in there talking about it now, wondering what was wrong with him.

"Then open the door," Darcy said.

Teagan stepped away from the door and turned on the nearest sink. Taking the handful of steps made his head swim.

It wasn't carpeted over by the sink. If he fell, he might crack his head on the tile. Maybe he'd die in here anyway.

"Teagan," Darcy said in a lower voice, speaking directly against the door frame. "I am not afraid to get out the fire axe and break this door down if you do not tell me *right now* what is happening. I'll do it."

He felt too unsteady on his feet to respond. Could he forget how to breathe? It felt like his body would no longer breathe without his conscious control. He gripped the counter, afraid that he would fall down.

His mother had done this. Been unable to walk, too many drinks into her evening. He'd come pick her up at a party or a restaurant, slip an arm around her waist, half carry her out. *Sorry, she's not feeling well*, he'd say. Maybe some people had even believed him.

The lock on the door was the flimsy kind, just a button, no key. It rattled for a moment, and then the handle twisted as Darcy got the door open with a bobby pin.

Teagan got just a flash of the worry on her face before he ducked his own to hide it. He lifted his hands from the counter to scrub at his cheeks, but he needed them to hold himself upright, and he had to quickly grip the counter again.

"Oh my God, Teagan," Darcy said, the fear in her voice sending a fresh bolt of shame through his stomach. She swept up against him, pulling at his tie to loosen it, fingers scrabbling for his pulse.

He got one hand free to ineffectually bat at hers.

"Stop," he managed. "It's not—it's not a medical problem."

Darcy ignored that. She pulled on his arm until they sank down to the bathroom floor, then got his tie all the way off and his shirt collar unbuttoned. Her fingers were solid and cold where they pressed against the pulse point in his neck.

"It's too fast for me to count. I think—I think you're having a heart attack," she said, voice tightening until it sounded entirely un-Darcy-like. "I'm calling 911."

Teagan grabbed for her wrist as she moved to get to her feet.

"It's not a heart attack," he said. "I know it's not a heart attack. I saw a cardiologist." He felt a little bit better on the floor. "Don't call anyone. Please."

"Then what's happening?" she begged, distraught like he'd never seen her.

"Nothing. Nothing is actually happening. This is all in my head," he said.

God, what would she make of that? He was on the filthy floor of the bathroom, hyperventilating as tears rolled down his cheeks, and the worst part was that nothing was happening to him.

"Did you take something?" she asked, voice only a little calmer.

He shook his head and nearly laughed. He wished he'd taken something, like he wished he was an alcoholic instead of a psychiatric patient, because if he took things that made him feel like this, then he might be able to *stop*.

"I won't be mad," Darcy promised. "You can tell me."

"No, I—I was just in that meeting, and I didn't sleep well last night, and—just give me a minute. Just give me a minute and I'll be fine."

He closed his eyes and leaned forward, resting his head on his knees. The spinning sensation was subsiding. He'd just stay here for a while.

He heard Darcy exhale and then rise to her feet. He heard the sink turn off. Her footsteps receded and returned. Darcy crouched next to him and gently wiped his face with a wet paper towel, then folded a second one over the back of his neck.

"Don't move," Darcy said unnecessarily. He couldn't go anywhere. He wasn't even sure he could stand back up.

He heard the door open and close. He tipped his head forward. The entire scene felt unreal, like it was happening to someone else. He had the sensation that he'd wake up in his own bed any moment now, still sweating but able to think again. Any second he'd wake up, and he would never have run out of an ordinary business meeting, because that wasn't the sort of thing he did. That wasn't the sort of thing any-one did.

The door opened, and he willed it to be Darcy without opening his eyes. Then he recognized the smell of her herbal shampoo, the now-familiar scent immediately soothing him. She slid a very cold object into his hands—a soda. When he simply held it between his hands, focusing on the solidity of it, she took it back and cracked the tab.

As though he was a small child, she pressed it to his lips.

"Here," she said, tone still thin and wobbly. "Some Sprite will probably help, huh?"

She probably was thinking about low blood sugar or stom-ach trouble, not panic attacks, but she happened to be right.

He sipped it, feeling his breathing regularize under the effort of coordinating the muscles in his mouth and throat. Darcy's fingers slipped around his free wrist, and he knew she was taking his pulse again, but he savored the point of contact. That irrational part of his brain whispered that she wouldn't let him die.

Someone else knocked on the bathroom door. Soft and tentative, unlike Darcy.

"Go away," Darcy yelled.

"Is everything okay?" Rose's voice came through the wood.

At the idea that anyone else would come in and see him like this, his anxiety crested again.

"We're fine," Darcy said.

"What's wrong?" Rose pressed. "Teagan?"

"Nothing's wrong. We're fucking in here," Darcy said. "Go away. We'll be out in half an hour."

Teagan made a small noise of objection as the other side of the door went silent. Jesus. If he hadn't been fired yet, he was going to get fired soon.

Darcy looked over at him, and he realized that he had straightened and opened his eyes.

"Not enough time?" she asked. "Forty-five minutes?"

"Workplace," he said.

"Oh, right," she said. She looked back at the door. "Just kidding!" she called.

Teagan managed a very small laugh, even though it hurt more than gasping for breath had. She patted his shoulder in approval, then wrapped her hand around the inside of his bicep and leaned into him. She minutely rocked back and forth against him at the tempo of her slower breathing. When he'd matched it, her head settled against his shoulder, the braid she'd put her hair in today slipping down to dangle over his chest. Darcy turned her face briefly into his neck, her hot breath steaming on his skin.

"You scared me there, Bear Bait," she said in a small, wobbly voice.

He nodded, feeling his eyes prickle again at the concern in her voice. Him too.

A few minutes passed, and the discomfort of sitting on a cold tile floor began to rise to the top of his list of unpleasant sensations. He could breathe. He could move. He could think. He couldn't think of how he was going to explain this.

"Did you get fired?" Darcy asked. It was a reasonable assumption, given how he'd acted.

"No. Not yet, anyway. Nora's got the majority of the board ready to let her sell off the art collection."

"I see," Darcy said, as though his reaction had made sense. It didn't.

It made him feel dirty that Nora was skimming five percent after the taxpayers took a huge loss on the art donations. It made him feel at once ineffective and complicit in the whole scheme, because the foundation wouldn't have had to sell assets at all if he'd been better at raising money. It made him feel like he'd been lying for years: first to cover for his mother, then to cover for himself, because hadn't he told everyone that he'd fix this?

But a rational person did not sprint from the room in response to a business proposal.

"Well, I'll go tell them you're puking your guts up because you had all that lox at breakfast, and I'll make them leave," Darcy said, beginning to rise again.

"Don't go," he immediately blurted, and Darcy froze. She slid back down and put her arm back under his, fingers rubbing at the downy hairs on the back of his wrist.

They couldn't just stay there forever, but he didn't have a better plan yet.

"You're going to blame the fish?" was all he could come up with, but Darcy gamely went along with it.

"Well, Pacific salmon stocks are down ninety percent in some places, and even the farmed varieties are spreading sea lice parasites to the wild population—"

She gave the impression that she was willing to sit in the men's restroom with him and discuss the environmental impact of salmon aquaculture for as long as was necessary.

God, he loved her. He wanted to listen politely until she was done, then promise that he would never eat another creature with a central nervous system if she'd stay with him after this. He wished he could think of a single other thing he had to offer her.

That wasn't the kind of worry that sent his heart rate spiking. It was the kind that felt like it would break his heart.

"Let's not tell anyone anything," he said. He didn't want to lie any more than he already had. "Let's just go."

twenty-three

IT BECAME OBVIOUS AS SOON AS THEY EXITED THE building that Teagan did not have a destination in mind, so Darcy set off for his condo. She'd mapped the route but had yet to go inside. His face was distant and remote as they walked, but he evidenced no surprise as Darcy brought them to the front entrance. He pulled out his keys and let them in without speaking about it.

The building was old and not tall, and Teagan's unit was on the third floor. Darcy hadn't really pictured what it would be like, but the smallness of it was shocking to her. It couldn't even be five hundred square feet, and it looked smaller in light of Sloane's luggage and boxes piled in the middle of the floor.

"Jesus, this is grim," she said, peering out the sole window, which opened into an air shaft. If she craned her head with her nose to the glass, she could just see a rhombus-shaped wedge of sky off to the left. "I thought you were rich?"

"Manhattan real estate," Teagan briefly explained. "I bought this place with my own money." He stripped off his shirt and undershirt and dropped them next to the neatly made full-sized bed at one end of the room. He had a futon,

a coffee table, and an entertainment console with a large
TV. No other furniture besides the bed and nightstand. There
were a few framed color photographs on the wall in IKEA
frames: other people's weddings, a picture of him and a teen-
aged Sloane smiling on a beach together.

As a place for a human to live, it obviously sucked.

She wished she had somewhere better to take him. Her
own apartment, some secret spot in the woods. Now that
they had reached their destination, she almost wanted to
take him by the arm and start moving again.

Teagan sat down on the bed to remove his shoes. Once
stripped to his trousers, he too seemed to run out of ideas
for what to do. Like a tree falling in the forest, he toppled
over onto his bed, then rolled on his stomach. He turned
his face to the mattress.

Darcy eyed his abject figure sprawled on the bed, then
went to sit next to him. Sober Sam had not covered this.
She had not been briefed on this mission. She was only a petty
officer third class, only a handyman, and her own family had
not provided good instruction on how to love someone who
was hurting.

"Do you want me to rub your back?" she asked.

"No, I'm okay," Teagan mumbled into the plain navy
duvet.

"Are you lying?" Darcy said skeptically. Who didn't want
a back rub?

Teagan's shoulders tensed.

"Yes," he admitted.

So Darcy stroked the palm of her hand up and down his
bare back, feeling the tension run out of him by degrees.
When they went to the gym, he usually swam laps, and most

of the muscle in his wiry body lay across his shoulders. Darcy liked to press her cheek there when he rolled on his stomach to sleep.

She wondered whether she could ever be good at this part. She'd never really gotten this far. She understood how things started, when she met someone at work or at a bar, and how they got going, when they went to get dinner and a movie or they went home together. She also knew how things ended, when someone stopped calling or cheated or moved away. But this part? Darcy didn't know about this part, where someone had a bad day or a series of bad days but then things got better, instead of worse. Where someone brought you a soda and rubbed your back.

She didn't know if she could be good at this part. She'd never had the chance to try.

After a few minutes, Teagan turned to his side and caught her hand between his own. He brought her knuckles to his lips and kissed them, breath playing out over her fingers. He looked up at her from the bed, and his expression was such a mix of sadness and care that it made her stomach flip over. She had that tiptoeing-over-the-edge-of-the-cliff feeling again.

"Thank you," he said. "I feel better."

It was as quiet as it ever was in the city. No footsteps from the hall or the neighbors above, and the street below was empty.

Teagan looked at her expectantly. *I'm in charge*, Darcy reminded herself. She was supposed to know what to do now.

"Do you have any alcohol in here?" Darcy asked, squashing her impulse to give him real estate advice or to demand answers about what had happened back at his office. First things first.

"I don't know," Teagan said. "I don't remember."

While Teagan went into the bathroom to rub his face with a wet washcloth, Darcy opened cabinets and the refrigerator. The refrigerator was full of science experiments, but none of the substances therein had begun as alcoholic beverages. The cabinets had little of interest either, but she found a bottle of Macallan 30 still in its box under the sink. It hadn't even been opened yet.

Teagan reemerged in a new shirt, his color improved.

He winced when he saw her standing next to the sink with the bottle.

"Sorry," she said. "I gotta."

"My boss gave me that with my bonus three years ago," he said. "Back when I was a bond trader. At least try it first."

"Is it good?" she asked, eyeing the bottle. "I've never drunk anything older than I am."

In lieu of answering, Teagan pulled a glass from the cabinet next to the refrigerator, then filled it with ice. He kept his head tilted in her direction, as though waiting for her to stop him. Darcy watched him like a hawk as he cut the seal off the scotch and unscrewed the bottle before pouring an inch into the glass.

"I don't know if I should," Darcy said reluctantly. She wasn't sure she ought to be drinking in front of him.

"Were you planning to never drink again either?" he asked, and his tone was very casual, but his eyes flashed with a stronger emotion that made her parse out what he might really be asking. No, Darcy had assumed that she'd occasionally have a drink. What he meant was, would he be in a position to see it? Would they still know each other? She didn't know if they would.

Teagan didn't own a kitchen table and chairs, so she hopped

onto the counter to take the glass from him. She took a small, thoughtful sip from the glass. Jesus, it was good. She wondered if she dared finish it.

"It's not that great," she lied. "It just tastes like wood chips."

"Hmm," he said. "Seems unlikely." Moving very slowly and deliberately, he stepped between her knees. He framed her face with his hands as he leaned down to kiss her. "I bet it's pretty good, actually," he murmured against the corner of her mouth. Keeping his hands cupped around her cheeks, he teased her lips open until they were pressed hot and slick against his. Together, they savored the taste of apples and peat that still clung to her tongue.

Darcy had now kissed him dozens of times, and she did it with no more thought than it took to pop a lemon candy in her mouth. She loved the little burst of sweetness she got from seizing Teagan by the arm and tugging him down to her. She loved the flash of surprise and pleasure on his face when he realized what she wanted, and she loved the moment it always took him to decide what to do with his hands. She couldn't recall him ever kissing her, even on a morning where they woke up curled against each other. She thought this might be the first time.

There was an edge of salt when she sucked on his bottom lip, and it had to have come from sweat or tears. That reminded her that only a little while ago, she'd been afraid she needed to call an ambulance. She needed to figure that out.

Darcy slid the glass further down the counter and curled her fingers into his shirt.

"Okay, Teagan, okay," she said soothingly, even as he continued to press kisses along her jaw line. "Um. We should talk, if you're feeling better."

Teagan pulled far enough back to give her a brief nod before busying himself with her lips again. His hands dropped from her cheeks and pressed against her waist only to fall further and grip her hips.

Darcy was beginning to feel affected by his closeness and the warmth of his skin radiating through his thin shirt. She also began to suspect that was a deliberate effort on Teagan's part. It occurred to her that in all those times she'd kissed him or pulled him onto the couch or into the shower, he hadn't simply been happy to do whatever she liked. He'd been paying attention to what she liked. And now, when she was trying to keep her wits about her so they could calmly discuss his crisis at the office—when he knew that calmly discussing was not one of her greatest skills!—he was giving her back everything she liked. He was asking her to want him.

He pulled her forward until her hips were spread around his thighs, and she had to hang onto his chest for balance. He licked into her mouth until she was breathless and distracted.

"Teagan," Darcy insisted, turning her head away. "Don't you think we should talk?"

"We can talk," Teagan said. His tongue traced a hot line up her neck to her earlobe as his thumbs brushed her inner thighs just beyond the frayed hem of her shorts.

"This doesn't feel like talking," Darcy said dizzily. "This feels like sex."

"It could also be that," Teagan agreed. He leaned back to give her a little more room to think, but he left his hands on her body, his fingers hot and tense where they rested on her bare legs.

She could tell him to stop, she supposed. And they could

rewind the discussion to an hour previous, when Teagan had been a vulnerable shape on the floor. Or she could let Teagan change the subject. Let him seduce her, pretend that she was so swept away by the promise implicit in his hands on her thighs that she could forget how scared she'd been for him.

She felt like she ought to know by now. Someone had probably figured it out and written it down somewhere, what she was supposed to do for someone who didn't want to be the person she'd already observed him to be.

But if all she had was her intuition, it told her that if Teagan was chasing her, she ought to let herself be caught. He felt like he'd lost some part of himself; she'd give it back to him.

He'd done the reading, and it said *if someone's holding on to you, hold on harder.*

So she twined her arms around his neck and turned her face up to his.

"If this is talking, I can't wait to see you argue," she said.

Teagan's exhale seemed to release all the remaining stiffness in his shoulders. His hands moved over her body more confidently, gathering the fabric of her shirt so he could pull it over her head. He took off his own and paused with his gaze on her body, fingers trailing down her arm.

Seeming to come to some determination, he took his wallet out of his back pocket, retrieved a condom from it, and set both on the counter next to her.

"Oh wow," Darcy said. "We're having that kind of a conversation, huh?"

Teagan nodded in agreement, head dipping to suck at the point of her collarbone.

"So it's going to be slow missionary with lots of eye contact?" she confirmed, joking to cover up her sudden nerves.
They hadn't actually done that yet, even though she thought
that was what sex had meant to Teagan before he met her.
She wasn't sure whether this was a step forward or backward.

"Are there other positions?" Teagan asked, playing along
and rounding his eyes.

"I'm not sure. Maybe we can experiment on my birthday," she said with mock seriousness, shucking the rest of
her clothing.

The stone of Teagan's counter was cold underneath her,
but his mouth was scorching wherever it landed on her skin.
His mouth carefully curled around a breast, pulling only to
the edge of intensity before it moved on. His fingers were
just as restless, stroking her thighs then sweeping around
her calves before rising almost but not quite to her core.

"We can pretend it's your birthday today," Teagan said in
a low voice. "This can go however you want it to go. I just"—
he knelt down so that when he spoke, his breath played out
on soft, bare skin—"I want to feel you. I want to be inside
you. I want to get something right today."

He spread her legs with his shoulders and leaned in just
enough to let his lower lip graze her. Darcy sighed and planted
her hands on the counter to hold herself up. Teagan's mouth
was always magic, and she felt a familiar rush of desire at the
sight of him on his knees in front of her. But the expected
relief of his tongue on her body didn't come.

"Do you want me to bend you over this counter?" Teagan
asked, tone still soft and smooth. "I could hold on to your
hair and make you guess when you'll feel me inside you."

Darcy restlessly shifted her hips, chasing his mouth, and resisted the urge to grab him by the ears to control his movements. Her pulse had begun to quicken at the featherlight touches he was alternating with his words, but it wasn't nearly enough to address the ache of building tension.

"O-okay," she agreed. Sounded good to her.

"Or you could sit on my lap and wrap your legs around me. I'd try to make you come by sucking on your breasts while you squirmed and begged me to move."

That also sounded just fine as an option. Teagan ran one careful fingertip in a delicate figure eight through her folds, using it to make a small wet circle around her clit.

"Yeah, let's do that," she said.

"Or you can get on top. I'd love to watch your face. I want to memorize the expression you make when you come," he said, fingers still stroking too slowly to do anything but slick his hand and her body both. "I like the sounds you make when you know you're on the brink but you want to draw it out just a little longer."

He was trying so hard to seduce her that she almost told him he really didn't need to *try*. She was seduced! She'd make this easy on him! He could have her any way he wanted her, just please, have her already. But the sweetness of serious-faced Teagan doing his best efforts at dirty talk while his fingers moved in and out of her body made her heart ache in a way she wanted to savor.

"I, um," she said. It was hard to think under the slow roll of Teagan's thumb and knuckle. "You know, I can get on board with the slow missionary. Or whatever it was you were planning. I want to accommodate *your* interests, for once."

"Anal it is," Teagan said in tones of great solemnity.

Darcy yelped with astonished laughter, tossing her head back and cackling so hard that Teagan stilled his hand and smirked at her.

Darcy put a hand on top of his to urge him to keep up with what he'd been doing and gave him a petulant look. "If you play that card, we're pretending it's *your* birthday, and then you have to wait a year."

Teagan raised his eyebrows significantly, then slid two fingers through much more favorable territory. He crooked them to make her keen, then followed them with a third. He studied her face as he slowly pumped them in and out. The stretch was welcome, but not nearly as good as what she was still anticipating. Darcy was about to whine that he was being cruel and withholding when he stood, slipped his fingers from between her thighs, and scooped her up off the counter.

The size of the apartment was such that he only had to carry her three steps before dropping her on her back on the bed. She still didn't know exactly what he was planning until he pulled her forward so that her legs dangled off the bed and he stood between her spread legs.

"My birthday is in two weeks," he announced, smile crooked. "I'll consider my options at that time."

All his big words aside, Teagan's face was vulnerable as he undid his slacks and kicked them off his legs, then peeled himself out of his boxer briefs. Darcy pushed up on her elbows to watch him, because Teagan was beautiful like this: his lower lip pulling inward with concentration, blonde eyelashes lowered in contemplation of her body spread out before him. The lean muscles of his chest and stomach were tight as he rolled the condom on.

It seemed to Darcy they both held their breath as he notched the head against her. They watched together as it disappeared inside her, the slow penetration pressing the air from her lungs until she gasped as a little twist of his hips drove it all the way home. He pulled back a few inches, checked her face, and slid in more carefully.

Darcy didn't have any leverage in this position, and she squirmed as she strove to accommodate the stretch between her hips, throwing him off his rhythm. Teagan put a cautioning hand on her stomach, skin nearly scorching against her own.

"I've got you," he said. "Just wrap your legs around me."

His voice was so peremptory that Darcy snorted and dug her heels into the round swell of his ass. His breath stuttered as the movement carried him infinitesimally deeper inside her. She giggled at him as he struggled to regain his balance.

She savored the imperfections of it. Every gesture that suggested this was a first time, not a last time, that she'd have him like this.

"Darcy, please. I'm trying to look cool here," Teagan begged, a rueful curl to his lips.

She spread her arms to him and scooted backward on the bed, briefly separating their bodies.

"Come up here, baby," she said. "I actually love slow missionary with lots of eye contact."

Teagan's smile widened as he crawled up the bed after her. He carefully lowered his weight back over her and swept the hair out of her face, hand cradling the side of her face.

"Oh, good," he said, dipping his head to whisper in her ear as he pressed into her body again. "I was totally lying about knowing how to do anything else."

· · · · ·

Teagan had begun to suspect that Darcy's willingness to accommodate his allegedly strenuous post-coital cuddling demands was less than totally selfless. The way she was drowsily splayed across his chest suggested that she didn't find it unpleasant. He scratched the gap between her shoulder blades with an arm that was slowly falling asleep under her weight, imagining that she might even find some corresponding satisfaction with the arrangement. She yawned in a kittenish way.

If he could do exactly what he wanted, he'd stay here all day, order some food, then propose round two. This was the best. This was what he wanted from life.

But it wasn't even lunchtime yet. He couldn't stay here all day, and he very rarely did exactly what he wanted to do. He had to go.

Teagan gathered all his resolve and shifted out from under Darcy's limp weight. He hesitated while looking at his clothes on the floor. He probably needed to shower if he didn't want to broadcast to everyone in the office that he'd taken a nooner, but getting out of bed and immediately going to clean up was also kind of a dick move, in his book.

"Where are you going?" Darcy asked, rolling over and pressing her cheek against his back. Her fingers slid under his rib cage, urging him back into the bed.

"I have to get back," he said, hoping his tone adequately conveyed his reluctance to do that.

"Mmm, false. There is literally nobody who will make you. If someone comes to make you, I'll fight them."

"I appreciate that. But if for no better reason than our workers' comp premiums, I'll spare them the necessity."

He sat up. Darcy did too, looking beautifully disgruntled with her long hair sliding down over her breasts.

"Spare yourself! It seemed like your office was really"—Darcy groped for a word—"freaking you out today."

"It's not the office," Teagan said, realizing too late that he was opening a door he wanted to leave closed. He sighed. Darcy never let anything go, so he might as well explain it now. "Or even Nora and Guillaume."

"Guillaume?" she asked.

"The short European guy she brought in. He's an art broker at Sotheby's. Nora asked me to work with him to sell off most of the art the foundation owns and to commit to soliciting more in-kind donations in the next quarter."

"And that was bad because . . ."

It was impossible to explain, because it didn't make sense. He could say that he disapproved of using a children's charity as a tax shelter. He could say that he felt incompetent when he tried to understand the art market. He could say that he felt awkward and exposed when he called strangers to ask them for money. But those things didn't add up to the full-body shock of fear and grief that had crashed into him in the middle of the meeting. He couldn't explain it. It was as though someone had wired a doorbell to blow up the garage when pressed.

"I just hate it," he said unsteadily and not very fulsomely. "That part of the job. Asking for donations. Especially when people are only giving for the tax benefit."

Darcy huffed in derision. "What part of the job *do* you like? Because as far as I can tell, you also hate the luncheons, the benefit dinners, managing people—"

"I like that it's a children's charity," he said.

"You like kids?" Darcy asked, looking skeptical.

"I like kids," Teagan said. "I used to coach a middle school softball team at the Y." Until he could no longer commit to Monday night practices in light of all the benefit dinners he was invited to.

Darcy leaned forward, loose hair dangling over naked shoulders. "Then where are the fucking kids, Teagan? I've been here a month, and I know you haven't seen any kids."

She looked angry at him, which he couldn't understand.

"It's not that kind of a charity," he began to explain. "We don't directly run the camp programs. We give out grants, we provide resources—"

"Okay, so you like exactly zero parts of your job," she said.

"Lots of people don't like their job." He stood, turning away to avoid her judgmental look and deciding that he'd just get dressed and take care to stand a few feet away from anyone else for the rest of the day.

"But you don't *do* anything else!" Darcy said. "You go to work, you go to these fake parties that you hate, you ride the train, and you go home to either your big empty house or this dinky little apartment. We haven't seen any of your friends, we've barely seen your sister—"

"I'm sorry this is all so shitty for you!" Teagan burst out. He only realized the volume of his voice when Darcy rocked backward in surprise. He wiped his mouth across his forearm as though that would erase the loudness of his voice and tried again. "I keep asking. What you'd rather do. But you won't tell me."

He wanted to bring the mountain to her, but he couldn't even find a restaurant she wanted to visit or a trail she wanted to walk. He was beginning to worry he didn't have a thing she wanted.

"Yeah, because it doesn't matter what I'd do," she said, looking puzzled. "This is your life. I'm here to help you figure out how to live in it without drinking."

That hit him low in the gut, the reminder that this was all just temporary to her.

He clenched his fists and turned away. None of this probably looked good to her. How'd he ever think he was going to convince her to stay with him in Manhattan when he couldn't even say that he liked it?

"I could sell this place and the one in Irvington," he said. "I could live somewhere closer to Peekskill."

"Okay," she said, still looking confused. "What's in Peekskill?"

It was the stop nearest Bear Mountain. But she hadn't been interested enough to look up the location this morning.

Teagan closed his eyes and pressed his palm against his face.

"At least the sex is pretty decent now, right?" he muttered. That probably couldn't last. He was going to need to start taking the Lexapro again if he couldn't make it through a nonconfrontational meeting with two other people without having a panic attack.

For a brief moment, he was uselessly, incandescently angry at his body. That it wouldn't do what he wanted. That it forced these kinds of choices on him.

"What?" Darcy said, obviously wondering whether she ought to be offended. "When wasn't the sex good? I've been nothing but spectacular."

"Never mind," Teagan said, biting into the side of his cheek. He needed to keep it together much better than this. "You are."

Maybe he could still find Darcy that park ranger job she'd

always wanted. It was a slim hope, but he hadn't been lying when he said he was good at applying to jobs. He hated asking for favors, but he'd do it even if he had to chase his leftover antidepressants with a Xanax kicker to do it.

"Anyway," he said, moving to change the subject, "you're right. I was supposed to see my sister more. Where the hell is she? It doesn't look like she's been here."

Darcy blinked a few times at the segue. "Um. I thought she was staying here? Her stuff is here."

"Sloane's never made a bed in her life," Teagan said, gesturing at the navy duvet. "Do you think you could track her down for me this afternoon? I'll just be in the office." Making calls to everyone he'd ever met who was even tenuously connected to environmental or animal welfare charities.

"Yeah, okay," Darcy said, still eyeing him distrustfully. "You sure you want to go back to the office today?"

"I feel better now," he said, which happened to be true.

Darcy snorted. "You had a soda, a walk, and an orgasm—of course you feel better right now."

He gave her a tight smile and pretended to open an agenda. "Then I'll pencil in the same before tonight's banquet to support the art therapy program at the children's hospital."

He knew it wasn't a nice thing to say when it left his mouth, but he was still smarting from her suggestion that she'd be gone as soon as this job was over for her. He saw her blink in momentary hurt before anger replaced the emotion.

Darcy's eyes narrowed.

"Fuck you," she said crisply. "You can pencil a short walk straight into the Hudson River."

Teagan opened his mouth to apologize, but Darcy grabbed him around the waist and tackled him to the bed. She pinned him on his stomach, twisted his arms behind his back, and rubbed her nose into the side of his neck as he squirmed and struggled to reclaim his dignity.

"Never done it in an office before, so you might get lucky," she said, and she bit his earlobe hard enough to leave teeth marks. "Shame about your crappy office carpet though. That's going to be hell on your back."

twenty-four

SLOANE DIDN'T ANSWER HER PHONE WHEN DARCY called her, and her text message back to Teagan was uninformative as to her whereabouts. Further investigation divulged that she was not showing up at whatever bullshit make-work volunteer gig Teagan had arranged for her at the Guggenheim. Darcy sensed that Sloane's well-being was climbing up Teagan's lengthy but fluid list of concerns.

The next time Darcy heard Teagan leaving Sloane a voice message, she plucked the phone from his hand.

"She's on your data plan, right?" she asked, taking a wild guess.

"She is," he acknowledged.

Darcy carried the phone into the other room and called the phone company to cancel Sloane's service. *That* yielded a flurry of angry text messages to Darcy once Sloane—who had been couch surfing in SoHo—found a cafe with Wi-Fi, Sloane correctly assuming that her brother would not have cut her off. Darcy was out of line, interfering, welcome to fuck off, et cetera. Darcy didn't particularly care, and she dictated as much right back to Sloane.

Darcy: Teagan is worried about you

Sloane: So? He worries about everything

That might be accurate, but that didn't give Sloane an excuse to add to it.

Darcy: Send him proof of life and start showing up at your job or I'll go after the credit card next

Sloane later sent Darcy a photo of the day's paper and an upraised finger, but Teagan was so relieved that Darcy didn't mind.

That Saturday they met Sloane for brunch in Brooklyn. The people crowding into the backyard patio where little wrought-iron tables were hidden among potted apple trees and loops of fairy lights were of a different tribe still from the ones Darcy had become familiar with over her weeks in Manhattan: thick of facial hair, strange of hat. Darcy, clad in cutoffs, hiking boots, and a T-shirt she'd bought used in a Jinhae street market, thought she might look more at home than Teagan in his chinos.

Sloane, who'd arrived half an hour late and still wearing pajamas, communicated mostly in grunts as they were finally seated. She wore very large sunglasses despite the shade, puffy face suggesting that the previous evening had not ended too long before.

A young waiter with an unfortunate mustache came by to take their orders. He had a variety of irreverent tattoos climbing his arms and neck, but his white, straight teeth said that he was waiting tables as a lifestyle choice on the way to some subsidized career in the arts.

Darcy waved at Teagan and Sloane to go first as she browsed the menu without much hope. Teagan had been excited about this place, even though it had taken them almost an hour to travel here.

"Tell us about the eggs," Teagan said to the waiter, glancing at Darcy out of the corner of his eye.

The waiter puffed up his narrow chest with pride, and Darcy sensed that he anxiously awaited opportunities to talk about the food in detail.

"All of our eggs come from a family farm in the Berkshires that raises heritage breed chickens on open pasture with nothing but organic feed," the waiter said. "The eggs are rich with omega-3 fatty acids and beta carotene and lower in cholesterol and saturated fat than commercial eggs. The farm supports local agriculture and social justice by training historically underrepresented farming groups in animal husbandry. All of the chicken waste is composted and reused in the experimental paw paw orchard on site. Paw paws are a native fruit, you know. You should try the paw paw smoothie. It's fantastic."

Teagan, who had been closely following the description of the wonders of the farm, passed his phone to Darcy.

"This is the farm's website," he said.

Darcy flicked through a montage of fat brown chickens gamely roaming through verdant green fields. The chickens looked reasonably happy, and there were no cages in evidence.

"Okay," Darcy said, encouraged. There was a big list of egg dishes down one side of the menu. Maybe she'd be able to eat something.

Teagan cracked a small, hopeful smile.

"What do you cook the eggs in?" Darcy followed up.

"Organic butter, from the same farm," the waiter replied. "The cattle are American milking devons, and—"

"Do you have margarine?" Darcy asked.

The waiter looked horrified down to the roots of his undercut. "Oh no," he said. "Everything here is natural. The chef only uses whole ingredients."

Teagan's smile faded. Darcy closed the menu. The waiter's face fell.

"I'll have the fruit plate," Darcy said. "And black coffee."

"I'll have the same," Teagan sighed.

Sloane made a disgusted noise, looking between them. "*I'll* have the corned beef hash, two eggs over hard, the blueberry Icelandic yogurt parfait, and a vac-pot of Kona coffee," she announced. "And the bottomless mimosas."

"*Sloane*," Teagan said, looking concerned at that last item.

"*Teagan*," she replied.

"Isn't it a little early to be drinking?" Teagan said, not taking the bait. "It's ten o'clock."

"It's Saturday. *Brunch*. And you made me come all the way down to Prospect Heights. I can have mimosas at brunch. I'm twenty-two."

"Please don't order bottomless mimosas in front of your alcoholic brother," Darcy said.

"I'm sure Teagan can handle it if I have some mimosas at brunch," Sloane said, scowling.

"I'm more concerned about you—"

"Don't do it as a personal favor to me," Darcy said, hunching her shoulders to appear larger and more menacing.

Sloane growled again and waved her hand. "Fine! Then I want extra turkey bacon too, extra crispy," she said.

"Very good choice," the waiter said, scurrying away from the family tension.

Both Darcy and Teagan looked at Sloane again.

"What," she said defensively. "Teagan, you're still eating meat, right? You're starting to look like shit again. Half that food is for you."

Darcy stiffened at that statement. Teagan didn't look great today, but she'd assumed that was just because he was hav-

ing trouble sleeping. She'd woken up in the middle of the
night to pee, discovered the other half of the bed empty, and
found him looking at his phone in the living room.

Darcy was starting to worry that she was fucking this up
somehow.

Teagan waved off Sloane's inquiry into his nutritional
habits, though as Darcy examined him more closely, she
thought he'd lost most of the weight he'd put on in Montana.

"You know, I wouldn't say anything if you wanted to eat
meat, dairy, whatever," Darcy said to Teagan. Not everyone
was capable of eating a peanut butter–based diet like she was.
Obligate carnivores and Teagan, she'd give them a pass. Everyone else could eat more bean dip.

Teagan put a cautioning hand on Darcy's knee under the
table, but Sloane leaped on the conversational thread.

"Yeah, Tiggie, you're a big guy. You can't live on the
food's food," Sloane said.

"Plenty of big people are vegan," Teagan said. "Anyway,
Sloane, the idea was that you'd go do something productive
every day."

"The job sucks, so I quit. Why would I spend this one life
I have to live passing out museum maps for stupid tourists?"
Sloane asked dramatically.

"Because you're majoring in art history? Where else did
you think you'd work after school?"

"*Mom* was an art history major, and she didn't have to
work at the museum. She helped fundraise for it. I could
do that."

Teagan gritted his teeth, and Darcy sensed that this was
an old argument.

"I don't think you understand what fundraising is really
like. It's not a fun job," he said.

"You don't want to work with me," Sloane accused him.

"That's not it. I could find you a job at one of the after-school programs," Teagan said, fatigue now dripping into his voice, "if you don't like the museum. I just don't think you should be bumming around the city with nothing to do—"

"I am not *built* for labor, and kids stress me out. Why can't I work at the foundation?"

"It's not a great time," he said slowly. "The board isn't happy about spending. They're not happy with me. I don't want to put you in the middle of that situation. We can't even afford to pay you."

"So you need more money. Fine. I'm fantastic at asking for money. I can call all of mom's stupid rich friends and kiss their asses, isn't that basically the job?"

"It's more complicated than that," Teagan replied.

"It really doesn't seem like it is," Sloane said, unconvinced. "I'd probably be better at it than you."

Darcy thought Sloane might be right about that, since she'd personally observed Teagan put both hands against his desk and stare into the void for at least five minutes before and after each fundraising call.

Teagan rubbed at the back of his neck. "If you'll come into the office to do it," he reluctantly offered. "I'll give you some of my call list."

Sloane dramatically rolled her eyes. "Fine," she agreed.

Despite his hesitation, Teagan looked faintly relieved, and he took out his phone to begin forwarding messages and calendar entries to his sister.

Darcy settled back in the uncomfortable iron patio seat as the two of them began to bicker about Sloane's work hours. She instinctively took her own phone out, but she caught herself before she could turn on one of her podcasts. Teagan and Sloane arguing wasn't stressful to listen to. Unlike in her own family, the stakes didn't feel zero-sum. They wanted good things for each other. Darcy had a pang of envy for Sloane, growing up secure in the knowledge that Teagan wouldn't let her destroy her life too badly. Nobody had said a thing before Darcy had made any of her terrible life decisions.

Darcy drained her glass of room-temperature tap water served in an artisan glass cup and clicked to her email. Other than bills, she rarely had anything of interest. Today, though, she had a new message with an all caps subject: OFFER LETTER ATTACHED.

She made a noise of surprise and pleasure as she sat up.

"Hey!" she interrupted Teagan and Sloane. "Teagan, it worked! Look, it didn't just go into the void."

She shoved the phone into his hand.

"What worked?" Sloane asked.

"Teagan filled out all the application forms for me," Darcy said. "At Yellowstone. And it worked." Nobody ever came through for her but Teagan. She should have known he would.

She beamed at Teagan, whose face was curiously blank. "What did they give me?"

He scrolled through the email without responding, then began to read it out loud.

"Snowcat tour operator," he said. He cleared his throat and began to read. "Seasonal. Full time, starting December 1. Ensures guests are provided with safe and enjoyable tour experience. Maintains and cleans vehicle for secure operation. Provides knowledgeable commentary about Yellowstone Park. Engages with guests and park personnel."

"Fucking fantastic," Darcy said, relief beginning to tingle through her body. The runway on her life was extended through March. "That's so much better than working in the rental shop. Is there housing?"

Teagan scrolled again. "In the dorms."

Darcy briefly closed her eyes. That would take her almost all the way through the next semester. The hours would be regular. She could take more classes. Maybe Teagan was right, and someday she'd graduate.

She turned to Teagan, ready to thank him profusely, but found that both Teagan and Sloane were both looking at her as though she'd just dropkicked a juvenile harp seal. Actually, Teagan looked like the kicked seal, eyes soft and betrayed.

Darcy quietly took the phone back from him.

"It's, um," she said. "You know, that's almost two months from now."

"I know," he said.

Darcy squirmed, feeling absurdly as though this was yet another fuckup on her part. "Do you have any better ideas? This is the only offer I have so far."

"No, I get it," he agreed, voice toneless.

He looked at her with patient expectation, but Darcy didn't know what he expected her to say. He was the one who'd put in the applications in the first place! He knew she didn't have anywhere else to go.

"This is the best job I've ever been offered," she said, feeling that she had to explain herself, even though it should have been obvious why she was pleased. "Well, working for the Goederts was supposed to be the best one, but that went pear-shaped. This'll give me direct education experience, and I'll get more familiar with the park, and—"

"No, I know," Teagan said. "I'm happy for you. I know this is what you wanted."

Both statements sounded like total lies coming out of his mouth. Darcy tensed in inchoate frustration, because what had he expected her to do? What had he thought she was going to do once she was no longer employed to keep him from drinking? He *knew* she didn't even have a car!

"I'm going to check with the waiter on what's taking so long with our food," Teagan said, pushing his chair back with a squeal of metal on brick.

He stalked away into the restaurant interior, not really looking as though he was in search of the waiter.

As soon as he was out of earshot, Sloane crossed her arms in an exaggerated flounce, glaring at Darcy with all the icy dignity she could muster for being clad in watermelon-print fleece pajama pants and one of Teagan's college sweatshirts.

"What's wrong with my brother?" she demanded.

Darcy tugged on the end of her braid, not sure whether Sloane meant generally or specifically.

"He hasn't been sleeping very well," Darcy began.

"Well duh," Sloane said. "He's basically three pots of coffee in a Burberry trench coat. He never sleeps. I *meant* what is wrong with him that you want to book it back to the stupid woods to wash snow cars when Teagan's already named your first three kids in his head."

Darcy snorted in shocked amusement. "Um, believe me. Active efforts are being taken to prevent kids. Don't worry that I'll make you an aunt."

"Not the point! The point is, women throw themselves at my brother. My friends in high school used to doodle his name in their notebooks and lie around my house in their swimsuits in case he dropped by."

Darcy didn't see why Teagan's appeal to teenage girls was really relevant to whatever point Sloane was trying to make. She was positive that Teagan would have been totally oblivious to any come-ons that did not rise to the level of taking off clothes and requesting sex in small discrete words, as that was what Darcy had basically had to do.

"He's *rich*, he's *nice*, he puts on headphones whenever he's watching videos on his phone—he's basically an urban legend," Sloane said, ticking off Teagan's advantages on her manicured fingers.

She was eliding some of Teagan's drawbacks, like the very recent crisis with alcoholism, but it wasn't like Darcy hadn't privately made a similar assessment. Who wouldn't want Teagan? Of course she did. But she wanted Teagan like she wanted to finish college or work for the Park Service: with a great deal of respect for the likelihood she wouldn't have him.

"You sound like you're trying to sell him to me," Darcy scoffed.

"Yes! I am! Except I thought I'd already sold him to you. You were going to come here and take care of him."

"I am," Darcy said, defensive at the idea that her performance might be criticized. "I'm being very careful with him. We talk about his sobriety plan for all the places he goes, and we've already managed the office and a bunch of lunches and dinners, and he hasn't had a single relapse—"

"You were supposed to do more than that," Sloane complained. "You made him go out and do stuff. And eat healthy shit. And like, be in the sun and not thinking about his job."

Darcy's lower lip twisted as she considered that. "He's not a dog I can walk. Recovery is about figuring out how to live without alcohol, and you're supposed to be cautious about making big changes—"

"It's going to be a big change when you ditch him in December!"

"I'm not ditching him," Darcy protested. "We said ninety days in the first place."

"So you want to go? You think living in a dorm and washing cars is better than being with Teagan?" Sloane asked incredulously.

"I didn't—look, if I find something else here, I don't have to go," Darcy said, feeling her back up against a wall. "But I don't even know how to look for work here."

"So you're still deciding whether you like my brother, is that it? You've known him for a couple of months, and he's totally obsessed with you, but you just can't decide whether you want to be with him?" Sloane was getting herself worked up, and other people on the patio were turning to look at them.

Darcy exhaled, considering the righteous fury of the hungover college student in front of her. It was hard to relate. Darcy had never in her life thought that she would get things just because she wanted or deserved them. What Darcy *wanted* was a consideration she rarely had the luxury of consulting in her constant scramble to keep herself housed and employed.

It didn't matter how she felt about Teagan. That wouldn't change a single thing except how hard it would hurt when this ended. She had no control over how long he kept her around.

"Some of us don't have trust funds. I don't have a rich brother who loves me. I don't have a car or a savings account or a degree—or friends with apartments in Manhattan. So what I have is a contingency plan. I know I have a job until December, and now I know I have a job after December. I can't afford to not have one."

Sloane stuck out her chin. "It's not like Teagan would make you start paying rent. He'd be thrilled if you just stuck around and lay by the pool and finished your degree. It's the dream, really."

"Sloane. Feminism *wept*," Darcy said, giving the girl the stink eye. "A little advice, from someone older, don't organize your life around a man wanting you around."

Sloane hooked a thumb at the restaurant, where Teagan had still not returned. "You really think my brother is going to flake on you? Teagan? Who is so addicted to fixing other people's problems that he's still doing our mom's job two years after she died—"

"I know how it ends though!" Darcy said, really wishing the conversation would end. "The same way it always does. I guess this is all great to start out with"—and she gestured vaguely at her face and chest—"but then after a while, the dude realizes that I don't cook, I don't clean, I don't *read*, I'm kind of a bitch . . ."

She fit in exactly zero of the places Teagan went in his normal life. That had to be grating on him already. It was only going to get worse when Teagan got better.

"It's okay to be kind of a bitch," Sloane said, making big circles with her hands. "In New York, at least."

"Maybe so." Darcy stared at the empty table. "But I guess what I'm saying is, yeah, Teagan wants me around now. And that's great. But he's just starting recovery, so of course he wants me around to help him out. But what if he gets out past ninety days, and he feels better, and then he doesn't? He's still figuring out who he is without alcohol in his life."

Sloane scrunched up her pretty face in a dramatic pout. Her mouth moved like she was wrestling with her words. Deep thought didn't seem like her natural default.

"He's not going to be a different person," she finally said. "Teagan is always like this. He's always been like this."

Sloane sounded very sincere when she said that, but Darcy thought, with a pang, that it would be a shame if that were true. Teagan had been going through it since she met him. *It* had varied, but Darcy had taken *through* as a temporary state.

Darcy was there for the temporary, to clear the way for the *someday* he'd have with someone else, when he was better, happy, ready for his permanent life. Remembering that was how she was going to keep her heart from getting broken when he told her they were done.

"Where is he, anyway?" Darcy said, spotting their server heading back with a laden tray. "Did he get lost?"

"Uh . . ." Sloane looked around. "I dunno."

"Crap," Darcy said, abruptly worried that Teagan was locked in another bathroom. She tossed her recycled linen napkin on the table and stood. "I'll go find him."

She dodged the server and jogged up the stairs into the restaurant, but the two bathrooms were free of anyone except hungover hipsters fixing their hair and makeup. She checked the kitchen and the basement. Beginning to feel some real panic, she walked out of the restaurant and scanned the street. She finally spotted Teagan halfway down the block, conspicuous mostly for being the only man in business casual.

He was leaning against a board fence between two brownstones, braced by his forearm.

"Oh no," Darcy said, rushing over. "Are you . . ." She wasn't sure how to refer to it, still. What had happened at his office. Freaking out sounded like a thing he could stop doing if he wanted to, but it was clear he really hadn't wanted to be hyperventilating in the men's room. "Upset?" she hedged.

Teagan barely turned his head to look at her, but he shook his head.

"No, I thought I might—but no. Not today. I'm keeping it together. I just—thought I'd stay out here until I could act happier for you than sorry for myself, and that's taking a minute."

At the idea it would be an act, and that he'd bother to do it for her, Darcy felt her heart stutter. Nobody else would ever have bothered to pretend. She didn't know why Teagan would.

"Teagan . . ." Darcy trailed off, chest feeling tight. "It's two whole months from now." Nobody else had still wanted her over that time frame.

Teagan straightened and turned to her. "It doesn't matter that it's in two months. It wouldn't matter if it was two years."

Darcy blinked at him, guilt and worry tossing against her own fracturing certainty that Teagan would get better and grow past her someday soon.

"I think—I think maybe we should try to get you a real sponsor. And maybe a group? Like AA? I don't know. I don't think I'm doing this right. I don't think it should be getting harder." She exhaled through her teeth, a more familiar sense of incapability leadening her body. She felt like she was failing him, and she didn't understand how.

"You know it's not your job to fix me, right?" Teagan said, one corner of his mouth tugging to the side. "I never thought you would. That's not why I'm dreading December."

Darcy rocked back on her heels. She hadn't realized that Teagan thought he was broken.

"Are you afraid you're going to start drinking again?" she asked.

Teagan tightened his lips and shook his head again, looking away down the street. Darcy put a hand on his arm, wishing she had some wonderful plan to help him fit back into his life. Or even a marginally plausible plan, if he'd actually try it. All she had were bad plans, because she'd only ever made bad ones for herself.

"How about—okay, I've got it. We'll move to Australia and work at one of those nonprofits that rebuilds coral reefs by planting baby corals on concrete pylons. Do you know how to scuba dive?"

"I don't," he said, smiling faintly. "And I get very seasick on anything larger than a sculling boat. Do you think that's an impediment?"

"Probably. Okay. Never mind. I'll keep working on it," Darcy promised, her eyes feeling hot and scratchy. "I'm sure the right job is out there for you and me. After all, you're very skilled at—well, I've been watching you for a month, and I'm still not really sure what it is you do. Answer emails. Look at spreadsheets. Brood."

Teagan forced the corners of his mouth into the shape of a smile, but his eyes were still distant and sad.

"Do you hate it all?" he asked. "Sometimes I feel bad that I ever asked you to come out here in the first place."

Darcy sucked on her lower lip, reluctant to be honest about

it. Because she was leaving in two months, and he'd never asked her to stay. He'd been very careful not to, she thought, to spare either of them the embarrassment of making promises they couldn't keep.

But maybe Sloane was right, and that's what he wanted. And if so, he ought to know how she felt, even if she didn't have any answers. She wished it wasn't all up to him to solve, but if she'd been good at planning, she wouldn't be perpetually two months away from having nowhere to live.

If she laid it out, she supposed, he'd at least know he hadn't done anything wrong.

"So, I hate going to restaurants because I'm just fine living on peanut butter and junk food, and I feel like a brat if don't order anything," Darcy muttered, feeling her face turn red. She shoved her hands into the pockets of her shorts and stared at her feet. "I hate going to parties because I don't like getting dressed up. I hate going to your office because everyone else is working there, and I don't have anything to do. I hate your condo because it doesn't have any natural light, and I hate your mom's house because you look so sad every time you walk in the door."

Teagan sighed. "I guess that's all of it, then," he said glumly. He turned his shoulders back toward the restaurant, opened his mouth to say they should go back inside.

Darcy reached out and took his arm. "But Teagan—I don't hate being with you. There's nothing I hate about that. Do you understand?"

Her heart hammered in her throat. It was as close as she'd ever come to saying *I love you* in her adult life, and she knew it probably wasn't as close as Teagan wanted to hear, but it was as much as she could live with having said if this ended the way it always did.

"Yeah?" he asked quietly. His eyes searched her face. And Darcy wished she could tell him it would all work out, even if she went back to Montana in two months. But he'd been honest with her, and she was trying to do the same. She wasn't sure he was going to be okay, and she wasn't sure that she would be either.

She nodded and hooked an elbow around the back of his neck, burying her face against his collarbone.

"I like this part," she mumbled.

It was very accommodating of him to be so tall, especially for situations where she felt vulnerable. Teagan closed his arms around her, and she got a little bit of that quiet feeling he'd once described, where the noise of the city fell away. She should have told him then that she felt the same way, but Teagan had chosen the wrong sober companion if he'd wanted someone really good with words.

She caught herself swaying back and forth as she held onto him, an instinctive rhythm not connected to the distant blare of taxis or rumble of the train. She wished they were back in Montana still, where she'd been certain everything she'd been asked to do was helping someone.

"Poached," Teagan said, apropos of nothing.

"What?"

"They could poach the eggs without using butter. Do you like poached eggs?" he asked.

Darcy leaned back and goggled at him. Teagan had a great portion of his mind devoted, at any given time, to worrying about other people's needs. She'd entirely forgotten about brunch, Sloane waiting for them, and Sloane's need for productive employment. Teagan hadn't. He was still solving those problems in the background.

"Yeah, I'll eat a couple of poached eggs," Darcy said slowly.

She frowned at him, recalling the hour on the train. "Did we come out here just for the eggs?"

Teagan ran a couple of affectionate fingers across the fluffy tip of her braid. He smiled at her, and this time, it reached his eyes. "Don't worry about it."

twenty-five

FRIDAY NIGHT FOUND TEAGAN IN THE BACK SEAT of his mother's car, head bumping against the driver's seat every time his sister approached a stoplight. She kept flooding the engine when she tried to shift gears. He wasn't even sure she had a driver's license, and he was too afraid to ask at this point.

He'd entertained the passing thought that *while driving Sloane and Darcy to the Westchester Zoo's annual Art Walk gala would be a very bad time to have a panic attack*, and of course, no sooner had he pulled onto Broadway than he felt that now-familiar surge of adrenaline course through his veins like snake venom.

He pulled over at a gas station, palpably aware of the stares that he drew leaning against the car in his tuxedo as two women in evening gowns argued around him.

"We should just go home," Darcy said. "I looked up the Westchester Zoo. It's a private zoo, owned by some eccentric finance jerk. Private zoos are terrible. They select for the most charismatic species rather than paying even lip service to captive breeding programs and species reintroduction. Everyone has a Bengal tiger when they ought to have a Przewalski's horse. And this dress is itchy."

"*Teagan* should go home," Sloane retorted. "I look hot.

You look hot. I got my hair blown out for this. We can probably hit up, like, a lot of donors if we work together."

"I have to go to this," Teagan said, struggling for air. "Just give me a minute."

Darcy and his sister regarded him with disappointment, and Sloane none-too-gently shoved him into the back seat.

"I'll drive," his sister announced.

The past two weeks had been hell. Nora was coming by the office almost every day to case the art on the walls like a Wet Bandit in Lanvin pumps, Sloane was making noises about changing her major a third time or possibly dropping out of school entirely, and, most ominously, Darcy had purchased a new pair of snow boots for the coming winter. The boots were stashed away in the coat closet of his mother's house, but Teagan felt their dire presence like a gothic heart beating under the floorboards.

His symptoms were all in his head. He was not having a heart attack. His terror was just a misfire in his brain. The woman crowding into the back seat next to him was real, and she cared about him, and if he just put his head down and worked hard enough at it, he could fix all the problems that were sending her out of his life.

These precisely dictated thoughts were launched at the invading mass of anxiety until it gradually began to retreat.

Darcy rubbed a soothing palm between Teagan's shoulder blades until he sighed and moved his head to her shoulder, feeling some of the storm in his skull subside. "Private zoos aren't even good at wildlife education," she gently chided him. "The animals don't perform their natural behaviors in the kinds of enclosures these zoos have room for, and they don't have enough individuals to maintain their typical social groupings."

"We can leave as soon as I've given my speech," Teagan promised.

"What speech?" Darcy asked.

"Mom was on the board of this zoo, and this was Mom's favorite event," Sloane called from the front seat. "She'd bring one of us as her date every year. There are pictures of teenage Teagan in a tuxedo, holding a lemur."

Teagan felt the weight of Darcy's judgmental stare, even though he didn't think it was fair to condemn him for not intuiting animal welfare concerns as a fourteen-year-old.

"Since she died on the way back from a board meeting, they decided to name the new tiger exhibit after her two years ago. I think they were afraid someone would sue them. As if Mom needed an excuse to get drunk. So, anyway, Teagan gives the annual update about the tiger exhibit now," Sloane finished.

"Jesus fucking Christ," Darcy muttered, hand still pressed against Teagan's back, the anchor he was clinging to. "This zoo basically killed your mom, and you have to give a speech every year?"

"Too many vodka sodas killed my mother," Teagan mumbled. He forced himself to sit up and take deep breaths. "I'm not worried about the speech."

He was worried about the speech. He'd spent ten minutes before the speech dry heaving last year. Public speaking didn't bother him any more than it did most people, but saying nice things about his mother and this nonprofit that he didn't really believe in did bother him. But his worries about the speech were not even visible over the pile of worries he was carrying for his other plans tonight.

If Darcy was serious about what she'd said—that she wanted to be with him, if all the other extraneous bullshit in his life didn't get in the way—he thought he'd put together something to offer her. He just had to keep it together for the next few hours.

They made it to the zoo's valet stand before Sloane could wear out the transmission. Darcy squinted suspiciously at the big flags depicting happy penguins dancing around bits of avant-garde sculpture while Teagan summoned every scrap of optimism he possessed. This could go well. He could end tonight happy. Maybe it would all work out for him this time.

His sister bumped him with her shoulder.

"Do you want a Xanax?" she asked quietly.

Teagan startled. He was holding off on all his prescribed psychotropic medication until after he'd convinced Darcy not to fly back to Montana for the winter.

"Do you have Xanax? Did someone prescribe you Xanax?" he demanded.

"No, but, I mean, I could get you some," she said, her expression stating that she thought she was being helpful.

"No, thank you," he said firmly, making a note to interrogate her later on who was selling drugs at these events.

They followed couples in evening wear through the roped-off entrance. There was an open bar and passed hors d'oeuvres in a pavilion near the entrance, but the dance floor was empty so early in the evening, and the band had not yet taken the stage. Teagan saw people he recognized: friends of his mother, donors to the foundation, other charity executives. Twenty million people in this town, but the number of people who liked to dress up and talk about how much money they might give away was small enough to feel like a terrible kind of high school class, one which held reunions multiple times a month. He saw the one person he'd been hoping to dodge until later tonight catch sight of him and stride purposefully away from the meerkat exhibit to intercept his path to the bar. Nora looped an arm under his and towed him off to a side path.

"Look at you two!" Nora said, gaze taking in only Teagan and Sloane. "Let me get a picture. Adrian, can you take their picture? We need to put a photo of you two on the website. Oh Sloane, my God do you look like your mother. You're gorgeous." Nora's fiancé gave Teagan a silent look of apology as he pulled his phone from his pocket and halfheartedly pretended to line up a shot.

"Ooh, hello, Adrian," Sloane said, wiggling her eyebrows at the artist, who winced.

Teagan put his arm around Darcy's waist as she tried to stomp away from the conversation.

"Nora, I think you've met Darcy?" he asked pointedly.

"Of course I met her," Nora said, checking the edge of her lipstick with a red-taloned finger. "Is that going well? Sobriety? You must be getting one of those little chip things soon. How many days has it been since you had a drink?"

"I'm not sure," Teagan said.

"Oh, really? I thought alcoholics always knew exactly how many days it had been," Nora replied.

"Seventy-seven"—Darcy looked at him oddly—"days since you were in the hospital, at least."

"Then it's seventy-seven," Teagan said, beginning to feel a little dizzy again. He hadn't had two panic attacks in a single day recently, but he was pretty sure he could manage it, if necessary.

Faking a history of heavy drinking was as good a reason as any to have one. Pretending to be sober for the rest of his life wasn't going to be hard—he just wouldn't drink—but pretending that Darcy was in his life for that reason needed to stop.

Tonight, he vowed. He'd tell her she could quit being his sober companion, and he'd handle his own sobriety from here on out. He'd start going to AA meetings, if necessary. He'd heard the coffee wasn't bad.

"I'm still so surprised you turned out to have a drinking problem," Nora said. "I can remember you driving out to pick your mom up when she'd had a little too much to drink. Oh well! She'd be so proud of you for continuing to support the Westchester Zoo, you know. She loved this party."

"She did," Teagan agreed, hearing ringing in his ears.

"You look very nice tonight," Adrian said to Darcy with the air of a man putting himself into the line of the fire.

"Thanks," she replied under her breath, fidgeting with a shoulder strap. Teagan would rather throw himself on a grenade than tell a woman what to wear, but Sloane had impressed on Darcy that she couldn't wear her typical button-down shirt and slacks to a black-tie event. The only dress Darcy owned was of the tube variety, so Sloane had furnished this long blue dress tied with gold cord under the bust and around the waist. Teagan vaguely recalled the dress on Sloane, some years past. It fit Darcy very differently, clinging to some of his favorite places on her. She looked like a Roman goddess with her wavy hair pinned loosely and hanging down her back.

Teagan hadn't said anything only because he didn't want her to think he cared if she ever put on an evening gown ever again, but Darcy's uncertain face said she hadn't been sure how she looked before Adrian spoke.

"Did Teagan buy that for you?" Nora asked Darcy, gaze assessing.

"No. I think Sloane wore it to prom," Darcy replied, wrinkling her nose.

Nora laughed politely. "Oh no. I thought so. I suppose there aren't many reasons to wear black tie in Idaho."

"Montana," Darcy said evenly. "And no, usually not."

"You must be headed back soon. Since Teagan's almost three months sober."

Darcy looked at him out of the corner of her eye. "Before Thanksgiving, probably," she told Nora.

Teagan gritted his teeth as Nora nodded in satisfaction.

"I'm going to get myself a club soda," Teagan said, taking a step to the side in an effort to extricate himself from the conversation.

Nora took a corresponding step to stay in his path.

"So, tonight would be a good night to announce that you're selling the John Currin paintings," Nora said. "While everyone's thinking about your mother. She has a lot of friends here. We might get a little premium for sentimentality."

"I haven't had a chance to look at the consignment agreement yet," Teagan said.

"Rose already reviewed and approved it," Nora said.

That was news to Teagan.

"I'd also like to review it," he said, trying to remain calm. "I'm not sure that's the direction I'd like to go."

"I can send it to you right now," Nora said, pulling her phone out. "What else are you addressing in your speech?"

Teagan resisted the urge to rub his face. "I was going to thank some of my mother's friends for their support of the zoo and the foundation."

"Do you have it written down? Let me see," Nora commanded.

Teagan sighed and pulled his index cards out of his jacket pocket. Nora plucked them from his hand and put them into her purse.

"There's a VIP lounge in the cabana behind the lemur house," she said, pointing out the building. "Why don't you meet me there in a few minutes, and we'll go over the speech and the other donors who are here tonight."

Teagan wanted to say no. He wanted to come up with some reason that he didn't have to do any of it. He didn't want to go sit in the VIP lounge with Nora, he didn't want to give a speech where he'd pretend that he had a single fond memory of pulling his mother out of this party or any other, he didn't want to talk to the people who'd handed her drinks and cheered her on as she spiraled further and further out of control.

"Yes, all right," he said.

"You're my favorite!" Nora chirped, finally stepping aside.

Teagan stood still until she was out of sight, mentally shouldering the other things he would do tonight, locking his knees and trying to refocus his mind on his existing plans.

This could go well.

Sometimes, things went well.

Nothing had gone well that he could bring to mind in that exact instant, and the gambler's fallacy dictated that the chances of things going well were no better because of previous failures, but surely he was due for something to break in his favor for once in a metaphysical way, if no other.

"I'm getting a drink and going to the VIP lounge," Sloane announced, giving Teagan a bright smile and walking fast after Nora.

That finally left Teagan alone with Darcy, under the judgmental eyes of many lemurs but thankfully few humans. Darcy glared off at the VIP lounge as though about to throw something at it, but she eventually wrapped two hands around his arm and shook him until he unlocked his knees.

"Hey, Bear Bait. Sometimes you need to make like Nancy Reagan and just say no," she said.

Teagan laughed politely. "If Nora offers to do lines in the VIP lounge, you have my word."

"No, I mean it," she said. "What are we doing here? You're not doing well tonight. You don't want to give that speech. I look ridiculous. The parrots by the bar were already freaking out about the music and the band hasn't even started playing yet—"

"You look beautiful," Teagan replied, choosing the statement he could refute. He needed to keep it together, look like he had a plan, focus on Darcy and how this *was* going to work, if he could get through tonight. "You're the most beautiful woman in the room, whatever you're wearing, but you look beautiful in that dress."

Darcy shook her head in faint amusement, her expression stating that she hadn't forgotten everything else in her list. "It doesn't fit. Sloane's three inches taller than me and like twenty pounds lighter. It's so tight around my hips that I couldn't even wear underwear."

"What—is that true?" He resisted the urge to look. Then he looked. He couldn't tell. It did look tight, but Darcy's hips could cause a traffic accident regardless of what she was wearing.

"Maybe you'll find out later," Darcy said, curling her mouth in a brief smirk. "We could go home now, and you could verify it."

That sounded like a fantastic plan, a hope he was going to cling to until this evening was over. That it would end with both of them at his home, Teagan taking that dress off her.

"Not yet. We'll be here a couple hours, at least. But this is the last gala you ever have to come to. You never have to come with me again," he said.

"Well no, that's not right. If you go, I have to go. Otherwise someone'll hand you a cocktail and all my hard work is wasted."

Teagan cleared his throat. "At some point you have to trust me to make good choices, right?"

Darcy fidgeted again with the strap of her dress. "I guess. I don't think you're there yet. Do you?"

"I think I am. I'm sober for good. I promise, I'm not even thinking about drinking," he said.

"Then what are you so worried about?" Darcy said softly, beautiful dark eyes wide with concern. She went up on her toes and kissed the corner of his mouth, then framed his face between her hands to kiss him more lingeringly. She pulled back to study his expression, leaving her hands loosely clasped around his neck, fingertips gentle on his jaw.

She was so good to him. She had to want this too.

Teagan exhaled, trying to think of a good way to start. He'd been working on how he'd ask her this all week.

"I'm actually—so—I wanted you to come with me tonight because there's . . . an opportunity."

Darcy stared blankly at him. He was falling back on business speak, and he probably sounded like he was asking for a transfer into the special situations group or a new corporate revolver. But now that he was in it, there was nothing to do but to keep talking.

"I want you to meet one of our donors, Yuna Park," he said. "Her latest husband is a small animal veterinarian, and he's retiring from practice to run a wildlife rehab outside of Beacon."

Teagan swallowed hard, even though Darcy's face said she still wasn't following this to its conclusion. "They want to hire someone to run a volunteer program at the rehab center. For local teenagers. I said you might be interested, and they want to talk to you about the position."

Darcy pulled back, her reaction leaning a lot further toward surprise and consternation than Teagan had hoped. She gestured at her cleavage.

"Jesus. You want me to go to a job interview in this dress?"

"It's not a job interview, it's just to meet them—"

"But you set this up? They know I'm coming? They knew about this?"

"I—yes, I talked to Mrs. Park a couple of times about it. But all you need to know about her is—"

"Give me a minute!" she shouted. "God. What even is this coordinator supposed to do? You know I don't have any experience actually working with animals. Or kids."

"I know, but—"

"What did you tell them? Did you tell them I did? Did you tell them I don't actually have a degree yet?" Color was rising in her face.

"I told them you were enrolled in a degree program for wildlife science, but nothing else," Teagan said, feeling buffeted by the vehemence of her reaction.

"How long have you known about this, again?" she demanded.

"Since last Tuesday?"

"Teagan! And you didn't tell me about it? I'm going to probably fall all over my ass when I talk to them."

Teagan bit down hard on the insides of his lips, trying to

choose his words carefully. "I wanted you to hear about the job from them, rather than me."

"Why?" Darcy began to pace. "Not cool, Teagan. Not cool, springing this on me."

"I wasn't sure you'd want to do it if you heard about it from me first."

"I'm not sure I do! If you work with migratory birds or endangered species, you have to get permitted by the state *and* the feds, there's probably even more paperwork if you work with kids, and—I'm sorry, Teagan. I'm sorry. This is probably not going to work."

"Wait, wait," he said, beginning to tense up at Darcy's agitation. "Please just hear it from them first. You don't think it might be better than driving the damn snow truck?"

"I know I can drive the snowcat! I keep telling you, I need to have a job I can actually do. I don't want to get arrested by the game warden because I didn't fill out the paperwork right."

"Please. Darcy. I just want you to consider it. Doesn't it matter at all that you could stay here if you worked at the wildlife rehab?"

"Of course it does. But I wouldn't be here very long if I got fired because I was terrible at managing volunteers. I've never managed anyone. Or anything. I'm pretty sure I'd be terrible at it."

"I wouldn't let you be terrible at it. If you have . . . *paperwork*, you could bring it home, and I'd help you fill it out. I wouldn't let you fail at it. Darcy, I'd help you," he said, trying to put his whole heart in his voice.

She wouldn't meet his eyes. "I can't take some job I can only do if you're coaching me through it."

"Why can't you?"

"Because, I assume, in this scenario you've dreamed up, I'm also living with you. I've never heard of Beacon, but I bet I can't afford to live there on whatever a wildlife rehab volunteer coordinator makes."

"Okay, yes, that's true, but that would just make it easier for me to help you until you get settled into the job."

"And if I don't settle into the job? If I get fired?"

"Then I'll help you find a new one."

"But what I'm saying, Teagan," she insisted, eyes round and scared, "is what if you and I don't work out?"

She said that like it was something that might be out of their control. It wasn't! He couldn't control when his brain would melt down like a graphite-moderated reactor, but he could commit to her, in whatever terms she wanted. He could do that even if she wouldn't offer up the same.

Teagan clenched his jaw hard. "You don't have to worry about it. You *know* me. You know it would never be me who left."

"I can't ever know that," Darcy said, looking down at her feet.

There was tight heat in a band around his throat and behind his eyes. Every word was harder and harder to force out.

"Then tell me what it would take for you to feel safe enough to take this job. It doesn't have to be this job. Tell me what would make you feel safe enough to stay here with me. If it's something that can be bought, I'll buy it for you. If there's something I can do, I'll do it for you. If there's anything you need to hear me say, any promise I can make, I'll say it to you. Here and now or in front of as many people as you like."

Darcy's shoulders heaved, but she didn't look up. He felt as though he was shouting up at her from a great distance below, somehow sinking deeper.

"I called the tow lot this morning. Your car's going to auction for tow liens next week. I could buy it for you. So that you could always move out, if you wanted to." He swallowed again. "Am I getting warmer?"

"I don't know," Darcy said, curling and uncurling her hands. "I need to think about it." She took a step away and turned toward the reptile house, and Teagan was abruptly certain that she'd talk herself out of it entirely if she had a chance to run off. He couldn't just let her go.

"Do you want to get married?" he blurted out.

"Jesus! Are you asking me?" she cried, spinning back to face him.

"No, I'm saying—is that what it would take? For you to be sure you could do this. That we could do this."

Her expression was appalled, and her reaction to the idea couldn't have been a sharper knife in the chest if she'd laughed at him instead.

"And if I said yeah, I'm not sticking around unless you put a ring on my finger?" She had her lips pressed so tightly together they'd turned pale.

There were right and wrong answers to this, he was sure. He wished he knew what she wanted to hear.

"Then—I'd get you one," he said softly. He thought it probably wasn't the right answer, but it was true, at least. Darcy gasped like he'd confessed some terrible misdeed.

"Why?" she said, throwing her hands in the air. "Why would you do that? Teagan, you're miserable, and you're only getting worse since we got back from Montana. I don't think I'm helping you at all with your alcohol dependency. I can't do anything to help you with *your* job, and your job's pretty all consuming. Don't you want to be with someone who makes you happy?"

"It's not your job to make me happy," Teagan said, jerking back in surprise. "I'm happy *with* you. I love you. You're that first cup of coffee that gets me out of bed in the morning. You're the song on my playlist for the drive home. You're every good thing that I promise myself to get through the day." He gripped his hair so hard it hurt, just to be able to keep talking. "You're the best thing in my life—and I mean it. I'll do anything. Ask me for anything."

At last something he said had landed. She was taking deep, gulping breaths, eyes wide and shocked, but at least she was considering it.

"Okay," she said. "Okay."

"Okay . . . what?" he was so dizzied by the conversation that he wasn't sure whether he was engaged or whether she was leaving him.

"Okay, I'll think about it. About what you said. About the job. And—and everything. Can you go drink some Sprite or something for a while? I just—I need to think about it."

She took another step backward, rigid and tense. He opened his mouth to beg her to stay, to promise he'd not bring it up again, but a big giddy knot of women came down the path, hands full of shrimp cocktail and cheap wine, and when Teagan moved out of the way to let them by, Darcy bolted.

twenty-six

DARCY FLED PAST THE HIPPOPOTAMUS IN HER BARE cement stall, the three-toed sloth marooned on his exposed bit of topiary, and the wretched jaguar stalking back and forth in his glass-sided exhibit.

She didn't know where she was going, but every turn led to another miserable creature displayed in an enclosure that maximized human observation, rather than animal welfare. She wanted to let every animal loose. The New York suburbs couldn't be worse for them than this place, which abruptly loomed dark and confining around her.

When she reached a cage full of reasonably content parakeets, Darcy lifted her phone and recorded a voice note, her tone the one that people use to report car accidents and shipwrecks. "Point number one: we never come back to this zoo."

That was an important stake in the ground. Teagan needed to cut off all association with the Westchester Zoo. This place was as bad for Teagan as it was for the animals.

If Darcy was making notes, though, she supposed that meant she was also making a conservation plan for one Darcy Albano, to be released in the marginally favorable habitat of metropolitan New York. She was thinking about what Teagan could promise that would let her say yes, she'd turn down the gig in Yellowstone and stay here indefinitely. Whether she dared stay with Teagan just because she loved him and he'd asked her to, and not because it made any kind of sense.

Kristin would be horrified at her. No, Kristin would be researching New York's alimony laws.

If Teagan had asked her to run away with him, if he'd ever said yes to a single one of her suggestions that they take up beet farming or beekeeping or vanilla bean orchid pollination, she would have done it in a heartbeat, as easily as she'd decided to come out here in the first place.

Because here was the thing about running away together: that was a story you could see the end of from the very beginning. When it inevitably didn't work out, when it proved to be a mistake, when they ran out of money or patience or love, she could look back and say *of course*. Of course that had been a mistake. Nobody could expect it to end any way but badly, *beet farming*. You ran off and farmed beets *for a while*.

There was no way she'd ever be able to look back and say that she'd expected it to end if she told Teagan she'd stay.

Darcy felt unprepared. Undersupplied. Untrained. She'd come to doubt whether her long string of temporary jobs, places, and relationships would ever lead to real ones, no matter how much she wanted them.

She rubbed her chest, where her heart was pounding like she'd just run a mile. She wished she wasn't terrified. She wished she didn't have to think about it. In any of the scenarios she'd ever daydreamed about a life with Teagan, it was always later. After she'd finished her degree, after he was sober, after he'd quit his job, after she'd found hers and she was standing, confident, on her own two feet—when somehow, implausibly, they found their way back together.

He had to know there were tangible risks if they did this now. Darcy might be terrible at her job. Darcy could get fired. Teagan didn't seem to be very good at his job, so *Teagan* could get fired. Darcy might always hate New York. Teagan could relapse.

But Darcy knew her own resilience, and she knew that she could slog through any of those disasters. Relapse was part of recovery, right? And if Teagan did relapse, which seemed like a thing that could really happen, Darcy could imagine herself driving him back to rehab (a better one, this time), picking him up a month later, cheering him on through all of it. She didn't worry about how to keep loving him, even if it got a lot harder to do that than it had been so far.

The real thing she had to worry about, the one risk she didn't know how to manage, was whether he'd keep loving her. Everything else fell apart if he didn't. Out of everything he might promise her, how could he promise her that?

That was the question that kept her pacing like the poor jaguar. What would Teagan do when it didn't get any easier to be with her? Could she really expect that from him on top of everything else he was already struggling with?

Darcy reached an area that was lit as bright as midday due to all the rented floodlights. Sucked to be a crepuscular species here tonight: the nearby flock of flamingos was probably going to get jet lag. A cheerfully painted sign announced that she'd reached the enclosure for the Asian small-clawed otter.

There was a crowd around a couple of zoo staffers, the guests squealing and whispering in the way people babbled at all infant mammals. Irritation rising, Darcy went up on her tiptoes to see over the crowd, anticipating some further outrage to the name of conservation biology.

Darcy gasped when she saw what was happening.

Mother*fuckers*.

The zoo staffers were passing around baby otters like they were canapés, reciting a robotic compilation of otter factoids under their breath as the partygoers ignored them in favor of fondling the little balls of brown fur. No reintroduction program at work here: if they were habituating the babies to this much human handling, they were never getting out of otter jail.

A short, skinny man in a loud suit was jiggling an otter in the crook of his elbow, mugging for his wife's flash photography. Another woman in an elaborately ruched red satin cocktail dress was trying to jam an anchovy into the protesting mouth of a second juvenile.

Darcy felt her hands curling into fists. She resisted the urge to wade in and snatch the otters away from the zookeepers. These were definitely the kind of people who'd call the cops on her if she attempted animal rescue.

She needed to document this. She'd take pictures, find Teagan, and tell him that if he was signing up for years of her paperwork, they were starting with a complaint regarding the Westchester Zoo otter exhibit. He'd know how to get it to the right authority.

"Point number two: we will get the otter exhibit shut down," Darcy said quietly into her phone. She knew she ought to be thinking about big picture things, like where they'd live, whether Darcy would stay in school, what they'd do if Teagan fell off the wagon, but the whole idea was so big and bright that she couldn't quite look straight at it.

"Shame on you," Darcy muttered at the otter handler. *He*

probably had the degree she hadn't been able to secure in more than ten years of trying. He knew better. But he hadn't even noticed her, so Darcy spun on her heel and walked on, urging the poor otters to hold on a few days longer.

Darcy reached a fork in the path, where one direction led back to the main pavilion and the other to the South American exhibits. She'd walked in a near circle, letting forward momentum substitute for action. There was a small chain partition partially blocking the second route, but she could see a few people drifting around beyond, and she wasn't done thinking. This area hadn't been lit for the evening event, and Darcy soon found herself mostly in the dark. She would have turned back, but she spotted the cherry-red glow of a lit cigarette in front of a large aviary.

How many animal welfare violations could she spot in one evening? Could she turn this into some kind of experiential learning credit?

She briskly approached the unknown smoker, halting only when close range revealed him to be Nora's fiancé, Adrian. Darcy scanned the area, but she couldn't spot the woman herself.

Adrian leaned against the wooden rails of the exhibit, holding the cigarette very gingerly between the tips of his first two fingers. As Darcy watched with folded arms, he flicked a graceful hand to dislodge nonexistent ash, then did it a second time, like he wasn't sure he'd done it right.

"Is that your first cigarette ever?" Darcy asked by way of announcing her presence.

The too-handsome artist jerked in response, nearly dropping the object in question. He hadn't noticed her either.

"No," he said when he recovered. "It's not. Thank you." His tone was curt and snippy.

Darcy hummed with skepticism. He sucked at smoking, if that was the case.

"I think I smoked three or four in college," Adrian amended. Then he sighed. "I just—I needed something to do with my hands, but I drove us here tonight, so I can't drink. I bummed a smoke from that guy over there." He nodded with his chin at an older man in rapt study of a cage overfull of turkey vultures.

"Birds are very sensitive to smoke," Darcy said, pointing to the exhibit behind Adrian. "You can't smoke here." She reached out and plucked the cigarette from his unresisting fingers. She stubbed it out on the rail.

"I've heard it's also bad for humans," Adrian said.

"Yes, well, I care less about you."

"Fair enough." Adrian spoke with enough bitterness that Darcy squinted through the darkness at the lines of stress around his mouth.

"Where's your better half?" Darcy asked warily, proud of herself for not delivering the phrase with the sarcasm she longed to salt it with.

Adrian's chest quickly rose and fell in the shape of a laugh. "I don't know. With yours, I suppose. She was hoping he'd announce the sale of a large portion of Margaret Van Zijl's collection tonight. It's a big deal for her."

"And so you are here trying to learn to smoke in the dark because . . ." Darcy trailed off, not sure she really wanted to know. She had enough to worry about.

Adrian exhaled again, then reached into his jacket to retrieve his phone. He tapped briefly on the screen and passed it to her.

"Nora apparently forgot that we share a photo account," he said evenly. "And tonight I was taking some photographs of the zebras to use as a reference." He swallowed, then continued speaking in a casual tone. "I recently got some feedback on the realism of the equine anatomy in my paintings."

Darcy ignored the implied dig at her ability to appreciate modern art and looked down at the screen. The photograph it displayed was pretty damn anatomical too. The face of the man depicted was just about the only major body part not on display.

"I take it that's not you?" Darcy asked.

Adrian gave her a pained expression.

Right, Adrian was a redhead, and this well-endowed gentleman had dark hair, at least south of his collarbones. Darcy didn't know from personal experience, but she'd heard that the carpet usually matched the drapes in such situations.

"I think it's that guy from Sotheby's that she's hoping Teagan will hire," he said.

Darcy grimaced. *Point number three: we are not going to see Nora in social situations*, she mentally vowed.

"She asked—she mentioned, at least—that she'd like to explore an open relationship," Adrian said, voice tense and fast. "And I said maybe someday. After we'd been married for a while. And that was it. That was six months ago. But maybe she thought I meant to just go ahead . . ." His voice trailed off. He looked down at his feet.

Point number four: We will have an extremely closed relationship. Like a ship's meat locker.

Darcy lightly cuffed Adrian on the shoulder, feeling awkward, because on the one hand, it sounded like his life was deep in the tank, and on the other, he'd picked Nora in the first place. "Hey. If she ran off and fucked this guy she's working with, it's not because of anything you said. She didn't really ask. And you didn't tell her to go for it."

"No. I didn't even really mean *someday*." He turned back toward the cage full of sleeping birds, tipping his head back in regret. "I should have asked whether she could handle that. Then at least I would have known."

Darcy nodded in agreement, but he didn't actually care whether she agreed, she imagined.

"What did you ever see in her in the first place?" She was morbidly curious. Nora seemed openly terrible.

Adrian shrugged without turning around. "I didn't even have to think about it, really. She was selling my paintings, and she started asking me to go with her to—oh, the symphony. Art openings. Cannes. Places I wanted to go. It was easy to say yes. She made everything really"—he exhaled—"easy."

Darcy supposed she could understand the appeal of a relationship that didn't make you try very hard. Part of her fear about the one she had was how hard Teagan seemed to be working for it, when she wanted so much more peace for him. "So what are you going to do? Beyond dabble in self-destructive habits?"

"Jesus. It was one cigarette," Adrian complained. He put his hands on the guardrail and braced himself. "And I don't know. We live together. We've lived together for *five years*. She's my gallerist, and friends with all of my friends; I barely have my own bank account anymore, and—I don't know now."

"I meant, like, tonight," Darcy said. "Do you need a ride somewhere? We can drop you off, if you don't want to talk to her."

"I don't have my wallet with me," Adrian said, face self-mocking. "We're staying in an Airbnb nearby. I don't have a key. So I guess I will put a pleasant face on and go home with her."

Darcy sighed. What a dork.

"You can come home with us," she said. "We have a lot of bedrooms. No need to play Stella Kowalski tonight."

She didn't realize until she spoke that she'd never doubted Teagan would risk annoying Nora by helping her fiancé leave her, if that was what Adrian ultimately decided to do. Her immediate belief had been that Teagan would take care of this too, even if she didn't add it to her list. Teagan wouldn't turn the poor guy away just to make his own life easier; Teagan did hardly anything to make his own life easier.

But that was probably an answer in and of itself. Teagan would never quit on her. Even if every disaster she could imagine did come to pass, she was never going to feel like she'd made a mistake in relying on him.

Every time someone had offered her something she desperately wanted, it had been a trap. A bait and switch. But Teagan didn't even realize he was what she wanted: gentle and serious and sincere, no matter what disasters befell him. Maybe nothing else would be what they expected, but if he was offering himself, she'd take him.

"I wouldn't want to cause Teagan any problems. He basically works for Nora," Adrian said, even as relief was beginning to color his face. What a shitty position to be in. He really had nowhere else to go, Darcy supposed.

"Oh come on. If Nora wants that open relationship, for all she knows we're dragging you home because I ordered a bunch of kink gear and Teagan heard redheads have a higher pain tolerance," Darcy argued.

He made a horrified face.

"Kidding! I didn't actually buy any whips or anything like that," Darcy quickly clarified, though Adrian didn't seem very reassured.

Maybe she ought to add something scary to the list as a

bluff, just to flush out Teagan's hard limits. Oh well, she'd just have to wait and see how he reacted to the stuff she *had* ordered.

Adrian hesitated, but he eventually agreed. "Yes, okay. Sure. Thank you."

Darcy offered him an encouraging smile. "We can leave as soon as Teagan makes his speech."

"It's very kind of you," Adrian said, still sounding disgusted to be in the position of accepting favors from her.

"Yes, well, us kept women need to look out for each other," Darcy said drily, and he chuckled, even if it was pained.

She was aloft on a wave of certitude. Tomorrow, she and Teagan would sit down like adults over a breakfast of peanut butter and bananas. Darcy would lay out her conditions, and Teagan would gracefully accept them. She wasn't asking him for very much. Just to promise he'd always keep loving her, no matter what mistakes she made, no matter what terrible ideas she had to follow through to their conclusion.

She stopped, a new idea already brewing. He loved her. He'd do this for her, even if she already knew it was a bad idea.

"Hey, one sec," she told Adrian. "Can we make a quick stop by the otter enclosure?"

twenty-seven

THE VIP LOUNGE WAS DECORATED AROUND AN AN-
imal theme. That wasn't unexpected for a zoo. But most of
the decorations were made *of* animals, and Teagan summoned a tiny drop of gratitude that Darcy wouldn't see the
chandelier made of antlers, the zebra-skin rug, and the ostrich-
leather seats. It didn't even register when it fell in the drowning sea of anxiety he was adrift in. Where was she?

"Do you think that when the zoo critters are bad, the
keepers bring them in here to scare 'em straight?" Sloane
whispered to him.

Teagan managed only a noncommittal grunt.

"I think your mother owned a couple of photographs by
Shirin Neshat. That would make a nice bundle with the
John Currin," Nora announced.

Teagan thought about going over to see what she was
talking about, but he couldn't gather the necessary attention.
Nora was rewriting his entire speech at the card table at the
opposite side of the room. Sloane was crashed next to him
on the couch, eating a pile of crustacean parts and flirting
with a forty-something capital markets lawyer with a reced-
ing hairline and a wedding ring tan line, who kept bringing

her drinks from the private bar. Teagan was frozen in place, unable to focus on either of these brewing disasters.

He'd told Darcy he was in love with her, and she couldn't get away fast enough.

"So where's Darcy, anyway?" Sloane said, draining her glass and handing it off with a winsome smile to her inappropriate new friend.

Teagan hadn't seen Darcy in two hours. She hadn't called. She hadn't texted. His mind was tearing itself apart, unable to latch onto the smallest thought and follow it to its conclusion.

"I think I fucked up," Teagan mumbled, more to himself than to his sister, but she startled to hear him swear.

"What happened?" Sloane asked, sitting up straighter.

"I asked her to talk to Mrs. Park about a job in Beacon—well, I asked her to stay here with me. Instead of leaving in December. But I think I said too much."

"Oh yeah?" Sloane said sympathetically. "You told her the whole alcoholism thing is bullshit?"

"What? No." Teagan hadn't planned to ever tell her that. God, if she knew that too, he'd never see her again.

Sloane laughed. "Then what did you say that could be that bad?"

"I accidentally asked her to marry me, I think."

"And what did she say?"

"She needed to think about it."

"Oh my God, and you're just sitting in here freaking out?" Sloane cried.

This was a failure of due preparation. He should have asked Mrs. Park to write—no, record—a job description, so that Darcy wouldn't worry about her qualifications. He should have put together a budget so that Darcy could see that she could afford to live here. If he ever proposed, he should have had a damn ring—Darcy'd probably want something low profile, just a recycled gold band, or—

He shouldn't have said anything at the zoo. She hated the zoo.

After he gave the speech, he'd find Mrs. Park and ask her to put together a formal job listing. No, he'd offer to draft the job listing, save her the time.

Maybe he should offer to stay down at his condo for a few days to give Darcy her space.

He could hire an independent appraiser for his mother's art to know whether Nora's valuations were legitimate. How would he find an appraiser?

His thoughts tumbled like socks in the dryer, and he didn't immediately realize Sloane was speaking. She had both hands on his arm, leaning in to him with her big blue eyes wide and excited.

"You need to go unfuck the situation. Find her and take her home. No, take her out some place she'd actually like, like, um, a boat or something. Maybe a forest? I'll cover for you."

"No, I've got it," he said. He couldn't throw Sloane to the wolves like that.

"I can chat up all the donors," Sloane insisted. "I've gotten a lot of pledges this week, and this guy over here said his firm could commit ten thousand dollars." She nodded at the lawyer, whose gaze skittered away from Teagan's suspicious frown.

Of course he'd talked about a pledge. He probably wanted Sloane to talk about it more over dinner at the Lower East Side crash pad where he lured his other barely legal girl-friends.

"I've got it," Teagan repeated. "In fact, maybe you should just go home now."

Sloane scoffed. "It's not even eight o'clock yet. I have like, ten other people Rose said I should talk to left on my list."

"Don't do that," Teagan said. "Don't talk to anyone. They're all going to ask about the art sale, and I need to keep the messaging consistent."

"What am I even doing here if you don't want me to talk to anyone?" Sloane asked, waving her hands in the air.

Teagan checked his phone for the fiftieth time, just to see whether he'd missed any messages from Darcy, even though he had the volume turned on. Nothing.

"I don't know what you're doing here, when you should be back in Claremont finishing college in something, in anything! Any major. Just pick one," he snapped at Sloane when he realized that she was waiting for a response. "But instead, you're here at the zoo, because I worry about you passed out in the alley behind some bar or *worse* if I don't know exactly where you are."

Sloane sharply inhaled. "You know exactly why I'm here," she said, shooting her eyes at Nora, who wasn't paying any attention to them. "And I am *trying* to help."

"There's nothing you can do for me," Teagan gritted out. He'd gotten to this position by not thinking things through, but how could he think when his brain was misfiring like a 1980s BMW with a hundred thousand miles on it? "*Go home.* Why don't you just get your own act together so that I don't have to worry about you on top of everything else for once? I can barely handle my own bullshit tonight," he said, using the sharpest tone of voice he'd ever employed with his sister.

Her face crumpled.

He felt it like a punch in the gut, the immediate regret. Here he was stone-cold sober, and he'd said more things he wished he could take back tonight than his mother had ever done while drinking.

Sloane scraped herself to her feet, moving with jerky dignity.

"You're so stupid, Teagan, you don't even know you need the help. No wonder she said no," she said, voice watery.

Teagan leaned forward and covered his face with his hands. "I'm sorry. I didn't mean that."

"You *did* mean that. You're just sorry you said it out loud. *You* should go home. I'm staying." She grabbed her purse, grabbed her shrimp, and grabbed the third drink the lawyer had left for her, clutching it all to her chest. Then she spun on her heel and stalked out of the room, leaving Teagan alone for the second time that night.

He ought to go after her. Both of them. He should have taken it all back both times, because there was no reason to put either woman in the position of making him feel better about how much he hated his life. He was torn between which direction he ought to run in, and he couldn't move.

Nora looked up, saw that Sloane was gone, and took the opportunity to plop herself down in the seat his sister had vacated. Her perfume was aggressive, and her imposition into his personal space was like a feedback loop to his senses.

"Can you give me a minute," he managed, holding up one hand, which Nora ignored.

"I just need a minute," she said cheerily. "I just finished with edits."

"I really don't—"

"I've got three options here," she said, putting the index

cards she'd taken from him down on the table. "Different dates, bundles, and pricing options. Can you pull up the cash flow forecast, and we'll decide which works best?"

Teagan stared at the cards helplessly, knowing that he ought to have opinions. The foundation might not meet its commitments for the next summer if he didn't come up with more money, and then it wouldn't really matter how much the paintings were worth.

"I'd rather talk to some experts about this first," he told Nora. "Can we talk about it on Monday? This isn't a good night."

Nora made a chiding noise. "That's why you're retaining Sotheby's to sell the art and my gallery to consult on the transactions. You don't need to be worried about it."

"Why does it have to be tonight?" Teagan asked stubbornly.

"A lot of people here are starting to think about their year-end tax planning. And investing in art is a great diversification strategy. I have a few people in mind, and so does Guillaume."

Teagan had to remind himself that he'd taken this job because he wanted to help kids.

He picked up a random index card containing a list of paintings and photographs. He had no idea what they were worth. He'd always been the wrong person for this job. He had no idea why Nora had asked him to do it.

"Ah, Margaret bought all of these pieces the summer she was with Sloane's father," Nora hummed, looking over her shoulder. "God love her, that woman had taste. In men, especially."

Teagan grimaced. He put the index card down. "I don't

think it's appropriate for the two of us to be negotiating your commission. We should get someone more independent to look at it."

Nora gave a polite laugh. "Rose already looked through all these contracts."

"Still, let's get one of the other independent directors to review these," Teagan said. "I don't know whether these commissions are standard."

"Honestly, Teagan," Nora said, feigning surprise, "your mother never worried about things like that. I've been doing the art sales for years. Just sign the contracts and you can go enjoy the party. That's what Margaret always did."

"I'm not my mother," Teagan instinctively snapped. Then he closed his eyes. He wasn't his mother. All he'd ever wanted to be was not like his mother. And he wasn't doing any better than she had. He was letting everything slip through his fingers, holding onto nothing. No wonder Darcy thought he couldn't come through with any of his promises. No wonder Sloane was putting her life on hold, trying to fix his.

No wonder Nora thought he'd do as terrible a job as his mother had.

"I quit," Teagan said, standing up. He had no idea what he was doing here. He didn't know what he'd accomplished in two years of trying, but it ended here tonight.

"What?" Nora said, taken aback.

"I quit," he repeated himself. "You can promote Rose. See if she'll sign *her* name to this. I won't. Excuse me. I need to go make sure my sister is okay, and then we're going home."

Two hours later, Darcy had committed a felony or two—she assumed that impersonating a game warden and grand theft otter were felonies—but she still hadn't located Teagan or Sloane.

She hadn't tried to call them. She hadn't seen many crime shows, but as she was in possession of three juvenile otters in a duffel bag which didn't belong to her (neither the otters nor the bag), she thought she should turn her phone off and leave less of an electronic trail before she, the otters, and Nora's runaway fiancé could make a clean escape.

Adrian was only barely on board at this point.

"I'll ask people at the valet stand if they're going past the train station. I can just take the first train tomorrow," he said, pretty face deeply depressed.

"Hush," Darcy told him absently. "I'm not giving you cash for a train ticket and sending you on your way. Are you sure you checked everywhere?"

She was seated in a narrow, shadowy alcove. The otters had settled down and fallen asleep inside the bag, no doubt exhausted by a long evening of being groped by people in formalwear. She longed to put them in her lap and tell them they'd be much better soon, but the less they were handled, the better.

"I walked around the entire zoo, twice. Nora's still in the VIP lounge. The Van Zijls aren't in there with her. I didn't see them. They must have left."

"Did you check the bathrooms?" Darcy asked skeptically. Teagan wouldn't leave without her, even if she had her phone off.

Adrian wrinkled his nose. "No, I did not look in the bathrooms. Why would Teagan and his sister be in the bathroom for an hour?"

Darcy gave him a flat, unappreciative stare. "Don't make that face. Sometimes people get sick." And sometimes Teagan had to spend time hyperventilating in the bathroom. She shouldn't have to explain it to Adrian, especially when she didn't understand it well herself.

She stood up and gingerly lifted the bag of otters, who chirped in protest at being disturbed.

"Sorry babies," she whispered. "Gotta find your dad, then we can go." Darcy poked Adrian in the shoulder. "*You* should be glad you have friends here. Things could be a lot worse. At least you have somewhere to go. Anyway, let's check the bathrooms." She straightened and attempted to exude competence again.

It didn't take long to find Teagan and Sloane with that search pattern. They were in a single occupancy stall in the back of the lemur house. Darcy heard them arguing before she tried the door and found it unlocked.

Sloane knelt in front of the toilet, stomach violently heaving as she attempted to pay further tribute to the porcelain god. Teagan squatted behind her, attempting to hold her hair out of her face.

Darcy's heart lifted to see him looking well, or at least not as distraught as she'd worried she might find him. God, he must have thought she was ready to break his heart.

". . . think you should think hard about going back to rehab," Teagan was saying as he dodged Sloane's heedless flails in his direction.

"Leave me alooone," Sloane moaned. "'M not even drunk. It's that awful shrimp, *fighting* me."

Teagan audibly sighed. "I can *smell* how many Long Island iced teas you had."

Oh, Jesus. Darcy was at once relieved and taken aback as she took in the scene. One thing after another, but this was, at least, a familiar problem, one she'd tackled before.

"There's a nice place in the Catskills. I could take you tomorrow—" Teagan happened to glance over to see Darcy standing in the doorway. His face went soft with surprise and pleasure. "Darcy."

Darcy braced herself and adjusted the strap of the duffel bag on her shoulder. She patted the top reassuringly. The pups were going to sleep. They'd be okay for a few minutes while she and Teagan dealt with this.

"Hey, sweetie, I'll be right there," she said gently to Sloane. She thrust the duffel bag into Adrian's arms and shut the bathroom door on his confused face.

Teagan's arms had gone slack at his sides with relief, and Darcy took a moment to go to her toes and press a quick kiss to the corner of his tense jaw.

"Hey. Everything okay?"

He brushed his fingertips against her loose hair as if reassuring himself of her corporeal presence. "Yeah. It is now. Or, I mean. I am."

Darcy nodded past the lump in her throat, then they both turned back to poor Sloane. First things first. Darcy used the elastic from around her own wrist to get some of the girl's hair pulled back out of her face. "Got it all out yet?"

Sloane wobbled as she looked up at Darcy, but she nodded. She grabbed Teagan's tie and wiped her mouth with it. Her brother's only sign of protest was to tilt his head and sigh.

"Let's get you home," Darcy said, bending to help her to her feet. She pulled and Sloane got more or less upright, teetering in her heels.

"It's food poisoning," Sloane said insistently.

Darcy made it a point not to argue with drunk people, but Teagan had somehow not learned that lesson.

"You checked out too soon. It's my fault. You should have stayed. But it'll be okay—"

"I'm not going back to rehab," Sloane insisted. "I never needed rehab."

Teagan's lips flattened as he looked to Darcy for support. It sent a little thrill of agency through her. Yes. They were a team. They would handle this latest snafu together.

Just get her home, Darcy tried to mouth to him. She had three otters and a cuckold to place tonight; she'd worry about Sloane tomorrow.

"I mean it!" Sloane said to Teagan when nobody agreed with her. "I didn't need it in the first place. Nobody goes to rehab just because they do a little coke at parties. I only stayed in Montana because *you* needed to stay."

"Did you do coke tonight?" Teagan immediately demanded.

"No! I haven't done anything since I got back! This is the shrimp. It was outside on the raw bar. I should've known. No outdoor shrimps," Sloane fuzzily insisted. "I'm not drunk. I didn't drink too much."

"I know it feels that way. But we can't do that in our family. Okay? I don't know if it's in our genes or . . . I don't know. We don't know when to quit. We're not good at knowing when things are bad for us. So I don't think you should drink. At all. Or anything else."

"I don't drink any more than anyone else does," Sloane said stubbornly.

"It's already affecting your life though," Teagan said. "Not showing up to work? Being hungover at noon? Throwing up at the zoo? This isn't going to work. You can't be doing this back in California where I can't help you. You need to make some changes. We can talk about it tomorrow, but you need to decide you're going to live your life differently from mom."

Sloane glared in a bleary way at her brother. "You should talk. *You* were in the hospital for a week. You were afraid you were going to *die*. You're still a mess. But the only thing that changed was you got a girlfriend. A girlfriend who's leaving you!"

"That's not true," Darcy blurted. Teagan shot her a grateful look, his face suffused with relief, before he focused on Sloane again. Darcy wrapped a sheltering arm around Teagan's hips and felt him automatically press back against her. "I'm not going anywhere. And it's not true that Teagan isn't doing anything to change his life. Teagan made the only big change he needs to be making for the next year—he stopped drinking. We'll work on everything else once he's past that. And I'll help you too—"

Sloane groaned with aggravation. "Stop it! He doesn't even drink! That's not even why he went to the hospital! Okay? He's not an alcoholic, I'm not an alcoholic, and neither of us are anything like our mom."

"What?" Darcy asked, not understanding the thrust of this argument, even coming from an overtly drunk person. The unflushed toilet reeked of triple sec. She met them both at rehab. She was still getting a paycheck to serve as Teagan's sober companion.

But Teagan's body stiffened next to her, going rock still.

Darcy turned to Teagan. "What?" she asked again.

Sloane answered for him, her eyes angry and teary. "You know he has panic attacks. Like earlier tonight? He had one in the subway and thought he was dying. It took a whole week for the hospital to stabilize him. You know? You didn't know. He didn't even tell you."

Darcy took a step back, eyes fixed on Teagan. She didn't need to ask if it was true. Teagan's face had drained of blood, leaving it gray around his round, scared eyes. His lips were parted, but he seemed to have lost his faculties of speech.

"You tried to kill yourself?" Darcy whispered, blood suddenly buzzing though her face and ears.

"No! No, I didn't. I never did. I wasn't suicidal. I thought I was dying," Teagan said in a jumble of words, too fast, too soft.

"And that's . . . different," she said, fear blooming in her throat like mushrooms after a storm.

"I wasn't dying. There wasn't anything wrong with me, physically, it's just a mental health thing—they said it's manageable, sometimes it goes away, and you can take medication," Teagan said, now tripping over himself to explain, even as he stared at her as though afraid to blink and lose eye contact.

"You aren't on medication," Darcy snapped. Then she startled in realization. "Oh my God, you stopped taking your medication. It was for this? Did you even talk to a doctor? You didn't."

Teagan didn't have a response to that. His face was silently pleading.

"You stopped taking your medication?" Sloane demanded, wheeling on her brother.

Darcy held up a palm between the girl and Teagan. "Go stand outside with Adrian and the otters," she growled at Sloane. "I'll deal with you in a minute." She was furious at Sloane *too*. Sloane had lied to her *too*.

Sloane jerked backward at the novelty of a command and, with a dark look at her brother, slunk out of the bathroom. Teagan sagged back against the wall as soon as she was gone as though seeking support from the cinderblock walls of the building.

Darcy curled her hands into fists and locked her knees.

"Were you ever going to tell me?" Darcy asked. "When?"

Teagan finally looked down at the floor. "I'm not drinking. I'm really never going to. I meant what I said to Sloane. I don't think we should."

"But you never did? You're really not an alcoholic—"

"I told you that. I told you that *several* times, that I didn't get drunk, that I'd never done drugs—"

"And then you told everyone else that you were an alcoholic. You said that to *me*. You *lied* to me."

Teagan swallowed hard, the muscles in his throat visibly clenching.

"I know," he said softly.

"Why would you lie about something like that? Why wouldn't you tell me what was really going on?" Darcy cried, trying to make it make sense. "God, the number of times I made you listen to that terrible alcoholism podcast—I would have done everything different. I've just been spinning my fucking wheels—"

"No, no, Darcy, it's fine, please, I couldn't have done anything without you. I meant what I said, you're everything good about my life," he pleaded until Darcy waved her hand at him to get him to stop talking.

"You're making it worse," she said.

She couldn't think. Everything was replaying in her mind, every time she'd told Teagan he was going to be okay because he wasn't drinking, all those things he hated about his life that she let him endure because he wasn't drinking. "You're making it worse," she repeated, not sure whether she was talking about him or her.

"No," he said, unconvincingly. It was what he wanted to be true.

"If I hadn't been here, would you have . . . kept taking your meds, gone to the doctor, therapy . . . something? Anything?" she asked.

Teagan's lips flexed. "I would rather have had you," he said, like she'd ever have made him choose. Darcy jerked back like she'd been slapped. How dare he put that on her?

"Why would you lie about something like that? Why wouldn't you just tell me you'd been sick?"

"It's not just that I was sick. It's my brain chemistry. It's . . . sometimes it's lifelong," Teagan said, face still tilted down to the floor.

"You were telling me to make a lifetime commitment two hours ago! You didn't think I needed to know?"

As if Darcy didn't come with her own baggage, with a whole lifetime's worth of damage too. Was that something he was weighing? Was it something he expected her to weigh?

"I came here with you to do a job you don't need done. And I don't know—I don't know what you need. I know I'm not trained for it. I don't have anything, Teagan. I don't have a job or a car or a family. I don't know how to do this!" she said.

One corner of Teagan's mouth pulled to the side in a grimace, the same side he smiled with. He made the same face when he was joking, but the only person he ever joked about was himself.

"I didn't tell you because I didn't think you'd come here if you knew it was something other than alcoholism," he said. His shoulders clenched. "And then later . . . I thought you'd leave."

Darcy covered her face with her hands. He didn't think

too highly of her, if that's what he'd thought. That she'd just quit when she realized she couldn't fix him. Everything she'd thought about him, he didn't think about her.

"And so you decided to worry about making sure I wouldn't leave, and nothing else," she said, her lips feeling heavy and numb. It felt true when she said it. That was the problem in a nutshell.

"I worry about everything," Teagan said quietly. "And you can always leave."

Darcy's chest heaved. That sounded pretty final. It was what he expected her to do. Teagan reached into his jacket pocket and fished around until he came out with the pink square of the valet ticket. He pressed it into her hand, their fingers brushing until Darcy jerked hers away.

She looked down at the ticket, not sure what he meant by the gesture.

"You can take the car," he said, voice so soft she could hardly keep up. "Don't worry about getting it back to me. I'll stay in the city or take the train. Keep it as long as you want."

When she looked back up, she met his eyes. They were hard and glittering like gemstones, holding onto her face as though he was trying to memorize it. He really expected her to go. He expected her to break both their hearts and walk away like none of this had meant a thing to her. That was the kind of person he thought she was.

"Okay," Darcy mumbled. "You'll need to get your own self home tonight, then."

Teagan nodded stiffly. He shoved his hands in his pockets, but not so fast that Darcy couldn't see them shaking.

"I'll get the otters," she tearily offered, before she remembered that she hadn't even had a chance to tell him about the problem with their enclosure here. Her nose was running. She was so angry she could barely see straight, and all the heartbreak she'd been so certain an hour ago that Teagan would never inflict on her was fracturing her chest. She didn't know how she was going to drive like this. She just needed to go.

Without another word, she spun on her heel and fled the bathroom.

Outside, Sloane was dry heaving over an azalea bush. Adrian held the bag of otters under one arm and Sloane's purse under the other, his face eloquently expressing a wish to be free of all members of the Van Zijl family, their friends, and their business partners. Darcy took Sloane's purse from him and took out her phone. She held it in front of Sloane's gagging face until it unlocked on the third try, then flicked to a rideshare app. She pushed the phone to Adrian's chest as she relieved him of the otters.

"I called a car. They both need to go home," she told Adrian. "Teagan and Sloane both. You're in charge. Good luck with everything."

Adrian called after her in consternation, but Darcy made it a point to get away from all her failures as quickly as possible, and she thought this was probably the biggest one yet.

twenty-eight

HE WOULD HAVE THOUGHT HE'D FEEL WORSE. TEAgan would have thought he'd have a panic attack or otherwise fall apart. Darcy had probably thought he would too. But he hadn't cried, wasn't even shaken. A soft, tired kind of calm had fallen on him.

He'd been staring at the television for hours in the darkened den of his mother's house. His sister had put on a streaming series when they got home, a romance involving beautiful Korean people who accidentally embraced at least once an episode. It was almost comically inappropriate to the household mood, but the background blur of the dialogue was better than silence.

Teagan's eyes couldn't pick out the television subtitles from the far side of the couch. He ought to go to the optometrist and get contacts or glasses or something. Use that gold-plated vision plan before his insurance cut off. He told himself he'd do it tomorrow.

Here was the silver lining about the worst thing happening: it had already happened. Everything Teagan had worried about had already happened. The love of his life had left him, he'd lost his job, he'd publicly embarrassed himself in multiple situations and locations, and his baby sister was periodically retching up shellfish and cocktails into a trashcan at the other end of the couch. So what was there to fear? It had all happened, and he was still alive. He could almost laugh about that. He'd survived a fucking bear attack! Of course this wouldn't kill him. So there was nothing left to worry about, and he hadn't even needed to open a prescription bottle to achieve this state of total numbness. It felt like clarity.

Sloane ineffectively spat into her trashcan, groaned, and took a swig from the bottle of blue Gatorade he'd positioned next to her. She sat up and put her show on mute with the remote.

"Have you heard anything from Darcy?" she demanded.

Teagan glanced down at his phone where it rested, screen up, on his thigh. Nora had called a couple of times and left messages, but nobody else had. *I'll listen to her messages tomorrow*, he told himself. Tomorrow he'd wrap up all lingering responsibilities from the first part of his life.

"She's probably halfway to Ohio by now," Teagan said.

He didn't really believe that though. All her clothes and things were still here in the guest bedroom. Darcy might leave him, but she was too practical to leave her snow boots and winter gear. He'd need to get Sloane out of the house to make sure there were no confrontations between the two of them tomorrow, let Darcy move out in peace.

"You really think that's it?" Sloane asked. "She's not even going to stay till December?"

Sloane was acting almost sober now, so Teagan guessed it was marginally possible that the shrimp were more responsible for her present condition than the drinks he'd watched her toss back earlier. Maybe the only lesson Sloane would take away from tonight was to not eat seafood served for a crowd.

"I think this is it," Teagan said.

He must have looked bad when he said that, because Sloane's face briefly crumpled up in anguish before she smoothed it again.

"If learning what was really going on with you made her leave, she was never going to stay," Sloane said with bitter confidence. "She didn't find out anything she shouldn't have already known about you. She knew you were a mess! It's not like you were hiding what you were like."

Possibly that was true in one sense: there was never anything Teagan could have said or done to make Darcy stay. Not after the way he'd gotten her here.

"She learned that I lied to her," he said softly. "That's probably enough, even without anything else."

Though all of that would have been enough too.

"Yeah, well, she should have already realized you're a big fat liar," Sloane said, even if the tilt of her chin was sympathetic.

"I am not," he protested. He'd lied to Darcy about *one* thing. He'd meant everything else he'd promised her. He could have come through with it, the same way he was going to have to get up tomorrow and take out the trash and call the optometrist and book his sister another stint in rehab as though his world hadn't ended tonight.

"You're a liar! You lie all the time! If you were a politician, your campaign slogan would be *I'm fine*. And you never are." Sloane's face slipped again, her eyes welling up. Teagan belatedly identified her expression as guilt.

"Sloane, Sloanie, it's not your fault," Teagan leaned forward and groped for her ankle, somewhere beneath the mohair throw he'd tossed over her. "You're right. She was always going to find out. And she was always going to be right to go when she did. It wouldn't have mattered if we'd already . . . I don't know."

He supposed that was a minor blessing. That she was leaving before he really thought she would stay. It still felt like it was his life she was leaving, not theirs. He hadn't gotten the chance to see what *their* life would have looked like, because she was always going to leave.

"She didn't *have* to go. There's a lot of worse things you could have been, like, you could have turned out to be a crypto bro or already married to one of those anime character pillows."

Teagan forced himself to smile at his sister. "Then I really wouldn't be able to live with myself."

Sloane shot him another worried look. "But you are, right?"

Teagan patted her ankle through the blanket, trying to look reassuring, because Sloane was only twenty-two and she was scared, and he knew she'd been trying as hard as he'd taught her how to do. Tomorrow he'd get up and do all the things he had to do again, and that's all life was and forever would be.

"If nobody else can stand me, I guess I have to," he said.

The battery on her phone was at twenty percent, and the front gate of the wildlife rehab in auspiciously named Great Swamp, New Jersey, was closed and locked, just like the first two places Darcy had tried. Darcy would have kicked the wall of the place for daring to be closed after she had navigated the Lincoln Tunnel to get here, but she was wearing a pair of too-large gladiator sandals borrowed from Sloane, and that would only break some toes.

She stomped back to the car and turned the ignition, not sure what her next step was. There was less than a quarter of a tank left, and Darcy wasn't inclined to fill the ancient Mercedes sedan up with diesel even if she could spare the money. The next nearest wildlife rehab was twenty-five miles away.

The duffel bag in the front passenger seat didn't move when she started the car, so Darcy quietly unzipped the top to check in on the otters. They were asleep in a huddle, totally unaware that they'd been stolen and then taken on a driving tour of the tri-state area. She zipped the bag again. She didn't know whether to try one more place or go buy them some food.

She slumped her forehead against the top of the steering wheel. In the Navy, every fuckup was swiftly followed by a critique. Darcy could nearly hear her chief petty officer's voice in her ear: *What were you thinking when you took the otters, Albano? Did you even read the manual first?*

Darcy felt tears leaking out the corners of her eyes again, even though she'd thought she was done with that before she left Westchester County.

She thought she'd be done with the otters by now. She thought she wouldn't be angry by now. She thought she'd be home by now, ready to hash this out with Teagan.

She could call him, she knew. She probably should have called him when the first place was closed, because she was sure he was a wreck now that it had been hours and she hadn't even told him she was coming back, but handling just *this one goddamn thing* on her own had taken on a talismanic importance in her mind.

She'd been so worried that Teagan was going to figure out that she was just a giant stack of unmet needs and unachieved aspirations, and that's when things would end. But of course he'd noticed—he'd probably clocked that at the point he got on the lawn mower and started clearing the weeds and her work schedule for her. Teagan was great at noticing when other people needed things. And since then, he'd doggedly gone about solving every single problem in her life, because he thought she'd leave him if he didn't.

That was the thing that hurt the most, more than the lying or the uselessness of all her efforts in maintaining a sober man's sobriety. He thought Darcy was the kind of person who dipped when she found out her partner had a serious illness, or even just that he had fucked up and then tried to cover it up.

Why wouldn't he think that though? What had she ever finished that she started? She didn't have any kind of track record, with him or anything else, even though she painfully wanted to be the kind of person who came through for people, the person who knew what to do in a crisis.

That was why Darcy was scrolling through Google Maps on her phone instead of going home to bawl him out and then tuck him into bed, because some irrational part of her brain thought she would show him when she got these otters squared away. Darcy was someone he could rely on. Look, she'd spotted and remediated an animal welfare violation, all on her own. *I love you too, Teagan, and everything is going to be okay. I've got you, don't worry. Nothing's more important than you.* And then he'd actually tell her what was going on and what he needed.

Possibly that's what he'd been trying to do, if not in simple enough terms that Darcy could pick up on it. He'd asked her to stay with him. Tonight, for sure, but he'd been trying to ask for weeks probably, every time he floated a vegan restaurant or a new apartment or a better job. And it was easy for her to say he should have asked for way more than that. He should have told her he was drowning in his life, that he didn't know how to handle his illness, and that he was worried about his sister, and asked for her help. Of course she would have helped him.

But he thought that asking her to stay with him was such a big request that he couldn't ask her for anything else, or he thought that it was such a weighty demand that he had to balance it out with everything else she wanted. That's why he'd done it in such a terrible, roundabout way.

Darcy sniffled tears back loudly, and one of the otters woke up, startling its siblings, who squeaked in protest.

"Shh, shh, it's okay babies, go back to sleep," she whispered, cranking up the heater, because she had a vague recollection that these otters were a subtropical species.

He was so wrong. He was enough by himself, without any of the other things he'd offered her. How was he ever going to believe that, though, if Darcy didn't show him she could handle a few things on her own? How was he ever going to believe she *chose* him?

That was the thought that had her beating the palm of her hand against the steering wheel hard enough to sting, because she didn't know what to do. What she wanted to do was just go home and figure the otters out tomorrow. She wanted to curl up around Teagan's long warm body in the guest room bed and go to sleep until she woke up. She wanted it to be okay that she didn't have all the answers today, because they had all the time in the world, actually. This job wasn't going to run out. This gig wasn't seasonal. This relationship wasn't temporary.

How did she convince him of that?

Darcy looked in the backseat. Her hiking sandals were tossed back there with a spare water bottle, an unopened pack of tissues, and Sloane's dress coat, which Teagan had made her bring in case she got cold from all the cutouts in her dress.

There wasn't an easy way to convince him. There wasn't a quick way either, even if she found someone to take the otters. She just needed to go home and get started. Teagan had been the one to tell it to her: the only way to teach him she wouldn't leave was by staying. If he was holding on, she had to hold on harder.

She put the car in reverse and checked that the otters weren't sliding off the passenger seat.

"Just a little longer, kiddos," she whispered to them. "Let's hope we have enough gas to get home to Irvington."

twenty-nine

WHEN SLOANE WENT TEN MINUTES WITHOUT PAY-ing tribute to the Hefty bag, Teagan urged her to try to get some sleep. It was way after midnight, and at least one of them was going to need to be functional the next day. He didn't think he could sleep. He worried he'd miss a message, a call—something.

The TV silently streamed more of the incomprehensible story. Several people got shot in the chest, but it seemed that they were all going to be okay. That was reassuring news, especially in relation to how he felt.

Sloane snored. After a particularly loud inhale woke her up, she flopped to her side, squinted at Teagan for a few moments to reassure herself that he was still there, and went back to sleep, just like she had as a baby. He felt a familiar pained tenderness at the sight. After they talked about rehab tomorrow, he'd call a charity to come collect all the bedroom furniture in the house, and then he was calling a Realtor. They were going to start everything fresh.

Teagan heard a noise from the backyard. He hit the power on the remote and listened again. Something from the pool house. He looked down the hall at the row of quiet bedrooms; he'd pointed Adrian to his own bedroom, but there wasn't an outside door, so it couldn't be the poor man trying to sneak out.

It was almost dawn, but probably not too late for the local teenagers to break into the only pool in the neighborhood. It was getting chilly this week, but Teagan had spent many summers chasing them and their White Claws out of his backyard.

He sighed and stood up, wondering if he ought to grab a lacrosse stick or something from the garage. He ultimately decided that getting his ass kicked if the teenagers objected to eviction would just be par for the course this evening.

It was pitch-black before Teagan flipped on the pool lights and the string lights around the cabana, and he blinked for a few seconds at the sudden illumination. Instead of teenagers, there was only Darcy, still clad in Sloane's prom dress, barefoot and wielding the netted pole for cleaning leaves out of the swimming pool.

Teagan could remember falling off his bike as a kid, slapping a hand to cover his skinned knee. That moment he'd lift his hand and see it bloody was always the moment it would start to hurt. This felt like that. He didn't know how much he had hurt until this moment.

"Oh," Darcy said, dropping her forearm from where she'd shaded her eyes. "I thought you'd be asleep by now."

Teagan swallowed hard at the useless lump of relief that caught in his throat. Her presence here now didn't mean anything, especially since he could see that her eyes were swollen from crying. He'd known she'd eventually come back for her things.

"I couldn't sleep," he said inanely.

She nodded.

"I'm cleaning out the pool," she said. "Have you put any chlorine in it recently?"

"A week ago," Teagan replied. He waited. Darcy usually explained herself if he gave her time and space.

Darcy looked into the pool as though answers would be found there.

"I had to find somewhere to take the otters," she said, voice very small and tired. "I . . . um . . . I took them from the zoo."

She hadn't come back for him. But he got to see her again, at least.

Near the back fence, Teagan could make out the large duffel bag she'd carried.

He could feel things tomorrow. He needed to focus.

"So you have how many—" She had a non-zero number of otters. It didn't matter how many. "What do they need?"

He saw her throat bob before she spoke.

"Just some bedding and a way to get out of the pool, for now," she said roughly. "I'll get the leaves."

Teagan nodded and went back in the house. He retrieved a pile of old towels from the linen closet and a large sheet of spare plywood from the garage. He got one of Darcy's sweatshirts from the front closet.

When he went back outside, Darcy was sitting with her legs dangling into the now-clean water, her skirt hiked up over her knees. The lights in the water cast shifting patterns over her skin as she watched the three otter pups, now released from the bag, peer warily at the first stair.

"Will this work?" Teagan asked, putting the plywood over the stairs to provide a ramp. The otters scattered.

Darcy nodded as he laid the towels down in a make-shift bed.

"I got them some cat food on the way. They'll be fine for a day or so," she said.

Teagan gingerly approached her and offered her the sweatshirt. It was cold at night in September, especially just before dawn.

Darcy looked up at him, eyes wide and hurt. She clutched the sweatshirt to her chest. Wordlessly, she patted the ground next to her.

It took Teagan a few seconds to process that she wanted him to sit down. His head felt stuffed full of cotton balls, and the fuel of adrenaline and grief that had kept him awake was bound to run empty at some point very soon. But he carefully pulled off his socks and rolled up the sweats he'd changed into so that he could put his feet in the chilly water too.

It took her another few moments to speak. "I didn't want you to think I didn't have any choice but to come back here," she said, voice tight. She sniffled and wiped her nose with an upward swipe of her palm. "But I couldn't think of anything else to do with the otters."

Teagan didn't know what to say about that; you could get almost anything in New York at any hour, but otter habitat was probably pushing that aphorism to its breaking point.

"I'm sorry," he said instead, because that would just about cover the entire field of what she might want to hear from him.

Darcy shook her head.

"Tonight really didn't need otters on top of everything else, did it?" she said. "I didn't think this through very well." Her face was glum.

"I think—in light of everything else—the otters barely register," Teagan sighed. "I probably owe you a few otters for your troubles."

"We can't keep them," Darcy said. "I may have said I was a game warden. Well, not me exactly. I gave a fake name at the zoo."

That sounded like a potential legal issue to be unraveled as quickly as possible, but Teagan could only wonder what she had meant by *we*.

"It's okay," Teagan said dizzily. "I'll call Mrs. Park tomorrow—I mean, later this morning. Her husband might be able to take them."

"Okay," Darcy muttered.

One of the otters, braver than its siblings, approached the edge of the water, sniffing suspiciously. After a moment of hesitation, it jumped in, landing with a small splash and swimming determinedly toward the other side of the pool.

"I was always going to come back though," Darcy said. "I just thought—if I could just handle one fucking thing on my own—but I guess not. I always think if I just get the next job, the right classes, a good start, then I'll have my shit together. Well, I don't. But I'm here anyway."

She leaned back on her palms, shoulders tense and arms flexed. Teagan didn't understand.

"You're not going back to Montana," he blurted, mostly as a guess.

"No, I'm staying here. I can't promise anything else, but I'm staying here."

"But you're still—you're going to take that job with Mrs. Park's husband," he hazarded, trying to understand her reasoning, what she thought was going to happen now. What was *here*?

"I mean, yeah. I will. I'll try, at least. But Teagan, I'm here because I want *you*. I'm staying with you."

There wasn't enough air outside. He needed to take great

big gulps of it, because he couldn't breathe. His lungs didn't work properly.

"You're sure?" he asked, even though he didn't want to ask if she was sure. He'd take her even if she wasn't sure. If he warned her off, it was only for her sake, not his. "I'm so— Darcy, I'm a wreck. You're right that things weren't getting better. I was getting worse. I'm so sorry."

Darcy exhaled. "Of course I'm sure. I love you. I'm not afraid of things getting worse." She closed her eyes as though about to cry. "I keep thinking about what Sloane said. About how I was going to leave. And I guess I do always bail out when things get hard. I don't want to do that anymore."

"Nobody would blame you. I wouldn't," Teagan said.

"I would. No place without you would ever feel like the right place to be. Even if it's not easy. Even if I can't hack it with the wildlife rehab or finish my degree or make it through a single boring party without an incident report—you'd never give up on me. I want to be that kind of person for you."

The first otter had made it to the other end of the pool. It loudly chirped when it discovered that the edge was too steep to climb out. They both looked at it with concern until it managed to turn around and swim back the way it had come. Teagan grabbed for Darcy's hand.

"It doesn't have to be this hard for you," Teagan tried to reassure her even as tears were beginning to overflow onto his cheeks. "I'll start taking my medication again. I'll—I'll follow up with a real doctor. I already quit my job."

Darcy shook her head, her own eyes scrunched closed. "No. No, I'm not making any deals with you. Not when you're what we're bargaining with. I don't want you to do it for me at all. I don't want you to ever think I'm with you be-

cause I think you'll get better or you'll be different or someday you won't have this illness. Okay? I'm here even if it's
always like this."

A wave of mingled relief and disappointment swept
through him—relief because he didn't know if he could
have promised her anything else, and disappointment because her hope for him, founded on false premises as it had
been, had been such a light in his life.

"You think it will always be like this?" Teagan gestured
at himself, but the movement took in his teary cheeks, the
stolen otters, the quiet house, the first gray streaks of dawn
smudging the sky.

"I don't know," she said slowly. "I don't know what
changes you're going to make in your life, and I don't know
if they'll work. Maybe there are parts of it you're always going to struggle with." She pulled her legs out of the water
and crossed them.

The other two otters had satisfied themselves as to the
survivability of the water, and they jumped in to follow the
first, all three beginning to swim in large, satisfied circles.

"But we've spent the past two months working on not
drinking when *you don't drink*." She gave a small laugh. "I'm
going to need an entirely new set of podcasts. It's like I've
been guiding you through a bamboo forest, but we've only
been watching out for polar bears. I was worried about the
wrong bears."

Teagan swallowed through his tight, dry throat as he
dimly imagined not feeling like this anymore.

"Was it—is it pandas? Are we worried about panda bears?"

"It's a fucking metaphor, Teagan," she said, glaring at him,
and he lifted his palms in surrender even as he was gratified

at the small upward tilt to her lips. "I know there must be other things you wanted in life besides me. Well, you've got me. What else?"

Teagan knew she was right, but the idea was so overwhelming at that moment that he couldn't even begin a response. He shuffled enough to the side so that he could lie down and put his head in Darcy's lap. He pulled his feet out of the pool and curled his legs up. When Darcy didn't object, he wrapped both arms around her waist and pressed his face into her hip.

"I'll think about it," he vowed, mumbling into the thick, soft fabric of her dress. "Once I can think again. But you may need to make all the plans for a while, because you're all I can think about right now." He wiped his face against the loose fabric, because he imagined she wasn't going to wear it again.

Darcy put a hand in his hair and stroked it gently.

"Yeah, okay," she said. "I'll do that." He heard her swallow. She took a deep breath, and when she spoke her voice was tremulous but determined. "Tomorrow all we'll worry about is getting the otters squared away, all right? And if it's a nice evening, we'll make smoothies and sit in the hot tub. Then on Sunday we can check out that bear mountain you mentioned."

That all sounded perfect to Teagan. She took another breath and told him what they'd do Monday.

Darcy's hand in his hair and her voice making small, soft promises were the only push Teagan needed to topple over the edge into sleep. He didn't care if it was cold out here. He didn't want to lose an inch of this, not even for a moment. He didn't care if the ground was wet, because his head was pillowed in Darcy's lap. But as soon as the otters were out of the pool and had found the pile of old towels, Darcy shook him awake and pulled him to his feet, and they both went inside and slumped off to bed.

When the doorbell rang just after eleven, nobody immediately went to the door, because nobody had been expecting a package. Sloane was still on the couch, feeding Gatorade to her hangover, Darcy was eating peanut butter off a spoon in the pantry, and Teagan was blending canned tuna fish with frozen kale to make otter treats. Everyone was in their pajamas, except for the otters.

When nobody else volunteered to get the door, Teagan went to open it. He wasn't sure who he'd expected to be there, but Rose Kelly was last on the potential list. Even though she was on his doorstep, she looked just as shocked to see him, or maybe it was that *teacher in the grocery store* moment of surprise, because Teagan was in plaid flannel and Rose wore floral joggers, a pink sweatshirt, and her curly hair up in a loose, messy bun. They stared off as each processed the other in a completely new context.

"Who is it?" Darcy called from the kitchen.

"Rose," Teagan said.

"Tell her you quit!" Sloane called from the couch.

Teagan nodded. "I quit," Teagan said, holding up his hands. "I'm not doing—whatever it is you want me to do."

"I heard about that," Rose said, almost as an aside. "And that'll be a treat to handle on Monday. Nora's been blowing up my phone all night."

"Sorry," Teagan said, even if he wasn't quite. He successfully kept his mouth shut over any offers to further involve himself.

Rose shook her head as though to reorient herself. "It'll be fine. Modeline was ready to take over two years ago. Congratulations on your retirement. No, I'm here for Adrian."

Teagan blinked. He looked over his shoulder toward the hall. The man had briefly emerged to drink coffee and be awkward, and then he'd retreated to his room again.

"Uh. Pretty sure he quits too. And if you're here to drag *him* back . . . Darcy will probably defend him."

"That's right," Darcy said, emerging from the pantry with the sticky spoon still in her mouth. She crossed the room to wrap a protective arm around Teagan's waist. "You ain't taking no one out of this house alive, not on my watch, et cetera." She smirked at Rose, as though hoping someone would try.

Teagan leaned over to kiss Darcy's temple. God, he loved this woman.

Rose rolled her eyes with great drama.

"Adrian's the one who called me. Something about your sister hunting him like a beast of the field?"

They all turned to look at Sloane, who pretended to be transfixed by the TV, where the beautiful people were now having a shopping montage against a background track of upbeat pop music. Her expression remained innocent, but she was blushing a little.

"Sloane, he just found out his fiancée was screwing around on him *last night*. Leave him alone," Darcy chided her.

"You're not my mom," Sloane muttered grumpily.

Adrian, who'd probably been waiting for his chance to make an exit, came out of the bedroom in Teagan's castoffs, his tux folded over his arm. He and Rose exchanged long-suffering grimaces.

"I'll take you back to my place," Rose sighed. She cast

another judgmental stare at Sloane. "Listen to this: we used to be roommates, and he made me clean out the garbage disposal every single time he clogged it. Didn't want to risk his dainty artist hands. You really want a man like that?"

Teagan hadn't even realized the two of them knew each other.

Adrian fled the Van Zijl house without a backward glance. Sloane pretended not to notice. Darcy stepped aside to let him go, then headed back to the kitchen and Teagan's forgotten tuna smoothie.

Rose didn't leave but hesitated in the doorway. She tapped her mouth with a finger.

"You know," she said, "I'm not telling you what to do, but your sister has the right to join the board now that she's over twenty-one. You two would probably have the votes to kick Nora off, if she did that. Not everyone approves of self-dealing."

"Why would you tell me that?" Teagan demanded. "I thought you and Nora were friends."

"What? No. We're not friends," Rose said fiercely.

"But she got you your job," Teagan said.

Rose rolled her eyes again. "It's called networking. Not all of us get to work at the entire foundation we inherited. *Adrian* got me the job—I've known him since college. He was the best man in my wedding."

"Oh," Teagan said, feeling ignorant. "I didn't even know you were married."

"I'm not. Which is why Adrian owed me a job. Where I'd prefer a little less Nora in *my* life too."

Teagan looked at his sister. "It's up to Sloane."

Sloane gave an aggressive thumbs-up as her lips twitched into a smirk. Teagan supposed Nora had that coming to her.

Rose nodded, slightly mollified by Sloane's agreement. "I'll call you Monday." She turned to leave, then halted again. She scanned the living room. An otter skittered out from behind the kitchen island, one of its siblings in hot pursuit.

Rose lifted her eyebrows but did not comment on the chase.

"You're okay, then? You're going to be okay?" she finally asked, eyes flicking to Teagan's face.

"Yeah, I'm fine," Teagan said, discovering after he said the words that, for once, he actually meant it. "I'm great. We're just hanging out and doing a couple of errands today. Probably going to grill some veggies out by the pool later."

"That's good," Rose said, looking like she actually meant it too. She turned her head to nod farewell to Darcy, then Sloane. "Just having a family weekend in, then? Must be nice." Her face was slightly envious.

Sloane turned the volume back up on the television. It was time for another survivable gun battle on her program, it seemed. Darcy hit the blender button to pulse the tuna one more time. Somewhere, an otter had caught scent of the fish and was starting to chirp for food.

"Yeah," Teagan said. "It is."

thirty

"HOW ABOUT THIS ONE?" SLOANE ASKED, PASSING her phone back to Kristin, who sat at the other end of the gray corduroy sofa that dominated the living room of the small house Kristin shared with her mother in Bozeman.

Darcy and Sloane had been in Montana for the past two days to retrieve Darcy's car from the tow lot and get it titled in her name. The quarters were close, and Darcy had been a little concerned that Kristin and Sloane would fight, as Sloane was not very used to even a temporary living situation where she was expected to clean up after herself, make her own food, and scrub her own bathroom sink.

But Sloane and Kristin didn't fight. Instead, they argued. They'd argued for two days straight about Darcy's wedding, even though Darcy had repeatedly told them that Teagan was going to have to come up with a ring and a less terror-stricken kind of proposal if he hoped to secure her hand in matrimony someday. On the third round of *who should be maid of honor*, Darcy had threatened to elope without either of them in the event she did get properly engaged. After a few moments of shocked, wounded silence, the two other women had moved seamlessly to arguing about Darcy and Teagan's new dog.

Darcy and Teagan were going to get a dog together. It was the first thing Teagan had asked her for, after a big wind-up of a speech about how quiet the house seemed without the otters. Darcy had been half convinced he was about to ask her to get with child. A dog was an easy yes.

"'Tater Tot is a six-year-old Lhasa apso-poodle mix. He takes twice-daily thyroid medication and is allergic to chicken and beef,'" Kristin read out loud. "I don't think so. Four references required. No."

Darcy pulled out her earbuds and paused Teagan's dictation of a handout on Fisheries and Wildlife Science 302: Systematics of Birds. "I have references," she protested out of sheer principle, even though she was only half listening to the other women's conversation.

For the first time, Darcy was fairly certain she could pass the scrutiny of the most discerning no-kill shelter. She had a permanent address at a tidy little two-bedroom home in Beacon with a fenced backyard, and Teagan certainly had the financial resources to support even a dog who ate nothing but forty-two-dollars-a-bag prescription kibble.

"Forget this prissy little thing," Kristin scoffed, turning the screen to flash a fat, fluffy white creature at her. "His beauty routine is probably longer than mine, and it takes four hours to dye my hair. No. You want a real dog. There's a nice big Pyrenees mix up in Helena—"

Sloane immediately squawked in disapproval of the idea of a weeklong trip back to New York with a hundred-pound dog, and Kristin protectively hunched over the phone, scrolling through the adoption app with all the furtive, judgmental confidence of a married man browsing Tinder.

"We're not getting a dog in Montana," Darcy said to put an end to the burgeoning dispute. She had her eye on a purebred Labrador rescue back in New York whose profile suggested, in so many coded words, that he would turn his home to rubble if he didn't get hours of exercise every day. But Teagan didn't start his new swim coach gig at the middle school down the street for another month, so they were waiting on the bring-your-pet-to-work policy to make a final decision. "Besides, there's barely going to be room for the three of us and all Sloane's luggage as it is," Darcy added, nodding out the window at her car.

"I'm not that bad," Sloane protested. "You should see how Teagan packs. Like he's worried he's going to spill tomato soup on himself twice every single day that we're gone."

"Where *is* Teagan?" Kristin asked, lifting her head again. "I thought his flight got in a while ago? Didn't you want to leave before noon?"

Darcy had been wondering that herself, but she didn't have to check her phone to answer, because she heard a taxi crunching the gravel at the end of Kristin's drive. She grinned and went to stand in the doorway. Kristin said it had snowed last week, but today was a beautiful, golden fall day in Bozeman, and the front door was open to allow Kristin's five cats access to the great outdoors and its hapless migratory bird population.

This was her favorite time of year in the Gallatin range. Frost in the morning, then enough sunshine to toast her cheeks in the afternoon. Darcy crossed her arms as the taxi parked next to her car.

Teagan's smile was a little abashed as he stepped out of the taxi, and Darcy guessed that the reason for it was the many plastic sacks of groceries Darcy could see crowding the back seat.

"So I stopped by Costco," he began to explain both his

tardiness and the groceries, but he didn't finish his sentence, because Darcy closed the distance between them at a sprint, put both palms flat on his shoulders, and used the leverage to propel herself up and into his arms.

She heard the grocery sacks hit the gravel just in time for Teagan to wrap his hands under her ass and catch her as she wrapped her legs around him. His knees sagged a little, but he kept his balance.

"Hi," Darcy said, locking her ankles behind his back and arms around his neck.

Teagan's smile was still crooked but sweet as honey as he took a quick half step back against the taxi to avoid dropping her. "Hi, Darcy," he said.

She kissed him, the kind of kiss you only gave someone you'd already kissed at least a couple hundred times and planned to kiss a couple million times more, all smooshed noses and aligned lips.

"I was afraid you'd been somehow beset by bears between the airport and Kristin's house," she told him once she thought he was properly impressed.

"Nothing bigger than a marmot," he said after a couple of blinks. "And I fought it off, somehow."

"The marmots are already hibernating," Darcy told him with faux indignation. "Must have been ground squirrels."

They smirked at each other in pleasant anticipation of annoying other people with their developing set of inside jokes for many years to come.

Darcy let go of Teagan and slid back down to her feet as the taxi driver grumpily opened his door to begin unloading additional groceries out of the trunk.

Darcy peered into the bags at Teagan's feet.

"Are we going on a weeklong road trip, or are we founding a survivalist compound right here in Montana?" she asked, pulling out a five-pound jar of peanut butter-filled pretzels.

"I . . . guess we can do either?" Teagan said, taking stock of the growing pile of groceries. "Sorry. I've never been through any of the states between here and New York. I didn't know if they'd have anything for you to eat there. I hear they're pretty big on dairy in the Upper Midwest."

"It's fine," Darcy said with studied nonchalance, secretly thrilled to eat five pounds of peanut butter-filled pretzels before they even got to Minnesota. She unlocked the trunk of her own car and began transferring grocery sacks on top of her luggage and Sloane's. "We'll just need to bring all our food in at night while we're in the park so that bears don't try to break in."

Teagan put his hands on his hips and turned to examine Darcy's car.

"Everything go okay? It wasn't damaged?"

"Runs great," Darcy said. "I had it inspected and got new windshield wipers and everything."

"And the title?"

Darcy nodded. She'd been a little skeptical of bringing Sloane along on the first leg of her trip when Teagan had to stay behind to close on the sale of his condo. But Teagan had been absolutely right that Sloane was an emerging expert at making her problems into everyone else's problems, and even if several employees of Montana's DMV would be happy to never see her again, Darcy now had all her paperwork fully in order.

They finished loading Darcy's car and over-tipping the taxi driver. Darcy pulled up her phone to check that she had enough podcasts downloaded to cover the next few days, then lifted a hand to shade the early afternoon sun.

"Sloane!" she yelled toward the house. "Are you ready to go? If we want to make it to the beaver ponds before dark, we gotta go now."

There was some dark muttering about beavers from inside the house, but Sloane and Kristin eventually emerged with the last of Sloane's things.

"Look," Sloane said, holding up her phone screen. "The city shelter here has puppies. Ten of them. Looks like they've got some golden retriever in them." Her phone displayed an image of a pile of blurry yellow fluff balls.

"We're not getting a puppy. Much less ten puppies," Darcy said, amused despite herself.

"I know! But I thought, maybe we could just stop and *see* them?" Sloane wheedled. "They're still being bottle fed. We could hold one. Take a bottle-feeding shift." She looked down at Darcy beseechingly.

God. That sounded fantastic. They should cancel all their plans and just play with the puppies. How did parents do it? Try to pretend like all the weird shit your kids wanted you to do didn't sound super fun?

Darcy crossed her arms, trying to look implacable.

Teagan took the phone from his sister and made big, soft eyes at the picture of the puppies. Then he snuck a glance over at Darcy to check whether she was tempted.

"I don't know," he said, ducking Sloane's imploring look. "We were planning to leave just after noon, and I made us late."

"And look, I promised your brother beavers," Darcy said, wanting to leave the decision up to Teagan. "At some point I've got to deliver."

Sloane sighed in a put-upon way. "That's why we reserved two rooms," she said. "Do whatever you have to do tonight. Can we stop and play with the puppies, *please*?"

Teagan's ears and neck turned bright pink, but he held onto Sloane's phone.

"Um. So, I recall that the beavers are crepuscular," he recited. "Which means they'll be out tomorrow morning too, right?"

Darcy kept her face stern even as a smile pulled at the corners of her mouth.

"We're only in Yellowstone for three days," she said thoughtfully. "And I've got a lot planned. Up to you though."

Teagan's lips pursed. *Go ahead*, Darcy mentally urged him. *Use your words*.

Teagan handed the phone back to his sister.

"I think we can stop by the shelter and see the dogs. We'll just take it easy today," he said. "We can always stay an extra day in Yellowstone, right? It's not like we have anywhere we have to be for weeks."

Darcy grinned and pulled Teagan over by the waist to bury her face against the side of his neck. It was true.

"Yeah, sure," she said, tossing her car keys in her palm. "We're on vacation. We've got time."

ACKNOWLEDGMENTS

Dear Reader,

If you have just finished something that slightly resembles a romance novel, I must admit that I too am shocked that it was not all a pizza dream. This eventuality still seems very unlikely—Sir! I am but a simple country pornographer! Why is my writing in a *book*?—but it would have been impossible without the help of many wonderful people I met along the path to publishing.

I thank Jessica Watterson, my fiercely competent and compassionately effective agent, and her team at Sandra Dijkstra Literary Agency. I am sorry I have told you so many irrelevant law facts. You know so many things; how have you also made room for what I think about the proper scope of force majeure clauses?

I thank my editor, Cindy Hwang, whose love of bears (They are fat! Fuzzy! Friend-shaped!) rivals that of the protagonist's and caused this book to exist. I thank the other supremely talented and hard-working people at Berkley who put this book together and got it out to you: editor Angela Kim, production editor Lindsey Tulloch, publishing assistant Kiera Bertrand, Elisha Katz and Fareeda Bullert in marketing, and Kristin Cipolla in publicity. I thank Vi-An Nguyen for the gorgeous cover.

I thank all the people who read this book as a manuscript and made it better: Lara Ameen for her thoughtful read; Jenna Levine and Celia for revising every single draft and adding extra love every time; Kate Goldbeck for reading this book when it was mostly bullet points and flop sweat; and my darling Beaubeau, Ashley Mackie, for her lack of shock when I confessed that I was thinking of writing a book, which is the only reason anyone else is reading this at all.

I thank Rebecca for knowing when to talk me out of the trees and when to send me into them, Anastacia Davis Bersch for being my very patient fine-art consultant, Beth Gordon for her solid academic advice for my fictional characters, and my sister for all the bear safety facts imparted herein.

I thank my mother for my first-class education that ensured that the face-sitting scene here was written at a graduate-school level. And also for not reading my book.

I thank Ali Hazelwood for so much, including my title, my agent, my editor, everything I know about publishing, and my uncomfortably heated feelings about the word *gland*. I thank Sarah Hawley for pointing out that the bear is a good metaphor (for getting dicked down by a bear).

I thank all my pocket friends in Hyun Bin's Burner Phone, SDLA Sisters, All That [G]litters, the Berkletes, and Fen'Harem.

I thank my cat. You're the best, Mr. Kitten.

I thank the things that helped me finish this book: Jeeno's linen closet, Celia's knitwear, BuSpar, Adderall, betablockers, Spotify playlists, the birds in Bozeman who wake up before dawn, Adam Driver's hands, Solas Dragon Age's cheekbones, Scrivener, passionfruit LaCroix, and spite.

Finally, I thank my beloved family, especially my husband and children, whose patience and delight at the idea that I will be a "real author" have carried me through this project. I hope none of you ever see this. If you have read this book, please take care not to let me find out about it, or I too will be forced to go live in the woods with the bears.

❤ Shep

KEEP READING FOR AN EXCERPT OF

SWEETEN
THE DEAL

*THE NEXT BERKLEY ROMANCE NOVEL BY
KATIE SHEPARD*

ADRIAN DID HIS BEST TO IGNORE TOM'S ANXIOUS shuffle around the kitchen when the other man arrived home before his usual hour. Adrian didn't react. He didn't ask why his roommate was home early. Privacy was only an illusion within the seven hundred fifty square feet of their poorly insulated Brighton apartment, but it was an illusion Adrian strove to maintain. He could offer Tom that much, at least.

Unlike Adrian, Tom had a regular work schedule and an active romantic life, so Adrian did not comment on Tom's comings and goings. (The former mostly took place away from the apartment, thank God, because the walls were *very* thin. Adrian had unintentionally Heard Things in college while sharing a double dorm room with Tom, and he didn't care to review the progression of Tom's technique during the intervening years).

Adrian kept his gaze focused on PBS Newshour as Tom put the evening's leftovers away in the fridge and paced. Tom was usually a chatty guy, which Adrian might enjoy at the end of a quiet day like today. But Tom's silence tonight was telling. It was a sign of more bad things to come for Adrian.

Adrian had therefore begun to worry even before Tom

ran a hand through his shaggy brown hair and announced, "We need to talk."

These were ominous words. Not least because Adrian had recently uttered the same ones to commence the conversation with his ex-fiancée that left him single, unemployed, and squatting in Tom's spare room. If Tom's typically cheerful expression had turned so serious, Adrian assumed his roommate had an unpleasant piece of news to drop and did not want to discuss, say, whose turn it was to take out the trash: Adrian's turn, always Adrian's turn, because Tom was a slob who expended all of his cleaning energies at the high-end Greek restaurant where he was a waiter.

Adrian flicked off the television and rolled to a seated position on Tom's couch, which had been serving as Adrian's base of operations since his late-night eviction from his home of five years. He schooled his features into an attitude of mild interest as Tom mixed a drink, added half a jar of maraschino cherries to it, and worked himself up to whatever he had to say. Tom rolled up the sleeves of his dress shirt over furry, muscular forearms and leaned back against the peeling linoleum counter.

"So, you know you are welcome to stay here for as long as you like," Tom began.

Adrian sighed. Of course Tom wanted him gone. Even though Tom's apartment was cleaner than it had ever been, and Adrian made himself scarce whenever Tom had dates over, no self-respecting adult wanted his former college roommate camped out indefinitely in his second bedroom, and it had been two weeks.

Adrian had thought he would have more time though. After all, ten years ago their situations had been reversed, and Tom had been the one sleeping on the couch and pondering how he'd fucked up his life so thoroughly.

"When do you need me out?" Adrian interrupted him.

His friend's thickly arched eyebrows jolted.

"I wasn't going to ask you to move out," Tom said too quickly.

"Okay," Adrian said, nonetheless beginning to calculate how many nights he could afford at a motel before he had to prevail upon friends who owed him fewer favors than Tom.

Tom's shoulders slumped before he consciously straightened them. He mixed a second drink for Adrian and carried it over to the sofa. He set their drinks down amid the tangle of Adrian's printed notes and revisions and sat next to him.

"The restaurant isn't doing well," Tom said softly. "And I need to get a roommate. A *paying* roommate. I'd prefer that still be you."

Adrian rubbed his face. "I'm broke," he reminded Tom. The shorter man shifted in discomfort.

"Can't you just sell a painting or something?"

Adrian groaned, because if he'd been selling more paintings, he wouldn't be imposing on Tom. He didn't understand why sales were down. His last exhibition had made it into Artforum. He'd assumed sales would follow, but he hadn't paid a great deal of attention to his bank account until he was standing on the curb in front of his former home, suitcases at his feet.

"I'm still under contract with Nora's gallery through the end of the year," he muttered. "And inexplicably, my art has not sold at all since I left." He hadn't gone by the gallery to check if anything was still on display since their breakup, as all of the gallery staff had come down firmly on Team Nora, but it wasn't like she'd asked for a forwarding address to send checks to.

Tom sighed and screwed up his lower lip. "Well, do you have any other ideas? Could you just go pick up a few shifts at Starbucks or something until things turn around at the restaurant? Have you even been going into your studio?"

"I'm researching for a new series," Adrian said, tapping his notes. "Historical scenes from the Anglo-Ottoman War."

"Uh huh," Tom said, unconvinced that this was a quick route to rent money. "That's, like, another step away from actually painting?"

Adrian thought that was a low blow, so he merely stared at his roommate mulishly.

The other man stared back. "Could you ask one of your parents to help you out for a while?"

"Do you remember that I could have been a doctor instead of an artist? They do."

"Or you could teach? You have an MFA," Tom proposed.

"Ha. Do you know what they pay adjunct art professors? I'd make more slinging coffee."

"Then sling some coffee, or we're gonna get evicted," Tom said, tossing his hands in the air.

Adrian appreciated the *we* in that sentence for its suggestion that they were in this situation together, even though the easiest solution would be for Tom to tell Adrian to get out so that he could move in someone that had a stable income.

Coffee. Jesus. The idea that he'd man a cash register would have been inconceivable to him just two weeks ago.

Adrian propped his forehead against his fingers. His swift descent from locally prominent artist to deadbeat couch surfer had happened so unexpectedly as to leave him feeling like he'd tumbled down a mountain and hit every boulder on the way down.

"I'll . . . apply for something," Adrian unhappily promised. "Some new grants. Or teaching, you're right. I still know a few professors here." It sounded pretty thin.

They both looked at the black television screen. Adrian imagined Tom was as disappointed in him as he was with himself. Until recently, he'd been the reliable one—the one whose life had gone according to his expectations. Tom slurped the rest of his drink and tipped his head back against the couch with his eyes closed, stress forming little lines around his mouth.

Adrian clenched his teeth as guilt hit him. It wasn't Tom's job to worry about his failing career and broken engagement. Two weeks was more than enough time to sulk about his breakup and his gallery and his declining sales.

"There's no reason I can't try waiting tables, I guess," Adrian said reluctantly. "Do you know if anyone nearby is hiring?" At least Tom's neighborhood was far enough from Adrian's former one that he wasn't likely to encounter anyone he knew here.

Tom didn't open his eyes, but his chest rose in amusement. "You'd suck at waiting tables."

"Why? I think I get the theory of it."

"Sure, *you* are going to hustle for tips." Tom scoffed.

"That's the point, isn't it?"

"Yeah, but the first time someone tried to order their bœuf bourguignon with the sauce on the side, you'd make a face—"

"What face? And how the hell would you do the sauce on the side, it's a *stew*—"

"That face! That one you're making right now. You'd make that judgy face, and boom, no tip for you. Plus, anywhere nice is going to want you to have experience. You'd have to start at, like, some hole in the wall, and you'll barely clear minimum wage."

Adrian waved a dismissive hand. "You figured it out. You managed to pay for your divorce waiting tables. I can come up with half the rent, at least."

Tom was silent for a moment, his mouth twisted to the side. He looked back over at Adrian, seeming to size him up.

"That's not how I paid for my divorce," he finally said. "Not waiting tables."

"I thought you were barely making a hundred bucks a week in the chorus," Adrian replied. He remembered that year clearly: his apartment in Back Bay, Tom present only long enough to sleep on the couch, shower, and radiate misery between restaurant shifts and rehearsal.

"Yeah. And I definitely wasn't making enough to pay for a lawyer at the first restaurant I worked at."

"Okay, so, what did you do?"

Tom blinked a few times, gave Adrian a guarded look, and then, after a long hesitation, grabbed his laptop off the coffee table.

"I'm not saying it was ideal. But it was fine for a while. And I think, you know, it's not as stigmatized these days—"

"What," Adrian said flatly, worried he was about to hear that his roommate had been selling Adderall to Harvard undergrads.

"For an artist, you are surprisingly conventional, did you know that? Practically bourgeois."

"Tom!" Adrian said, now impatient to hear about it.

"I'm just saying, hear me out." Tom typed something into the search bar, then spun his laptop to show the page to Adrian.

A young woman in a short party dress laughed and displayed her white veneers to a middle-aged, tuxedo-clad man with a chiseled jawline and graying sideburns. *A relationship on your own terms*, the site's slogan promised in lacy white font. The login prompt was discreetly tucked at the bottom of the page. Adrian reeled back from the screen, hoping he was vastly mistaken about what the site advertised.

"Jesus Christ," he said automatically.

"You don't know what it is."

"It's an escort site," Adrian said.

"It's not that. It's different."

"Okay, what is it, then?"

"It's, like, a sugar baby thing—"

Adrian snorted, the noise ripping unwillingly from his throat. "That is the same thing! Jesus, Tom, you were *hooking*? You should have said something."

Tom winced. "Yeah, this reaction? Is why I didn't."

"No, no, no, I'm not—Sorry. I'm not upset at you. *I'm sorry.* I wish I could have—done something else. I thought you were just upset about Rose. If I'd known you had to—"

"I didn't *have* to do anything. And you were doing plenty. You were already feeding me, housing me, listening to me whine about my divorce—"

"I would also have done something to keep you from taking a job that leads to your dismembered body turning up in the Mystic River!" Adrian said, catching his voice just before it turned into a shout.

"You've got the wrong idea about it. It's not sex work," Tom insisted, shoving his shoulder lightly.

Adrian gave him a long, skeptical glower.

"I mean it," Tom said. "Not this site, anyway. Not even all the men I went out with thought they got to sleep with me."

"So it's just a dating site then?"

"Sort of. I mean, it's dates, yeah, but for money."

"Which is . . . different from sex for money," Adrian repeated, still alarmed.

"Because you don't have to have sex with them! That's not what they're paying for."

"What are they paying for, then?"

Tom relaxed a little. "Well, there are an amazing number of rich people who are divorced, widowed, single, whatever, and they just want someone hot to stand next to them at their fancy rich person things and impress their friends. You don't have to sleep with anyone. You're not meeting people in hotel rooms. You're getting paid for going to parties and stuff."

"What do you mean *you*," Adrian said, stiffening. "Do you mean *you* like you or *you* like me? Because I am not doing this, and I don't think you should either."

"Hmm. So. You can either serve clam chowder to tourists for an entire week, or you can look pretty for just a couple hours. How do you want to earn five hundred bucks?"

Adrian paused. His mind had already illustrated forty hours at a restaurant, and it didn't look like Renoir's *Luncheon of the Boating Party*, but like someone throwing iced tea in his face because he didn't bring the drink refills fast enough. Unwillingly, it began to sketch an easier job, one that would still leave him time to paint.

"Five hundred dollars? Are you serious?" he said, wishing the words back as soon as he uttered them.

"As a heart attack. That's what we'd ask for. You'd only have to go out with someone a couple times, and we'd be clear on rent."

It still sounded dangerous and unlikely to Adrian, even

if toiling in food service was not exactly appealing either. "You were making that much money to go out with people, no expectation that you would . . ." He didn't finish. He wasn't sure he really wanted to know.

"Well, I was making a few hundred dollars a week, but I think you could do better than that," Tom said.

"But why?" Adrian regretted saying that, because that made it sound like he was really considering it, which he wasn't.

"Because you look good!" Tom said. He eyed Adrian, who was dressed in jersey pajama pants and a bleach-spotted Mountain Goats T-shirt, because he hadn't gone outside today. "I mean, maybe not at this exact moment. But you are, like, the most attractive person I know in real life. You're *hot*—hotter than I was at twenty-three, even. Take advantage of that."

"You sound like you're trying to get me into the back of your van so you can take photographs of me," Adrian deflected, uncomfortable every time his looks were mentioned. Too many of his old reviews had been organized around the theme of *pretty man makes pretty art*. Which didn't lend much to his reputation as a serious artist.

"If I owned a van, you could be driving for some rideshare app, and we wouldn't have to have this conversation," Tom said airily. "But you know, the more I think about this, the better of a solution I think it is. Why should you get a *job* job? Let's just bridge the gap until you can sign with a new gallery or the restaurant can give me more hours."

Adrian closed his eyes tightly and rubbed his forehead with his palm.

"I could get a job," he mumbled.

"You've never *had* a job. But you have spent five years sucking up to a really terrible rich lady—"

"Tom," Adrian warned him, because he didn't want to hear Tom trashing Nora. Or suggesting that they'd been together because of her money. Which wasn't true. Or at least, hadn't been true to start out with.

"Oh, fine, you know I didn't like her. But you have to admit you get along with those people. Better than you would with the average fast casual restaurant diner, anyway. Picture yourself getting paid to stand around and be handsome. Now picture yourself, still on your feet, still handsome, but you're in a seafood shack, you're earning four thirty-five an hour, and your table of twelve is yelling at you because they had to wait ten minutes for their lobster rolls . . ."

It might be the best bad option, put that way.

"What would be involved, exactly?" Adrian said, trying to stress the reluctance in the question.

Tom beamed at him, newly energized by this horrible scheme. "First, we make your profile. You still own a tux, right? Let's dress you up. Like you're going to a silent auction to benefit the Society for the Advancement of Shrimp Cocktail and Prevention of Testicular Cancer."

Adrian did own a tux, even though he had loathed Nora's charity ball circuit. It always felt like performance art: a dance performed for some of the worst people in the world, who didn't actually care about supporting the arts, but liked the idea of rubbing elbows with artists. He supposed putting clothes on for money was marginally better than taking them off though.

"You can do it," Tom urged him. "You're exactly the arm candy a certain kind of woman is looking for. Didn't Nora always complain about those art groupie people hitting on you at gallery openings?"

"I hate those people."

"Don't be so prissy about this. Come on," Tom groaned. "It's bumming *me* out to see you on the couch all day long. This is depressing, you know? You look like a very depressed person. Let me just set you up a profile. It'll get you out of the house at least."

Adrian demurred.

Tom insisted.

Adrian offered to sell some plasma.

Tom told him he could keep every single bodily fluid to himself.

Eventually, Adrian felt exhausted from the longest conversation he'd had in weeks, and he gave in. At Tom's instructions, Adrian dug his tuxedo out of his luggage, put it on, and stood against the wall. Tom had one of Adrian's old paintings hung over his sofa—a sentimental one, lush florals and bright colors, the sort of thing he hadn't done in years—and it was going to serve as proof of his bona fides as artist arm candy. Adrian uneasily shifted from foot to foot as Tom tried to take a decent picture under the cheap CFL track lights.

"Just use an old picture," Adrian complained. "Grab the one off my gallery page."

"Uh, we are not going for pensive and temperamental. No. In this fantasy, you are charming. Look at the camera and smile. Come on, look happy. You're at a cocktail party, you just said something hilariously mean about Jeff Koons, and everyone is laughing."

Adrian suppressed a scowl and tried to fix his features in

an expression he could barely remember making naturally. It seemed to satisfy Tom, who uploaded it to his laptop and then turned to filling out Adrian's profile, greatly embroidering Adrian's preferences regarding black-tie galas and long walks on the beach.

"What if someone I know finds my profile?"

"Then you know a bunch of people who pay a hundred bucks a month to check out sugar babies. Nobody ever found out about *me*. Relax."

Adrian did not relax. He gritted his teeth and peered over Tom's shoulder.

"And why *Women* and not *Any*?" Adrian asked, pointing to the *Seeking* drop-down menu. He imagined there were a lot more men looking for paid companionship than women.

Tom gave him another long look. "You need to pick a struggle, buddy," he said. "If you're gonna start dating men, maybe try it for free first? I wish I had."

"If it's not about sex, though—"

"Well, obviously, it's a *little* bit about sex, or at least the *idea* of sex . . ." Tom's voice delicately trailed off as he pursed his lips.

Adrian groaned and stuck his hands in the air, backing away from the laptop. "I'm not doing this," he said. "I am not! I'll start looking for a job tomorrow."

"I just uploaded your profile," Tom said firmly. "At least take a look at who's on here?"

"Take it down, Tom," Adrian instructed him, going to the kitchen to investigate the leftovers Tom had brought home. The tuxedo felt a little tight, and Adrian didn't know if that was because he'd been in drawstring pants for two weeks or because Tom's leftovers all seemed to contain a great deal of béchamel. Adrian found a paper container of braised chard, which couldn't be too bad for him, and dumped it into a bowl to reheat in the microwave.

"Okay, how about this lady? She's going to the Cape soon, her sister is bringing her ex-husband as a date, and she wants someone to spend the week rubbing suntan lotion into her shoulders and asking her ex pointed questions about his real estate portfolio. She says there's only one bed at the beach house though. Is that weird?"

"Take it down," Adrian repeated, watching his dinner circle in the microwave. He'd apply at the retail shops on their block, and maybe he could make some extra money teaching those paint and sip classes for seniors or something.

Tom clicked again. "This lady is in her eighties, but she's flying to Arizona for the Ring Cycle, and I know you like opera. You can lift fifty pounds, right? She has oxygen tanks." He paused. "Oh, and she's into BDSM. Huh."

"Take it *down*, Tom!"

The microwave chirped, and Adrian stirred the greens. He took a bite. Bitter. Just roughage. It tasted like penance. Mentally vowing that he would go to the gym the next day, he opened the fridge and got a carton of moussaka out. He put the food into a new bowl and started the microwave again.

Tom continued clicking on his laptop. When dinner was done, Adrian arranged it on the tiny kitchen table and was sitting down to eat when Tom stood up.

"Look," Tom said triumphantly, turning the screen of his laptop around to show him. "What about her?"

Adrian paused with his fork halfway to his mouth.

Tom had expanded his potential patron's photograph until it filled the entire screen. The blonde woman's face was obscured by the shade of a visor, but she was wearing a short white tennis dress and sneakers, her racket held at the ready.

The picture had been taken on the court, the sun shining on the woman's long tan legs. She looked way too young to be hiring a sugar baby.

"That picture's probably thirty years old," Adrian said.

"So?" Tom said. "At least you know she used to be hot. Maybe she still is."

Adrian ignored him for a minute as he chewed his reheated dinner, and Tom browsed the rest of the woman's profile.

"What does she want?" Adrian finally asked, unable to immediately discard the concept of going out with the tennis player.

Tom smiled in suppressed triumph. "She's new in Boston, and she wants someone sophisticated to show her around the city."

Adrian waited for him to continue, but he didn't. Instead, Tom began typing. Adrian worried that Tom was now going full Cyrano de Bergerac: Tom did regional theater when he wasn't waiting tables, and he had a large flair for the dramatic.

"What's the catch?" Adrian asked suspiciously. He thought he was broad-minded, but he had some firm lines he was not going to cross, even if Tennis Girl had grown up into a reasonably attractive Tennis Woman.

"Hmm?" Tom said, typing, deleting, typing again.

"What's the weird thing she wants that she can't get for free?" Adrian demanded. With his luck, it was something painful or illegal.

"Nothing weird. It looks like she checked every single interest box. Art, music, theater, *and* fashion, plus everything else under the sun." He peered up at Adrian, a grin tilting the corners of his mouth. "Fortunately, you're a total snob.

I'm sure you'll fit right in at whatever bullshit charity events she wants you to impress people at."

Adrian bit down an objection, contemplating the potential arrangement as he finished his dinner. Maybe it wouldn't be worse than his relationship with Nora. She'd paid the bills, handled all of the business of selling his art, and demanded very little in the way of emotional engagement. In return he'd managed the house, let her dictate their social life, and—until two weeks ago—been so absorbed by his art that he failed to notice her cheating on him. It could have continued indefinitely if she hadn't saved someone else's nudes to their joint photo account.

Tom stopped typing and shut his laptop.

"I'll think about it," Adrian promised him. "Maybe I'll contact her tomorrow."

"Okay," Tom conceded. Too easily.

"What," Adrian said with deep alarm. He crossed his arms over his chest, feeling his heart rate pick up along with his anxiety. Tom beamed at him, his dark brown eyes cheerful again.

"You have drinks with her tomorrow at seven. She's open to paying a thousand a week. Her name's Caroline Sedlacek."

Katie Shepard is, in no particular order, a fangirl, a gamer, a bankruptcy lawyer, and a romance author. Born and raised in Texas, she frequently escapes to Montana to commune with the trees and woodland creatures, resembling a Disney princess in all ways except age, appearance, and musical ability. When not writing or making white-collar criminals cry at their depositions, she enjoys playing video games in her soft pants and watching sci-fi shows with her husband, two children, and very devoted cat.

CONNECT ONLINE

KatieShepard.com

🐦 YTCShepard

📷 KatieShepardBooks

Ready to find
your next great read?

Let us help.

Visit prh.com/nextread

Penguin
Random
House